INCENSE
AND
SENSIBILITY

A NOVEL

SONALI DEV

WILLIAM MORROW

An Imprint of HarperCollinsPublishers

P.S.™ is a trademark of HarperCollins Publishers.

INCENSE AND SENSIBILITY. Copyright © 2021 by Sonali Dev. All rights reserved. Printed in the United States of America. No part of this book may be used or reproduced in any manner whatsoever without written permission except in the case of brief quotations embodied in critical articles and reviews. For information, address HarperCollins Publishers, 195 Broadway, New York, NY 10007.

HarperCollins books may be purchased for educational, business, or sales promotional use. For information, please email the Special Markets Department at SPsales@harpercollins.com.

FIRST EDITION

Designed by Diahann Sturge

Library of Congress Cataloging-in-Publication Data has been applied for.

ISBN 978-0-06-305180-5

21 22 23 24 25   LSC   10 9 8 7 6 5 4 3 2 1

Praise for *Incense and Sensibility*

"This book holds a galaxy of depth in its pages; it is powerful and loving, sensual and layered. Sonali Dev's writing is glorious."

—Christina Lauren, *New York Times* bestselling author of *In a Holidaze*

"*Incense and Sensibility* is a tender, well-crafted novel, as much about finding purpose as it is about falling in love. Dev writes with such rare empathy and humor that I often found myself holding my breath on one page only to be giggling by the next. This is the kind of book you finish with a whole-body, happy sigh and a warm ache in your chest where the characters will live on. Yash and India's story will stick with me for a long time."

—Emily Henry, *New York Times* bestselling author of *Beach Read*

Praise for *Recipe for Persuasion*

"A delight from start to finish, both for Jane Austen fans looking for a fresh take and readers seeking deeply felt relationships and complicated family dynamics. In Dev's world, the past is alive in the present; I was wholly engrossed and had plenty to think about. At the same time, the reality TV story line added a thread of pure fun escapism—something all of us need right now."

—Joshilyn Jackson, *New York Times* bestselling author

"Nuanced and powerful . . . balances the toe-curling romance with high-octane family drama. . . . Dev's candor and sensitivity in both story lines set this family-centric romance apart."

—*Publishers Weekly* (starred review)

"A sumptuously multilayered story about the ways love gets tangled in family life and romantic relationships. Highly recommended."

—*Library Journal* (starred review)

Praise for *Pride, Prejudice, and Other Flavors*

"With humor, insight, and culinary descriptions so rich the tantalizing aromas practically waft from the pages, Dev's latest draws readers into a tangled world of class, cultural, and political issues in a delicious riff on *Pride and Prejudice*."

—*Library Journal* (starred review)

"Vivid and deliciously enticing, Dev's storytelling is layered with emotional depth. . . . A flavorful harmony of cross-cultural unions, familial love, and an entertaining ensemble of characters that will leave readers with a serious craving for more."

—NPR

"I don't know what I loved the most about *Pride, Prejudice, and Other Flavors*. Was it how well Sonali Dev writes about family ties and how meaningful and painful they can be? Was it how passionate and dedicated her characters were for their chosen careers? Was it the fully realized love story between two complicated and sympathetic people? Or, my goodness, was it the food descriptions, which had me swooning? I can't choose: all of these things came together to make a truly wonderful and joyous book."

—Jasmine Guillory, *New York Times* bestselling author

INCENSE
AND
SENSIBILITY

Also by Sonali Dev

Recipe for Persuasion
Pride, Prejudice, and Other Flavors
A Distant Heart
A Change of Heart
The Bollywood Bride
A Bollywood Affair

For Gaelyn.
For always always being the voice at the other end of the line when I need to be talked off the ledge. Some sisters are ours by birth and some sisters we find in striped pants and bobby pins in a Mumbai local train.

Chapter One

From the day he was born Yash Raje had his entire life planned out for him and he was wholeheartedly on board with the plan. Sure, there was the prophecy—your life tended to leave the realm of mediocrity when you had a clairvoyant cousin who saw great things in your future—but the real reason was that Yash wasn't an ungrateful prick.

There were those born under the diamond-studded blanket of privilege who were tortured by it. Then there were others who took it as their due. Both those types of people struck Yash as asinine. Yash looked at his privilege as a test. How worthy could he make himself of all these opportunities, and how much could he change with them? Yash had always been a great test-taker. Perfect scores on the SAT, ACT, and the LSAT, thank you very much.

"Ready to go get them?" Rico Silva, his media strategist, strode into the holding area behind the stage of Santa Clara University's soccer stadium. His enthusiasm matched the purposeful energy coursing through Yash. Rico was a World Cup–winning soccer player and media darling, and hiring him to handle his press and messaging was one of the smartest things Yash had done for his campaign.

Not only did Rico possess an uncanny sense of what voters needed to see and when, but being a star athlete also made him the perfect person to introduce Yash at rallies with talk of dreams and pushing the limits of human potential. Running for political office was a test of how well you could sell that dream. The dream of hope. Yash had every intention of acing that test as well.

Rico's introductions always fired up the audience, and a fired-up audience was exactly what Yash needed three months before California's gubernatorial election. Yash was still doing a back-and-forth two-step with his opponent for a lead in the polls.

"Always ready," Yash said, adrenaline drowning out everything but his goal: that podium, that audience, and owning them both.

"Ready to go get them?" His sister Nisha echoed Rico's words. Nisha had managed all of Yash's campaigns since his very first one as the youngest person running for state senate.

He mock-frowned at her. "Actually, can we cancel? I have a tummy ache."

She made a face. "Funny."

As a little girl Nisha had used tummy aches as an excuse to get out of anything she didn't want to do. Usually this involved activities that might ruin her hair (swimming with her siblings) or her clothes (literally, any physical labor). When it came to Yash's political campaigns, however, his sister was an unstoppable force. "Where is Abdul?" Her eyes swept the room for Yash's bodyguard.

"He's checking the stage one last time. Rico and I were ironing out some tweaks to the speech. Did you check up on Naina?"

"Your girlfriend is just fine." Nisha started tapping on her iPad with her usual focus. Everyone was in the zone. Yash never left the zone. The zone was his dominion. "She's seated next to the university chancellor. I'm sure she's charming the pants off him."

Of course she was.

With one last tap, Nisha finished what she was doing. "I just texted Naina and she thanks you for checking up on her and wishes you luck even though she knows you don't need it." Then, eternal romantic that she was, she sighed and gave Yash a smile that said you-two-are-so-adorable.

Rico threw him a wary glance. As a man newly in love, he wasn't quite as convinced about Yash and Naina's romance. And people liked to claim that women were more intuitive than men.

Rico was right to be skeptical. Sometimes Yash wondered how more people didn't see through his arrangement with Naina. They'd been together—more accurately they'd been pretending to be together—for ten years. It had started off as two friends trying to help each other get their parents off their backs about marriage, and it had worked out perfectly.

Naina was off in all parts of the world studying how to structurally dismantle the gender imbalance caused by centuries of systemic economic dependence of women. Yash was here trying to change the world from the only place where it could actually be done: California.

Which made Yash a thirty-eight-year-old who was hanging on to a deal he had made with his friend when they were twenty-eight, so they could live life on their own terms and circumvent their overbearing families without hurting them. Sure, it sounded a tad bit cowardly, but only if you didn't know their families.

The added bonus of not needing to expend energy on a relationship had meant undistracted focus on their work for both of them. Sure, it was unromantic, but romance hardly got things done.

Rico pressed his phone to his ear. "They're ready for us. We've got to kill this one, Raje. We've got to put some distance between Cruz and you in the polls. I'm going to go get the crowd excited.

Try to keep up." Thumping Yash on the shoulder in his star-athlete way, he jogged out.

Abdullah Khan, Yash's security guard, entered the holding room. "Rico's about to pour fuel on them. You ready to throw the match, boss?"

A little morbid, but Yash loved it. He nodded. "Always ready."

"Hey, Abdul. How's the baby?" Nisha asked.

The burly giant, who could snap your neck with his bare hands and shoot you dead from five hundred feet, went as soft and fuzzy as the teddy bear Yash had brought Abdul's newborn daughter yesterday. After seeing him hold the tiny pink bundle, Yash could not for the life of him stop thinking of the man as cuddly.

"She's amazing. Has quite the lungs, just like her ammi." Abdul winked.

"Thanks for being here," Nisha said, hand on heart.

They had tried to get the man to take the week off after the baby was born, but he'd refused to let a new bodyguard take over just months before the election. Abdul had been with Yash since the start of the campaign and knew only too well how hard it was for Yash to trust new people.

"Where else would I be? Let's go, boss, let's get you elected." Abdul hammed up a salute, then pointed with a flourish to the exit.

Nisha gave Yash a quick hug and hurried off to take care of the next thing, her pregnant belly not slowing her down in the least bit. Yash marched out behind Abdul.

This was Yash's favorite part. This charged moment offstage, able to see the audience when they couldn't see him, just before he went out into the bright lights. All the things he planned to address today were laid out in a precise grid in his head ready to be retrieved and articulated. Fiscal reform. Social reform. How the two intersected. His plans to tie them together.

A college campus was his crowd. Young people excited at the prospect of not having someone their parents' age running things. All that raw hope that hadn't yet been pounded down by cynicism and bills. *Right* and *wrong* still meaningful words not blurred by single-minded economic focus. Yash's talking points about dismantling accumulation of wealth as a systemic norm were an easy sell here. Actually, it was a surprisingly popular opinion in the Bay, with its combination of greed and guilt.

The challenge was communicating the idea outside the bubble of the Bay without coming across as a hypocritical elitist. Being pro-business wasn't a problem. It couldn't be, in America. The problem was how businesses reallocated profits to affect economic change in communities where social change was most vital.

Talking points scrolled across his brain. His body vibrated with all that could be. Potential. Power. Purpose. This gave him life. This connecting with people. This knowing that he could change things for them.

Onstage, Rico had the crowd eating out of his hand. A chant of, "Yash is us," started up and boomed across the arena like drumbeats. Excitement thrummed in the air like an electric force.

Abdul's shoulders took up the rhythm of the chant even as he scanned the crowd with laser focus. Rico called out Yash's name with all the aplomb of a sportscaster announcing a reigning champion before a big fight, and the cheering turned deafening.

"You're a rock star, boss," Abdul said, his fist bumping against Yash's as they ran out onto the stage.

"I Love you, Yash Raje!" someone screamed from the crowd as though Yash really were a rock star.

It was the first sound to hit him as he faced the crowd, anticipation rising from it and rolling over him like a wave.

The second sound blew out his eardrums just as fire exploded in his arm.

Two more shots followed the first and Abdul's body slammed against Yash's, pushing him out of the way. Yash fell back, his legs flying out from under him as he watched Abdul slam his head on the podium and crumple to the floor across Yash's legs. Everything inside Yash braced for more shots. When none came, he felt his heart start beating again, but when he tried to move . . . nothing.

Why have I never googled what happens after you get shot? That should not have been Yash's first thought after the deafening blasts rang through the stadium. But it was.

Scattering footfalls thumped across the ground beneath the stage. An endless ringing, like a suspended beep, was trapped deep inside his ear. Outside, everything was too bright, washed in white light. He felt like he was in a movie. How did filmmakers know how this felt? How many of them had experienced being shot?

His hands twitched for his phone in that internal tug that had become part of the human condition, the need for an immediate answer uncontrollable. The memory of crisp encyclopedia pages slid against his fingertips. As a child, he had found answers in his father's library. The beloved knowledge-filled tomes had swallowed his questions, fueled them, and now they crammed landfills because of a machine that fit in his hand.

The weight across Yash's legs twitched, pulling him from the tightly packed thoughts in his brain. This time when he tried to move, his body responded and he pushed himself up on his elbows. Abdul was lying across Yash's legs, face down.

Abdul? The word left his lips but didn't reach his ears past the suspended beep. *Abdul!* Was his bodyguard not responding because he didn't hear him, or because he couldn't hear him?

Should I move? God, sometimes questions were the bane of his existence. To stop and think before acting, it was supposed to be his gift. Controlling your emotions was the only way to control anything else. It might be the first thing Yash remembered his father ever saying to him. A lesson so early and strong that it had become twisted into the helixes of Yash's DNA.

Animals operate on instinct. Humans temper their actions with intellect. A leader reins his emotions better than everyone else. A leader thinks.

His father's voice crackled in his head. Yash had always known that when death came it would take the form of his father's lecturing.

A man was lying on top of him, and *reining his emotions* was doing Yash zero good. "Abdul!" This time the sound had to have left his throat, because Yash heard it at a distance.

Abdul didn't move.

Why am I not feeling anything?

He could feel Abdul's weight across him. He could smell the dust and blood. But *inside*, where there should be terror and panic, nothing—just thoughts crashing against thoughts.

As gently as he could, Yash leaned forward and pressed a hand into Abdul's shoulder. His body was utterly still. Blood pooled under them, springing from a gash on the side of Abdul's neck, just above his vest. Damn it.

Bending forward, Yash reached for the wound but his hand hovered over it. Pressure seemed the most logical way to stop the blood, but what if touching it made something worse.

"Abdul," Yash shouted into his friend's body. The wetness

under him made a squelching sound. Abdul was losing too much blood.

Pulling off his jacket, Yash bunched it up and pressed it into the wound as lightly as he could. Almost instantly red soaked through the pale gray linen.

Déjà vu soaked through Yash's brain. It had been a full twenty-three years since his accident. He'd been all of fifteen when a driver had jumped a stop sign and hit Yash. He felt his belly bounce as he was thrown off his bicycle into the air. The sight of blood always made the collision come alive inside him, so he avoided it. Now every cell in his being felt like it was soaked in the memory.

Beneath his hands Abdul convulsed once. A sign of life. Yash increased the pressure just a little bit. Abdul had brought him a box of burfi this morning to celebrate his daughter's birth. Naaz, they had called her. It meant pride. A beautiful, beautiful name. A name Yash had tucked away in the vault where he kept things that belonged just to him. Just in case a day came when he might have children. Oh God, Abdul's wife hadn't even gone home from the hospital.

"Come on, *wake up*." Yash wanted to shake him, do something, but he was too afraid to take his hands off the gash in Abdul's neck.

"Sir, are you all right?" A man ran up the stage and suddenly Yash was aware of the chaos around him. Screams and scrambling footsteps.

The man tried to pull Yash's hands off Abdul, but Yash couldn't let the spring of blood start up again. "You have to let go. We have to get him off you and get you looked at. The paramedics are almost here." The man was another guard from the security company. Yash couldn't remember his name.

"Don't touch him." Finally, Yash's voice reached his own ears, loud and forceful. He should have felt relief. He needed to feel something. "Where's the ambulance? Do you know what the golden hour is? If we don't get him to a hospital right now, his chances of survival will fall by seventy percent. Do you realize what seventy percent is? Where's Rico? Rico!" He looked past the guard who was crowding him.

A crush of bodies moved in a wave toward the back of the stadium, leaving overturned chairs in their wake. Twenty thousand. Twenty thousand young people with their lives ahead of them. At the mercy of a shooter. Because of him.

Where was Rico? Had he made it off the stage when the shots went off? Yash's hands trembled on Abdul's wound. What if Rico was bleeding somewhere too? Rico wasn't just a friend, wasn't just Yash's media wiz. He was dating Yash's sister. Technically Ashna was his cousin but Yash only ever thought of her as his sister. Rico was family. Ashna was happy. It had been years since Yash had seen her happy. Just this morning Yash had teased Rico about his intentions toward his sister.

I intend to let Ash use my body for her shagging pleasure for the rest of my life, mate.

Had Ashna been at the rally? Why couldn't he remember who else was here?

He turned to the guard. "I need you to find Rico Silva for me. Right now."

"I'm here, mate." Rico's face came up behind the guard whose name Yash couldn't remember.

Yash never forgot names. Ever.

He was also never this cold. Rico was alive and Yash could feel absolutely nothing. *I should be feeling something. Something!*

"Abdul needs to be in an ambulance," Yash said as Rico squatted next to him.

He looked unhurt. The only sign that this wasn't just another day at just another rally was that the giant YASH RAJE FOR GOVERNOR button on Rico's jacket had come askew and was hanging lopsided.

"You need to let Abdul go," Rico said, face tight with so many emotions that the emptiness inside Yash doubled down. "The ambulance is here. They need to look at you." Rico looked over his shoulder as paramedics rushed at them with gurneys.

"This way," Yash shouted, but they were already tugging his hands off Abdul and lifting him off Yash to a stretcher.

A paramedic helped Yash up and onto a gurney. "You need to let us look at you." He tried to get Yash to lay down but Yash wouldn't let him.

"I'm fine. He was hit." Yash didn't recognize his own voice, but something about his tone was familiar. "Why did it take you so long to get here?" Just like that Yash knew why it sounded familiar. He sounded exactly like his father. Yash had spent his life trying not to sound like his father.

He tried to soften it, tried to sound more like himself. "He's within the golden hour. That means he's going to be okay, right?"

The paramedic gave Rico a look and Rico pushed Yash back with a "Please, Yash."

Yash resisted but suddenly pain shot through his arm making him lightheaded and he lay back.

He didn't want to be on a gurney. The last time he'd been on one he'd ended up in a wheelchair for a year. His blood-soaked clothes, the pain throbbing in his body, all these paramedics. The numbness in his legs. He wasn't fifteen, this wasn't that day. He didn't even have real memories from that day. Just these splashes of sensation.

It took some effort to stop himself from searching his surroundings for his bike. The one that had become as twisted and mangled as his broken spine.

"They're taking care of him." Rico pressed a hand into Yash's chest to keep him on the gurney.

Before Yash could respond a woman screamed his name and ran at him.

Yash knew the woman.

He couldn't for the life of him remember her name.

"Yash, honey. Oh no." She was sobbing. Mascara ran down her face. She looked like she'd lost someone she loved.

That's how I should look. That's how I should be feeling. But nothing. He felt nothing.

"Naina, he's going to be okay," Rico said.

Naina. Of course.

Naina and Yash. Spoken for. The words made him laugh. They made him think of his parents. *How would Ma survive it if he died?*

Spoken for. Ma had come up with that label when Yash and Naina had said they wouldn't get engaged. Ma, who always found a way to make things okay.

Spoken for. And he'd forgotten her name.

Naina kept stroking his arm. Then she leaned over and kissed his forehead. Mascara-tinted teardrops splashed onto Yash's face. A light flashed with a sound Yash knew so well it could wake him from the dead. A camera.

"Honey, please let them do their job." Spoken-for Naina sobbed as more cameras clicked.

"Their job is to make sure Abdul doesn't die." He tried to catch Rico's eye, but Naina had wrapped herself around Yash and he couldn't see. The smell of her perfume was so strong he couldn't breathe.

Twisting in her embrace, he spoke to the paramedic who was clamping a monitor to his finger. "What's taking so long? That man needs to be in a hospital. Don't you understand? He has a bullet inside him." His father was back in his voice.

"Actually, sir, he doesn't," the paramedic said, pressing something into Yash's shoulder, making it feel like he'd taken an ax to it. "The bullet went through him. You're the one with the bullet inside you."

Chapter Two

*I*ndia Dashwood loved her life. She lived for the joy she experienced every time she led a yoga practice and watched her students connect with parts of themselves they had never accessed before.

"Namaste," she said to the room filled with twenty glowing faces.

They had just completed the final session of the two-week long *Namaste Yogi* camp she'd come to Costa Rica to teach.

That name always made India cringe, but it wasn't something she had any control over. Calling yoga students "yogis" was quite a stretch. A yogi was someone who had harnessed their mind and body, so it was never regulated by desire. India had spent her entire life aspiring to this. Growing up in a yoga studio and being raised by a mother and grandmother who were yoga gurus meant India had lived the yogic practice since before she could walk, and she still couldn't claim the title of yogi.

"Namaste," her class chorused back in one harmonious voice. Fifteen days, and the texture of their namastes had changed. India had worked them hard. Relentless breath work, meditation that dug deep, poses that reset bones held long enough to bring out the strength of the very soul. Yoga brought together the entirety of a person's experience being them. The body, the mind, the consciousness, all brought into awareness and experienced at once. If you gave it time, it gave you a glimpse of your whole self, your very humanness.

The enthusiasm of their first few days was sweet. The exhaustion of the middle slog that they hit on day seven and struggled through until day thirteen was heartbreaking but hopeful because India knew the outcome. It was this deeply relaxed and rooted "Namaste" that India waited for as she led them through their camp. Her grandmother would be proud.

They each stopped by to thank her and she pressed her hands together as she thanked them in return. Some of them just wanted her praise, others wanted her reassurance that they could hold on to what they had learned here. She gave each one of them what they needed, what the voice inside her told her would help them best.

There was very little you had control over in the world. But your own actions, those you could make exactly what you chose to make them. Staying connected to her inner voice was the only way India knew to make sure she kept her actions what they should be.

After the last of the students had left, India made her way to her suite wrapped in the kind of peace that came with giving a job your all. The resort was located at the edge of a cliff in Punta Quepos overlooking the Pacific coast of Costa Rica. She walked past the infinity pool that dropped into the ocean. Of all the resorts in the Manuel Antonio region this was the only one without a bar.

Most of her students would be headed to one of the other resorts today, to the places with multiple bars. India didn't begrudge them their enjoyment. During her retreats, however, she preferred that her students not imbibe, and try to stay vegetarian. The body stayed better focused on itself with food that was easier to digest, and the mind stayed better focused on itself without alcohol messing with the nervous system. You emerged more refreshed and energized after a meditative retreat if you didn't drink or eat meat; and India had never had a student who didn't wholeheartedly agree, even if they'd started out trying to prove her wrong.

Inside her suite, she pulled off the turquoise shrug she'd worn over her white yoga pants and tank and put the kettle on in the kitchenette. Then, she retrieved her phone from her nightstand and let herself out onto the balcony. The coolness of the slate floor soaked into her bare feet. The resort was built on terraces tucked into a hill slope rising from the ocean and the briny sea breeze caught speed at this height and pummeled harder. Her hair caught every bit of salt in the air, making the short cropped strands stiff and heavy against her fingers as she tried to push them back in place.

Her thick, straight, jet-black hair was a gift of her Thai genes, and she was grateful to her birth parents for it, whoever they were. When India was younger she would search her own facial features in the mirror to piece together what they looked like, and wondered where they lived, and if they ever missed her. She did it only rarely. Not often enough to feel like she was betraying her mother, but just enough to bring awareness to the people who'd brought her into the world.

At sixteen India had finally asked her mother if she had any records that told India something, anything. But keeping true to her nature, Tara Dashwood had saved none of the paperwork. It didn't matter. India loved her mother more than words could describe. A mother who drowned her children in love, who drowned anyone and anything that crossed her path in love, was hard to not love. Growing up, India remembered not a word of criticism, nor a harsh experience of any sort. Her childhood had been suffused with the sweet scent of incense, the soothing sounds of chanting, and the warmth of being wrapped up in hugs and unconditional acceptance.

If a serious illness ever befell India or her two siblings (an eventuality Tara never foresaw, because: yoga!), they'd have no idea if it was genetic predisposition. Because Tara had adopted children from three countries with an equal disregard for parental history for all three.

The kettle whistled and India poured herself a cup of hot water and took it back to the balcony, and finally checked her cell phone. Her mother used technology as little as possible, but as expected, there were missed calls and a string of texts from India's sister, China. Their brother, Siddhartha, hadn't checked in, but that wasn't surprising either. He was off photographing birds-of-paradise in Papua New Guinea, and as Sid loved to say, a cell signal and birds worth photographing didn't go together.

Instead of reading through her texts, India called China. Wi-Fi calling meant international calls wouldn't bankrupt her. These retreats did make more money in a week than a month's worth of classes at their studio in Palo Alto, but she needed every cent to pay the mountainous debt from recent renovations to her family's studio.

"India!" China always answered calls with your name, as though you had to be reminded that caller ID existed.

"China!" India said, mirroring her tone, and couldn't hold back the smile that split her face. "All well? Is the studio still standing?"

China was the one who had goaded India into doing the retreats, because India had never shown any interest in leaving the studio. She loved Palo Alto, loved the studio and their apartment above it that she shared with Tara and China. What was the reason to ever leave? But they'd recently had to renovate the studio because parts of the structure had become hazardous, and renovations in Palo Alto basically cost more than a small Greek island. The reason India knew this was because Sid had checked the prices and suggested they buy the island instead of renovating.

"Actually, the studio's crumbled to the ground. It refused to stay standing without you holding it up on your tiny but mighty shoulders." China enjoyed teasing India, but between how little China cared about anything but her work (which was *not* teaching yoga *or* taking care of the family incense business, thank you very much) and the fact that their mother hadn't been her usual energetic self recently and had been forgetting little things like turning off the stove and locking up, India's fear was not entirely unjustified.

"And the classes are going well?" India asked. She couldn't wait to get back to her students. Their mother's style of instruction catered to students who were more interested in loving themselves than pushing themselves. This was the point of yoga, obviously, but the point was also growth. Every mind and body was stronger than it believed. And, in Palo Alto—the chosen home of so many tech billionaires—India had learned to braid together self-love with growth so it best benefitted her clients.

"No, Mom and Tomas suddenly forgot how to teach with you gone," China said, sounding cheeky enough, but something was off in her tone. India could tell that China's brain had already moved on to the next thing. "I do miss you, though," she added, voice suddenly wobbly.

"Something wrong, Cee?" India was instantly in big-sister

mode. Even though China was almost thirty, India would always be three years older. Every time China sounded like something was bothering her, it would always take India instantly back to when China was a toddler who woke up in the middle of the night needing to be held.

Instead of answering, her sister let out a sob.

Worry rolled through India, even as she listened carefully to determine if there was any real cause for alarm. "It's going to be okay. Are you alone? Is it work? Is it Song?" China was equally passionate about her family, her work, the weather, their pug, her new girlfriend.

"Do you believe it's possible to burst with love?"

India relaxed and took a sip of her hot water, a relieved smile nudging at her lips. "You mean physically, like a balloon popping? I've never actually heard of a case where that happened."

"Funny. But I don't expect you to understand. It's just . . . it's just . . . I'm just filled all the way up, you know? Like my feelings for her are pushing against my skin in every part of me. Even the tips of my fingers tingle with it, India!"

India dropped into the circular chair bed overlooking the ocean and crossed her legs. "You're adorable, Cee."

"I am, right? So, it's not strange that someone as perfect as Song likes me?"

"You're the one who's perfect here," India said, making sure China knew she meant it. If they had to play the who's-luckier game, anyone who earned her sister's love was the lucky one. "Has Song decided to stay back?" India tried not to sound worried but she wasn't sure she succeeded.

China had recently started seeing Song Ji Woo, who was a famous Korean actor. China was a producer at the Food Network and Song had been a contestant on China's TV show last season.

Problem was, Song had moved to the U.S. only for the show. Just like her choice to be addressed by her last name instead of her first name, being here was a temporary thing she was escaping into. Her life and work were back in South Korea. To say nothing of the fact that Song was quite firmly in the closet and China had been out and proud her whole life.

"Why does that matter?" China tried not to snap, India knew that, but keeping her emotions tempered had never been her sister's strong suit.

How could it not matter? If the person you were giving your love and trust to wasn't interested in giving you theirs, how could that not matter? There was no way to ask China that without sounding disapproving of this great love she was experiencing. So, instead, India said, "It only matters if it matters to you."

"I knew you'd do this. How can you of all people not understand that if you love someone, you love someone. It can't be conditional on what they can give you in return. It's the journey, not a destination. Isn't that what you spend your days teaching people?"

Sure, life, like yoga, was a practice. You stayed in the moment. Lived it with mindful actions. That was the only way to experience it fully and do it justice. That didn't mean you jumped off a cliff onto rocks just to know how that felt.

"I'm not saying you can't have the feelings or that you shouldn't take joy from them. I just don't want you to get hurt," India said gently. The expectations, the hopes, the dreams, all the things China wanted from Song were clear in her voice, in the way she breathed when she talked about her. "You can only live in the moment with yourself. But that's not what you want. You want those feelings returned."

"She returns my feelings."

"I know she does. But, sweetheart, she's not planning to stay."

"This isn't the nineteenth century. Every relationship does not have to end in marriage."

"Okay." Strong as the urge to fix this for her sister was, India knew it wasn't in her hands.

"Did you have to ruin it?"

"No. I'm sorry. I do think you're great together. And you're so much more fun when you're getting some," she added, needing to diffuse the tension between them.

That made China laugh. Her sister was quicksilver, her temper burning hot but her need to return to joy even more stubborn. "Hah! Yes, speaking of getting some. The girl is insatiable." China's laugh got all husky and India knew her anger was forgotten. "I think I might have set a record. And you know that I'm already somewhat of a legend."

"Also somewhat lacking in humility?"

"I came seven times in one night, India! And I wasn't the one who came the most number of times."

"TMI, Cee!"

China didn't care, she filled India in on the details. Which were undoubtedly impressive. India had to admit that she'd never seen her sister this happy. China's naturally high capacity for joy stretched beautifully at the seams.

Maybe India didn't need to worry about Song breaking China's heart. Only the most foolish person would let feelings so precious slip from their hands. Maybe Song would realize how fortunate she was and the two of them would find a way to be together.

Once China had caught India up on every single detail of every single thing Song and she had said and done over the past few days, India gently turned the conversation toward their family.

True to form, Sid hadn't been in touch with China either. As soon as their brother had access to a network he'd call.

"Mom canceled her classes yesterday," China said absently. "Nothing to worry about, though, Tomas picked them up."

"Is it her back?" Tara's upper back had been bothering her for weeks. No matter how much Mom insisted she was okay, recognizing signs of pain was India's job. She should never have left without making sure that her mother saw the doctor.

"I think it is. But you know how she is, she will neither confirm nor deny, but her heated buckwheat pad has been going nonstop. She won't go to the doctor. I tried."

Obviously China hadn't tried hard enough. "I'm canceling next week's session and coming home."

"I hate when you do that." India knew what China would say next. "Act like you're the only one who can fix things. Act like you're the only one who wants to fix things."

"That's not what I'm doing. But Mom has to see the doctor. It's not a choice."

China made an infuriated sound. "I will drag her there if I have to. You don't have to come home."

"You sure?"

Another infuriated sound. "Of course I'm sure. I get that you run the family business, that you've taken it all on because Sid and I weren't interested, but you do it because you love it, right?"

"Yes." The family and the studio were what made her *her*. It was just that she found it easier to take care of things herself instead of relying on someone else, even her siblings.

"You know I would help you with the studio if I could bear to," China said, her distaste at having to do such a thing palpable in her voice.

India didn't need another rundown of all the reasons why her life was boring, why she was passionless for toeing the family line. "Mom and I don't need your help with the studio, we're fine. It's just not like Mom to miss classes. She needs to see a doctor. In fact can you call Trisha and run this by her?"

Trisha Raje was a neurosurgeon, so not quite an internist, but Trisha was one of China's closest friends. Trisha's cousin Ashna lived next door to the Dashwoods. The Raje cousins and the Dashwood sisters had been friends for years, their friendships solidifying in adulthood because both families tended to be private and slow to trust strangers.

"I'll call Trisha and Mom's doctor as soon as I get off the phone with you. You stay right where you are and don't worry about it. You know I can be an adult when I focus really, really hard."

India had another week-long corporate gig coming up with a week's break before it. It was much less work than a full retreat because she just needed to lead morning yoga sessions and then give a couple lectures about stress management and she'd get paid several times as much as the retreat paid. "Thanks. It would be unwise to give up that kind of money." But something about not taking care of Tara herself didn't sit right inside her.

"Yeah, no need to . . . Hold on . . . Oh God . . ." There was a scrambling sound and India heard the television volume turning up at China's end.

"China, what's wrong?"

"Oh my God." That was not China's emotional drama voice. It was real horror.

"Cee! Will you please stop saying that? You're scaring me. What's wrong?"

"Oh my God," China said again. "Oh no. It's Yash Raje. Something is wrong."

A sharp and dark feeling twisted in India's heart.

"What are you talking about?" It had been a decade since India had seen Yash. In person. You couldn't avoid him on TV no matter how hard you tried. She was friends with his sisters and his cousin and they thought the sun shone out of his . . . well, out of one of his orifices.

She had thought so too. For precisely one day.

She hated the panic that gathered in her body. By all accounts, her experience with Yash Raje had been some sort of aberration. With everyone else he seemed like a perfectly stand-up guy. Not that any of it had mattered in a very long time. No matter how angry she'd been with him, she most certainly did not want anything to be wrong with him.

Please let nothing be wrong with him.

"Is it the polls? Has he dropped in the polls?" India tried not to follow politics, and she'd avoided it even more since Yash announced his candidacy, but she wasn't an ostrich either.

Over the phone, China let out a gasp. "It's not the polls." Her voice was shrill with tension. This was bad. Really bad. "Oh God. Oh no. I think Yash has been shot."

Chapter Three

The last time Yash had emerged from general anesthesia he'd been fifteen years old and surrounded by a roomful of family. Every one of them with swollen yet dry eyes. No doubt because his parents had warned his siblings to make sure they did not cry in Yash's presence because he needed them to be strong.

This time when Yash regained consciousness he was all by himself. Disorienting as this was, it was also a relief, considering how on that day twenty-three years ago he'd been told he would never walk again. He wiggled his toes and moved his legs just to make sure he could.

"You're up!" Someone ran into his room. Hands were thrown around him with no regard for the shoulder that felt a bit like a boulder was balanced on it.

"It's you," he said, poking at his brain for her name. It was gone again.

Fortunately, his sister Trisha followed close on her heels. So he hadn't forgotten everyone's names, just the name of the woman who was supposed to be his girlfriend. Fabulous.

"Hey, Yash." His sister tapped the woman's arm, obviously trying not to show her impatience, which was usually not something Trisha bothered with.

His girlfriend squeezed Yash's hand and left the room with an "I'll be right back."

Trisha pushed his hair off his forehead. "You're awake."

"Was that not what you were expecting?" He tried to remember the details of what had happened, but the fog blanketing his brain was too thick.

She smiled her amused-doctor smile. "No, drama queen, we were fully expecting to not be rid of you just yet. Then again, we were also not expecting you to go and get yourself shot." She looked like she wanted to smack him upside the head.

Right. He'd been shot. "Abdul. How . . ." Yash tried to sit up.

Trisha pressed him back down. "He's in the hospital too. We're treating him."

Yash waited, but she said nothing more and just kept petting his hair like he was a puppy she'd found on the street. All this out-of-character coddling was more than a little disconcerting. Trisha was his least warm-and-fuzzy sister.

"And . . ." Yash prompted, not bothering to hide his impatience.

"And you need to worry about your own healing right now. How's your shoulder feeling?"

Yash was the most bullheaded of the siblings. Trisha ought to know that. "But he's okay? He's conscious?"

Her hesitation made it clear that they'd had a family meeting while Yash was out and strategized how much to tell him and when.

"He's out of surgery."

Usually Yash could outmaneuver his family's strategizing in his sleep, but he was so not in the mood for that. "How bad is it?"

Before Trisha could answer, his girlfriend came back into the room. Behind her his entire family followed. Could someone please tell him her name?

"You're awake." Mina Raje was not given to crying, but her swollen eyes meant she had been.

"Ma, I'm fine."

Their father squeezed his foot. Other than the squeeze, Dr. Shree Raje was as regally stoic as ever. Yash's father had been born a prince, and the staff at the Sripore Palace, the Raje's ancestral home in India, still referred to him as His Royal Highness. It was so fitting that Yash and his siblings had always called him HRH behind his back. The shadows under HRH's eyes were the only tell of his worry.

Now that they were adults, at least he wasn't glaring at Nisha and Ashna for crying. And, man, those two were making up for the rest of them. As soon as she saw them, even Trisha's eyes filled up.

Yash could bet his life having a bullet enter you after hitting someone else made it much less serious. For you, not for the person who'd saved your life.

"Will someone please tell me how Abdul is doing?"

His sisters all looked at one another and refused to meet his eyes. He turned to their significant others: DJ, Trisha's boyfriend, looked at Trisha, and something passed between them. Something that kept DJ from answering Yash.

Next he looked at Neel, who was married to Nisha, the sister who was also Yash's campaign manager, therefore also an employee (not that Yash was brave enough to remind her of that). Neel had been one of Yash's closest friends since they were in diapers, but the traitor did the same thing DJ had done, he looked at his wife and then studied the walls.

Were his sisters puppet masters? Looking at Rico yielded the same results. Rico looked at Ashna, who gave him a wide-eye, and the man promptly turned to studying the many monitors in the room.

"For shit's sake! . . . Sorry, Ma. Will someone tell me what is going on with the man who took a bullet for me?" Yes, he yelled, and it made him break into a cough, and that made the worried faces multiply their worry twenty times over.

"They don't think Abdullah Khan is going to make it," his girl-friend said, impervious to the glares that went flying around the room.

"What Naina means," Nisha said in her intimidating-mom voice, "is that his condition is critical right now but the doctors are trying their best to save him."

Naina. Of course.

This memory-lapse thing was annoying as hell. Yash fought to reach for the rush of relief knowing her name should have brought, the hope Nisha's reassurance about Abdul should have brought, but all he felt was parched emptiness in place of all the emotions he should be feeling.

All around his bed were faces he loved, looking at him with absolute adoration and gratitude that he was alive. A tightly squeezed circle of all the reasons his life was far richer than any-one deserved. He knew this. Logically. Intellectually. Up in his head. In his heart there was nothing.

"I want to see Abdul," he said, and the circle of faces turned all shades of indignant.

"Let's have your doctor look at you first," Trisha said. Then she turned to the rest of them. "Can everyone clear out? We're not all supposed to be here. He's fine. Seriously. We're overwhelm-ing him."

He was not overwhelmed. He should be. He was not.

That didn't change the fact that this was a hospital. It was Trisha's domain and DJ squeezed her hand and headed out. Rico and Neel followed him. It was also their father's domain, but Ma took his hand and tugged him out. Which meant there was a strategic plan at play. Yash studied the people left in the room and tried to calculate who'd been assigned to manage him.

"Naina, beta, let's wait outside," Ma said to Naina in a far kinder tone than the one she used on her own children. It was her children-in-law voice and it was always extra-kind toward Naina.

"Yes, Mina Auntie." Naina dropped a kiss on Yash's lips and smiled sadly.

Did he and Naina kiss? Was that part of the deal? Then why did it feel so strange? Did their kissing always feel so . . . so . . . dry?

He smiled back, managing only to highlight the fact that there was nothing where his feelings should have been. Nothing where her kiss had landed.

Once they were all gone, it was just him and his three sisters. Strategically speaking, he had to admit it was a smart choice.

"I'm not overwhelmed." Honestly, any degree of whelmed would be great. "I just need to see Abdul."

"I think they're only letting family see him right now." This from Nisha. Other than Yash, she was the one who had spent the most time with Abdul. She knew him. And Yash knew her. There was no way she hadn't gone to see him.

Nisha studied his face. "His wife, his parents, and his in-laws are with him. They're hopeful."

"And Naaz?" Yash asked.

Nisha went just a little bit green. Her hand went to her pregnant belly. A baby having her father shot two days after she was born was a dose of reality no expectant mother should be exposed to. "His little girl is healthy. So is Arzu."

"Good. Then I'd like to go see them." Yash moved to stand, and for the second time today Trisha held his shoulder—the good one—keeping him in place.

"It wasn't your fault. You weren't the one who shot him," Ashna said.

"I'm aware," Yash snapped. "But Rico was there with me. If he'd been standing closer. If he'd been hit, would you still think it wasn't my fault?"

Her fingers twisted together. "Yes," she said after a long pause. "I would still blame the person with the gun, not you. You're a victim here too. There's a hole in your shoulder too. And a rip in your arm."

That, too, he was aware of. As if on cue, the wounds in his shoulder and arm gave a throb. Good thing the bullets had struck his left side. Since there was no more space for scars on his right side. The accident had already taken care of that. Automatically his hand went to his chest; the hospital gown covered his torso and shoulders, but he still pulled his blanket up to his neck.

Nisha picked up a bag from a sideboard. "Ma brought you your pajamas." Obviously, Ma knew he'd need his clothes as soon as he woke up.

For a moment the discomfort of unspoken things, unspeakable things, silenced them all.

This wasn't a time to wallow in old wounds. He turned to Trisha. She was his only hope. "I need to see Abdul. You know you can make it happen."

Trisha looked at Nisha.

"Fine. I'll talk to the family," Nisha said. Then the three of them exchanged another one of their loaded looks.

"What now?" he said. "I'm fine. Just spit it out."

"You haven't asked about the polls." Ashna was the one who spoke.

Right. The election. Another thing that felt several lifetimes away. He wondered if he should tell someone about the numbness. What would he say? *I'm not feeling anything? I can barely remember the election.*

His family would only argue that not feeling anything was a feeling in itself. Then they would freak the fuck out.

"Yash?" One of them prodded him. He wasn't sure who. All of a sudden he couldn't bring himself to focus. The fog in his brain had thickened to sludge.

They stood there, his wall of sisters, watching him so intently that he had to respond. He pushed through the sludge and racked his brains for what they wanted to hear and came up with, "What are the polls looking like?"

Last he remembered Joshua Cruz, his opponent, had been leading by a narrow margin. Cruz sold himself as the blue eyed *and* blue collared, father of four, "all-American" candidate. If Yash had a penny for every time the man used the term "middle class family values" Yash may never need to do another fundraiser again. Cruz had played in the NFL, so *middle class* was pushing it.

"What?" he asked when no one answered.

All three of them looked at him like they were going to explode.

Finally Trisha squealed, like a child who'd just received a long coveted present. "You're leading in the polls! By ten points!"

What? "Leading Cruz?"

"That is who you're running against. So, yes." Nisha retrieved her cell phone and navigated to a video, bouncing on her heels.

"The entire state is in an uproar over the shooting. Vigils everywhere. For you. For Abdul. For Naina."

"For Naina?"

"Yes, she's a damn hero!" Ashna said.

At the cost of repeating himself: *What?*

"The footage of Naina leaning over your gurney and sobbing as you bled all over her has hit the public hard. It's everywhere. She's Jackie Kennedy."

"Except. She isn't. I'm not dead in her lap." Neither was he her husband or the father of her children. He was, in fact, no more than her friend. A partner in crime. Someone who had conspired with her to cheat their families so they didn't have to deal with their pressuring tactics.

On the phone Nisha handed him, Naina was crying mascara-stained tears into Yash's face. She looked devastated, and he looked quite near death. Were they more than friends? Had he forgotten more than just her name?

"The video has been playing on the news cycle nonstop," Ashna said.

"Is Rico responsible for this?" His tone must have been harsh, because the wall of sisters turned their joint frowns on him.

"You got shot. What exactly is that question supposed to mean? Are you suggesting Rico made that happen?" Ashna, who was the least mean person on earth, snapped in a tone that sounded pretty darn mean. "You're acting very strange," she said more gently. "Are you feeling okay?"

Not at all. I feel like a block of ice encased in paper. "Of course I'm okay. I'm great. I can't feel my shoulder. A man might be dying because of me and no one will let me see him. But I'm just peachy, thank you very much. You're right, we should all be celebrating the polls!"

"Yash," Nisha said with all the gravitas of someone who had dedicated her entire adult life to his career. "We are all heartbroken about Abdul, every one of us. We're praying that he wakes up. He believed in you. He was obsessed with you winning this election, just like the rest of us. We will do everything we can to make sure he and his family are okay. But did you not hear us? With these numbers and the outcry so close to the election, only an act of God can stop you from winning in November. The election just became ours to lose. Everything you've worked for—*we've* worked for—it's going to happen."

Trisha wheeled Yash down the eerily quiet hospital corridor. Nisha and Rico had done a great job working with the hospital to keep the press out.

"Stop here," he said to Trisha, when they got to the door of the private lounge where Abdul's family was waiting for him, and stood. He didn't need a wheelchair, but Trisha had refused to let him leave his room if he didn't use one. God save us all from bossy sisters.

This one was looking at him as though he were breaking her heart. "I'm fine. I'm not going to do anything irresponsible. Don't worry."

"I know that. You're Yash. Do you even know how to do something irresponsible?" She smiled at him kindly enough that he knew she was hurting for him. "I know how hard this is on you. But it's not your fault. Abdul was doing his job."

"His job was to keep people from getting too close and familiar. Taking a bullet was never in the job description."

"Taking a bullet is always in the job description. You just wish it wasn't."

They had arrested the shooter. Your garden-variety white supremacist who didn't want his state handed over to a *foreigner*. Yash should have been angry, but he was still having that little problem of not being able to feel anything. Plus, dealing with bigots was half his job. It was half the job of anyone not born white in this country. He could do it in his sleep.

The good news was that the man was going away for a very long time. The bad, but not surprising news was that for all the outrage and sympathy that had landed Yash at the top of the polls, there was no shortage of people on social media turning the bastard into a martyr and supporting his "cause" and wishing death upon "browns who conspire to steal America."

"You have five minutes. Then you need to be back in your room," Trisha said. "I'll be back to get you."

"Doesn't a fancy surgeon have anything better to do than wheel patients around?"

"She does. But there's this dumb kid sister getting in her way because her brother won't stop being a stubborn ass." With that she kissed his cheek and hurried off, leaving him to enter the waiting room.

Arzu, Abdul's wife, sat flanked by an older couple.

The man stood and shook Yash's hand. "I'm Hafiz Khan, Abdullah's father."

Yash took the man's hands in both of his. "Thank you for seeing me," he said, looking at Arzu, whose eyes were so dry and stoic they should have been a sledgehammer to Yash's numbness.

Next to her, in a baby carrier hooked to a stroller, Naaz was rolled up in a pink blanket and fast asleep. Her head was covered in a cap, leaving open nothing more than cheeks, a button nose, and tightly closed eyes.

"How are you?" Hafiz said, and the ice inside Yash went even colder. He was here, standing on his own two feet, the wounds in his shoulder and arm nothing more than a few stitches. While Abdul was hooked up to a ventilator, a head injury and major blood vessels and tendons in his neck torn and sewn up. His brain unable to process that his body was alive.

Yash bent over Naaz. *She's so beautiful*, he wanted to say, but nothing came out, so he simply stroked a crooked finger along her baby carrier, too afraid to touch something so fragile.

"They're not sure if he'll wake up," Arzu said, her strong voice at odds with the words she was saying.

"He'll wake up. He has to." Yash turned to her.

Nisha had warned him to be careful about what he said. To not give her hope when the doctors were being so cagey. But doctors didn't know everything. Who knew that better than Yash?

"They aren't sure they can keep him on the ventilator much longer." Every time they'd met, Yash had noticed the spine of steel under her easy banter with Abdul. They were a powerhouse together. Now she had to be fierce enough for the both of them.

"We'll keep him on the ventilator for as long as it takes him to wake up. You don't have to give in to pressure. I will make sure no one makes that call but you. If there is anything in this world that can be done to get him to wake up, I'm going to do it. I promise you that."

That did it, that made her shoulders slump. Just for a moment. Then she straightened again, eyes still dry.

For a moment he thought she would tell him to stuff his promises. For a moment he thought she'd thank him. She did open her mouth to say something. In the end she just nodded, then she bent over her baby and stroked her cheek as Yash let himself out of the room.

Chapter Four

India had canceled the corporate retreat and rushed back home early because of her mother. Yash Raje had nothing to do with it. No, he did not. She would never change her plans because of some politician being shot. Even though that politician was her friend's brother. Correction, he was her friends' brother. Plural, not singular.

Ashna, Trisha, and Nisha had all responded to her texts and assured her that they were fine and that Yash was on the road to recovery. That's what the news said as well.

It was a relief. Not just to her, but to all of California—all of America. Her relief was no different than anyone else's. Being relieved was natural. The fact that the man's tongue had been the first tongue to ever be in her mouth had nothing to do with it.

Settling into the yoga mat in her room, she dragged a breath deep into her lungs and held it. Energy traveled all the way down her arms, her legs, filling up her fingertips, her toes. Then she released it. Emptying herself out. So it went for a while. Keeping time while meditating wasn't her way, so she didn't know how long it took. In the end when it released her she felt much more centered.

The first thing she'd done after she got home yesterday was take Mom to the hospital, where they'd spent the day doing test after test.

"That's what you get when you go to a Western hospital," her mother had said. Tara always said "Western hospital" as though she hadn't been born and raised in California.

West of what? India would have asked, if Mom hadn't looked so fragile. She had lost twenty pounds. India kicked herself for not noticing. Her mother had always been on the thinner side. They all were. A lifetime of yoga and vegetarianism would do that to you. According to the doctor, the weight loss might not have been visible because it was mostly muscle mass loss. India should still have noticed.

After rolling up her mat, she made her way up the narrow wooden stairs to the third-floor attic that housed the incense work-shop and Tara's room. The yoga studio and India's office took up the first floor, with a public entrance in the front that opened into a lobby and a private entrance in the back that opened to the staircase that led up to the private apartment. The second floor was occupied mostly by the family room and open kitchen with India and China's rooms tucked away in the back along with a guest room that Sid used when he was in town.

As India entered Tara's room she was flooded with the smell of incense. Naturally it was strongest up here, even though a hint of it always permeated the rest of the apartment and studio.

Their family had owned this three-floor block since the early part of the last century. India's great-grandparents had bought it to open a barbershop on the first floor and live on the upper floors. When the business grew, they had hired an immigrant from India who in his spare time practiced a strange form of stretching and breathing called yoga that they'd never heard of.

The couple had become intrigued when their joint pain disappeared when Ram taught them some poses and helped them practice every day. The more they practiced, the more obsessed they became. They cleared a part of the barbershop and tried to get their neighbors to join in. Their efforts were met with suspicion and accusations of practicing pagan mystical arts, but it hadn't stopped them from continuing to practice themselves.

India's grandmother had grown up in love with both yoga and the man who brought it into their lives. Ram was a good fifteen years her senior, and marriage to him had been not just scandalous, but also illegal. In the end, the town's hatred had driven Ram out.

After he left, Romona had found out that she was pregnant with Tara. Romona was the one who finally turned her parents' barbershop into a yoga studio. San Francisco and the surrounding Bay were a vastly different place in the sixties than it had been in the forties, and Romona had been able to raise Tara, who had inherited her father's black hair and brown skin, with only an undertone of disapproval from the neighbors and a steady supply of students to make a living.

When she turned eighteen, Tara had traveled to India in search of her father. She hadn't found him, but she had spent ten years in a yoga ashram in Jammu. She'd come home with Siddhartha, a four-year-old boy she'd adopted, and joined her mother in running the studio. Two years after that she'd adopted India from an orphanage in Bangkok, and two years after that China from an orphanage in Nairobi.

India hadn't known there was anything different about her family until a substitute teacher in her kindergarten classroom had looked at her with an expression India would come to know well as she grew up, and asked, *Aren't you one of that yoga teacher's kids? The ones with the cleft lip scars adopted from three continents?*

When India had told Sid about it on their way home from school, he'd said, *But India and Thailand are on the same continent.*

It's how India had learned that adults, even teachers, didn't always know everything. To India, their family was how families were supposed to be. Many years later, when China was in her rebellious phase, she had asked Tara why she had felt the need to adopt children from three countries.

I took a lifelong vow of celibacy. How else was I supposed to have children? That had been Tara's answer.

"India?" her mother said, bringing India back to the present.

India was sitting on her mother's bed massaging her feet. Chutney, their pug, was squeezed into Mom's side snoring in long whistles. She barely stirred as Mom moved her so she could sit up.

Now that Mom was awake, India scooted closer and lifted one foot into her lap and started to massage in earnest.

Tara moaned a long, satisfied sigh. "That feels wonderful. You have magic hands, baby girl." She shifted her stance and India could tell her back was hurting.

"Did you take ibuprofen this morning?"

"I drank the turmeric milk you made me." The whites of Tara's eyes were almost as yellow as the turmeric milk, and she looked exhausted. Anyone who knew Tara would know how terrifying that was.

"That was hours ago, and it's not going to stop the pain."

"Why don't you rub some of your eucalyptus oil blend on my back? That usually brings the pain down," Tara said as though speaking to a class full of students.

The next thing India knew, Tara was elbows-deep into a story of how her guru in India had brought down someone's fever by hanging onions from their ears.

India smiled. All had to be well with the universe so long as Tara was telling her bizarre stories, right? Nodding along, she handed Tara a pill and some water.

"Great men cured fever with onions, we have little white pills for aches." Tara's sigh was deep, but she took it, which was telling.

"The doctor's office hasn't called with results yet," Tara said. "I know you've been obsessing over it all day and dying to ask me. Wouldn't I tell you if they had called?" She took India's hand. "You're a silly girl to come running back from Costa Rica to take care of a mother who is fully capable of taking care of herself."

But Tara hadn't taken care of herself. India wouldn't have had to come home if Tara had gone to the doctor herself, or if China weren't so wholly preoccupied with Song right now. China had barely spent a half hour with India since she'd returned. Plus, there was the feeling that had flared inside India after she'd heard about the shooting. What exactly it meant, she didn't know. She wasn't even sure if it was the shooting or Mom, but something had told her that she had to come back home.

"Once we get the results and figure out what's going on, I can still go back for the corporate retreat if I want. The organizers have a substitute, but they want me to try. There wasn't anything to do there this week anyway except attend some dinner parties."

"And see one of the most beautiful countries on earth, at someone else's expense."

"I go every year, Mom."

"You've only gone for the past two years. Because of the renovation. And you've barely stepped out of the hotel to see anything. This was your first chance to. How is Sid the only one of my kids who has any interest in seeing the world?"

India picked up Tara's other foot and started massaging it, gauging the tightness of the pressure points so she could loosen them. "You made us love our home too much."

Tara sighed and gave her a too weak smile. "My sweet baby girl. What did I do to deserve you? Well, I recognized the shape of your ears." She reached over and stroked India's ears. "Even as a baby your lobes reminded me of the Buddha."

They sat there like that for a while. India massaging Tara's feet, Tara stroking her ears and reminiscing about her babyhood. It was heavy on the diarrhea stories, because Tara was Tara. But for all her love for the gross and the macabre, she never talked about the surgeries. With three children with cleft lips, there had been a lot of surgeries in those early years. Tara just never touched those memories.

Tara's phone buzzed. She made no move to pick up, so India reached for it.

"Leave it. It must be someone trying to sell us something again. Or threatening to send us to jail if we don't send money to the fake IRS."

Tara knew perfectly well that the doctor's office was going to call today. When India answered, all Tara did was sigh heavily and lie back against her pillows.

It *was* the doctor's office. They wanted Tara to come in for the results, and they happened to have an opening in an hour.

"Why would the doctor want to give you the test results in person?" India asked, helping her mother get dressed.

Tara was trying hard to hide it, but her dragging movements were impossible to conceal given her usual energy. Even her vibrant green aura had turned muddy brown.

From the rideshare, India called China, who was with Song.

"We're on our way," China said without a second of hesitation. "See you there."

Tara and India smiled at each other as the car made its way down the short stretch of palm-lined road to Stanford Hospital. If you could call deep worry manifesting as a lip stretch "smiling." A little like how gas manifested as smiles in babies.

China had barely ever given a relationship the time of day. Even the family knew to give her space or she got crabby. Now she was joined at the hip with someone 24/7. And that someone had a life waiting for her almost six thousand miles away in an entirely different country.

"Maybe Song will figure out how to risk her career for China," Tara said, stroking the thick silver braid slung across her shoulder.

India was all about trusting people to do the right thing, but she was not given to flights of fancy. Celebrities were ambitious and the ambitious always put their goals before everything else.

"China has the high forehead of the blessed. It signals that she's going to find her soul mate." Tara said that about India too, and about Sid. It was her motherly hope finding anchor in superstition.

When India didn't respond, Tara patted her clasped hands. "Or maybe they'll enjoy what they have for now and move on as richer people for having experienced love, even transiently."

If it was transient, how could it be love? Nonetheless, Mom was right, every experience did make you richer. That's what India told herself when she couldn't get a relationship to last more than four or five dates. It always felt transient, and that wasn't what India wanted.

She was pretty sure China wasn't feeling transient with Song.

"China has three friends," India said. "She still drives the first car she bought straight out of college. She sleeps with the quilt she slept with as a child, in the bed she slept in as a child. She's changed jobs once, and you know how hard that was for her." Her sister was not given to moving on. She had never moved on from anything in her life. To her, love and loyalty were absolute.

When they made their way to the consultation room, China was already there, Song by her side. As soon as she saw Tara, she ran to her and wrapped her in a hug. "Mom! You look terrible. Why didn't you tell me it was so bad?"

"It wasn't until a couple days ago. How's the new season? How was Yosemite?"

The worry in China's eyes didn't eclipse the fact that she was glowing. Her flawless skin and dark eyes were even more sparkly than normal, veritable gemstones. Their joy was so contagious, India smiled at her sister and returned Song's hug.

The petite actress was wrapped in a hoodie three sizes too big and wore sunglasses indoors. Huge ones. The kind you might wear if you needed a disguise. Oh, and her hood was pulled up over her head.

Some of India's trepidation settled when Song took both of Tara's hands in hers and complimented her on her flowy elephant pants. It was a particularly kind thing to do, given how her daughters had been so focused on how sick she looked that they had to have been making her feel several times worse.

As they sank into the waiting room chairs—gorgeously modern but lacking in any warmth or comfort—Yash Raje's face flashed on the TV hanging in the middle of the room.

China jumped up and raised the volume. According to the news anchor, Yash had been scheduled to attend a rally that morning. And he'd just canceled his appearance at the last moment. It was the first event he had ever missed in his relentless campaigning. His energy levels had been dialed up to a hundred for months now, if not years. The person on TV seemed to think that someone trying to do an event five days after he had been shot was surprising. But who in their right mind thought Yash was like anyone else?

"Have you spoken to Trisha or Ashna?" India asked China, who was looking as stricken as India was feeling. "Is he okay?"

China squeezed in to Song and Song threw a nervous glance around the empty waiting area. "I spoke with Ashna yesterday. She said he was out of the hospital and she sounded like everything was okay."

"And the bodyguard?" India and Tara asked together.

"He's still critical."

India twisted in the stiff chair. "Ashna would not lie about how Yash is, right? I mean, it's not like him to miss a campaign event. If he's fine, he's not the kind of person—I mean, he doesn't *seem* like the kind of person who would miss a chance to speak to an auditorium full of voters."

China and Tara cocked their heads in unison and looked at India as though she had suddenly taken off all her clothes and exposed an unfortunately located wart.

"You know what I mean," she said, making the effort to sound less distraught than she had just sounded.

Obviously they did not know what she meant.

China blinked. "Why would Ashna lie about Yash being okay?"

Fortunately India didn't have to respond to that because the TV was flashing footage of Yash's girlfriend and they all turned to watch again. Naina Kohli was practically perched on top of his gurney, screaming his name, spilling tears into his face. India felt her throat constricting. Then the screen switched to a montage of pictures of the two of them doing all sorts of happy-couple things one might do if one had enough money to own a small country. The clothes, the chandeliers, the rocks in her ears, it was like thumbing through a catalog of a lifestyle magazine. Was this really the time for this?

"That woman is gorgeous!" Song said on a worshipful sigh. "But she should switch to waterproof mascara."

China smiled smittenly. Song wasn't wrong. Yash's girlfriend was gorgeous with or without runny mascara. She looked like someone had engineered the perfect being using genetic material from Padma Lakshmi and Halle Berry with input from every fine-boned, perfectly proportioned woman who ever lived. As if the genetic lottery weren't enough, she wore wealth and beauty with the effortless poise of someone who'd always had those things.

She was also an activist who had dedicated her life to rural women in all corners of the earth, as the person on TV was detailing with that oddly benevolent expression news anchors always wore when talking about charities and tragedies. Anyone with even a modicum of sense would choose Naina Kohli over anyone else. By all accounts, Yash Raje was a man of great sense.

The nurse called them in, and all thoughts of Yash and his lady love left India's mind.

They said bye to Song, and she pulled her oversized disguise hoodie lower over her face and left. India and China flanked their mother as the three of them went in to see Dr. Kumar. He was one of those doctors who smiled a lot. This was more disconcerting than you'd think in a doctor.

"So," he said, displaying eerily perfect teeth. "It's not all bad news."

What kind of tone-deaf thing to say was that?

"What is that supposed to mean?" China snapped. God bless her unfettered tongue.

"We have confirmation that it's not pancreatic cancer."

China sucked in a breath. Tara's face turned into a mask. India shifted closer to her. Had they been expecting it to be cancer? Did Mom know they were looking for cancer?

It took some effort to remember how to move her lips. "Do we have confirmation of what it is?" India asked.

Dr. Kumar took their confusion in stride, which India took as the first sign of his competence, despite his misplaced smiling. He explained that with the back pain, exhaustion, and yellowing in the eyes, pancreatic cancer was what he'd checked for first. Fortunately, it wasn't that, but Tara's liver enzymes were elevated and based on her fibroscan she had cirrhosis in her liver.

The word dropped like a cold rock in India's belly, but the doctor didn't look like he was delivering a tragic diagnosis, so she waited.

"Mrs. Dashwood, do you—"

"Ms.," Tara interrupted calmly. "It's Ms. Dashwood."

"Oh. Of course." Dr. Kumar blushed and ran a quick hand over his bald head. "I apologize. Your records said you don't drink and you've never done IV drugs. I just want to confirm that you never have."

"I might have tried some wine once," Tara said, her voice still utterly calm, the voice she'd used to respond to rude questions about her variously raced children. The quietness of a predator stalking her prey. "But that was more than thirty years ago."

If Dr. Kumar smiled again, India was leaving. He smiled. "Have you ever visited a third world country?"

"Third world?" Tara said in a tone that made Dr. Kumar look like he was cursing the day he'd decided to skim over his diversity training. "I lived in India for ten years. But as far as I know it's in the same world we all inhabit."

To no one's surprise, the doctor smiled. "That would explain it."

The three of them leaned forward, waiting for more.

His smile turned just the slightest bit smug. "Did you get a blood transfusion when you were in India?"

Mom was visibly startled at that. For a few moments she said nothing, then she closed her eyes and focused inward, almost sliding into a trance. "I did fall out of a rickshaw when a cow ran into it."

India and China turned to her, mouths agape. When she opened her eyes they were twinkling, as though the memory were a joy.

"The rickshaw landed on me, but I wasn't hurt. Well, there was the broken ankle. Then we tried to pull the cow upright because she'd rolled over. She kicked the driver, but she seemed to like me."

"Mom?" China was the one who prodded.

Dr. Kumar seemed captivated.

"I think the bells on her horns sliced my hand. Then she just sauntered off. Have you ever noticed how well cows handle trauma?"

"Mom, the transfusion?" This time it was India who prodded.

Tara stared off into space, trying to remember. "I think it was the sliced hand. Oh, and the overturned rickshaw also cut my thigh. I don't remember much more than the cow. But I did wake up in the hospital and there had been a transfusion. I think." She chuckled, her eyes alight with the memory. A memory of something that might have made her sick thirty years later.

"You said the news wasn't all bad," she said finally, coming back to this moment.

"Er, well." God, please could he stop smiling? "I think you might have hepatitis C, so I want to do the labs for that today and we'll also need more imaging to confirm the extent of the fibrosis."

"And what happens after all these tests?" How could their mother sound so calm right now? China looked like she was going to throw up. India reached over and took her hand.

"Let's not jump ahead of ourselves, but Hep C is treatable now. And cirrhosis is not reversible but a transplant is always an option. Let's wait to consider our options once we know more."

A curtain of calm had fallen over Tara's face. "How much will the treatment cost?" she asked, while her daughters sat there struck speechless. To think India had thought she was bringing her fragile mother here so she could be strong for her.

"Well, why don't we wait until all the tests are completed before we discuss a treatment plan," the doctor said.

"Do you have a ballpark?"

Finally India spoke. "It doesn't matter, Mom. Insurance should cover it."

Tara's jaw worked. It wasn't her way to contradict family in public, but the set of her face told India that she was going to fight this. What was there to fight? No matter what, Mom was getting treated.

India turned to Dr. Kumar. "And we can expect a full recovery?"

The smile he gave her this time was laced with sympathy. "Let's get the results. It's a long road. In the meantime, a lot of rest. It would help for someone to stay with her."

"We live in the same home," India said, more relieved than ever with the fact that she and China had never moved out. "We'll take care of her."

THE DRIVE HOME was barely a mile, but the silence in the car made it seem endless. It wasn't like either China or Mom to be quiet, but they had barely said a word since they left the doctor's office and waited with Tara as she made her way through blood draws and scans.

"I hope neither of you fed Chutney," India said as cheerily as she could. "I fed her this morning."

China hadn't been home since yesterday, so she couldn't have fed her virtually, and Mom had been in bed all day, but the mention of Chutney would snap everyone out of their funk.

"I did, uh-oh," Mom said, a smile touching her lips. India should've known she'd get out of bed to feed their dog, when she forgot to feed herself most days.

"I thought Chutney was on a diet. Aren't we supposed to cut back how much we feed her?" China spoke finally. "You two are going to cause her to die of obesity if you don't stop being obsessed with feeding her."

"We're not obsessed. A dog has to eat," Tara said simply.

"I'm gone for a few days and it's like no one can do anything right." China pulled the car into a parking spot in front of the studio. "What if she gains even more weight? She can barely move now." Her tone was too harsh, too filled with guilt to have anything to do with their dog's obesity.

"You are allowed to go out and do things," Tara said. "This did not happen because you were living instead of babysitting me or because India had to come back and force me to go to the doctor."

"But I was here. I was the one who should have done it. India shouldn't have had to come back. And now you're both trying to kill Chutney with food." With those words she stormed out of the car and took off down the street.

"China, sweetheart, come back. Chutney is going to be fine," India called after her.

"Let her go." Mom leaned on the car. A sight so heartbreaking, India didn't know what to do with it. She offered Tara her arm. How had the illness progressed so fast? "You know she likes to walk when she can't handle her feelings." It was how China had done everything from throwing tantrums to thinking through decisions. If she didn't get out and walk, she started to act like a caged tigress, and that was no fun for anyone.

India punched in the security code and unlocked the studio. They had left the original turquoise-painted glass-paned door as is during the renovation but added electronic locks. The sign in the door was flipped to CLOSED. India wasn't teaching a class today. She wasn't on the schedule for the next two weeks because she was supposed to be in Costa Rica. Tomas—the instructor they had hired last year when they had expanded their schedule to help pay for the renovation—had a class at seven and it was barely four.

As they made their way across the studio to the apartment stairs, the smell of home—floral incense mixed in with the aged-wood scent of an old house no renovation could erase—seeped into India's lungs. She grounded herself in it.

"It's just this one lifetime," Tara said, yanking her out of her peaceful place. "It's going to start and end when it does. We're just here to aid it along the best we can while we're here. Worrying won't change anything."

As always, Mom was right, and India refused to transfer her own worry to her.

At their first footfall on the stairs, the familiar pattering of a four-legged dance began on the upper floor and Chutney's scrunched-up face appeared at the top. Over the years the dance of excitement had turned more into a slow plodding roll. Chutney could no longer go up or down the stairs, but you could not enter the apartment and feel like it really happened without seeing her face at the top, and smelling her slobbery breath. She was the sound of their tree falling in the forest.

Despite the inducement at the top of the stairs, Tara's climb was slow and it made a restless determination churn inside India.

Mom was going to be all right. One step into the living area with its timber rafters and cozy furnishings, and Tara's shoulders relaxed.

India pushed her into the couch and tucked a quilt around her. "I'll make you some tea and then get dinner started. Soup sound good?"

The family room and kitchen were one continuous space and India watched Tara as she put the kettle on.

"Will you burn some of that kashi agarbatti?" Tara asked crossing her legs into the lotus pose.

India grabbed incense sticks from the ceramic jar on the tiled island. Holding them over the stove flame, she waited for the ends to light, then shook out the flames that left embers at the ends of the sticks. Twisted ribbons of smoke wafted up to the ceiling as she poked the sticks into an inlaid wood holder designed to collect the ash drippings. The kitchen filled with earthy scent.

Carefully, she chose vegetables from the fridge and laid them out on the cutting board. It was a good day for soup. Soft light filtered in through the rattan blinds. Barely audible sounds of Tara's practiced breathing spun around the room as she settled into her meditation, connecting with the only thing that was going to get her through this, her indestructible inner self.

On the surface it was just another day unfolding around them, but underneath it had a strange texture, an arrogance, as though it knew it was different from all the other days they'd spent doing these very things. India thanked the voice that had compelled her to come home and sliced through a carrot. Then like Tara she let her mind slide inward to the place that was strong enough to take on whatever life was getting ready to throw at her.

Chapter Five

"It's okay to admit you're in pain. We can get you meds." Rico looked more nervous than Yash had ever seen him look before a public appearance. Or maybe Yash was assigning emotions to Rico, since he couldn't seem to manage any on his own.

"I don't need meds." Maybe it was part of the relentless numbness, but Yash had expected a bullet wound to hurt more.

He stared out at the crowd from behind the stage. The Orpheum was packed to capacity. Everyone was carrying a candle, flameless naturally. Wave upon wave of flickering electronic wicks lit up the darkened auditorium.

"Maybe it's too soon. You're looking a little green." Rico followed Yash's gaze to the too somber crowd. Yash didn't think he had ever seen such a large audience be this quiet.

"I feel perfectly normal." *Physically.* "That bullet barely made it inside me. It hardly even broke skin. The other one just about grazed my arm." Someone started singing *Imagine* and the crowd started swaying with their candles raised up and hummed along. "What is the vigil for? What is all this sympathy for? I'm standing. And Abdul's not dead either."

"It's a vigil against hate crimes, against the gun culture. It's one of your biggest platform issues. It's time to get people to see sense."

"People haven't seen sense through fifteen hundred school shootings. Now a politician gets shot at and you think it's going to make a difference?" The NRA had poured another giant cash infusion into Cruz's campaign the day of the shooting.

Rico threw him the look that everyone in his family had taken to tossing his way all the damn time. A look that told him they weren't quite certain how much to push him, or even who he was anymore, really.

"It's an opportunity. It's not how you wanted to get here, but that shooter practically handed you this election." Rico had grown up in Rio de Janeiro and lived in London for the past decade, and his accent tended to go all over the place with the enunciating and lilting when he was upset.

"That shooter, who you think has handed me the election, might have taken a little girl's father from her before she was old enough to know him. She'll have no memory of him if he dies. All she'll know is that her father died because some damn politician made some damn fanatic angry enough to shoot at him."

"That's not what I meant and you know it." Rico gave Yash one of his coach-before-a-game looks. "You did not cause this. But you can make something good come out of it."

The man may be a recently retired soccer star, but Yash wasn't a nervous rookie in need of a pep talk. "Of course I caused it. I don't look like these people. I don't pray like them. From the first time I announced that I might have hopes of doing this, of running this great state, I was warned this was going to happen."

When the news of his candidacy first came out, someone had put a dead squirrel in his car with a note that said people who tried to step out of their lane ended up as roadkill. It was one of those letters that had been pasted together from magazine cuttings.

"Do you know how many threats I've received? How many creatively phrased messages telling me to go back to where I came from? More than I've bothered to count."

"And you decided to fight them. To make sure that people stop seeing the color of our skin when they see us. To prove that elections should be won for what we believe and how hard we're willing to work, not because of how we look or how *relatable* we are."

Yash backed away from the wings, then spun around and returned to the green room, Rico close behind him. "What if that's not possible? What if it was just hubris, me thinking I could do any of that? What if more people get hurt?" As a young boy Yash had exhausted everyone's patience with his questions. There had been so much he wanted to know that it used to fill him up and make him feel like he would burst if he didn't find out.

That wasn't how he felt now. These weren't questions. Even if he was phrasing them as such, they felt like answers. In fact, he knew for sure that none of what Rico had just said was possible. That knowledge felt so absolute inside him that he couldn't imagine how he'd believed it until now.

Once, while hiking in Yosemite, he'd wandered off a trail and gotten lost. The disorientation had felt like this, like he hadn't just lost his way, but like the path he'd been on had disappeared, like it had never existed in the first place.

Was it hot in here? He loosened his tie. A black one—Nisha had put it on him when she had picked him up this morning.

The black tie was a protest against the shooting. A statement of support for Abdul. Both he and Rico were wearing black bands around their arms. The sea of people filling the stadium were wearing black bands. Yash pulled off his tie. The breath in his lungs had grown thick and hot, fire trapped inside him building into a backdraft. He wiped his face against his sleeve. It came away damp. He was covered in sweat.

Someone called his name. It had to be Rico. But his vision wasn't doing what vision was supposed to do.

"I can't breathe." That's what he tried to say, but it wouldn't come out. Or it probably did, because suddenly there were several people in the room. Nisha, Ashna, his mother. Naturally, everyone had insisted on being here for his first event after the shooting.

Finally Trisha hurried in. They were all dissolving around the place like an oil painting left out in a heat wave. Someone pushed him into a chair and shoved a paper bag in his face.

Great, he was hyperventilating into a paper bag. Like a nervous boy. Something sharply cold hit the back of his neck, jolting him. Someone was pressing ice against his neck.

"Yash, beta? It's okay. We're here." Words his mother had always said to him anytime he needed support. Even if it was just her, she always said, "We're here," her attempt at reinforcing the support she was providing by multiplying it.

"What happened?" he asked, when he could finally speak. What the hell had that been? "Did I have a heart attack? Did the bullet move something that damaged my heart?"

"Your heart is fine," Trisha said, "but we should get an EKG to make sure." She was squatting in front of him and asked him to walk her through what he'd experienced.

He told her how it had felt like leaving his body or maybe like having his body leave him.

"I suspect you had a panic attack," she said, pulling his eyelids apart and staring into his eyes.

Ashna was squatting next to Trisha, worry pinching her forehead. "That's what it looked like. I had them for years." She took his hand and stroked it. "You're going to be okay. It just doesn't feel that way right now."

Damn straight. "I feel fine now," he said, lying. Nothing felt fine. He couldn't seem to remember what the hell fine felt like.

"Are you sure?" Nisha asked, far too gently. "Do you think you can go onstage? Those people have been waiting for hours to hear you speak."

And there it was again. His heart started to thud in his chest cavity like a stampede of rogue elephants. His mouth felt like he had gulped down his tongue and left behind a vacuum he couldn't swallow around. It wasn't exactly emotions, but at least it was something.

"He can't. We're going to have to cancel," Trisha said, staring into his eyes again.

"I'll go speak to them," Rico said, giving Yash's good arm another squeeze. "You're going to be okay, mate."

"What will you tell them?" Yash asked.

Nisha's phone beeped and she looked at it. "I think we have something we can give them. Abdul's blood pressure is falling. It's not looking good. We should head to the hospital."

HAVING YOUR FAMILY talk about you like you weren't in the room was never fun.

"My son have a panic attack? How is that even possible?" their father asked Trisha.

Why don't you tell me how it's possible, Dr. Raje? Yash wanted to say, but evidently His Royal Highness Shree Hari Raje, the patriarch, had completely taken over Dr. Shree Raje, the physician.

"He's obviously in shock from the shooting, which isn't surprising. He needs help." Trisha tried to sound patient. Yash knew what she really wanted to do was tell Dad to stop being pushy. But no one spoke to their father that way.

"He's leading in the polls. This is the miracle we've been waiting for," HRH said as though it weren't the single most abhorrent thing to say in this circumstance.

They were all gathered in Trisha's office because there were too many of them to wait outside intensive care, where Abdul was struggling for his life.

If one more person said anything about the polls right now Yash was going to—ah, forget it, he did scream. For the first time in his life he raised his voice while speaking to his parents. "He might die!"

Yelling in a hospital, even though it was just barely yelling, was bad form. Yash knew that. Which was why he swallowed and lowered his voice. The family, who had turned to him as one, gaped at him.

"A man might die. A father, a husband. That is not a miracle. That's a travesty," Yash said in a voice that took all his strength to keep down.

"We know, beta," his mother said, stroking his arm and giving HRH a placating look, as though it were Yash and not HRH who had just said something completely despicable.

They had all rushed to the hospital. All hands on deck. That was the Rajes. The room closed in around Yash. All he wanted was to be alone. Just for a moment. Yash had never felt suffocated by them before. He needed to breathe. Could everyone let him breathe for just one moment?

"That's not what your father meant." It wasn't surprising that Mom was supporting Dad. Usually Yash appreciated the devotion between his parents despite their vastly different personalities.

"Mina kaki." Ashna wrapped an arm around Ma and moved her away from Yash. "Trisha is right. Yash needs help." Ma saw something in Ashna's face, because she waited for her to finish. Even HRH watched her, his face softening for the first time.

"You know I started having panic attacks after Baba died." Ashna's father, Yash's uncle, had shot himself when Ashna was eighteen, and she was the one who had found him, minutes after he'd done it.

Ashna had spent the past ten years buried in guilt and trying to revive her father's restaurant. There was something in the way she looked up at Yash that hooked into him and told him what she had to say was important. "I was only able to work through my panic attacks because I knew what they were and how to get through them. You have to get help."

"Ashna's right. He needs therapy," Trisha said with all her directness.

"That would be all well and dandy if it didn't involve the therapist knowing that he's having panic attacks. No one is going to vote for someone who's actively losing control of himself." No one but HRH could say that without a bit of hesitation a week after his child had been shot.

Yash reminded himself that he loved his father and that his father had done everything in his power to give Yash the best possible life any human being could have.

"Yes, but his health is more important than the election." Trisha again. She'd been Dad's pet when they were young and she seemed to have the easiest time going up against him.

"His health is fine. He has a lifetime to take care of his health. The election is in a matter of months. He can't lose this momentum." Dad doubled down.

"Yes, but if he has a nervous breakdown, he's going to lose

more than momentum, he's going to lose the election." Nisha joined in. "The public sympathy is high enough right now that we have some time. If we don't use that and take care of this now, and he has an episode in public, we're throwing the election away."

HRH stood surrounded by two daughters and a niece who was as much his daughter as the rest, the wall of sisters shooting daggers at him like superheroes facing off a supervillain.

"Okay, warriors, stand down," Yash said. "This is my election and my life. You can all stop acting like I'm some sort of robot you all get to control."

The wall of sisters turned their eye daggers on him and he rolled his eyes. "I had one panic attack. One. I'm not going to have a nervous breakdown."

"And where did you get your medical degree from?" Trisha, naturally.

Nisha held her hand out to him. "Well, then, let's go. You have another event scheduled for today, at San Jose State. If we leave now we can make it there. Rico's told them we're canceling your appearance, but Rico is still speaking, as are other supporters. I'm sure everyone will be happy to see you."

His heart started to race and, damn it, sweat broke out across his forehead.

"That's what I thought," Nisha said, smug as ever. "You need to see someone." She turned to HRH. "Dad, surely you have psychiatrist friends you can trust. Plus there's doctor-patient confidentiality."

"There's no one I trust enough so close to the election. This cannot slip out. The media is far too hungry and the other side is spending an obscene amount of money digging through every single thing they can get their hands on," HRH said.

In this Yash agreed with him.

"If I go to a psychiatrist, I'm going to be honest with the public and announce it. I'm not keeping something like that secret."

HRH looked at him like he had lost his mind. Again, he wasn't wrong. It definitely felt like he had lost something.

"Actually," Ashna said, "going to a psychiatrist didn't help me that much. The person who really helped me was . . . well . . . you all know India Dashwood, right?"

Yash fell back in his chair and pretended it was exactly what he'd intended. In the midst of all his numbness, a jolt of discomfort punched deep inside him. A feeling. His first since the shooting.

"Isn't she your yoga instructor?" Ma said to Ashna. "China's sister?"

"Actually, she's a trained yoga therapist and one of Northern California's foremost stress management coaches," Trisha said.

"When I first got back from Paris and was struggling, India was the one who helped me out. She taught me everything I know about meditation and grounding myself and working through episodes. This is very much in her wheelhouse," Ashna said.

"I'm not having episodes," Yash said, just as Dad said, "He's not having episodes." Saying it together like that seconds after he'd had an episode did not help their case at all, and the wall of sisters made sure he knew it with their glares.

"There is no point skirting the truth." Ma fixed her son and husband with the master glare that his sisters had trained from, then turned to Ashna. "She did help you, didn't she?"

Ashna nodded. "I wouldn't have made it without her."

Ma threw a look from Ashna to Nisha to Trisha. "And you girls have been friends for many years now. You think we can trust her?"

"I'd trust her with my life," Trisha and Ashna said together, because suddenly his life was a theater production.

"She was with me at Berkeley and she punched Rick Nugen in the nose when he called me . . . well, he used a word I'm not repeating, but it was offensive to people with developmental challenges," Nisha said.

Despite himself, Yash wanted to smile. Of course India had done that.

"Haven't I met her?" Ma said. "Wasn't she at Nisha and Neel's wedding?"

"Yes, I remember she wore that lovely lilac ghaghra." Nisha remembered every single thing anyone had ever worn in their entire life. How she had any space left in her brain after storing the entire world's fashion choices, Yash had no idea. Who remembered what someone had worn ten years ago?

Hypocrite.

He pushed away a vision of India in what he'd always thought of as not quite blue and not quite pink. So the color had a name. Lilac.

India Dashwood in that ghaghra was probably the only thing Yash remembered about Nisha and Neel's wedding. A memory too long past, water under the bridge. Or not. Because no way would she give him the time of day. Not after the way he'd behaved.

Another faint brush of feeling rolled through him. Was he feeling things again? A wave of relief crashed on hope so intense, he stood and started pacing, trying to hold on to it. Just as quickly as he had felt it, it was gone and he was cold again. Filled with nothing again.

It was getting a bit annoying, all of this nothing filling him.

"How do you remember the color of her ghaghra?" Trisha asked, blinking at Nisha.

"Hello! It's Nisha. She remembers what everyone wore to her wedding, including all the aunties," Ashna said.

Their father cleared his throat.

"You can all relax. I do not need to see a therapist. I most certainly do not need to see some woo-woo yoga self-help life-coach guru person who manufactures incense in the middle of Palo Alto and travels around the world lecturing people about how to breathe."

The attention of the room shifted to him like a spotlight. Every brow rose. The silence was so intense he could hear himself breathing. Not in the correct way, no doubt, but who needed training on how to breathe? What kind of scam was that?

"I only know those things about her because I've heard Ashna mention them so many times." Actually, he knew because he'd read about India in the *Daily Post* last month. It was his job to read the local papers.

Ashna frowned at him. She had never mentioned India around him until now and her narrowed eyes told him exactly how well she knew this. But she kept her mouth shut. Which meant Yash was in more trouble than if she'd said something.

"Then you'll agree that I know what I'm talking about. It won't hurt to meet her once," Ashna said. Was that a threat in her eyes?

He had nothing to be afraid of. Knowing what a family friend did with her life was not a crime. Especially for an information junkie like him. Sure, he usually focused on things like the unemployment rate or global health care statistics, but India Dashwood's work was unique enough to stick in anyone's head. Plus, she'd ended up doing exactly what she'd dreamed of doing, what she'd talked so excitedly about that night.

"There are behavioral therapies that can help you deal with

what you're going through. A set of steps that can walk you out of your moment of panic," Ashna said.

"Clearly you know what works. Can't you just walk me through it?" Yes, that was the answer. Ashna could help him.

She squeezed his arm. "What works for me may not work for you. Our cases are completely different, and I'm not qualified to know what will work for you. India is."

Avoiding going out into crowds and speaking to voters was not an option. Unless he wanted to walk away from the race and let not just the people in this room but all his supporters down.

His family watched him, worry etched into their faces.

They'd had the scare of their lives when he got shot. If it happened to any one of them, if he thought even for a moment that he might lose any one of them, he didn't know how he would handle it.

His family had dreamed of him winning this election for as long as he could remember. Now they could almost touch the dream. Unless he messed it up.

Ashna sat down next to him and laid her head on his shoulder, a very Ashna gesture. She was the gentlest of them, the most empathetic. Just having her hold you made the world a better place. But today, nothing. Until she'd mentioned India.

"Chances are it's just shock and it won't last long," Trisha said.

"But you can't take the risk of having a public panic attack months before the election," Nisha added. "Not when your chances of winning are the best they've ever been. Think about what this means. All that we've put into this campaign. It's going to pay off."

Nisha had spent more days and nights than he could count working on his campaigns, prepping for interviews and debates, strategizing responses to mudslinging in the press. She'd been tireless. This time she was doing it pregnant. With swollen feet and needing to take breaks to throw up.

"Go see her once. If it doesn't help, you don't have to go back," Ma said.

"Don't forget why you're running. You can't do any of those things if you don't win," Dad said, but Yash could no longer remember what his reasons for running were or why he had even decided to go into politics. "Your sisters might be right. Going to see this girl makes sense. So long as we can trust her."

"We can trust her," Yash said before he knew he was saying it. Then, because he wasn't interested in more probing looks, he added, "I mean, if Trisha, Nisha, and Ashna trust her, we should too." Then, without waiting for a response, he excused himself and left Trisha's office.

Nisha followed him out. Of course she did. "You got a minute?" she called after him, and he turned to her.

He did not like what he saw in her face. "I already said I'll see India. You don't expect me to rush off there right this minute."

"You're right. This minute I need you for something else."

"Fine, hit me."

"I need you to meet your new bodyguard."

Over his dead body. "What the hell, Nisha! We talked about this."

He started walking and slammed his hand into the elevator button. When had his family completely stopped paying any heed to his wishes?

Nisha waddled after him into the elevator, face as patient as a saint's.

"I told you I don't want to talk about a new bodyguard, and I meant it," he said as the elevator slid shut. "At least wait until I'm campaigning again." *Until Abdul wakes up.*

"And I told you that not doing this right now is not an option, and I meant it."

They stood there staring each other down. "Are you questioning my professional opinion as your campaign manager?"

"As my campaign manager you're supposed to work for me, which, you know, involves taking my wishes into consideration. At least every once in a while. You're basically freaking out as my sister, and I'm telling you that I will be fine. I don't need security to walk from my car to buildings."

She took a step closer to him, but her pregnant belly kept her from actually getting close enough to breathe down his neck. "You will be fine?" Her voice did a high-pitched wobbly thing that was all sister and zero campaign manager. "You're not a superhero. This is not you going to prom by yourself so you could dance with all the girls who have no one else to dance with. Get over yourself. You have no way of knowing that you will be fine."

"So you think someone is going to shoot at me twice in one campaign cycle?"

Sticking out her hand, she started counting off on her fingers. "Reagan, Johnson, Nixon, Carter. They've all had over fifty assassination attempts. Some over a hundred!"

His sisters were the earth's most annoying creatures. "Those are all presidents. And they all *survived* the attempts."

"William Goebel, gubernatorial candidate. George Wallace, gubernatorial candidate."

"You're in the wrong century."

"And you're underestimating the power of racial hatred," she snapped.

"Bill Richardson, Deval Patrick, Bobby Jindal, David Paterson, Susana Martinez, Michelle Grisham—"

"And listing all the minority governors from this century proves what?" she snapped again.

"It proves that we can run for elections without ending up dead."

The elevator stopped and he waited for her to get out. "California's economy is larger than almost every nation's in the world," she said, heading off across the lobby.

"No way, really? Is that on Wikipedia?"

It was a miracle she did not wring his neck. "Really? Being a patronizing prick, that's your response, because you have nothing intelligent to come back with? I haven't lost you a single election in ten years. I'd like you to show me some respect."

"And I'm the one who won those elections. I'd like you to show some respect for what I want."

With a sigh, she grabbed his arm. "Yashu, think about this. It's three months to the election. And we're going to have to do this with a ground game, door-to-door, like we've won the rest. There's no way you're doing that without security. Not after what just happened."

"If someone is going to shoot me again, I'd rather not have anyone take another bullet for me."

Her eyes filled with sympathy. "Oh, Yash." Her thumb stroked his arm.

"How can you not understand this?" Of all his siblings, Nisha and he were usually on the same page. She would, in fact, tell anyone who'd listen that she knew what Yash was thinking better than he himself did. It wasn't untrue, and was terrifying as hell.

"I do understand it." Her voice was entirely nonconfrontational now. "I just want you to meet this person. Just say hello. She's here. Don't waste her time, at least."

That stopped him in his tracks, as Nisha had known it would. She was such a sneak.

"You found me a female bodyguard? And you thought that would somehow make the job of bullying me into it easier?"

She had the gall to grin. "Bingo. Wait here while I text her. We've made her wait long enough."

He sank into a couch off in a private corner of the hospital waiting area. "I really pity poor Neel, you know that?" he said with all the spitefulness of a sibling who'd lost an argument.

Her grin widened, a damn whoop of victory if he'd ever seen one. "You're so easy."

He narrowed his eyes at her, deploying one of her own favorite strategies for getting her way. "You know Ma loves me more than you, right?"

"Sorry, buddy, I'm the favorite by miles. Substantiate your claim by getting her to admit it, or shut up." With that she grinned widely at the woman approaching them with long, powerful strides.

Brandy Hennessy (yes, that was her name) was not what Yash had expected. Although he couldn't say what it was he had expected. She had cherry-red hair cut into short spikes and biceps that pushed into the sleeves of her muscle shirt. If you wanted your security detail to be visible, she was your person.

"Isn't it your job to disappear in a crowd?" Yash said as soon as Nisha had introduced them, being deliberately and uncharacteristically ornery.

"I don't believe that is part of the job description. In fact, I would say warning people off is the job description, sir."

"Okay, let's cut to the chase. There is only one condition on which I would hire you. If there is a shooting I need your assurance that you will not jump in front of any flying bullets."

Nisha knew better than to interrupt, but she threw him a look that would have maimed a man who hadn't dealt with her his entire life.

Ms. Hennessy met his stubborn gaze, stood, and shook his hand. "Well, it was nice meeting you, Mr. Raje. I hope you find someone who does the job the way you want them to." With that, she turned and strode away.

Nisha ran after her. "Brandy, listen, could you hold up a minute?" Before Nisha disappeared out the giant glass doors, she threw Yash the nastiest glare.

With a deep, deep sigh, Yash followed the two women out. Both of whom were moving a little too fast. And Nisha was pregnant.

Fortunately, Brandy noticed that Nisha was chasing her down and turned. Good, because the woman gave off a Terminator vibe, one that said she could outrun them if they were driving cars.

"I'm sorry," Yash said, catching up. "Can we come up with a compromise?"

"A compromise?" Brandy said, as though it were a word Yash had just made up out of thin air.

"Yes, in case of an assassination attempt, could you just shout me a warning or something? Oh, and could you wear a bullet-proof body suit—head-to-toe?"

Not a single muscle on her face moved. She looked as though the question were too far beneath her dignity to address.

Yash raised his brows in a do-we-have-a-deal? gesture.

"No." Just that. A single word.

"No to one or both?" he said, and tried to ignore the fact that Nisha looked like she was going to kick his shins, even as she texted away furiously on her phone. What was she up to now?

"Both." Another single-word answer from Brandy. He could

work with this woman. Especially if she trained everyone else in his life in the skill.

"Have you ever been shot?" he asked, determined to not sound like a scared little boy.

"I've never been hit by a bullet."

"So you've been shot at?"

"The person under my protection has been shot at." The woman seemed to be entirely unfamiliar with these things called emotions. In other words, she was Yash's inner world right now.

"What did you do?"

"I pushed him to the ground and the bullet missed." Still no emotion. None at all.

"How many times has this happened?"

It took her a few moments, during which her face blanked out even more. She was actually counting the number of times in her head. "Four."

"Why do you do this job?"

"Someone has to do it and I can do it better than most."

Nisha looked like a cat who had swallowed a giant tub of cream.

Yash threw his sister a look that said, *Don't you dare say one single word*, before turning to Brandy again. "You can start tomorrow."

He was about to leave, glad to be done with this, when Nisha spoke. "Actually she's starting today." She turned to Brandy. "Yash needs to go see someone in Palo Alto today. Now, as a matter of fact."

Yash didn't even bother to glare at Nisha. How had she and Ashna managed to even get through to India so fast? "I'd like to do that by myself. Thank you."

"So you're going to hire someone else for this job, then?" Brandy said.

God, he hated his life.

"No, he won't," Nisha said before he groaned out loud. "You'll go with him. Your first assignment." As if he didn't know that Nisha had already hired Brandy before bringing her here.

Yash sighed. "I didn't say I was going to go see India today."

"You need to be back on the campaign trail. You don't have the luxury of waiting until tomorrow." Nisha no longer sounded smug, just worried. "Brandy and you can wait in the car. I just texted Ashna. She's on her way down, she'll take you over to India's."

Nisha and everyone he knew had spent a lifetime working to make his goals a reality. It was time for him to stop being a baby.

"Fine." They walked in silence to his car.

He hadn't seen India Dashwood in ten years, and now he was going to have an audience when he did see her.

At least there was zero chance that she would want to work with him. Which meant he had to show up, have her tell him she didn't have time for him, and then . . . and then what, he didn't know.

For the first time in his life, when he looked into the future, he hit a wall. A wall that loomed as dark and endless as the numbness inside him. For the first time in his life, he had a problem and no idea how to fix it.

Chapter Six

India handed her mother a cup of steaming ginger and turmeric tea. The shadows under Mom's eyes were deep and her aura was still completely off, but between the meditation and the medication her pain seemed to have eased. "Is China back from her cooling-off walk?" Tara asked just as the doorbell rang, startling them both.

Their doorbell never rang. Not ever. Why would China ring the bell? Both the entrances had a security keypad with a code. Only the front studio entrance had a doorbell.

"The keypad must not be working," India said, dropping a kiss on Tara's head. "Get some rest. I'll let China in and then I need to file some patient records."

Making a mental note to get the keypad checked, India took the stairs down and made her way through the studio to the front door. She pressed her face to the mullioned glass to see who it was and threw the door wide open. The bells on the doorknob went off in a jingling frenzy.

"Ashna! I'm so glad to see you." She wrapped her arms around Ashna. "How is your cousin? I was so worried. Is everything okay? Did you need a session? How is the bodyguard? Is he going—"

Ashna quickly returned her hug, then pulled away and looked over India's shoulder at someone standing off to the side. India spun around.

Oh.

She had forgotten how tall he was. How long-limbed and athletic. How thick his hair. How stark the gray of his eyes against his dark skin. How wide his shoulders.

She'd forgotten the sheer force of his presence.

Like an absolute and utter idiot, she made a sound that belonged to no language on earth.

His lips did the barest twist. She had no idea if it was a smile or a grimace. Raising his hand, he gave her a wave.

A wave! As though he were onstage and she were one of his political groupies lapping up his speeches and waiting to shake his hand. Now that he was standing here all healthy and as vibrant as ever, she wanted to shove him away and slam the door in his face. She'd been waiting a long time to slam the door in his face.

"I texted you and tried to call. But you didn't answer," Ashna said, and India spun to her, praying that the embarrassment burning her face wasn't visible.

She had turned her phone silent at the doctor's office and forgotten to turn it back on.

"Do you have a moment to talk?" Ashna asked.

They wanted to come in? Both of them? Why? "Absolutely. Come on in."

Before India could step aside and let them in, a woman in a black muscle shirt and an earpiece stepped out from behind Yash. "Is there anyone in the studio?" She had red spiked hair and the palest blue eyes. The word *assassin* came to mind.

"This is Brandy, Yash's bodyguard," Ashna said, sliding a quick look at Yash. "His new bodyguard."

The lines around Yash's mouth tightened. He looked away when India caught the punch of pain in his eyes. Now that she was past the initial shock, he seemed drawn. His angular face had filled out, all of him had broadened and gained gravitas. The streaks of silver radiating from his temples took the gravitas to the next level. Despite that, there was a hollowness to him. Not even a hint of the energetic sparkle she remembered in his eyes.

Don't think about his aura.

His golden aura had been a magnet to her. The only aura that she had ever read wrong. It had dulled to a tarnished bronze.

He'd just been shot, and the rate at which he'd been campaigning was nothing short of frenzied, so maybe she shouldn't be surprised. Gauging people was her job, intuitively knowing what ailed them was her greatest skill, but there was something in his face that she couldn't put into words.

The bodyguard extended her hand and India took it. "It's nice to meet you." She hated how much she loved that his bodyguard was a woman.

India could carry a grown man up five flights of stairs without breaking a sweat. She could bench two-fifty. Not many people realized how strong a lifelong yoga practice made you. The last thing she needed flashing in her head right now was that first time she had met Yash at his sister's wedding. It had been years since she'd thought about how dazzled he'd been when she'd helped him move those heavy boxes.

"Likewise," Brandy said. To no one's surprise she had an impressively assertive handshake. "Is there anyone else in there?"

"The studio is closed." India threw a look at the CLOSED sign hanging on the door. "My mother is upstairs and we don't open again until six."

Yash was watching her. The awareness of it fell like sparks on her skin. She was glad for the tie-dye yoga jacket she'd thrown on over her usual yoga wear to go to the doctor's office. No one needed to see the goosebumps that danced down her arms. He hadn't said a word, but his presence was a hum in the air. Exactly like the breathing of a sleeping dragon in a fairy tale.

"Are there any other entrances to the place?" Brandy asked.

"There's an entrance in the back that leads up to our home on the upper floors."

Yash looked up at the facade of the studio and the late afternoon sun caught his eyes. A crystalline gunmetal-gray she'd never seen anywhere else.

She had been to the house he'd grown up in. Just the pool house on the Raje estate was larger than the Dashwood studio and apartments put together. But it was hers and she loved it. Childish as it was, she stuck out her chin as he looked at her, but he gave away nothing.

"Is that entrance secured?" Brandy said, studying the building as though it might blow up if touched.

"It's locked and has a touchpad that unlocks it. This is the only public entrance."

"I'm going to go around the back and check it out. Please keep this door locked."

It's a pretty safe neighborhood, India wanted to say, but Yash had just been shot, so India was happy for Captain Marvel here and her paranoia.

"I will. Come on in. Please." She pushed the door open and Ashna walked in. Yash pressed his hand against the door and held it, waiting for India to go in before following her. He still hadn't said a word.

She led them through the waiting area past the registration

desk and the benches with cubbies for shoes and hooks for bags and jackets.

Yash took in the place with that utterly flat expression he'd been wearing this entire time. The kind of expression a guilty person might paste across their face when invited to testify in front of a grand jury. Trying to get people to plumb the depths of their emotions was what India did for a living. Resistance was her daily companion. He was not here of his own free will. This was not in the least bit surprising.

"Let's go to my office." Her office was her sanctuary. She loved what she'd done with it during the renovation. Self-consciousness kicked in her gut when she thought about the dramatic beauty of his parents' estate. She kicked it right back and led them past the yoga rooms and showers and threw her office door open.

Fading sunlight streamed in through the wall of windows lined with shelves that held her grandmother's bonsais. They were now her bonsais. They had been since Grandmona died almost ten years ago. White walls and white furniture were offset by an orange couch and carpet. The perfectly balanced beauty of it made her feel just a little bit less off-kilter.

Ashna sat down on the couch, but Yash walked straight to her bonsais, mouth slightly agape. A universal reaction to the miniaturized trees her grandmother had tended for fifty years and India would cherish for as long as she lived. She would not let the fact that he looked awestruck by her cherished trees affect her. It was perfectly normal to be fascinated by an art that harnessed the splendor of a giant life-form.

"Is this a banyan tree?" Those were the first words he uttered. The first words he'd addressed to her in ten years. Not that it was anticlimactic or anything.

The way he talked had changed. There was a deliberately understated quality to his diction now. The boundless enthusiasm that had struck her as so endearing was completely leashed. This new voice was the one she'd heard on TV. His jaw barely moved and each word came out laced with careful sincerity.

"It's the bodhi satva tree," she said, her voice even more dead-pan than his.

"The one Gautama Buddha meditated under when he achieved nirvana."

She met his flat look with one of her own. "One doesn't achieve nirvana, they attain it."

He stiffened so slightly she only noticed because she was trained to notice. It was a professional hazard.

"Didn't you break your arm while swinging from the roots of a banyan tree in Sripore once?" Ashna said, a smile in her voice from the memory.

India wanted to give her a hug. How terrifying the shoot-ing must have been for the Rajes. Especially since they'd been through something like this with Yash when he'd had that ac-cident in high school. Did the man have to be ambitious about being accident prone too?

"There's this three-hundred-year-old banyan tree on the grounds of our ancestral home in Sripore," Ashna added, with all the fondness of a doting sister. "As kids we loved to swing by the hanging roots. Yash liked to pretend he was Tarzan."

Color crept up Yash's neck, past his tightly buttoned collar. He cleared his throat and turned back to the bonsai. So he'd started to take himself quite seriously, then. What she'd found most ap-pealing about him was how self-deprecating he'd been, how filled with humor.

Enough. Time to stop with the Spurned Lover's Tragic Mus-ings. It had been one day. Fine, one day and one night. One magical night. But that didn't make them lovers, not even close. He'd ghosted her, long before the word *ghosted* was minted. No one said he wasn't a trailblazer.

"Tarzan grew up to wear a suit," India said, and Yash stiffened again.

He wasn't wearing a suit right now, just a crisp blindingly white shirt, and a long gray coat that looked like it cost as much as the studio's monthly earnings.

"There are hooks behind the door, if you'd like to take off your jackets."

Ashna took off her red leather jacket and hung it up. Yash pulled the lapels of his coat tighter around himself. A faint memory of something pricked at India's mind, but didn't fully form.

"Do you want to sit down?" she asked, because suddenly exhaustion seemed to drag at the body he was holding so tall and proud.

He turned away from her bonsai and looked at her funny. Admittedly, her voice had sounded a little too concerned. She barely knew the man. *I care about everyone. You're not special*, she wanted to tell him. It was time to rein in her Mother Earth instinct. He didn't need it. Even though he looked like he needed something.

"I'm fine, thank you," he said in his new voice.

"As you know, Yash was shot," Ashna said, every bit of her horror at the memory clear in her voice.

India had already established how much that fact had bothered her when she'd first opened the door and vomited her concern to Ashna, so she nodded.

"We need your help."

We?

Yash cleared his throat. "I. *I* need your help." For the first time today his voice sounded real, tinged with the vulnerability she sometimes still heard in her dreams. He turned to Ashna. "Can I talk to India alone?"

Ashna blinked as though he'd asked if he could take off his clothes and take a nap on India's couch. The cousins exchanged a look. During the exchange, Ashna obviously didn't find the answers she was searching for. His face was so stubbornly set, India would have been surprised if Ashna had argued with him.

She turned to India. "Is it okay if I go visit Chutney and Tara? I'm guessing China's not home." China and Ashna were best friends, so naturally Ashna knew that China had barely left Song's side in a month.

"Mom's upstairs. She's not been feeling great. She's resting, but she will be happy to see you and so will Chutney."

Ashna threw another gauging look at Yash, then squeezed India's arm. "Thanks. Just holler if you need me."

Yash didn't like that. He frowned as though Ashna had called his integrity into question.

"Your mother's sick?" he asked as soon as Ashna left. "I hope it's nothing serious." His politician's voice again, the concern in it too smooth.

"Thanks," she said, and turned away. How badly she wanted it to be nothing serious was none of his concern.

"You have someone named Chutney upstairs?" So his voice could still smile.

Stop it. Stop overanalyzing every little thing about him.

"My dog."

"You have a dog named Chutney?" She couldn't be sure if that sound coming from him was a laugh, but when she turned around his shoulders were shaking and he'd buried his face in his hand.

"Why is my dog's name funny?"

He looked up, his laughter barely brightening his eyes. "It's a condiment."

He looked around the room and discomfort zinged through her. Being judged was a feeling India was familiar enough with. Hippie-dippie? Woo-woo? Mumbo jumbo? They ate labels for lunch in her family. "I am aware," she said calmly, because snapping at people was not her way. And because she'd show him her emotions again when the netherworld froze over.

"Would you call a dog Mustard or Relish?"

"I'm sure people do." She sounded every bit as indignant as she felt. Although why she was feeling this indignant, she had no idea.

"But Chutney," he said, and it made him laugh again, and then grimace.

"Are you okay?"

"Yes. It just hurts to laugh."

"I'm sorry." It came out automatically, the apology for the fact that he was in pain.

"Why are you sorry?" Was there an edge to his voice? Not that she didn't understand it. She'd be livid if someone shot her. "I'm the one who should be sorry. I shouldn't have laughed. Sorry." He spun his finger around his head. "Things have been a little weird up here."

Which explained why he was here.

She spun a finger around her head. "Generally the only reason people seek me out."

He'd have looked less like she'd kicked him if she'd kicked him.

"Is it okay if I ask you a question about the shooting?"

"Sure." But he didn't look at her, just stared at his hands.

"Is your bodyguard okay?"

Now he looked at her, guarded gray eyes not doing a damn thing to hide how he felt about a bodyguard taking a bullet for him. "He's alive. But no, I would not say he's okay."

She was about to say, *I'm sorry*, again, but the look he threw her stopped her. "You said you needed my help," she said instead. "How can I help you, Yash?"

Instead of answering, he started pacing. "I'm sorry we barged in on you. I'm sure you were busy." It was the third apology between them, which was ironic, given their history. Or their lack of history.

"I didn't have any appointments today, or classes."

"You teach yoga."

"Technically it isn't teaching, it's leading the practice. It's a yoga studio. That's what we do here."

He looked around the room again. "Looks like you do a lot more here than teach—I mean, lead a yoga practice."

She'd told him about her dream of running a holistic practice where she helped people with all aspects of wellness. He'd teased her about using the word *holistic*. How easy all the teasing had felt, how heady the laughter.

Perfect timing for every detail of their conversation from ten years ago to light up her memory. While he, on the other hand, barely seemed to remember that they'd ever even met.

"I believe that to truly heal you have to treat the whole individual. Yoga is one part of that."

"What's the other part?"

"Understanding yourself as a human being."

"You mean therapy."

"I mean digging into your emotions. Understanding yourself, who you are, how you function. Taking yourself apart like a machine and finding the rusty parts and oiling them."

"Ashna says you helped her with panic attacks."

Oh. "Would you like to sit down?"

"On your therapist's couch?"

"If you'd like."

He smiled at that, but she couldn't tell if he was just amused or amused at her. "Psychiatrists really do that."

"I'm not a psychiatrist."

"Therapist, then. They really do act as though they're putting every ball in your court."

"I practice as a yoga therapist, actually, and a wellness coach." If he was accusing her of something, she might as well live up to it. She left the ball in his court.

"Ashna thinks I'm having panic attacks and she thinks you can help me deal with them. Quickly."

"Ashna thinks you're having panic attacks?"

That seemed to annoy him, which was interesting. He paced the length of her office again. "I'm not sure this is a great idea. I don't want to waste your time. You seem like a busy person."

Was he mocking her again? Her office was only empty because she was supposed to be out of the country.

"Why don't you tell me what happened, and we'll go from there?"

"The part where someone tried to kill me?"

"We can start there."

"Let's." He looked at her as though she'd thrown him some sort of challenge and he was picking it up. "I was at a rally and some gun-toting asshole thought I'd lived long enough. And, well, when I tried to go out on a stage for another rally it didn't go so well. And now my family thinks I can't handle campaigning anymore. Which obviously means that I can't win the election."

There, does that about sum it up? That last part, his set jaw and general stance finished for him.

Since he refused to sit, she sank into the chair across from the couch. "What happened when you went out onto the stage after you got out of the hospital?"

"Basically"—a pause for breath, a too shallow breath—"I thought my heart was going to explode in my chest." His voice was flat again. "I had no control over my limbs." He started pacing again, frustration coloring his aura in murky hues. Under the dull patina sitting over it, it was still as golden as ever. The only golden aura India had ever witnessed.

"You got shot at a rally. What were you doing trying to get on a stage and in front of a crowd so soon after that?"

"Campaign events are set up months in advance. And the election is less than three months away."

"And that makes you a robot?"

"If you call fulfilling your responsibilities being a robot."

"Your responsibility is to be whole so you can run a state. Not to cut out your feelings."

He was standing over her. "You don't follow a whole lot of politics, do you?" The smile he gave her was a travesty of smiling in general and it made her more angry than it should.

She stood, leaning her head back and facing him, eye-to-eye. "I thought you didn't want to be a politician. I thought you wanted to be a public servant."

He froze. They both did.

Those were words he'd said to her ten years ago.

Way to bring up that night, India.

His face went so steely and blank that suddenly India was absolutely certain he was not the same man she'd met that night.

And she wasn't at all sure there was anything she could do to help the man standing in front of her today.

Before he could respond, a scream sounded outside the window. India ran to it. Outside, China was facedown on the concrete pavement and Yash's bodyguard was straddling her with China's hands pinned behind her back.

AFTER THAT EVERYTHING moved really fast. India banged on the window and China and Brandy's heads snapped up and looked at her. China's eyes were filled with terror and Brandy's with military-level focus.

Yash was already across the office trying to get outside. India ran past him and flew out the back door.

"Let her go!" she yelled, yanking at Brandy's arm.

"That's India's sister. She lives here," Yash said to Brandy, who was already pulling away.

China sprang to her feet, breathing heavily. "Get off me, you psycho! What the fuck is wrong with you?" she shouted into Brandy's face, and shoved her with both hands. Not that it was easy to budge the woman, who was almost six feet tall and built like a tank.

"I'm sorry." Brandy looked neither guilty nor apologetic. "But you shouldn't have attacked me," she said with deadly calm.

"Shouldn't have attacked you? I caught you climbing the windowsill of my home. Why would I not pull you down? I thought you were trying to break in." China dusted off her jeans, they were ripped at the knee. She picked up her cell phone. The case was cracked. "This was a limited edition case from the Laurel & Hardy museum," she said with a sob.

India wiped China's cheek, trying to remove the streak of gray from being pressed against the concrete.

Yash extracted a handkerchief, of all things, from his coat pocket and handed it to China before turning his attention back to Brandy. "Why were you climbing the windowsill?"

It was hard to tell if Brandy was embarrassed about any of this. The woman had the iciest blocked-off energy, a pale, almost white-gray aura. "I was checking if the windows were breachable."

"Why the hell would you care if our windows are breachable?" China, in complete contrast to Brandy, was in full raging splendor. Flaming red fire to the bodyguard's gray ice. "Who the hell are you, and what the hell are you even doing here?"

Suddenly she seemed to register Yash's presence. "Yash? Oh my God. What's going on?" Forgetting about everything else, China threw her arms around him. Since when were they this close? "I was dying of worry. Well, bad choice of words, not dying, just worried. I'm so glad you're okay. What are you doing here? How are you up and about so soon after . . . well . . . Do you know this psychopath?"

"This is Brandy. She's my new bodyguard." He took the handkerchief from China and wiped a streak of dirt from her jaw. "I'm sorry."

Before China could respond, Ashna ran out through the open door. "What's going on? I heard shouting." She was carrying Chutney in her arms, and the poor baby was doing a yelping thing that was half trauma and half excitement.

"Wow," Yash said, staring at their admittedly unattractive dog. Chutney was slobbering all over herself and her usual undeniable smell engulfed them like a methane cloud.

India braced herself for disgust, the common, and quite frankly not entirely unwarranted, response to their drool girl. When, to India's horror, Chutney reached for Yash and slurped a slobbery tongue across his hand.

With the kind of laugh that India had never expected to hear from him again, Yash reached for the bundle of skin folds. "And who do we have here?" Every bit of deliberate enunciation was gone from his voice. Instead his pitch jumped to that strange voice people reserved for babies. "Hey, there, beautiful baby!"

And, damn it, the sun chose that moment to shoot a bright ray through a tree at his face.

"This is Chutney," Ashna said in a matching high pitch, presenting Yash with the pug as though she were a particularly delicious ice-cream sundae.

Chutney paused in her mouth-breathing to start lapping at Yash's face.

Indian and China gasped. India reached out to take her away, but Yash was smiling into Chutney's face. Not his politician smile, not even his you've-amused-me, peasant smile. This smile yanked her back through the years, eyes disappearing into slits, too much teeth and gums. An explosion of unadulterated joy. Tremors rippled low in her belly, high in her heart.

Meanwhile, a besotted Chutney went at his face with nothing held back. Most people scrunched up their noses when Chutney entered the room. Her kisses weren't for the faint of heart, though India lived for them. They had named her Chutney because she smelled like a mix of too many things. None of them pleasant.

It's how she had smelled from the day they had brought her home, an abandoned year-old puppy with balance issues. They had changed her diet several times, switched to feeding her homemade food, bathed her every day. Nothing worked. It was the slobber. There was just some sort of genetic thing that no vet could figure out how to mask. Tara had declared that there was something magical about having a dog with an odor problem living in a home that made incense.

Chutney was also not a fan of people, given how they usually reacted to her. This person, however, seemed to not have received that memo. Did the man not have a sense of smell?

The kiss fest continued and India found her hand pressed into the odd wobble in her chest. Brandy came up to Yash and put a hand on his shoulder, the unhurt one, she hoped, because that hand was not messing around.

"We need to go back inside," the cause of all the trouble said with the calmness of someone who had not just pinned someone to the ground outside their own home.

China glared at her. "I'm sorry, who invited you inside? This is a place of peace. We keep violent psychopaths outside."

"China," India said. Because, to be fair, the woman had been doing her job.

"Why do you need a bodyguard to come to our home?" China asked Yash, who was scratching the exact spot behind Chutney's ear that she loved having scratched.

"He was just shot," Icy Brandy said. Did she think a single person here was unaware of that fact?

China slapped a hand to her chest and gasped. "No! When did this happen?"

Again, the mocking landed on the bodyguard like a torrential downpour against slick rock. "What I meant was that the election isn't over yet, so the reason he was shot isn't over either. He's not going anywhere without security."

Yash did not look happy with that declaration. "Let's please not push people to the ground when they're trying to enter their own home, okay?" he said, not unkindly, but with all the authority of someone used to giving orders.

Brandy's face was still a brick wall, but her shoulders slumped by half an inch and it was hard not to feel sorry for her.

"Actually," China said, a hint of sheepishness creeping into her face, "she didn't push me down when I was trying to enter. I pulled her off the windowsill, and she flipped me onto the ground."

Brandy swallowed, letting the first flash of emotion crack through her face. A tiny blue hue in the gray aura. "Thank you."

China spun on her, hands on hips. "Don't you dare thank me! Who flips someone in the air like a pancake? You could have broken my back. I need this damn back."

"With all due respect, ma'am, if I wanted to break your back, your back would be broken."

China threw her hands up in the air. "Wow, were you raised by wolves?" Then without waiting for an answer she took herself inside, muttering, "Who the fuck calls people ma'am?"

"I was just doing my job," Brandy said, sounding so sincere that India's anger died inside her. "I didn't mean to hurt her."

"She'll be fine," India said gently.

"I'll go make sure she's okay," Ashna said, lobbing a look to Yash and then India. "How do you guys want to do this?"

"I'm not sure he needs my help," India said, just as Yash said, "I want to give it a try."

Oh.

"We can give it a try," she said, just as Yash said, "Well, if you'd rather not do it."

The awkward silence that followed was the most uncomfortable thing India had experienced in a long, long time.

Ashna studied them. Brandy studied the windows. Chutney licked Yash's face.

This time they both opened their mouths and then waited and said nothing.

"Okay, then," Ashna said verbalizing a shrug, if such a thing were possible. "Why don't I check up on China and then head off home, and you two can decide what to do." She spun her hands between them in a confused rolling gesture that was painfully accurate, then made a run for it.

"Let me take her." Chutney had to be getting heavy in Yash's arms and that shoulder had to be hurting.

Without argument he dropped a kiss on Chutney's lopsided head and handed her off. "Why does she angle her head like that?"

"She was abandoned as a puppy. When the shelter got her, they found a maggot infestation inside her ear. Her right eardrum's permanently damaged and it messes with her balance and makes her tilt her head like that."

"Poor brave girl." He leaned over and dropped another kiss on her head. Chutney let out one of her love-grunts. Okay, great, that sealed the deal. India was going to help the man. Even if he decided to fight her on it. She was going to help him and then she was going to kick him to the curb.

"Do you want to come inside?" she said.

Just as he said, "Sorry to have wasted your time."

God, this was getting tiresome. They stepped back and away from each other at the exact same time, like a darned choreographed musical.

Mortification bloomed inside India at having done it again, at having invited him in, when all he wanted was to leave.

"Take care, Yash," she said finally. She wouldn't get to kick him to the curb after all.

"Take care, India," he said, and with nothing more than that he walked away, his measured strides doing nothing to hide the fact that he couldn't get away fast enough. Again.

Chapter Seven

Yash missed the solitude of his apartment, but expecting Ma to let him go home from the hospital to an empty apartment would have made him certifiably delusional. So Yash had been living at the Anchorage, their family's estate in Woodside in his childhood room since leaving the hospital a week ago.

That morning he'd woken up too early. Okay, that was a lie. You could only claim waking up if you were able to fall asleep in the first place. After another night of tossing and turning, he'd gotten out of bed at four, paced restlessly around his room, and then made his way up to Esha's suite on the uppermost floor.

Esha was the oldest of the Raje cousins, HRH's oldest brother's daughter. Like Ashna, who was his younger uncle's daughter, Yash only ever thought of Esha as his sister too. Esha shared the suite with their grandmother. She and Aji had moved in after Esha had survived the plane crash her parents had been killed in along with every other passenger on board. Her miraculous survival had been followed by seizures and visions triggered by any human contact. The only way to control the seizures was to not expose Esha to human contact outside the family. Esha hadn't left the five acres of the estate in decades.

As usual, she was up and waiting for Yash in the suite's living room in her bright white pajamas. How she always knew when he was going to visit, he had no idea. When they were younger and he couldn't sleep he'd always make his way up here, and she'd always be waiting for him on the couch. Back then they talked. About everything on Yash's mind.

This past week they'd sat together in silence for hours, as though Esha could sense the emptiness inside him. Emptiness that had only eased in one harsh rush yesterday when he'd watched a face press to the glass of a mullioned door. Emptiness that had crawled back into him as he'd walked away, self-preservation pulling him away even as it pulled him back. Now the emptiness sat inside him again like dead weight.

There wasn't anything Yash wanted to discuss with anyone. Least of all with yoga instructors whose eyes had collected old anger like gemstones in long-lost treasure. He hadn't gotten where he was by digging up things. You couldn't walk on dug-up dirt without stumbling.

Usually, when Yash left, Esha told him everything was going to be all right. This morning she didn't. She just patted his cheek sympathetically and went back into her room.

After a quick shower, Yash made his way to his father's office. It was detached from the main house and empty because HRH was at the hospital.

The smell of leather-bound books and furniture polish wrapped around him. The year that he'd spent in his wheelchair, the entire house had been fitted with accessibility features. He'd asked his father not to make his office wheelchair-accessible. HRH hadn't questioned Yash—a courtesy he seldom afforded his children. He'd understood.

Maybe Yash had wanted it to be his carrot, this room that

he loved and coveted. Maybe Yash hadn't wanted to taint his memories of this cherished place with a time he wanted to leave behind. Whatever the reason, Dad had understood.

Sometimes Yash thought he had managed to survive the accident by the sheer force of his father's faith in him. When Yash had decided that he would prove the doctors wrong and walk again, not everyone had believed him, but HRH had.

Calling Yash's relationship with his father complicated was putting it mildly. HRH's particular brand of bulldozing when faced with obstacles in Yash's "path" was something Yash had always ignored because he believed his goals were his own.

I thought you didn't want to be a politician. I thought you wanted to be a public servant.

Who was the person who had said those words?

Where had he gone?

Suppressing the need to pace again, Yash opened his laptop. The speech he'd been working on stared him in the face. Page upon page of goals turned into policies then spun into dreams.

He wanted to erase it all and replace it with one word.

Abdul.

He didn't need a therapist to tell him what that was. Survivor's guilt.

Yash had always navigated guilt by setting goals and shutting out noise. When you had a family like his, goals tended to get snarled up with expectations. Esha's vision of him in a certain white building in their nation's capital when he was nine had sealed his fate. Her visions were never wrong. She'd seen him in a wheelchair before it happened too.

For the first time in his life threads had come loose in the securely woven fabric of his dreams. Tugging at them could unravel everything. Yash hadn't built his life to unravel it.

It was time to get to work. Two speeches waited for his attention, along with Rico's notes about his health care talking points.

The next time Yash looked up from his laptop, the sun was high in the sky. J-Auntie, his parents' housekeeper, had slipped in and dropped off his favorite chocolate-glazed donuts. Freshly fried.

He'd made his way through most of the plate and was contemplating popping another one in his mouth when footsteps sounded on the stairs outside. Sitting up, he quickly fastened his top button. No one ever saw Yash with his shirt unbuttoned. What lay beneath his clothes was no one's business but his.

"Yash?" Naina knocked on his door the way she did everything, impatiently and without entertaining the possibility of not getting what she wanted.

"Come on in," he said, standing to greet her.

She flew into the room and gave him a hug. A new practice since the shooting. Naina might be one of Yash's oldest friends, but touchy-feely she was not.

"How are you?" she asked, looking genuinely concerned. Nurturing was another thing Naina was not, so this was all a bit awkward.

"Please tell me you're not going to go all concerned-auntie on me. The bullet barely even made it past my epidermis."

She dropped into the leather armchair across from the desk and crossed her denim-clad legs. She was wearing a red YASH Is Us sweatshirt, and despite his impatience at having his work interrupted it made him smile.

"I love when you go all science-nerd on me." She picked up a donut and bit into it. "Seriously, though, doesn't it hurt? How are you up working already? No wonder your poor mother is having conniptions in there."

He did feel bad for Ma. If she had her way she would wrap her kids in cotton wool and keep them locked up in the safety of her home. Yash had tried to tell her it wasn't her fault when she'd sat by his hospital bed for two days and he could practically hear her mentally kicking herself for not doing something to prevent the shooting.

"Whatever you decide to do with the campaign, I'm going to support you," Ma had said to him when they came home.

"Why would you think he wants to do anything with the campaign but win it?" HRH was not kicking himself for anything. He was congratulating himself for the excellent security firm he had hired. The firm Abdul worked for.

Naina waved a hand in front of Yash's face. "Where did you go? I thought you were okay talking about the shooting. Is it giving you PTSD?" She recited the letters as if it were a new hashtag. How could a woman who was so empathetic with her work, which involved an ocean of strangers, be so disconnected from the people she was supposed to be close to?

"Obviously I'm okay talking about it. It only hurts the way a scraped knee hurts. I'm fine. My life isn't going to change at all." He sat back down and fidgeted with the notes he'd made. The speech had been fighting him hard, and speeches barely ever did that.

"Speak for yourself, buddy," Naina said, with the kind of smile he hadn't seen on her face since they'd been in grade school and she used to get into all sorts of mischief that he then had to get her out of by taking the blame. They'd had fun together. It would've made everything so much easier if they'd felt anything other than friendship for each other.

"Prince Yash to the rescue," she'd loved to say.

He hated that nickname. Monarchy was the most abhorrent of all forms of government. Even dictatorship was more respectable; at least dictators worked their way into power. Their power wasn't dropped into their lap by a genetic accident. Not that Yash could say any of that without insulting his ancestors, who believed themselves *chosen* and worked to justify that belief by making themselves worthy of their gifts. A combination of entitlement and guilt. His legacy. They should have put that on the Raje crest Instead of *Victorious Through Truth*.

"The polls are continuing to climb," Naina said. "If the election happened now, you'd be a shoo-in."

Yash didn't want to be a shoo-in because of a sympathy vote. He'd worked too hard for that. Especially when the sympathy came from Abdul's life hanging in the balance and Naina's tears that everyone assumed were a lover's tears.

Why was the deception suddenly sticking in his throat like a bone? It was a harmless arrangement.

Or it had been meant to be.

Harmless to everyone but one person. One person he had completely shut out until now.

Naina leaned toward him. "Don't be tiresome, Yash. Why are you always so brooding about any good fortune that comes your way?"

"Good fortune coming my way would pretty much define my entire life. Both our lives, as a matter of fact."

"You were just shot. What part of that is good fortune?"

Yash stood and walked to the window. A spectacular view of the mountains stretched before him. Mountains he'd always thought of as his. As though he were Simba and his life were *The Lion King*.

"The part where another man took a bullet for me."

Joining him at the window, she touched his arm. "What happened to Abdul is sad. But it's not your fault."

What was wrong with all of them? How could they not see how unfair it was for him to be standing here when Abdul was hooked up to a ventilator? Suddenly he was tired. "How has your day been? When do you head back to Kathmandu?"

She bounced on her heels. "What if I said that I'm considering not going back?"

"Not going back?" Their arrangement worked because they were never in the same place together. The whole damn point of the arrangement was that she could go wherever she wanted and do whatever she wanted.

"What if I told you that I'm considering staying in California for a while?"

"In California? For a while?"

"Okay, echo, you sound like my mom when my dad speaks. Except without the question marks you're adding."

"Why would you do that? I'm fine. I've come out of this as though it didn't even happen."

"Except with a ten-point lead in the polls," she said, a smug smile splitting her face. "You're welcome, by the way."

"Thank you for being so distraught when you thought I might have died, by the way."

She didn't like that. "You're my best friend, Yash. How would I not be distraught? I had no idea what I was going to do if . . . if . . ."

"If I wasn't around to be your fake boyfriend."

She went to the door and checked if anyone was outside, then shut it and glared at him. "That's unfair. Our friendship is the most *real* thing in my life." She spun a finger around his face. "How long is this brooding going to last?"

It was a question he'd very much like an answer to as well.

There was an endless list of things to do, and brooding was putting a damper on all of that. The desolate, restless fog that wrapped itself around him when he thought about the yoga studio was no better than the cold nothingness it had replaced.

He apologized and she waved it away, her excitement returning. "Never mind all that, because I have something to cheer you up. Aren't you at least a little bit curious about why I'm saying I want to stay?"

Curious would be one way to describe it. "I'm all ears."

"You know how hard we've been working to get the foundation funded and it's been like trying to fill a silo with pennies? Well, Jiggy Mehta called me this morning."

Yash sat up. "Jiggy Mehta? The billionaire, Jiggy Mehta?"

"The gazillionaire, Jiggy Mehta." She laughed delightedly. "Isn't he one of your donors too?"

"Yes, he's been very generous."

"Well, you can say that again. He's donating thirteen million dollars to my foundation. That size of endowment means we can put the plans we've been struggling with for a decade into action, no compromises."

"That's terrific, Nai."

"Thanks. And you know what this means, right?"

"It means all the hard work you've done for all these years is going to come to fruition."

"Yes! And that means the foundation gains the kind of visibility that can spell . . . it can spell . . ." She took a breath, so deep it made her look like she was going to explode. "The Nobel!" Reaching across the table, she took his hand. "Can you imagine what that means for us as a couple?" She squeezed it. "It means we'll be unstoppable. We'll be the ultimate power couple."

Proud as he was of her, his hand felt heavy and cold in hers and he pulled it away. "But that was never the deal. We never meant to be a power couple."

They had never meant to be any kind of couple, other than one who kept their parents from pressuring them about finding someone to be a couple with. A way to avoid her father from controlling her life. A way to avoid his own weaknesses from controlling his life.

"We meant to get what we wanted. I'm fully aware that I was the one who bullied you into doing this because I wanted to go to Nepal," she said without a whit of guilt. "But we've both benefited from it."

"You did bully me into it." He tried to smile at her. The rebellious girl who'd stood by him always. Sticking it to her dad might have been higher on her list back then than rural microfinance reform, but right now Yash couldn't quite manage the hypocrisy of judging her for it.

No one had ever told him he couldn't do something he wanted because of his gender. No one had ever held his sisters back either. In all their bulldozing glory, his parents had pushed them all equally brutally. They weren't like Naina's parents. Subverting people like that, people who refused to evolve their views no matter the evidence, it had felt right.

It no longer felt right. Not when a private deception that was meant to help a friend was misleading the electorate.

"So, our deal . . ." She walked around the desk and leaned her hip on it, staring down at him. "What if it's time to adjust it? Our goals have changed, shouldn't our deal change too? We can achieve things we couldn't even imagine back then." She hadn't changed one bit.

"Like winning the Nobel?"

Excitement flashed in her eyes. The kind of excitement for one's work that Yash had always taken for granted. Now it was gone, and he couldn't seem to retrieve it from the hole that had opened up inside him.

"Like winning the Nobel. Like running California. All we have to do is figure out how to make living in the same city work."

Or maybe it was time to figure out how to get out of the arrangement. Living on different continents and getting together for the occasional photo op, that was easy enough to fake, and harmless. It was a different thing entirely to perpetually be around each other and pretend to be something they were not.

It was a different thing entirely to profit from people's sympathy for a sobbing lover over a fallen body.

The excitement on Naina's face told him that they were not on the same page. "How long would you stay in San Francisco?"

"Indefinitely, at this point. I'd manage the project from here. You'd mostly be in Sacramento. And I'll be there when you need a first lady."

"First lady?" He jumped out of his chair. Maybe he should not have sounded so horrified, but what in the hellish hell?

"Keep your boxers on, I'm not saying we have to get married. At this point I don't think the public cares if we get married or not. I think being partners actually makes us more relatable to young voters."

"And our parents? The reason we've been able to avoid marriage without them losing it is because we've never lived in the same place." He squeezed his temples.

"It's not about our parents anymore. We're too old to not be able to just tell our parents to butt out of our lives."

"Actually, we were too old for that at twenty-eight, by normal people standards," he said.

"Well, we aren't normal. My parents certainly aren't. How is it normal to hold your daughter's career ransom to marriage? The only reason Dad let me take off around the world for my career is because I was with you. The prized catch of the community wanted his daughter. He thinks it's his greatest achievement."

This was doubly preposterous, given that Dr. Kohli was credited with pioneering the imaging of certain parts of the human body using an MRI.

Naina's laugh was too sad by half. The laugh of a child who'd never felt like she was enough for her parents. It was this determined laugh that had made Yash go along with all her shenanigans when they were kids.

"MRI machines don't have vaginas that you get to hand off to the most deserving member of the next generation," she added with fiery bitterness.

"And yet you never figured out how to say any of this to your father."

She looked at him as though he were being willfully naive. "Truthfully, I can tell him to go to hell now. I can support Mummy, so she doesn't have to put up with him. I really don't care about him anymore. But I do care about you. The election is on the line now. So is my foundation. Don't you see?"

He did see.

"I thought you'd be excited for me. Why are you acting like you don't want me here?"

"I'm saying having you here means we'd have to fake a relationship in full public view on a daily basis. Do you really think we can do that?"

"Why not? We like each other, which is more than most real couples."

"We aren't a real couple, Nai. We tried, remember? It didn't work out."

"We can try again!"

Without thinking about it, he stepped back and away from her. Annoyance, even hurt, tightened her mouth, and he kicked himself for not controlling his reactions.

"Friends with benefits" was a phrase Naina had thrown around a lot in the early years of their arrangement. They had even tried it, but sex had been such an awkward, mechanical experience, they'd given up.

He knew she was right that it would make everything easier. Sleeping with anyone else would be perceived as infidelity. An affair would have ended his hopes at running for any public office.

This hadn't been much of a problem for Yash. The idea of physical intimacy froze his insides, and not thinking about it was usually the best way for him to deal with it.

His early experience with intimacy had shredded his ability to trust. Julia Wickham, Trisha's college roommate and best friend, had drugged him, and taped him having sex with her. She was underage, and his intern. Then she'd used it to blackmail him.

Yash would never forgive himself for putting his family through the amount of money and legal corralling it had taken to make Julia and her threats disappear. So, forgive him if intimacy did not come easily to him.

Yash started to pace, hating that the discomfort of the memories made it necessary to move. Naina had picked up pretty quickly that Yash wasn't quite into it. She'd tried to help, she'd tried keeping it light, keeping it purely physical so his head didn't get in the way. He trusted her enough that the physical release wasn't bad. But the work involved in getting there was exhausting. For both of them, and when she'd given up, it had been the greatest relief.

Naina's eyes softened. "We don't have to try again. There's a lot of couples who don't have sex." She smiled. "It's like we're already married."

He stopped pacing and leaned on the desk next to her. "Wait, this is sounding more and more like a proposal."

"Hell, no! What this is, honey, is opportunity. Do you know how many women can become financially independent as a result of this endowment? Quarter of a million, directly. That means, in terms of generational trickle-down, millions. This is what we always wanted. This is us changing the world. We've lied to our families for ten years so we could do this."

Every time she said *we* his insides turned. Why did that word sound so jarring suddenly?

"What happens to your endowment if I don't win?"

The look she threw him was a warning. "The two things aren't related," she snapped. "Mehta is interested in the foundation's work. No strings. I've already made that clear. And at this point you not winning is a really negligible possibility."

Except the idea of going out on a stage and speaking to a crowd still made his knees buckle. The one person who might have been able to help him, well, obviously she couldn't.

Or, rather, he couldn't let her.

There was a knock on the door, and without waiting for an answer Nisha hurried in, coming to a stop when she saw Naina and him standing there shoulder to shoulder.

"Sorry. I had no idea I was interrupting."

Naina waved her over. "Come on in. We're done."

The two women air-kissed. "He's all yours." With that Naina picked up her bag.

"You didn't interrupt anything," he said with so much gruffness that Nisha frowned. "Did you need something?" he added much more gently.

"Umm, yes, I wanted to, you know, check in on that thing we're working on." She scratched her head. "What was it again? Yes, your campaign."

Naina backed away, hands raised, as though she wanted nothing to do with their sibling drama. It was why their arrangement worked. They got to focus on their own stuff without having their legs tangled up about each other's stuff like real couples.

"I'll see the two of you later. Yash, listen to the women in your life. They know what's best for you." Before leaving, she threw a smile at Nisha and Nisha returned it.

Yash couldn't tell if it was a patient smile or a fond one. His sisters were always courteous to Naina but never close. Was that them or her? How had he never given a thought to any of this? How many things had he trampled past without giving a thought to?

"Do you want to run the speech by me?" she asked, studying him.

"Do you want to get to the reason why you're really here?"

"Fine. How did things go with India?" She picked up his last remaining donut.

Terrible. Amazing. "Okay." He took the donut from her and took a bite.

There it was again. His heartbeat. Feelings. Sensations. Memories that didn't make him fold inward.

She took the donut back. "When are you seeing her again?"

Never, he wanted to say. *Right this minute*.

Instead, he said, "Let's go over the speech."

Chapter Eight

*I*ndia threw open the doors of her closet. Unsurprisingly, it was lined from top to bottom with yoga wear. A few dresses hung from hangers. She riffled through them, checking to see if . . . okay, so she wasn't checking for anything, just looking at them. Not every action needed a purpose.

Her hand stopped short of the plastic-covered hangers all the way at the very back corner. The lilac silk embroidered with silver thread looked faded behind the aging plastic. Next to the ghaghra hung the white and silver palazzo pants with the halter top. In the months after Nisha's wedding, India had refused to bring what she'd worn back from the dry cleaner's, unable to bring herself to look at the clothes she'd worn when she'd met Yash. Clothes she'd let him touch her in.

India had always taken her physical being seriously. Human touch was a powerful thing, and her body always told her whom to trust. Yash Raje was the only person her body had ever gotten wrong.

Tara had picked the clothes up from the cleaners for her and left the hangers hanging behind her door. It had taken her months to move them to her closet. Since then she hadn't touched them. Not for the first time, she considered taking them to Goodwill. But that would involve touching them. Touching the feelings she'd buried with them. The casual rejection. The confusion that had followed.

At least he'd walked away again, which meant she didn't have to deal with any of it. She was ten years older. Ten years wiser. Ten years stronger.

At this point the only thing that mattered was that he was okay.

But he's not okay.

Slamming the closet shut, she went to the kitchen and laid out vegetables for today's soup. Mom was keeping soup down. She was spending all her time in the incense workshop upstairs churning out incense sticks by the hundreds. She was also being extremely stubborn about not wanting to discuss treatment and doctors.

This was the mother who'd laid out every form of menstrual product and birth control on the dining table and given her children the sex talk in great detail, in middle school, with illustrations. Tara did not avoid conversations. Tara was avoiding this conversation. For someone who had no experience, she was really good at it too.

India really needed to clear her head, not to mention her chakras. This feeling of being blocked up was not a good one. Making her way down to one of the studios, she laid down a mat and went through a few sets of surya namaskar. Then she made her way into a sirsasana. The headstand required full focus; any shift in concentration could result in falling out of the pose wrong, and that could result in injury.

She'd been in the pose a little longer than was advisable when the doorbell rang. India took her time coming out of the pose.

When she came up to standing, her head felt completely reset. Good.

It lasted all of thirty seconds. Because when she pulled the door open, tortured gray eyes met hers.

The impact was full-bodied, hitting her like the blood rush after a sirsasana held too long.

He waited for her body to absorb the impact, as though he felt it too.

Behind him Brandy stood utterly still.

"Hi." India waved to Brandy and she waved in response. "Did you want to come in?"

Was there a stupider opening line? Given that he had knocked on her door. Then again, it was Yash Raje, so his actions and intentions weren't exactly interrelated. They obviously weren't something she had any skill in interpreting.

Instead of coming in, he gave her another tortured look. Then he made it worse by trying to cover it with stoicism. "That depends," he said, voice low enough that she had the urge to lean in.

On what? She wanted to respond, but not responding was probably a better approach if she wanted to convince him that it didn't matter if he came in or not, if he'd called or not.

"Do you have time to talk?" He sounded tentative and hopeful, not studied and strategic, and it reminded her of the man she'd met years ago. Before the Yash on TV took over.

Wasn't he the busy one? Then again, maybe he was here because he couldn't do the things he was supposed to be busy doing. She couldn't imagine how devastating it must be for him to not be out there campaigning right now.

"I can leave if this isn't a good time."

She did want him to leave. Not because it wasn't a good time, but because she couldn't take him on as a client. Ethically she would never cross professional boundaries with a client. Neither as a yoga therapist nor as a stress management coach. Not that there was any danger of crossing boundaries with him, ever. The real issue was that India never brought her own feelings into the equation with her clients. Helping clients was sacrosanct, it was about them and them alone. She wasn't sure if she could do that with their history.

She stood there staring at him, wishing she didn't see every bit of the restlessness inside him. He was asking for help. He hated that he was. She couldn't not help. It wasn't in her. *Learn, then, life is about growing.*

"The studio is closed until five." She looked at Brandy. "No one else is here except my mom." Then she turned back to Yash. Silence stretched. If she made this awkward, if she let him see, she would never forgive herself. "I have to cook dinner for my mother. If you don't mind me doing that while we talk, you can come in." That meant they'd just be talking. She'd just be helping a friend's brother, not a client.

"You don't mind?"

"I wouldn't have asked if I did."

He turned to Brandy. "I'll stay indoors. You're only supposed to be guarding me in public places. I'll call when I'm ready to leave."

The entire tortured thing must have gotten through Brandy's iciness, because after a quick sweep of the studio she left.

India led him across the studio, up the stairs, and into her home.

His keen gaze searched the place and she steeled herself. This was not going to work out if she let every little thing he did get to her. That wasn't who she was anymore.

"Where's Chutney?"

There it was, the god-awful electric spasm that zinged through her heart.

"She's with my mom."

He looked disappointed. Damn him.

"Something to drink?" Hurrying to the kitchen, she grabbed a coconut water from the fridge and put it in front of him without waiting for an answer.

He thanked her and took it without giving one.

She picked up a carrot and stared at it. Why was the carrot so large? Why hadn't she noticed that bulbous tip? And why in heaven's name was she holding it up like that?

His mouth quirked. He looked away.

Slamming the unnecessarily humongous thing on the cutting board, she picked up a knife and chopped it in half.

It wasn't clear if Yash cleared his throat because she started slicing, fast and furious.

How on earth was Yash here ten years after she'd humiliated herself for his entertainment? Why was she letting him watch her mutilate a carrot? What had she been thinking, letting a stranger into her kitchen?

Although the definition of *stranger* might be a bit of a problem. That's the thing she remembered most about him, the fact that their first encounter had felt like she'd known him her whole life. If that regularly happened to people, it just proved what India knew, that she wasn't entirely normal. It had only happened to her that one time.

"May I help?" he asked, rolling up his shirtsleeves to reveal forearms that she absolutely would not stare at. How did one get forearms like that working on speeches? How many hands did you have to shake?

She slowed her hands. No point losing digits over unfairly

ripped forearms. "There's really not that much to do. I'm going to chop the vegetables and put them into the pot and then let them cook. But thank you." Also, thank you, God, for making her voice sound so calm that even she wondered if it was coming from her.

The rhythmic chopping seemed to hypnotize him, and he watched silently without any further response. Cutting vegetables relaxed her. She tried to remember that.

When was the last time you slept? she wanted to ask, but it felt too intimate for an opening question. It was just two people in a kitchen. Nothing had the right to feel this intimate.

He has a girlfriend.

"How is Abdul?"

His shoulders rolled back as though his skin had suddenly become too tight around him. "The doctors don't know if he will regain consciousness." He swallowed. "The patient waking up from surgery within forty-eight hours is what you hope for. It's been over a week already."

"And what do they do in a case like that?"

"It's too soon after the surgery to do anything more just yet. Right now hope is the only action we can take. That's what they tell me." His jaw worked. Obviously, he hated saying those words.

"How is his family doing?"

"They're strong." His hand went to his hair, but he pulled it back. "He has to wake up. His little girl is not growing up without a father." He grabbed the carton of coconut water and it dented in his grip. "Aren't you going to tell me how it isn't my fault?"

"Excuse me?"

"Everyone keeps telling me Abdul getting shot isn't my fault. That I shouldn't blame myself."

"Don't you think it's natural that you would blame yourself?"

"It is, isn't it?" The strength of his relief at having her give him permission to feel how he felt melted something in his eyes.

She scraped the carrot pieces from the chopping board into the saucepan and added ghee. "Yes, it is."

"But?" he asked.

"But nothing. It doesn't matter that you weren't the one who pulled the trigger."

"It does feel like that."

She started on the cabbage and waited. There was obviously more. He was stretched at the seams with how much more there was.

"It does feel like I pulled that trigger," he said finally.

"Have you ever?"

"Have I ever what?"

"Pulled a trigger. Shot a gun."

"When I was little. My uncle—Ashna's father—took me hunting once."

"How did that go?"

"Other than the nightmares it gave me for days? Not well. My uncle called me a girl. Actually, I believe the word he used was *girlish*. I suspect he meant it as an insult." He leaned his hip into the countertop, obviously more at ease talking about something other than his bodyguard. "His exact words were, 'I'm glad our monarchy was abolished, because God help a country with a girlish boy like you for a king.'"

Her slicing took on force and she controlled it. "How did you respond?"

"I didn't." He shrugged. Obviously he thought a statement like that didn't deserve a response. "My uncle wasn't a person you won arguments with."

"But you never went hunting with him again," she said, causing him to study her.

"Not even when he offered to make a man out of me. It wasn't hard, because doing all I could to avoid my uncle was something I was always good at. And I . . ." The rat-a-tat of her knife filled the long silence that followed. She wondered if he would win the battle to not say what he wanted to say. "And I swore I was going to be king someday."

Her hand stopped, and the sound of his words rang in the silence.

He shifted his weight. "But not the kind of king he meant."

"Then what kind?"

"The kind who didn't have to kill animals so he could feel powerful. The kind who didn't think it was his due because he was born into it."

"How old were you?"

"Eight."

"So you've always known what you wanted."

His expression said, *Doesn't everyone?* and she wanted to laugh. "It wasn't like that. Back then I think all I wanted was to stick it to my uncle. Not that I said anything to him. I never stood up to the things he said." She couldn't quite tell if that was regret she heard in his voice.

"Why is that?"

"Because he was the kind of person who never listened. Actually, I don't think I was afraid. It just felt like a waste of my time."

She smiled. "An eight-year-old who was aware of time management."

"I'm told I was precocious." He returned her smile. "Time is our most finite resource. We can replenish or increase almost everything other than time."

"I can't argue with your brilliant eight-year-old self about that." She slid the cabbage into the pan and reached for a basket of green peas, immensely grateful for the number of steps involved in vegetable soup. "Is that the only reason?"

"The only reason to not argue with my uncle and try to change his mind? Yes. Because my time was better served proving him wrong."

"And you didn't tell your parents or anyone."

"No. I didn't want anyone else getting in the middle of it." If loneliness were a tone, this was it.

She started shelling the peas, although what her hands really wanted to do was reach out and comfort him, stroke his tight shoulders, ease them.

He stepped closer and picked up a peapod. "Aren't you going to ask?" The plump glossy peas slid from the pod into his hands. They were as strong and capable as she remembered, fingers long and graceful, palms etched starkly with just a few lines.

"Ask what?"

"Why is that?" He mirrored her tone. Another smile. Everything about that smile reminded her of a warm summer night with wedding lights strung by trees and flower garlands strung from gazebos.

"Why is that?" she asked, mirroring his mirroring of her tone.

"I don't know why. But something tells me you do."

She moved the basket she was using for the shelled peas closer to him and he dropped the peas into it.

"Is that why you're here? Because you think I have the answers?"

They both reached for the same peapod, fingers almost brushing.

"I was led to believe that you do."

The pod was cool and smooth in her fingers; she clutched it tighter even as his grip got firmer. "Something tells me that if I gave you the answers, you'd have a harder time accepting them than if you came up with them yourself."

His gaze fell to where their fingers were fighting over a vegetable, where heat was sparking between their skin. His voice got low, determined, filled with something she couldn't quite identify, but it sent the spark between their fingers racing up her arm. "Are you trying to tell me that I have control issues?"

Chapter Nine

*I*ndia let the peapod go, and Yash felt an absurd sense of loss. Of all things, asking her if she thought he had control issues was the question that shook her. Pushing the basket of peas at him, she picked up a zucchini and tried not to look self-conscious.

How had he never noticed that so many vegetables were phallic in shape?

This time she placed it on the cutting board with a little more gentleness. Then she sent the knife slicing across it with the controlled movements of a professional chef. It wasn't in the least bit surprising. India Dashwood was the kind of person who did everything as though it were a precise art.

What did I say? he wanted to ask. But already he'd said everything that had popped into his head. Something he never did. He'd told her about his uncle. He'd never told anyone else that.

Maybe it was the tapping of the knife. Maybe it was a hypnotic trick to loosen the tongue.

"You think this is about control," he said finally, and just saying the words, acknowledging them, made something far too powerful move inside him, even as that same thing darkened her eyes.

Was she proud of him? Impressed? Why was the impact of

it the same as if she had pinned a medal to his chest and then dropped a kiss on it?

Turning away, she dumped the chopped zucchini into the soup and spooned in some powdered spices. Her pale yellow yoga shirt formed a complicated pattern of crisscrossing bands across her back. The need for her to turn around and face him again was a tug deep inside him.

The way he felt when she did turn to him again made alarm bells clang in his head. Before she could speak, he raised a hand to stop her. "Please don't turn the question back on me."

"Fine." A stray pea had stayed stuck to a pod in the basket. She eased it out, carefully, thoughtfully. "Why did you agree to your family's demand that you come and see me?"

"I'm sorry?"

She popped the pea in her mouth and met his eyes again. Her eyes were an almost black brown, her irises so unusually large that they gave her beauty an uncommon blend of wisdom and innocence. It was her eyes, with their lack of armor, that had disarmed him years ago. Here it still was, the naked vulnerability that had drawn him in. Was she afraid of nothing?

"Ashna was probably the one who suggested it and Trisha and Nisha probably agreed that I might be able to help you. But you wouldn't have come unless you wanted to. What scared you enough that you agreed to come?"

Fair. Enough.

"I told you the last time I was here. I tried to get on a stage at a rally and I couldn't."

"Couldn't how?" The sparkling brown of her eyes changed when something caught at her thoughts. What he'd just admitted had clearly snagged at her sympathy, and naturally those transparent eyes showed it.

"Couldn't because my legs wouldn't move and my heart felt like it was going to race right out of my chest. It felt like, well, I felt like I had disappeared into myself. Like I wasn't even there."

"And you've never been afraid of getting on a stage before?"

"Hell, no." It was embarrassing how much he loved it. Laying out his plans and policies, explicating problems and their solutions. Watching the audience react to his words. Reaching out. People never really understood how much you needed to love campaigning to run for any kind of office.

"So you felt out of control," she said softly, as though she knew how loud the words would sound in his ears.

Each word was a scream. He didn't answer.

It's the only thing I've felt, really felt, since the shooting.

He couldn't say those words. Feeling out of control had scared him even more than the panic attack. The empty space in place of feelings was the most terrifying thing he'd ever experienced.

He was feeling things now. Here.

Feeling so much that it was like his emotions were actors hamming it up, auditioning for India's attention.

"When did you feel like you had reappeared? When did those symptoms alleviate, the elevated heartbeat, the inability to move?" Her soup was boiling and she turned down the flame and put a lid on it.

"Only when Rico went out to announce that I wouldn't be speaking."

She didn't respond. He really needed her to respond.

This felt strangely intimate, the kitchen filled with the scent of spices, the faint gurgling of boiling soup. He rifled through the basket of peapods, but they were all shelled.

India's gaze lingered on his fingers digging at empty peapods.

She knew there was more. She waited for him to find the courage to say it. He couldn't.

"Is there anything else you need help with?" he asked, when he really wanted to ask if she let all her clients into her kitchen like this.

"Have you ever done pranayama?" she asked in the quietest voice, as though he'd spoken the turmoil he was feeling, as though she needed to ease him of it. "It's yogic breathing."

"I know what pranayama is." Snapping the words made everything worse, so he evened out his tone. "Our grandmother does it every day. When I was young and visited her in Sripore, she'd make us kids sit down with her and do it every morning. After she moved here, we joined her for it on weekends."

"Do you mind sitting down for some breathing with me?"

It was such an absurd question, made even more so by the formality of her tone and the fact that they had just shelled peas together, that he almost smiled. "Now?"

She almost smiled back. "I promise it's nothing too woo-woo."

"But it is a little woo-woo?"

"Just a little." She went to the living area adjoining the kitchen and unrolled a couple of yoga mats stacked up in a corner.

She sat down on one and he sank down across from her on the other.

The artistic line of her spine made her look like she was floating. The way she held herself was a thing of beauty, everything about her was graceful, almost poetic.

Don't think the next part.

He thought the next part. This was how she'd been even ten years younger. Completely in possession of herself. Her movements, her body, the way she treated you, there was a cohesiveness to her. Not a hint of the dissonance he saw in the world around him.

Sitting by her, Yash felt stiff and clunky. A legal brief next to a haiku.

She shifted until she was facing him. It was impossible not to be drawn into the circle of peace that emanated from her as she folded her hands together in her lap, one over the other as though she were hiding something precious between her palms.

"I want you to close your eyes." She closed her own. Her spare but long lashes spiked up in all directions when they pressed against her smooth high cheeks. As soon as it was gone from sight he missed the warm brown of her eyes.

Something about the trust that let her sit there with her eyes closed was exactly what he needed to be able to let his own eyelids drop shut. "Okay." Then he couldn't help but open them again to make sure she didn't open hers now that he'd admitted to closing his.

She didn't. Her face was a lake of calm, not a line marring her soft forehead. He closed his eyes again.

"Okay." Had she known he'd check and given him time to? "Do you mind breathing with me for a bit?"

He wanted to say five silly things about how they'd been breathing together for the past hour, but her voice was too soft and soothing for that. She was too wholly immersed in this. "Are we going to chant, 'Om'?"

"Do you want to?" Her tone only made his attempt at lightening things feel like mockery.

"Let's stick with what you were planning."

"Good. Let's breathe in for four breaths. Hold for four breaths and then breathe out for six."

Sounded simple enough.

Before he knew it, a shimmering peace had spread through him.

"Now I want you to stay right here. In this moment, and I want you to think about the first time you ever got on a stage to give a campaign speech. Do you remember it? Bring it to you, here into this room. It's coming to you. You're not going to it."

He remembered it in vivid detail. He was running for San Francisco supervisor. "It was in a church in the Mission. It was a Saturday afternoon, a rare sunny day in January, and there was this one leaded window that scattered a pattern of light across the empty pews. It looked like birds in flight. Yes, there were more empty pews than filled ones. There was a group of Indian high schoolers there. I kept wondering which of my parents' friends' kids they were."

"How did you feel?" she asked.

"Excited. I was finally doing what I was born to do. There were nine people there, it wasn't an empty church."

"Not nervous?"

"No."

"Not about forgetting your speech or about the questions the audience would ask?"

"I always know my speeches by heart. And I want to engage with the audience, so the questions are never scary."

"Can you tell me how you felt physically?"

"Strong. Powerful. I had gone for a five-mile run, so I was kind of exploding with energy."

"And emotionally?"

So she did know he was hiding something. "Exactly the same as I did physically. I felt connected to every person in that church, and all the others outside it."

It had felt fabulous. Instead of dwelling on that, she walked him through other memorable speeches. Convocation ceremonies. Award acceptances. Rallies. His entire body throbbed with all the emotions he'd lost these past days. Pride, excitement, jubilation, even sadness and anger at all the things people suffered. All the reasons they came to see him. And yes, also power that he could do something.

Before it could all slip away, she spoke again. "Can we go to another day now? Can you bring the day in the Orpheum in here now? The day when you couldn't go out on the stage and speak to the crowd, bring that to yourself."

"I know what the day at the Orpheum was," he said too sharply. A dark sense trembled inside him. "Are we done with this?"

"Can you stay with the discomfort for another moment?"

He made a grunting sound, and that just made him feel like an idiot.

"Did you have a speech prepared?"

"Do you know how many speeches I've given just these past six months? Forty-nine. I can give that speech in my sleep."

"So you were perfectly prepared."

"I don't need to prepare. It's not student government. This is my thing. I'm always prepared."

Silence. Then, "So it was like every other time."

"No. I had no idea who was out there. I never thought about that before. I trusted everyone who came to see me."

An even longer silence. "We're jumping ahead of ourselves," she said finally. "You haven't told me how you feel. Physically."

"I feel like throwing up. Like I couldn't move if I tried. Like someone's taken all the strength out of my limbs. Are we done? How is this helping?"

"Stay here, Yash. Just a little bit longer. Stay inside yourself. Just one more time, can you go with me to the last democratic convention in Florida when you gave that speech to the delegates?"

One of the best days of Yash's life. He relaxed.

"What do you remember?"

"Noise. Delegates love to talk. Who would have thought?" He chuckled and felt her smiling in response even though his eyes were closed. God, was he buying into her woo-woo? "I remember deafening cheering and a lot of red, white, and blue balloons and streamers and confetti. It was everything I'd dreamed of that day in the church."

He'd never realized that he carried that day in the church into every public rally he ever attended. It felt somehow significant to know that. "And, no, I wasn't nervous at all. It was an opportunity I'd been preparing for my whole life."

"And you always have your speeches memorized, and this was your crowd."

"Yes."

"And how did you feel—"

"Physically?"

"Yes."

"Strong. I'd gone for a run that morning. I was bursting with energy."

"And you're feeling that now. As if you're there?"

"Inasmuch as I can feel like I'm there when I'm actually here."

"Right." There was a smile in her voice. A smile she was trying to resist but couldn't. A smile that made him feel so full, so rooted, that it made him want to stay right here, sweet-earth incense caressing his senses, throbbing purpose filling his body.

Emotions swirled inside him and around him. Tangible emotions that didn't feel slippery.

The moment Ashna had knocked on India's door and India

had run at Ashna with questions about him, in that moment something had bloomed inside Yash. The belief that he would feel like himself again, that he hadn't lost himself. Like he knew what to do with people. Like the beating heart inside his chest was more than an organ. Like he was more than the blood that circulated through his blood vessels. All the things he hadn't been able to feel since the first gunshot went off. All the things he stopped feeling when she wasn't there.

He jumped off the yoga mat.

"I . . . I have to go. I'm late for something." Yes, he sounded like an absolute coward.

India opened her eyes slowly. It was possibly how she would have liked him to do it. He felt like a jerk, but he embraced it. Because, hey, you were who you were. He could feel things now. Their work was done.

Touching her own chest in some sort of ritual, where she looked like she was pushing something back inside her heart with her palms, she stood, looking as floaty and grounded as ever.

"I think we're done here," he said, not proud of his harsh tone.

"If that's what you want." Her expression did not alter, but deep in her eyes disappointment flashed. So the yogi wasn't quite as yogic as she'd like to be.

"Thank you. That was very, umm, very insightful." He turned toward the door. Something tugged at him, pulled him back. That wasn't why he turned back to her, though. "Can I have you invoice me, or do I pay now?" He reached for his wallet.

Without looking at him, she started rolling her mat. "There will be no invoice. We're good."

"Excuse me?"

Her focus stayed on the mat. "You're my friends' brother. You needed help and I helped you. Or tried. Ashna, Trisha, and Nisha are like family." She put away both mats.

"You provided a service. This is not up for debate." HRH's imperiousness was in his voice again.

She had this thing she did, like she was tightening something deep inside, the very core of her being, without moving a single visible muscle. "You're right, there's no debate. We had a conversation. You didn't feel like you wanted to stick it out until the end, but basically we had a conversation, and I don't charge friends or their families for talking to them. Now, if you're ready to leave, please call Brandy so she can escort you home."

Her tone was nonconfrontational. He doubted she'd ever been confrontational a day in her life. Then why the hell did it feel like he'd done something wrong and she was confronting him about it? This particular form of treatment wasn't working for him. So he'd stopped wasting her time.

He texted Brandy. "I just texted Brandy."

"Good." She stood there all perfectly erect and still, smooth glowing skin stretched tight over lean muscle. That long bare neck at once proud and humble.

"Can I ask you a question?"

"Only if you don't offer to pay me for the answer." So she did do confrontation. She just did it in this utterly unruffled way. How had he offended her by offering to pay for her time? He was running a political campaign, for shit's sake. Knowing what not to say to people was supposed to be his topmost skill.

"If I hadn't jumped off the yoga mat like . . ." He wasn't sure if he paused because he wanted her to finish that for him or if he just wanted to extend the conversation because suddenly he didn't want to leave.

"Like someone who was uncomfortable with what he was feeling," she filled in, soft pouty lips barely moving, the effort stretching the faint scar marking the vulnerable Cupid's bow.

He would have said, *Like an utter coward.* He wasn't sure he liked her version better. "Well, if I hadn't stopped, what would we have done next?"

The eyes that met his told him that she had a good mind not to answer, but then her generosity won out, because he probably looked as tortured as he felt.

"Yash." She said his name the way his family said it. To rhyme with *rush*, not *dash*. The way she'd said it the very first time. "What you're experiencing isn't technically panic attacks. Panic attacks are usually random. There can be identifiable triggers, but they aren't obvious. And they don't go away immediately when the triggers are removed. What you had was an anxiety attack. Given what you went through, that's to be expected."

"Are you saying I'm not actually going to die from a heart attack if I step on another stage?"

"Anxiety attacks, especially so soon after trauma, can feel absolutely physically debilitating."

"So you're saying time will take care of it." But time was the one thing he didn't have.

"It usually does." She paused, weighing how to say the next part. "The more you bury things, the more you have to dig to get to them."

That wasn't an issue, because putting things away had worked out just fine for him.

She studied him, then let a breath go. "But, yes, there are ways to aid our natural healing process."

"But it takes time? The election isn't something I can postpone. What do I have to do to speed things up?" Impatience rolled through him. He hated this. Whatever this was.

She seemed to see exactly what it was. "You've had stitches?"

He nodded.

"So, if you didn't have a doctor around to sew up torn skin, your wound would still heal. The stitches just make sure that the wound heals the way it's supposed to. You're basically just helping your body by securing the cut in the position where you want your skin to thread back together. The actual regeneration of cells to heal the cut is done by your own body, which has the natural ability to heal most injuries. Your mind is somewhat like that."

"Wounds don't always heal right if you leave their healing to chance," he said.

The barest nod.

"Or even worse if you scratch it wrong or bandage it too tight or put something on it that holds an infection inside." He ran his hands through his hair. His worry tell. Nisha and Ma had worked hard to have it trained out of him. "You can cause gangrene. Even—"

"Yash." She reached out to touch him but withdrew her hand. Her gaze was the gentlest touch, a calming caress. "You don't have gangrene. You just need to talk to someone about how you're feeling. Just in case there's something you need help with. What you experienced was traumatic. You're human. It is possible to heal yourself, but there's nothing wrong with getting help."

"I don't have time." He should be out there right now campaigning. "Other than talking to someone, is there anything else I can do to help myself heal correctly? Quickly?"

That she smiled at. An indulgent smile. The kind you'd give

a tantrumy child. "I don't know if I'd use the word *correctly*, but those two might be at odds. If you wanted to do this by yourself, I'd give myself some time to collect myself. I wouldn't force myself to go out on a stage before I'd let what happened sink in. If you keep falling on a wound because you're in a hurry, it will take longer to heal. You have the public's sympathy right now. They will understand if you need a moment. You're not broken but you are hurt, and you need time to heal until you can stand back up again. Focus on healing first, not on getting back out. You're good at focusing on things."

He pulled his hand away from his hair and found it shaking as he shoved it into his pocket. "Thanks," he said, unable to come up with another response.

It was good advice. Focus. That he could do better than anyone. He could focus so hard he could force himself to heal. It wouldn't be the first time either. He'd done it with his body, surely he could do it with his mind too.

Chapter Ten

*I*ndia had fallen off a horse once. It was nothing as glamorous as being thrown by a horse. She'd just been trying to get on it and she slid right off the other side. India was not used to being clumsy. Falling off a horse while trying to climb it was a few levels past clumsy on a scale of incompetence. Need she add she did not enjoy incompetence? Now, competence? That she found incredibly hot.

No.

She was not going to think about Yash Raje in terms of competence being hot. More importantly, she was not going to equate how she was feeling about him with falling off a horse.

Good lord, though, the man took competence to a whole different level. He had slipped into the zone like that, then boom, boom, boom. That breakthrough had taken minutes. Anyone else would have taken a year to come around to it. Her insides did a god-awful melty thing at the thought.

Stop. It.

He'd only been here because he needed help. The man had been shot. He was terrified. There was obviously too much going on inside him that he needed to navigate. The second he'd left last evening, she knew what she'd seen in his face that she hadn't been able to put her finger on. His guilt was haunting him.

She wished she could visit Abdul, know how his family was coping. How brave did you have to be to risk your life for someone else's? Lighting a bunch of incense sticks, she stuck them into the holder in front of the Ganesha statue in her office. Then she joined her hands and said a prayer for Abdul's family and made her way up to the second floor.

As she entered the living room, giggles and heated moans greeted her. China and Song were entwined and kissing. Loudly.

Mom is at home! India wanted to whisper-hiss, her inner ten-year-old jumping to the surface. But she wasn't ten, so instead of clutching her dress-up pearls she cleared her throat and said hi.

Making a smitten sound that could only be called tittering, they pulled apart, their lips mimicking suction cups in overdrive.

"Hey, India," they both singsonged, bouncy as kittens—fine, adorable kittens—high on catnip.

"What's new in the yoga guru business?" Song asked with a sparkling smile that transformed her beauty into something true and lovely. No wonder China walked around looking like someone had sledgehammered the back of her head. When India had first met Song, her energy had been a dusty faded rose, tinged with underlying sadness and a determination to not let it shine through. Now her aura glowed pink and joyful. There was no reason for that to scare India, but it did.

"Oh, the usual. Breathe in breathe out breathe in breathe out," India said.

Song laughed like it was the funniest thing she had ever heard.

"How are things in the superstardom business?"

Song dropped a kiss on China's lips. They locked gazes like Lady and Tramp over a bowl of spaghetti. Then Song twisted around and settled into China, who wrapped arms and legs around her. "What superstardom? Everything I need is right here."

China dropped kisses behind her ear, eliciting another giggle.

Her sister had never looked so happy. That shouldn't scare India either. *This isn't the nineteenth century. Every relationship does not have to end in marriage.* India reminded herself of her sister's words. China was an adult. She knew what she was doing. Song was in this as much as China. She had to be.

After finding out about Mom being sick, they had started to hang out here rather than at Song's hotel. They'd been snuggled into various corners of this couch constantly, except for long disappearances into China's room.

But it was 11:00 A.M., on a *Monday.*

"Can I get you something? Tea? A snack?" India asked. *Also, China, why aren't you at work?*

Holding that last part in wasn't easy, but she needed to figure out how to work it into the conversation without putting China on the defensive.

"I'd love some tea. That Indian spices thingy from Ashna that you made yesterday was lovely. I need to get myself some of that."

"Sure. Anything for you, Cee?" India went to the kitchen and filled the kettle. "What's the plan for today?"

China, who was usually fabulous at picking up the nuances in India's voice, made *nmnmn* sounds as she dropped another string of kisses behind Song's ear, and completely ignored India's question. "Oh, could you put extra honey in Song's tea? I think it was a little less sweet for her yesterday. She's too polite to say anything. You should tell people what you want, baby."

"Your sister shouldn't have to wait on me, baby," Song said. "We should get up and help her." To her credit she did try to stand up, but China pulled her back.

"India loves to take care of people. Seriously, we're actually helping her. She's been terribly grumpy these past few days. I wonder what's wrong." China said casually, but India felt her cheeks warm. She refused to let her mind wander to the restlessness that had wrapped around her recently.

"Thanks, Song. It's just tea." India poured water from the whistling kettle onto a tea ball with Ashna's *Deepest Breath* blend that Ashna had made especially for India. She added a goodly amount of honey to it. Then another spoonful for good measure. Everyone deserved as much sweetness in their life as they wanted.

She handed Song the tea and threw her sister a pointed look. "Is today a vacation day?"

"No, Song wanted to binge *The Witcher*. That Indian actress . . ." Song filled in the name "Anya Chalotra." "She's smoking hot. And deliciously ruthless." They went off into a discussion about this show they wanted to binge. A show her work-obsessed sister had missed work for.

"Don't look so disapproving," China said, gazing at her girlfriend with so much adoration that India almost relented and rethought her concern. "We're only prepping for next season. Shooting won't start again for two months." India had never heard China sound so offhanded about *Cooking with the Stars*, her show.

"But didn't you say that today was the big meeting where you're finalizing the lists so the network can start putting together the pairings?" The show paired chefs with celebrities and last season China had talked of nothing else for months.

"Shit." China sat up, Song still pressed into her. "Shit, shit, shit!"

Song turned to her. "Kitten, take a breath." She cupped China's face. "They're lucky to have you. That show would not exist without you." Song had been a contestant on the first season, but she had no way of knowing who the show could and could not exist without. "You are allowed to take time for yourself. You work so hard. You'll totally make up for it tomorrow when you go in."

"Tomorrow?" India said. "Don't you want to call in and make sure everything is all right? Song is right, this is the show you worked your butt off to build."

China looked at her watch. She did look stricken. It was not like her to forget about her work. India was much more used to worrying about her sister working too hard and being too focused on her job, to the detriment of everything else. "At least call in and make sure everything is okay. I'm sure they'll understand that you needed a break."

China smacked herself on the head. "I was supposed to call in sick and I forgot."

Are you on drugs? India wanted to yell, but watching China and Song stroking each other's faces, India knew that she was. Love was definitely a drug. Anyone who fancied themselves in it certainly seemed to display all the restraint and common sense of an addict.

China extracted herself from behind Song and got off the couch and India felt like the worst kind of killjoy. All cuddled up with someone and entirely focused on them did seem like the perfect way to spend a day.

"I'm sorry, puppy, I'll just call my boss and make up an excuse." China started searching for her phone, another alarming thing.

"Fun! What will you say?" Song said excitedly. "Can you tell them your girlfriend was dying of love and you had to take care of her?"

"I'm supposed to be making up an excuse, not telling them the truth," China said with all the glee of someone who believed there was no better life on earth than the one she was living right now.

Song jumped on her and they kissed some more. Despite herself, India smiled. Their joy was palpable and India had to stop trying to control everything just because she was afraid. It was time to acknowledge her worry for her sister, then leave the rest to China and the universe.

"I'm going to check up on Mom," she said.

The only response she got was more kissing sounds.

Mom had not left her room all day and India entered as silently as she could.

Instead of finding her mother in bed, she found her sitting cross-legged on the floor, going through a trunk of old sweaters India's grandmother had knitted for them. India dropped down across from her, and Chutney rolled up to her and climbed onto her lap.

"Hey, there, beautiful girl. You been keeping your mommy company, yes, you have?"

"She's been helping me decide which sweaters to start with."

"Start with? Were you going to donate these?" These sweaters were their childhood. Grandmona was an artist, no matter what the rest of the kids in school had said about their sweaters.

"Don't look so sad. I would never donate them. I'm going to take them apart."

"Wow. That's so much better."

"Hah. My funny girl. I'm not destroying them." She picked up a marsh-green turtleneck that Sid had worn in middle school. "Well, I am destroying them, but only temporarily. I'm going to unravel one sweater each for the three of you, one each of Mom's and mine, then I'm going to use the yarn to knit squares to make a quilt."

India picked up a rusty red cardigan she had worn on her first day of high school. The wool was soft and fine and it had worn away at the elbows. She'd loved that cardigan, with its too-long sleeves that gathered at her wrist.

A project. Not surprising at all. Tara was constantly coming up with projects. All the walls in their home and studio used to be hand-painted with murals. They'd lost them all to the renovation. But instead of being sad, Tara had been excited to get to paint new murals. Already the studio had a giant Buddha across one wall. The living room had the beginnings of a forest that Tara had been working on for the past year.

The mosaic backsplash in the kitchen. Beaded borders on all the lamps. Even the mandala rug in India's room was hand-hooked by her mom. Never had India seen her mother sit still. Not even these past few days when her movements had gotten just a tad slower.

"I was lying down and I realized that having a blanket with all of us woven into it is exactly what I need."

"It's a great idea." India ran a hand over the sweaters scattered across the floor between them.

"You're worried about something," Tara said. A statement, not a question.

"How can I not be?" She reached out and touched her mother's forehead. No fever, but her batik caftan hung on her and the whites of her eyes were far too yellow. "How are you feeling?"

"You know, I'd rather feel a little bit stronger and have a little more energy. But I've been breathing and you've been giving me Reiki, so I'm going to be okay."

"And Dr. Kumar will have the results today and we're going to figure out a treatment and everything can go back to normal," India said.

Her mother patted her face and smiled. "Is China's lady love still here? Doesn't a fancy star have her own home?" She held up China's ocher-yellow poncho and India nodded in approval. "Is it mean to say that?"

"Yes, a little bit. She's here because she wants to spend time with China, and I'm sure she feels welcome." India hoped she hadn't made Song feel unwelcome. She was hanging out here so much only because China felt guilty about leaving Mom.

"You're always such a good girl. Always so kind. I should have named you Empathy."

"Emotions instead of countries? What a novel idea!" India reached across the sweaters on the floor and took her mother's hand. "Guess I wasn't feeling all that empathetic just now when I basically scolded China about blowing off work."

"China missed work?"

"And forgot to call in to let them know."

Their mother looked sufficiently horrified, and India felt a little less terrible about being a killjoy. "I thought she was home because it was some sort of holiday."

"She was supposed to take the day off. She just forgot to inform anyone that she was taking it."

"China? Our China? Are you sure? That does not sound one bit like her." The worry in their mother's eyes was exactly the worry in India's heart. The kind of worry you felt when something beautiful happened to a loved one but you knew it was tenuous and the fact that it was so beautiful was what made it so much scarier.

China had no experience with emotional disaster and heartbreak. For someone who took herself and everything she desired so seriously, she'd never taken a relationship seriously. Her obsession had always been her work.

Plus, Mom dodging the topic of her diagnosis and treatment did not bode well at all.

"Stop worrying about everyone else," Tara said quickly, as if sensing the direction of India's thoughts. "Look at you. You don't wear stress well."

"I'm not stressed. Concern for loved ones and stress aren't the same thing. Are you ready to go to the hospital? They'll have the results and we can finally have an action plan."

"Oh, the appointment is canceled." Tara started packing up the earthy rainbow of sweaters that hadn't made the cut for the quilt.

"Mom? What are you talking about?"

"Well, I'm starting to feel much better and I made an appointment with the Chinese herbalist Tomas's aunt recommended."

"You canceled the appointment? Why? Why would you do that?"

"You know how Western medicine is. I'm not sure it's for me."

"Since when? You never missed a single well appointment or vaccination for us with Dr. Sarkar. We use holistic remedies for wellness and symptoms, not for infections and illness. Since when do you not believe in Western medicine? What's going on?"

"Since when are you such a suspicious person? You don't wear it well. It's not part of your true nature." Tara patted India's cheeks with both hands.

"And avoiding the truth is not part of your true nature. It's natural that you're scared. It's terrifying to know that you might have something that will take months, maybe years of treatment. But you're the most courageous person I know. You're going to fight this. Dr. Kumar will fit us back in." She pulled out her phone to call his office.

"Stop. I don't want to go." Tara took the phone out of India's hand.

Not leaving people to do things at their own pace was not India's way.

I don't have time. What do I have to do to speed things up?

The purpose on Yash's face had been so unhesitating. She'd always envied people who knew exactly what they wanted and put it before everything else.

The sense that time was important here had been nagging at India. Taking the phone back, she scrolled to the doctor's number.

Tara snatched the phone back. "India! I said I don't want to go. What has gotten into you? This is not like you at all."

Playing tug-of-war with a phone was not like Mom either, and yet here they were. "Not going is not a choice. We have to find out what it is and treat it. Look at the life you've lived. Everything you've ever put in your mouth is healthy. You've practiced yoga and meditation since before you could walk. Whatever this is, your body is primed to overcome it, reverse it. Your body knows what to do." These were things Tara had taught her, things she'd woven into their core. Without these beliefs, India didn't even know who she was.

Tara stared at the phone they were both gripping like a baton they couldn't pass. "That's not how it always works."

"I can't believe you're saying that."

Tara let the phone go, and hurriedly—angrily?—started pressing the sweaters into the wooden trunk and slammed it shut. Then she stood and carried it back into the closet, but when she tried to lift it up to the shelf, it wasn't as effortless as she wanted it to look.

India gave her a hand. "Are you really angry with me for wanting you to go to the doctor when you're this sick?"

When Tara turned to India there were tears in her eyes, and something else that India had never seen there before.

"Mommy?" India had been adopted when she was sixteen months old. She had no memories of her birth mother, but through most of her childhood she did remember waking up at night with a racing heart, covered in sweat, with an indescribable terror that would only be quelled when she walked around their home and made sure that China, Sid, and Mom were still there.

She felt that same terror now.

Tara blinked her tears away. "Oh, my darling child, I'm not angry at you. I'm never angry at you. How can I ever be?"

India took Tara's hands and stroked them, thumbs against skin, the way Mom had always done to soothe her, tracing the familiar tendons and vein patterns, the strong sharp knuckles. "Tell me. Whatever it is, we'll take care of it. Together. Don't be afraid."

Her mother had said a version of this to her so many times. Enough times that nothing had ever felt like a crisis because of her.

"I . . . I dropped my health insurance six months ago."

"What are you talking about?"

"When we did the renovations. You kids spent all that money. You drained all your savings."

"You drained yours too. And you're helping pay for the home equity loan." Mom had insisted on paying into that.

"When I took that on, I thought the incense sales would cover it. But, well, Whole Foods didn't renew the contract. They decided to import from China, where they could get the incense sticks for less than half of what it costs us to make them. That was our biggest contract."

India let Mom's hands go. "Why didn't you say something? Why didn't you tell me?"

"You've already taken on so much. You're single-handedly running the studio, teaching classes and those retreats, running your practice, helping with incense production. I couldn't put another thing on your shoulders, strong as they are."

"But health insurance, Mom? You're sixty-two."

"I know. But those things you said to me are true. I've practiced yoga all my life. I've lived as healthfully and mindfully as anyone can. I thought I of all people had nothing to worry about. I was only going to go off it until we got a new contract for the incense." She reached out and took India's hands and started stroking, tracing the veins and tendons, caressing the knuckles. "I am so sorry."

India pulled her close and held her tight, her heartbeat mimicking her childhood nightmares. "Please don't say that. It's going to be fine. We're going to the doctor. Let's find out what we're faced with. Our theory about our lifestyle isn't just a theory. Our bodies are strong. Our minds are stronger. We'll find a solution." Smiling, she wiped her mother's wet cheek. "It's only money."

That was what Tara had always said to them, when she paid for their college, when she paid for trips and supplies and shoes and backpacks. All the latest styles that China wanted. All the camera equipment Sid needed. All the reasons why there had been no money saved up when the structure of the studio was crumbling and they had to rebuild. Loans on the studio were how they had made it through all the early surgeries and tough times, and now they were borrowed out and already it wasn't easy to make the payments.

"We will figure this out."

Tara studied her with her kind eyes. "This is health care we're talking about. Apparently no one can figure it out." She smiled, more defeat in it than India could stand. "We're already deep in debt over the renovation."

"Stop it. I want you to stop this negative train of thought. Our business is solid. Didn't you read the *Daily Post* last month? I'm the undisputed leader in stress management coaching in the Bay area? Do you know how much stress there is around here? It's a gold mine. We're going to keep our focus on what we can control, and the universe will take care of the rest."

Chapter Eleven

It had been years since Yash had sat in the gazebo on his parents' estate. As a matter of fact, he couldn't remember the last time he'd just sat anywhere without actively doing something. Lying in a hospital bed drugged out of his mind didn't count. It had been two weeks since the shooting, four days since he'd shelled peas in India Dashwood's kitchen. He'd spent that entire time working on the policies his team was getting ready to post on his campaign website. Fortunately, there had been no more scheduled events to cancel until next week.

The wound on his shoulder barely hurt as he pressed a finger into it. The doctor had removed the bandages today and left just some strip dressing on. Same with his arm. Both wounds were almost healed.

"They're going to leave a scar," the doctor had said, and they'd both laughed. *Sesame seeds in a river*, his grandmother would say.

After he'd seen the doctor, he'd sat by Abdul for the rest of the morning, trying to block out all his scars, the new ones, the old ones. It had been years since he'd let himself think about how alive they felt on his skin. Like organisms crawling over half of his body, leeching at something. The only way he'd ever known how to deal with his own ravaged skin was to separate himself from it, to cut off the oxygen that gave it power by concentrating on the things that did need the oxygen of his focus.

Then Rico had come to get him. Did his family not trust that he would show up for his own campaign meeting?

Today was one of Ma's Family Teas™. Which was basically code for an all-hands-on-deck meeting to recap the past week of the campaign and make plans for the upcoming week. Usually Yash looked forward to the meetings; they relaxed him and got him ready to take on the week ahead.

Today, however, Rico had to drag him out of the hospital and bring him here. If that wasn't bad enough, he'd asked Rico to go inside and join the others because Yash had needed to come to the gazebo to gather his thoughts. Now he couldn't get up off this bench.

It wasn't like he didn't want to be with his family. He did. He missed them, even though they were all right here, a few steps away, inside the house he'd grown up in. He'd never been able to go too far from them, yet he felt miles away. How did Vansh do this? His kid brother had gone to boarding school and then never truly returned home. Yash scrolled to his brother's number on his phone and called him.

"Hey, old man," the brat answered.

"Hey, brat."

"Are you hiding in the pool house?"

"No!" Not a lie. He was hiding in the gazebo.

Vansh laughed. "I just spoke to Trisha. They're all waiting for you upstairs."

"How can you be so up in everyone's business all the way from Africa?"

"Because I don't have the weight of the world on my shoulders. How's Abdul?"

Yash filled him in on Abdul's condition.

"When are you coming home?"

"Aww, you miss me. Or then you need me for something. Distracting HRH? Figuring out what to do with the police union? Trouble in paradise with Knightlina?" Vansh was the only one who used Naina's birth name and got away with it. She hated the name her dad had given her and would kill anyone else who dared to use it.

Vansh might believe himself to be the problem-solver extraordinaire, but to solve a problem you had to identify it, and therein lay the problem.

You're not broken but you are wounded. Why would her words not stop playing in his head?

"I just miss you, gym-rat."

"I'll be home in a couple months. You're in luck, dad-bod."

Yash had to laugh at that. "Such a brat."

"I know. You should try it."

"Not all of us can pull off living only for ourselves."

"Why not? How can you live for anyone else if you can't even live for you?" And with that wisdom that came to him so very easily, he was gone.

Yash leaned back against the railing and trailed a finger along the worn wood of the bench. This was where he'd been sitting when he'd first held India's hand. His first time holding a girl's hand. Romantically. When he was all of twenty-eight.

He hadn't exactly been precocious with his dating life. Then again, his lack of skill was more than proven by the not-quite relationship he'd been in for the past ten years.

How had he put a night that magical away so easily?

By the time he'd met India at the mehendi ceremony the night before Nisha's wedding, the path of his life had been set. Anyone with a modicum of sense, and integrity, would have walked away from her after she'd helped him out with those boxes he'd been staggering under.

She'd done it with such ease.

Lift with your legs and carry with your core. It makes it easier on your back.

The memory could only be described as staring into a blast of sunshine. She'd dazzled him. A girl who looked as delicate as spun glass, white and silver chiffon spilling around her like liquid light, with herculean strength.

"*I'm India Dashwood,*" she'd thrown over her perfectly sculpted shoulder as she carried the box to the pool house, tempering her pace so he could keep up.

"*I'm . . .*" For a second there he clean forgot his name.

"*I know who you are, Yash.*" There was an almost artless direct-ness to the way she spoke.

"*Have you seen me on TV?*" Why? Why on earth would he ask something so juvenile and needy?

"*No. Sorry.*" Her smile was far too kind, and for the lack of a better word: delighted. "*You were moving boxes dressed like that.*" She lifted her chin at the silk and gold angarkha Nisha had picked out for him. "*So I assumed you live here. And you look like the rest of your family.*"

When she put the heavy box down—gently, not with a thud the way he did—the blouse straps that went around her neck snapped.

She pressed a hand to the fabric to hold it up, the wardrobe malfunction painting pink streaks across her cheeks and brightening her eyes with mortification. He averted his eyes and pointed her to the restroom. Then he waited for her outside the door.

And waited.

And waited.

After waiting twenty minutes, he finally knocked on the door. Maybe the right thing to do would be to fetch one of his sisters in case she needed help. But he couldn't. What if she came out and wondered where he'd disappeared to after she'd helped him?

Who was he kidding? The idea of leaving her didn't enter his mind. Who could leave a girl like this? With a smile that dipped divots into her cheeks at either corner of her mouth, and hair so shiny it was like she had a halo.

"India, umm, do you need help in there?"

An embarrassed laugh-sob sounded on the other side of the door.

"It's okay. I have four sisters. I'm practically a woman. You can tell me."

She laughed then, and even across a door something inside Yash shook free. *"I'm going to need a safety pin. The . . ."*—she cleared her throat—*"hook on my halter has fallen off."*

While he had no idea what a halter was, it felt safe to assume she was talking about her blouse. *"Okay, I can go find you a safety pin."* He actually had no idea where he could find one.

Asking one of his sister's meant a million questions about why he wanted one. Which should have been easy enough to answer. India was their friend. He'd heard his sisters talk about her, but he'd just never met her until today.

"Do you know where to find one?" How she knew that he was still standing there on the other side of the door, he had no clue. His breathing did feel different, so maybe she could hear it?

"*Not really. But I'll figure it out.*"

"*There should be one in Nisha's room.*"

"*Thank you. You'll be okay in there?*"

"*Why? Is there something I don't know about this restroom?*"

He pressed his forehead to the door, not even sure why he was smiling. "*I'll be back in a minute.*"

"*Okay.*"

"*Okay.*"

Inside the house, Nisha's mehendi ceremony was in full swing. Some two hundred women dressed in all sorts of glittery things (none of which were the exact incandescent white and silver of India's clothes) filled the great room, where an army of artists piped henna on hands.

A dance floor had been put in for the ceremony and was filled with dancers letting loose as a band of women played the dholki drums and sang wedding songs on a raised stage.

On another platform lined with a thick mattress sat Nisha, flanked by two artists, one on each side, painting both her hands. Her already painted feet were propped on a padded stool. Ashna, Trisha, and Neel's cousins sat surrounded by a bunch of friends having their hands done as well.

India had probably left them in search of the restroom and then lost her way and found him fumbling with the boxes that contained the surprise gift he'd ordered for Nisha and Neel. Replicas of Kamasutra sculptures from Khajuraho, an inside joke because Neel loved to tease Nisha about honeymooning at the erotically carved caves, much to her horror. Yash certainly did not want their parents to know.

The mehendi was traditionally a women-only celebration. The few men in the house were in HRH's office, drinking scotch and smoking cigars. Yash had hurried back to the house when the incompetent delivery people left the packages in the middle of the entrance porch. He had needed to hide the boxes before someone found them.

That's when the most beautiful girl he'd ever laid eyes on had stopped by—almost causing him to lose his toes by dropping the box he was carrying—and asked if she could help.

Before Yash could say, *No, thank you,* she picked up the second box—the one he hadn't been able to budge—with considerable ease and asked where they were taking them.

No, with the way he was feeling right now, asking anyone who knew him—especially his busybody sisters, who had no concept of boundaries—where to find a safety pin and telling them why he needed it was out of the question.

Avoiding the gaggle of aunties, Yash made his way up to Nisha's room. Nisha had spent the past few months talking incessantly about everyone's outfits for each wedding event. That's how Yash knew what he was wearing was called an angarkha. For all the complexity of that name, it was simply an embroidered silk kurta with buttons running down one side of his chest instead of the center.

India was right, if anyone in this house was going to have pins that could substitute for malfunctioning hooks on a *halter*, then Nisha was the one.

He went to her dressing table and started riffling through her cabinets.

"Do you need something?"

Shit. He should have known that he wasn't cut out for sleuthing.

"Hey, J-Auntie," he said to their housekeeper. *"Did I tell you how lovely you look today?"* She wasn't dressed in her usual severe black-on-black uniform but in a navy-blue sari with all sorts of . . . wait for it . . . sparkles.

"Thank you, Yashu." Much to his sisters' chagrin, J-Auntie doted on him and his younger brother. It was legendary, the things they had gotten away with because she had cleaned up after them without breathing a word to anyone.

"What are you looking for? Does Nisha need something? You're such a good brother, to help your sister on her mehendi day when all the men are off in the den." He heard the worshipfulness in her voice and felt like a prized fake.

"She needs a safety pin." He hadn't said Nisha, so that meant he wasn't lying, right?

She hurried over, her movements just as efficient in a sari as they were in trousers. Within seconds she had extracted a handful of safety pins from the back of one of the drawers, all crammed with more trinkets and gizmos than he'd seen in his entire life. Usually he hated when someone acted like his sisters were somehow different from him. *But, man, Nisha, get a grip!*

He gave J-Auntie a quick hug, making sure he didn't thank her quite as profusely as he wanted to, because he did not want to make her suspicious. He didn't break into a run until he was outside the house where no one could see him.

"You still here?" He leaned in to the bathroom door and tried not to let his voice sound breathless.

"No." Just that one word.

It wasn't even that funny.

Come on, it was hilarious. And incredibly sweet.

"If you open the door, I'll slip it to you."

She did, and he did.

Another silent minute went by.

"Yash?"

"India?"

"Have you ever secured a halter with a safety pin?"

"Do it all the time."

He heard her smile across the door. Then it opened.

Her cheeks were still flushed. And smooth, and glowing. Her head was held high as though she were trying to convince herself that this was not at all embarrassing. One hand held the straps of her halter top at the back of her neck, the other one held the safety pin out to him.

He took it and she turned around, giving him her back. A gesture of trust that hit him square between his ribs.

"You just hold the two ends of these straps I'm holding together and then run the pin through them to secure them together."

"Easy," he said as breezily as he could manage. She trusted him to do this and he would rather die than let her feel uncomfortable for even a moment.

In two quick movements, with all the focus he was famous for, he accomplished the mission and stepped away, giving her space. *"There, done."*

When she turned to him she had the oddest expression on her face. *"You look like you climbed a mountain."* With that she burst into laughter.

For a few moments they stood there, winded with laughter, and the exertion of wrestling fashion, and whatever else was spinning around them. Then she thanked him and started to walk to the door and he realized that he did not want her to leave.

"India?" When he'd heard his sisters say her name, he'd thought it a bit strange to name a child that. Especially a child who had no apparent connection to the country. Now he found that there was a magic to saying it and a perfection to the way it fit her.

"Yash?" She said his name the way his family said it.

His brain raced. All he knew was that he did not want her to leave. *"I need help with something, do you mind helping?"*

"Sure. What is it?"

Crap. Usually his brain worked faster than this. *"The boxes, thanks for helping me move them. I think we need to move them again."*

She raised one eyebrow. God, she was totally on to him. *"Sure. Where are we taking them?"*

His back groaned. *"If we leave them here and someone comes in before I can get them to Nisha and Neel's home, then the surprise will be ruined."*

"Where did you want to move them?"

That's how they spent the next half hour, moving boxes that weighed as much as an overfed horse back and forth across the pool house, just so he could learn more about her. She'd just finished grad school, but she only ever wanted to work in her family's yoga studio. There was a clarity to her thoughts, an almost economic focus to her words that exposed an infinite wealth of understanding. He felt like he'd stumbled into a new universe that was waiting to unravel before him.

"Yash?" she said finally, once again putting down a box much more gently than he had.

"India?"

"I'm really having fun, but I don't think anyone is going to find these boxes if we throw a blanket over them."

"A blanket."

"Yes."

"That's actually brilliant."

"Thanks. Also, we can still talk even if we stop moving the boxes. I'm strong, but I think I might need to rest my arms now."

"Sorry." He was such an ass.

"Don't be." She smiled and touched his hand, then pulled away when something zinged between their bodies. Something bright

and electric that made his entire existence matter and burned away the usual discomfort that surfaced when women flirted with him. His entire being was seized with urgency. Not being able to speak to her again felt like too big of a risk.

"I have to go and get henna on my hands, otherwise someone's going to come looking for me."

He picked up her hand, another zing, and studied how wondrously beautiful it was.

You're twenty-eight years old, he reminded himself. *Get a grip. This does not happen to grown-ass adults.* Doubt nudged inside him, but with the way her hand felt in his, as though he were holding it with his entire being, he didn't let any other thought form. *"How long does henna take?"*

"I'll ask for very little."

God, how was she so perfect?

"I'll wait for you in the gazebo."

"Okay."

"You'll come, right?"

She nodded. *"I'll try my best."* Then she left.

He sat in the gazebo, the ball of anticipation in his gut fighting for space with the fear that she might not return.

She did.

They talked all night. Gazes clinging, fingers tangled, studying each other's lips as words they'd never said to anyone else formed on them. Childhood dreams and misadventures. Adult insecurities and missteps. All that they hoped to accomplish with their lives.

He had never wanted to kiss someone so badly. There was such an inevitability to it, and yet when he imagined it, the hunger and wonder of it terrified him. He didn't let the terror take form. Fear had controlled him for too long. It had locked him up.

What he was feeling now was too precious to stay locked away from. So he pushed down every memory that had torn up the connection between his mind and his body.

He let himself imagine kissing her. Somehow he knew how kissing her would feel. It could erase everything ugly inside him. Hope was a magnet. It tugged him forward, then pulled him back to slow down, to not mess things up.

As they talked, their gazes returned again and again to skim lips, desire glowing in the air around them. He took her to all his favorite places on the estate, exposing parts of him he'd let no one else see. But he couldn't bring his lips to hers.

When she left him the next morning just as the sun peeked over the house because they had to get dressed for the wedding, he told her he'd wait for her near the pool house after the wedding ceremony.

"You'll come, right?"

She dropped a shy kiss on his cheek, sending heat coursing through his body. *"I'll try my best."* Then she left.

A mix of fear and anticipation churned inside him all morning as he got dressed, all afternoon as he smiled at the guests, struggling to remember their names.

Seeing her again was a burden slipping off his shoulders, but also a breath caught in his lungs. The silk that wrapped her body was neither pink nor blue. A color he could swear had never existed before this moment. The brown of her eyes brightened when she caught the way he drank her in.

They snuck around catching moments, exchanging whispered words, stealing glances across the crush of wedding guests. Just the two of them in a celebrating crowd. It wasn't until much later, after the rituals were performed, the meals eaten, that they found each other in an isolated spot behind the pool house where the music from the reception wafted over. They found their way into each other's arms and danced, holding each other and swaying under the brightly lit night. That's when it happened.

After twenty-four hours of yearning, India went up on her toes and kissed him. It was soft at first, slow, then they fell into it body and soul. Reaching for each other with their lips, hungry for what lay beyond the heat of their skin, beyond the wet melding of their mouths.

Everything Yash was made of turned into that kiss. Weightless and searing and wide-open. His existence turned new and untouched. For a moment he thought he could hold on to it. Then the sound of faraway guests yanked him back to earth, the disorientation of it, yanking other things inside him out of place. For one ugly second, it wasn't India's hair gripped in his fingers, it wasn't her lips saying his name. He squeezed his eyes shut and brought himself back to this moment, but inside his belly was the nauseated swirling of whipping across time.

She stroked his hair, his jaw, he could tell that she sensed the confusion inside him but she couldn't articulate it into a question. As they walked back to where the guests were dispersing he wanted to do something to put her at ease, to put everything back. Taking her phone from her, he'd called himself from it and then saved the numbers on both phones. She told him where she lived but he'd always known. Her family's yoga studio was next door to his uncle's restaurant.

In that moment it felt as though they'd always been aware of each other, homing devices in search.

His family was leaving for Sripore the next day to celebrate Nisha's wedding at the Sagar Mahal, their ancestral palace.

"I'll see you after we get back," he said, looking into her hope-

soaked eyes, her fingers tangled in his, hating that suddenly the coming week felt like a lifeline. Too long. Too short.

Letting her hand go felt like a premonition. The weight of things he'd let out into the light started to wrap around his throat again, heavier and tighter.

"You'll come, right?" She borrowed his words from last night, confusion at the sudden storm she sensed inside him too clear in her voice.

As much as he'd wanted that kiss, the struggle to hold on to the beauty of it took up too much energy. *"I'll try my best,"* he said, borrowing back the words she'd said to him in return.

He'd never gone. Never called her.

What happened in Sripore the following week changed everything, brought back the things he'd let himself forget when he met her. After returning he'd allowed himself to wonder fleetingly if she would call. But of course he knew she wouldn't, not after she heard from his sisters about his being with Naina. Then he'd put it away and never let himself think about it.

It had felt like a dream. He told himself that was all it had been.

THINKING ABOUT NISHA'S wedding all these years later was a mistake. Yash knew the shooting had weakened him. Keeping his thoughts well leashed and where they needed to be was his superpower. Even the enormity of what had happened in this gazebo with India had been no match for his focus, because twenty-four hours did not define you.

An hour with her just redefined you.

He had to stop this. He had to get out of the gazebo. He needed to feel things again.

Feeling things gave him something to control. But the emotions had stopped again the moment he'd stepped out of that glass-paneled turquoise door.

"Penny for your thoughts." Nisha made her way into the gazebo and sank down next to him.

"Why do people say that?"

"For obvious reasons. Everyone wants to get rich, and people zoning out on you seems a plentiful enough resource." She smiled her worried smile. "It could be a profitable enterprise."

He grunted in response, and she elbowed him in the ribs. "Yash! You know the best thing about you is that you focus on people. You've always made even us, your annoying younger siblings, feel like we mattered, even when we pestered you."

Turning to her, he made eye contact, hoping it was his usual. "What makes you think I'm not focusing on people?"

She widened her eyes in a very Nisha way, infusing the action with more censure than most could withstand. "Trisha and Ashna were saying you're not returning their calls either. Rico said you've basically been *hmmm*-ing through your briefing calls. And you're sitting here in the gazebo when everyone is gathered upstairs."

"So I can't take a moment to myself? Every waking moment I need to be this robot everyone wants me to be. All the damn time." His tone was so sharp she flinched, and he should have felt terrible, but there was the little problem of his feelings being lost.

"You can totally take a moment to yourself. Is that what you want me to tell Ma and Aji? Our mother and grandmother have been worried and waiting with everyone for the past half hour." Nisha held up her phone.

He squeezed his temples. "Why the hell is everyone in this family so manipulative?"

That made her squeeze her temples too. "Okay, Yash, come on. I was not being manipulative. I understand that this isn't easy for you, but listen . . . Never mind. Do you want us to cancel?"

"Now you're just babying me. That's not what I need from you right now."

She took his hand, and if she hadn't done it so gingerly, he might have pulled away. "Then tell us what you need. We already canceled the last two weeks of appearances."

He stood, leaned on a column, and stared at the mountain beyond the house. Anchorage point, where he'd loved to hike as a boy. Where he'd taken his younger siblings when they needed a place to make them feel rooted, because you got a perfect view of the Anchorage from there. Where he used to go when he needed to think. Where he'd taken India that night, because he'd had to show her how the sun rose from behind the home he'd grown up in. Where he'd waited all night to kiss her but hadn't been able to.

"Yash?" Nisha said behind him.

"I need time. Someone hated me enough to shoot me. I'm not broken but I am wounded, and I need time to heal until I can stand back up again." Saying those words, her words, felt like being in her presence again, and the warm prick of emotion bloomed inside him. "Put out a statement that I need another few days to recover. Ask people to pray for Abdul, not me. We have a big enough lead in the polls that I can take a little more time." With that, he made his way out of the gazebo.

"Okay," she said behind him. "At least tell me where you're going."

"To get help."

As Yash approached his car, he found Brandy waiting by it. He still wasn't used to seeing her, or rather he wasn't used to not seeing Abdul. He checked his phone to make sure there was nothing new from Arzu. A new trauma surgeon had seen Abdul today.

Brandy straightened up when she saw Yash. Actually, that was a lie. The woman had a way of being incredibly erect and alert at all times, but she did look up from her phone and there was something suspiciously like a smile in her eyes. Naturally, as soon as she saw him she put it away and looked at him in that icy assassin way again.

"Everything all right?" Yash asked, looking pointedly at her phone, and there it was again: the softening of her eyes.

With nothing more than a curt nod, she asked where they were going.

"I'm not sure. Hey, is it okay to ditch this today? Take the day off? We need to renegotiate our hours. I'd like to engage you only for rallies and events." If he could ever do those again.

"Nisha's orders are that I accompany you to all public places," she said, emphasizing Nisha's name like the leverage it was.

The urge to dig his fingers through his hair was strong. "I'm not really going to go out in public."

"The yoga studio is a public place."

"Wow. Umm. Is that where I said . . ." Never mind. If being surrounded by sisters had taught Yash anything, it was that Brandy totally had his number and arguing with her would gain him exactly nada.

He got behind the wheel and Brandy settled into the passenger seat.

He must have looked as defeated as he felt, because her tone gentled several notches. "Nisha said I only have to accompany you to places that don't qualify as your family's homes. She also said that we'd revisit that once you start doing events again."

He let out a sigh. What Nisha meant was that he could have his independence back when he got his head out of his ass. "I really need space right now." He tried sincerity, because if anything was going to work with Brandy, something told him honesty would.

"You can ignore me. Pretend I'm not here." There was something about the way she said it, as though that were her dearest wish.

Being the center of attention was something Yash had always been comfortable with. *Attention whore*, Trisha very politely called it. This need for isolation was entirely new to him. Apparently his new bodyguard had the skill by the balls.

For a few minutes they drove in silence, then her phone buzzed and the ice in her eyes did a little tremble.

"We're in a car. Unless someone is going to drive up alongside like a gangster movie, you can take that."

She looked at her phone. Yup, the eyes warmed over again. With her usual quick efficiency, she typed something on her phone and put it away.

"Everything all right?" he asked for the second time that day, and she threw him a look that said, *Which part of "ignore me" involves being all up in my business?*

"I'm sorry, I didn't mean to pry." He merged onto I-280 and was met with an ocean of cars. Traffic was a sign of a vibrant economy, he didn't begrudge it.

"It's my daughter. She's—" She cleared her throat. "She's getting ready to ask a boy to a dance. And she's . . . um . . . she's never nervous about anything."

"Wow, things must've changed since I was in high school."

"She's in middle school. Sixth grade."

"That's somehow even more impressive. Do the girls ask now? Or is it one of those turnabout dances?"

"No, she just likes this guy, so she's going to ask him."

He had never asked anyone to a dance his whole life, so this child had his respect. "It's pretty impressive to have that kind of self-confidence so young."

Her smile completely transformed her face. "She's a special kid. Actually, I lied earlier. She isn't nervous at all. I . . . I kinda was the one who was nervous, so . . ."

"So you asked her to keep you posted." Yash found himself smiling. "And she's keeping you posted? That's a great kid."

"Yeah."

"Do you have only one?"

"Yeah."

So they were back to the monosyllables. Her phone beeped again and she looked at it.

"Did she do it?" he asked.

"It's done," she said.

"Yes!" they said together, with the same kind of excitement he felt when the Niners scored a touchdown.

"Details?"

That got him a smile. "Apparently I was being *extra* with my concern. She asked, he said yes, and that's that."

Without doubt she was the least extra person Yash had ever met.

"Your daughter should meet my mom if she thinks you're extra. Not that my mom ever had to worry about me asking a girl out."

"Come on. With the famous Yash Raje charisma, you probably had to fight them off."

"Quite the contrary." The Raje kids were most certainly not allowed to date in middle school. The only one who'd possibly even considered breaking that rule was Vansh. There wasn't a rule the brat had met that he believed was meant for him.

Through most of high school, Yash had been preoccupied

with trying to get out of a wheelchair, and through college he'd been just too driven to care about anything but proving everyone wrong about everything. "What about you?"

She made a snorting sound that he would never have associated with her. "When I was in high school you couldn't exactly show up at a school dance with a girl if you were a girl. Or at least not in Chattanooga, Tennessee."

"It couldn't have been easy," he said.

She made a grunting sound.

"Did you meet your . . . girlfriend? wife? . . . here in California, then?"

She went impossibly still and Yash knew he had crossed a line. "Sorry. I'll ignore you now."

A long silence. Then, "That's fine. I'm surprised you don't already know everything about me. It's all in the background report."

"Nisha takes care of all that."

"I don't have a girlfriend or a wife." A jaw clench. "She died two years before we could have married in the state of California. Ellie is her daughter. Well, she's mine now."

Chapter Twelve

India had been poring over their accounts for two hours. They were already over leveraged on the studio and the incense orders were low. At least the classes were filled to capacity and India's client list was full, but it wasn't enough. A bubble of anger sprang to life in her chest and started to fill. She traced its growth and squeezed it inward until it popped.

What would anger accomplish? Nothing. She'd forced Mom to the doctor. He'd confirmed that Tara had Hep C and advanced fibrosis. The treatment was going to cost a few hundred thousand dollars at the outset.

Mom was so ashamed about having canceled her insurance that she didn't want China or Sid to know, so asking them for help wasn't an option. India knew her siblings didn't have the money to help and she didn't want them weighed down with guilt. The check from the retreat would cover part of Mom's first payment. India would figure out the rest.

Not having to count on others simplified life, and India valued simplicity over most things. Sure, it was lonely, but she knew that her sudden loneliness had little to do with not being able to share her financial troubles with her siblings.

This same loneliness had devastated her ten years ago. It had taught her that waiting on someone else for happiness was the surest way to never be happy. Forgetting that lesson was a path to heartbreak, a path lined with the gravel of unforgivable recklessness.

When China stormed into her office, interrupting India's thoughts, she was beyond grateful for the distraction.

"Why are you upset with me?" China dropped into a chair as though she owned the room. The sisters had spent hours in the office "plotting world domination," as China called it. Starting from China's college projects and presentations to every job she'd gone after, India had played many a tough interviewer, many a disapproving panelist for China.

"I'm not. What are you talking about?"

"You know you can't lie." Getting straight to what was bothering her was China's way. Even though this recent lovestruck avatar had mellowed her manifold. "It's probably the one thing you're awful at."

"I'm awful at a great many things," India said.

"Yeah? Like what?"

India looked off into the distance as though thinking really hard. It made China laugh, so it was worth it.

"I'm an average cook at best."

"Come on. Who else can put cocoa in avocados, call it cookies, and not make you gag? Who else can make wheat-germ muffins taste like actual food instead of cardboard?"

That made India laugh. "That's me, skilled at making food that doesn't make you gag *and* doesn't taste like cardboard."

"See, you've got nothing."

China was wearing a well-fitted jacket over jeans and her hair as always was perfectly styled into a pony tail. To say nothing of the gorgeous hot pink lipstick.

"I'm horrible at dressing up," India said.

"That's because you rock yoga wear to a point where it looks like high fashion. You know, I don't know how an active wear brand hasn't asked you to model for them yet."

"No one has asked me to model because they're usually actually interested in selling stuff."

"Oh, India, India, India," China said in her dealing-with-a-lost-cause tone. "Then let's just say you're amazing at anything you happen to have an interest in."

"Everyone is good at things when they're focused on them. No one as much as you, though," India tried not to make it sound like a reprimand. She wasn't upset with her sister, but she was worried sick. "You're the best television producer in the business. There is nobody on earth as good as you." China had said those words herself so many times.

India had always pushed China to think about work-life balance, but China had been far too obsessed with the work half of it. India couldn't remember the last time China had talked about her work.

"I know. I know. Stop looking so worried. I still love my job. But I've never felt this way in my life. My whole self feels awake. You know how you and Mom are always going on about life force? Even the insides of my cells, the very nuclei inside my cells"—she made little pinching actions with her fingers—"even those feel lit up. I feel all the things we spend a lifetime wanting to feel, like the life force inside me is an inferno. I feel . . . consequential when I'm around Song. Being removed from her presence feels violent. I know you've never felt that, but how can I not be true to that?"

Every word sliced through India like a hot blade, cutting far closer than it should. She was happy for China. She focused on that.

"That's beautiful, Cee." China had a right to these feelings no matter how much it hurt afterward. India had no right to assume hurt was coming for her too. "I'm really happy for you."

"Are you? Because I need you to be. I can't contain all this happiness by myself. I need you to not be ashamed of me."

India reached across her desk and cupped her sister's cheek. "Listen to me. There is nothing on earth you could ever do that would change how incredibly proud I am of you. But please, you've given so much to this job. Don't give them an excuse to take all that hard work away from you."

"Cynicism? From you, India? What's wrong?"

The need to talk to her sister, really talk, about their mother, about everything, rose, but it had been a while since China had been interested in talking about anything but Song. Also, India couldn't break her word to Mom.

"It's not cynicism, it's pragmatism. Just because I don't always buy into the way the world works, doesn't mean I deny it or its impact on us. You have the gift of passion for your work. I just want you to protect yourself."

China groaned and stared moodily at the windows. "I wish I was more like you. How do you do that? How do you live inside your armor and turn off your feelings?"

Before India could respond, China's phone buzzed just as the ding that announced someone had come through the back door went off.

"Speaking of the world, Song's here," China said with a moony smile, and then shouted, "We're in here, baby."

Within seconds the door flew open and Song flew in and China flew into Song's arms. They had left each other a few hours ago.

"I missed you, puppy."

"I missed you more, kitten."

Once they had convinced each other that they had missed each other at least an equal amount, they pulled apart and turned to India.

"You look well, India," Song said.

"As do you. How was your day?"

"Heaven!" Song beamed. "Had the best training session with Boadie—you know Boadie, right? Boadie of Boadie Sculpting?"

As a matter of fact, India did not, but she appreciated a bad pun as much as the next person.

China gasped. "The trainer you've been trying to get to take you on? Why? Why would you want to torture yourself? I've heard the man is a sadist. Didn't Priyanka Chopra tweet that she couldn't walk for a week after her session?"

Song's smile was appropriately smug, given how impressed China looked. "But she was ripped after just a month with him."

"Ripped? Why would you want to be ripped? Your body is perfect." Eyes locked with Song's, China ran a hand up and down her arm. India decided this was a good moment to examine her bonsais for new growth.

"Thanks, puppy," Song said. "Boadie usually works out of L.A. He's been spending just one day a week in San Francisco. Jiggy Mehta, the tech billionaire, roped him in because he's on a health kick." Song dropped down on India's couch with a moan. "Priyanka was right. I feel like I've been put through a blender. Sitting down and standing up is excruciating and my shoulder feels like there's a vise around it."

Sure enough, Song was holding her shoulders at a misaligned slant.

"Didn't you stretch?" India sat down next to her.

China's face lit up. "India can do a session with you." She

squeezed in on Song's other side. "India has magic hands. Can you do some Reiki work on her?"

India rubbed her hands together and nudged them in front of Song. "This okay?"

Song looked delighted. "Yes, please."

India put her hands on Song's shoulder, the one she was holding as though it didn't quite belong to her. Pressing into the soft tissue around bone, India felt around for alignment. The muscle was so tight it was basically one big knot. She cupped her palms around the joint. Almost immediately some of the tension in Song's shoulder eased.

"My God. That feels amazing." Song closed her eyes on a sigh as India focused on the muscles, bones, and connective tissue under her hands, and let the healing energy inside her flow out through them.

It didn't take long for Song's shoulder to relax completely. Energy was a healer and touch brought awareness to the part of your body that needed attention, and that had its own power.

India removed her hands from Song's shoulder slowly, then pressed them into the middle of Song's back before pulling away and pressing them into her own chest and absorbing the remnants of energy.

Song rolled her shoulder. "My God, I can move it. You're a magician!"

"Rest it today. Tomorrow I'll show you some stretches to do before and after your next session with your Body . . . Boadie."

Song gave India the most grateful smile just as the doorbell dinged, startling them all but making fear flash in Song's eyes.

"Were you expecting someone?" China asked.

"I don't have any appointments because I was supposed to be

in Costa Rica. And we're done with classes for today." She patted Song's shoulder, trying to calm her and made her way to the front door.

The stuttering way in which her heart raced was totally unacceptable.

Don't be idiotic, India.

She checked herself in the hallway mirror. *So, so idiotic.*

The giant full-bodied jolt she felt when she pressed her face into the glass and saw Yash wasn't idiotic, it was pure lunacy.

His hands were stuffed into his pockets and his eyes were filled with so much unfettered anticipation that for a second India imagined his lips moving. *You'll come, right?*

How could she be foolish enough to think about that right now? *He has a girlfriend.*

He belongs to someone else.

A sick sensation gathered in her belly.

Shoving it down, she pulled the door open. "Yash? Is everything okay?" Relief flooded his eyes at the sight of her, turning the gray dark and intense.

"I . . . I need to talk to you. May I come in?"

How she had loved how formal he was. How polite, how *gallant.* *Stop it. Stop.*

"Hey, Yash!" China said behind her, making her jump.

Yash started too. Inasmuch as this new Yash would show being startled to anyone.

Brandy was close behind him, her usual icy demeanor firmly in place. "Hi, Brandy. I didn't mean to be rude. I just wasn't . . . well, come in." Moving aside to let them in, India gave herself the hardest mental shake in history.

Brandy got right to her usual sweep of the place. "Is there anyone else here?"

China glared at her. "Why? Have you not pinned anyone to the ground in a while? Missing it?"

India placed a big-sister hand on her arm. Holding China down when she wanted to fly at anyone who pissed her off had always been one of India's jobs.

They crowded into the entrance foyer lined with empty shoe racks and coat hooks. Which didn't stop Brandy from studying everything as though it hid moats from which someone might ambush them. Or, more accurately, ambush Yash. When India thought about it that way, she was completely fine with Brandy's paranoia.

China caught India's eye and slid a glance at her office, a silent plea for India to not mention that Song was here.

"Yes, there is." India never lied and she wasn't comfortable skirting the truth either. Brandy was just doing her job. But Song had a right to privacy. "Our mother is upstairs." Mom was in the incense workshop working tirelessly on incense sticks they had no orders for.

"I . . ." Yash hadn't looked away from her even for a moment. His expression was impossible to interpret. Or at least, her interpretation was highly unlikely. The last time he'd been here, he'd run out of here as though she'd thrown gasoline on him and lit a match. "If you're busy I can come back later?"

She made a sound that could be interpreted as a yes or a no. She wasn't sure if she was relieved that she had the week off or if she wished she had an excuse to not see him. Oh, who was she kidding? She'd cancel everything to help him, but only because: one, she'd help anyone who needed help; and two, she wanted him to win the election. It was time for someone to fix the mess their state was in. Yes, she'd read his health care policy, and, yes, it had caused her entire body to be seized with hope.

All eyes were watching her and she realized that they were waiting for her to lead them to her office. Or somewhere.

The pleading in China's eyes bordered on threatening. The office was not an option. "Do you mind if we talked upstairs again?"

A full-bodied relief rolled across him. "That sounds good. Thank you," he said, just as Brandy started walking toward India's office.

"Is there anyone else here?" Brandy repeated.

"No." China was in front of Brandy in a second. Blocking her path.

Nose-to-nose, they stared each other down, neither looking like backing off was an option. India was pretty certain they'd both missed the backing-off gene. China, in fact, looked like she was itching to return Brandy's favor and flip her to the floor.

"Do you mind if I check?" Brandy's tone made it not so much a request as an order.

"Yes, we would mind if you check." China did a perfect imitation of Brandy's tone.

"If there's no one there, why can't I check?" Brandy said, piling her stubbornness on top of China's.

"Because you just marched into our home and invaded our space and, generous as we are, we prefer to be the ones to decide which parts of our home we'd like violated." Even in her sputtering rage, she threw Yash an apologetic look. "Not that *you* can't come here whenever you want, Yash."

"No, you're right," Yash said. "I . . . I shouldn't have just barged in like this. We'll leave."

"That's not what I meant at all." China sounded torn, and Brandy studied her with an extra layer of iciness falling over her iciness.

"Let's just go upstairs," India said.

"Yash can't stay until I've secured the premises."

"That's not necessary." This from Yash. "I'll call when I'm done. You can leave now."

"I can't do that, Yash, I can't leave you here until I've made sure the premises are secure," Brandy said.

"Will you stop saying *premises*? It makes you sound like a psychopath. This is our home." China looked ready to wring Brandy's neck.

"Cee, sweetheart, please," India said.

"These are not *premises*. Who says *premises*? Is this an episode of *Homeland*?" China was not in a mood to be curbed.

"China's right," India said to Brandy. "This is our home. But you're right, this is also my office. A lot of people who come here take their privacy very seriously."

"So someone *is* in there," Brandy said with some satisfaction.

"Yes, and if you wait in the yoga room, they'll leave and then you can secure the premises."

That seemed to satisfy everyone and made Yash look at her in a way that he really should not be looking at her. Ignoring him, when her entire body had decided to do the opposite of that, she ushered Brandy and him into the yoga room. As soon as she shut the door, she knew she'd made a mistake.

The room was lined with mirrors on opposite walls. Seeing Yash reflected across mirror upon mirror almost knocked her back. Those haunted eyes, that velvet-thick salt-and-pepper hair tousled by his fingers, that perfectly shaved jaw that didn't know how not to be determined. Having him look at her that way, as though she were the answer to his questions, having that multiplied to infinity, it was a visual India really did not want to carry to the end of her living days.

Chapter Thirteen

As Yash followed India up the narrow wooden stairs to her apartment, the oddest sense engulfed him. What exactly the sense was, he didn't want to inspect. He let it dance there, at the edge of his consciousness. Her hair was shorter than it had been ten years ago, and it tapered in the back to her long graceful neck, leaving it bare.

The moment they entered the cozy living room with its teal sofa lined with orange pillows, an already familiar smell—fine, stink—hit him, accompanied by a panting sound. Chutney's slobbery face came into view.

One pat on her scrunched-up head and she promptly rolled over and whimpered. Dropping down on the top step, he gave her what she wanted, a belly-rubbing for the ages. In return she closed her eyes and gave him her unbridled ecstasy, and for the first time in days he laughed. And felt like himself.

"If you don't stop, you could be doing that for the rest of the day." India folded the throws that were strewn around the sectional couch and stacked them up. Then she picked up cups sitting on the worn wood center table piled with books and took them to the kitchen.

Sunlight filtered through a tree and streamed in through the wall of windows, kindling warmth in long-forgotten parts of him. There was a sense of peace here and it settled around him like the perpetual smell of incense threaded together with Chutney's smell.

"Would you like to sit down?" India said. Her calm tone disturbed him and wrapped around him in equal measure.

The way she held herself was open and loose-limbed, as though he hung out in her living room every day, as though anyone and everyone walked in here and was welcomed. Meanwhile, his heart was beating out an entirely unfamiliar pattern directly at odds with her even breathing, and he couldn't quite find the strength to fight it. Especially when something else inside him felt . . . it felt as even as her breathing.

Extracting a large glass bowl of something orange from the fridge, she placed it on the tiled island as he joined her, leaving a very satisfied Chutney behind.

"Can I help?" He'd never in his life had the urge to shell peas. Now it was a god-awful tug inside him.

"I need to take my mom a snack." She filled a bowl with what had to be orange yogurt with unidentified clumps of something mixed in. "I'll be just a minute." Tightness slipped into her voice. She was working hard to appear relaxed and realizing that made a weight settle on his chest.

"What is that?" he said, pointing at the goop in her hands.

"Mango chia overnight oats."

He tried not to, but he blanched.

"What?" His reaction made an amused smile push at her lips, and that made the sense of lightness that had wrapped around him when he came up those stairs return.

"That's a lot of pressure on the mango," he said seriously, making her amusement lean into delight.

She waited for an explanation, as though she didn't already know exactly what he meant.

"Well, mangoes are delicious. But can they really help those other things go down?"

She mock-frowned, trying hard to keep the amusement from dancing in her eyes. "I'll have you know that this is my signature dish. No one who's eaten it doesn't love it." She pulled out another bowl and spooned some into it and pushed it toward him.

No way! He jumped back. "Um, that's terribly generous of you, but I'm not here to impose."

Naturally she didn't buy that and stood there, arms crossed. "No imposition. Try it."

Over my dead body. "I had a big lunch. Really big. I'm full." He touched his belly in that way a bad actor would if he were trying to convince someone that he was full.

When she narrowed her eyes, her cheeks had a way of pressing up and crinkling them. "Seriously? You won't even take a bite?" *What are you, two?* She didn't say that last bit, but her tone did.

"I . . . um . . . oats make me gag." Frankly, he didn't understand people who ate them voluntarily. Even the word made him gag.

"When was the last time you ate them? Have you ever had them soaked in yogurt and not cooked?"

A horrified tremor went down his spine. And, damn it, she saw that too.

"Who would've thought?" she mumbled, reminding him of J-Auntie when she had to clean his room, a tone that could only be described as abject disappointment, if not horror. Then she took the bowl to the stairs.

"What's that supposed to mean?" he called to her back.

"You had donuts for breakfast, didn't you?" she threw over her shoulder.

"No!" he said with all the indignation of a liar. And hell if he didn't make it worse by trying to sound imperious, like HRH when their mother caught him bypassing the salad and he denied it. India was wrong. He hadn't eaten a donut. He'd eaten a croissant. So what if it was chocolate-filled?

"But it was some sort of sugary pastry."

Without his permission his spine lengthened, giving off more of that imperiousness. "I was shot. Cut me some slack."

"Ah." Balancing the bowl in one hand, she scooped Chutney up with the other, making the entire thing look like a ballet move. Then she ran up the stairs to her mother.

What on earth was "Ah" supposed to mean? He didn't like that "Ah" one bit. He had nothing to be ashamed of. Hardworking people deserved their treats.

"Ah," he imitated, and turned back to the kitchen island.

The bowl of orange goop taunted him from the tiled countertop. He ignored it and moved his attention to the ceramic jar filled with incense sticks. Pulling one out he smelled it. The strong sandalwood scent reminded him of the Sripore palace and the childhood summers he'd spent there. Before his mind drifted to the week of Nisha's wedding when Naina had fought with her father and come to Yash for help, he turned back to the *mango chia overnight oats*.

It was still taunting him. He glared right back at it. Then he checked over his shoulder and leaned over and smelled it. It smelled like . . . like, what was the word he was looking for?

"It won't bite," India said behind him, and he pulled away and straightened up. An action that was impossible to execute with any sort of dignity.

"I was just trying to figure out what that smells like," he said, giving up on dignity.

She had a particular smile she smiled when he was honest. Her reward smile. She raised a brow. "And what did you come up with?"

"It smells, well, it smells"—he made a face that couldn't quite capture the undesirability of the smell—"fruity, but not in a good way . . ." *Like Skittles*, he wanted to add, but he wasn't an idiot. "It's a little too, um . . ." *Cloyingly healthy?*

"Perhaps the word you're looking for is *fresh*? *Wholesome*? *Unprocessed*?" But her eyes were dancing, so he'd take the disappointment writ large in the way she was shaking her head. "You sure you won't even try it?"

More sure than I've been of anything in my life. "Maybe later."

The way she smiled at that made him want to press a hand into his heart, it made him want to step closer, it made him want to . . .

She stepped back, going straight from playful and unguarded to scared. Scared of what she'd just seen in his face. Her withdrawal felt like pulling a patch of skin off with the tape on a wound.

Maybe he'd just offended her. Some people were sensitive about people not eating things they'd made. Nisha would've shoved it down his throat. Fortunately, Nisha stuck to baking cookies and brownies.

Was not offending India important enough to try orange-colored sludge with . . . with . . . *oats*? All he knew was that he wanted that easy teasing smile back.

Her fingers fiddled with the spoon in the bowl she'd filled for him. Without thinking about it, he touched the spoon with a finger. Her fingers lingered on the cool metal for a moment and something tingled all the way up his arm. Then she pulled back, that fear back in her eyes.

He drew back too, stepping away from the island. The sugary tart smell of mangoes and yogurt was suddenly overwhelming. "How's your mother?"

"She's upstairs working." That wasn't an answer to his question. Which meant her mother was not doing great. India never outright lied. Not even in the small, seemingly harmless ways people naturally did.

It's what had struck him that first time he met her, when she'd picked up a box that was obviously too heavy for him with ease. It hadn't struck her that some men might see it as emasculating or threatening. She wanted to help him and she had. For the rest of the time they'd spent together, she had been more honestly herself than anyone he'd ever met.

It was what he'd always strived for. How easily it came to her had been yet another thing that dazzled him. Her core of truth, of goodness. Back then it had been raw, unformed. Now she'd turned it into a practice. A lifestyle.

"Do you know who Yudishtir is?" he asked.

That threw her. Her lips quirked again in curious amusement. How much he loved that reaction wasn't something he had the luxury to analyze.

"Isn't he one of the Pandava princes?"

It was his turn to be thrown. Self-satisfaction glittered in her eyes at getting that reaction out of him.

"Yes," he said. "He was the oldest of the five princes in the *Mahabharata*."

"The rightful heir to the throne."

"Yes. He was also the most virtuous of all men. He followed Dharma—the righteous way of living—to the letter. Never told a lie in his life, never stole or coveted what wasn't his, never reneged on a moral duty or shirked a responsibility. So strong was his virtue that his chariot floated a few inches above the earth when he rode."

She smiled. It was dangerous how much he loved that smile. "An inbuilt air-suspension from the fuel of his virtue."

"Yes."

"Didn't he lose that inch of air-suspension when he lied during the war?"

"Well, technically he never lied." The *Mahabharata* was the Hindu epic that ended, as all epics do, with a war of good against evil. With the Pandavas on the side of good and Kauravas, their cousins, on the side of evil. "The commander of the Kaurava army, Drona, was unbeatable on the battlefield, his will as strong as his incomparable skill. The only weak spot in his otherwise indestructible emotional strength was his son Ashwathama.

"The Pandavas knew that the only way to defeat Drona in battle was to break him emotionally. If Yudishtir lied and told him that his son was dead, Drona would believe him, given that the prince never lied. But Yudishtir refused to lie.

"So the Pandavas named an elephant Ashwathama and killed him. Yudishtir repeated this news on the battlefield. 'Ashwathama—the elephant—is dead,' he told Drona, whispering the words 'the elephant' under his breath so Drona didn't hear them. As a battle strategy, it worked. Drona, broken by the news, let down his guard and was defeated and killed. Yudishtir never technically lied," Yash said, watching her watch him tell the story, utterly absorbed. They were standing almost toe-to-toe, he could feel the warmth radiating from her body, but he didn't remember moving closer.

"Nonetheless, his chariot no longer floated above the ground after that," India said, jet-black strands falling across her forehead. "Because you can't win a moral argument with the universe on a technicality. Truth is truth." She was staring up at him, absolute clarity in her eyes.

"You would get that. I've never seen you lie."

That made her swallow and step away. "You barely know me, Yash."

That might be the first lie he'd heard her tell. At least it felt like a lie. From the first moment he'd met her it had felt like he'd always known her.

There was this way she had of shaking her head, as though dusting off one conversation and resetting herself before moving on to the next.

He complied. "What is your mother working on?"

A shadow passed in her eyes. "She's working on her incense sticks."

"Words one doesn't hear every day."

She smiled again, with more patience than humor. People being amused by the woo-woo-ness of her life had to be something she was used to. "So, did you want to do some breathing?"

"Also not words one hears every day. And yes, please."

She rolled out a yoga mat. Following her lead, he did the same. One orange and one turquoise, stark against the dark gray wood of the floor.

He was struck by how little he had noticed details the last time he was here. Now he couldn't stop noticing everything. Storing it away.

"Let's stretch first today. That okay?" India said.

"Sure." The idea of following along relaxed the knots he'd been tied up in. Then again, they'd started to relax the moment he'd walked through her door.

India crossed her legs, spine stretched tall, legs almost poetically contained in that compact fold. The way all her lines came together was effortless. On her it was no wonder why they called it a lotus pose. Yash followed, working hard to mirror her. His legs were stiffer than he'd like them to be. Definitely more cactus than lotus.

He always stretched before his runs, but these past few years he'd stretched in a hurry, too strapped for time to take away from the run itself. Since the shooting, he hadn't stretched or run at all.

A groan escaped as he pulled his knees toward himself. With her usual grace she ignored it. "Let's pull our knees apart and bring our feet together."

He did as he was told, and somehow it released the tightness in his hips.

As he relaxed and focused, the strong earthy-sweet smell of incense caught his senses. "So your mother makes incense sticks? Like agarbatti?" That was a little much even for a place this comfortable with woo-woo-ness.

"Yes, we have a workshop upstairs, with all the equipment and supplies you need." Unlike his, her feet met flush together and her knees fell outward and touched the floor. She folded her hands around her feet and stretched forward, bringing her jaw to her toes, her eyes signaling him to follow. "My grandmother learned how to make them from Ram—he was, well, he was my grandfather. My mom's father. She taught my mother, and Mom taught us."

"Seriously?" He forgot about the pose and sprang upright. "Your grandfather was called Ram?" This was so bizarre, he laughed.

Her body stayed languid, but something inside her stiffened. Something too much like anger pursed her lips as she too straightened up. "Why? Because if I have an Indian ancestor, it makes it harder for you to mock my family's lifestyle?"

"What? No. Do you really think I mock you?" Did he?

She closed her eyes, obviously wishing she hadn't reacted the way she had.

"India?"

Her eyes opened again, but she focused on her feet. "No, I don't think you mock me. But . . ." On a deep breath, she threw a glance around the apartment. "You find the way we live amusing. I understand. Most people do. Our lives are nothing like each other's. I get that." Was that a reference to what had, rather hadn't, happened between them? She looked at him again. The anger was gone, but something defensive lingered. "You also think of a lot of this as something you own, culturally. Indians do have a chip on their shoulder about other races and yoga. I get that too. It's their chip to have. But . . ."

"But what?"

"But, when *you* do it, it feels more . . . more judgmental."

"Because I know you and I should know that everything about you is authentic."

Color rose up her face. She fought to keep herself composed. "No, you don't know me at all," she said again. "But this is the only life I've ever known and I feel blessed to have it. I'm proud of it. I can understand that for a man like you this feels too out there, but you're running for governor and you should be everyone's governor, and being judgmental doesn't support that." It was the most she'd said to him about herself since they'd met again.

At Nisha's wedding, she'd chattered on unencumbered. Unafraid to share herself. She'd shown him her hand, all of it.

Ever since they'd met after the shooting, she'd been the opposite of that. Shuttered. Focused on playing a stranger. Focused on helping him. The way she was looking right now told him she wasn't happy that she'd said so much. Her fear of making the same mistake again, of not holding back, it was obvious.

She was not wrong.

"I'm sorry. I have sounded mocking before and I shouldn't have." Their gazes ended up locked together again. "But I wasn't mocking or judging you just now."

The skeptical twitch of her brow said she didn't believe him.

"Ram was my grandfather's name too." That got her attention. "Well, it was one of his names. Shree Ram Chandra Haridas Raje. I might be missing a few more in there, but he was called Ram by his family."

She looked embarrassed, and that made him feel as small as a rice grain, because it wasn't like he hadn't found all this woo-woo a little bit entertaining, and what she said about running for public office with a closed mind was absolutely right.

"I'm sorry for jumping to conclusions. That's an incredible co-incidence, though, isn't it?" The tiniest spark of the wonder that had captivated him all those years ago lit up her face, then was gone just as quickly.

It was wrong how much he wanted it, wanted her openness, her innermost feelings, her wonder, her trust, considering how he'd thrown it away with so little regard. "It is an incredible coin-cidence. So, no apology needed."

With nothing more than a nod, she placed her right hand on her left knee and twisted into it.

Again, he followed along, his stretches as tight as hers were fluid. "I never knew him. He died just before I was born. My aji—my grandmother—says I look like him. She loves telling stories about him. He was quite the revolutionary in the fight against the British. He specialized in"—Yash lowered his voice to a conspiratorial whisper, the way his siblings did when dis-cussing this, an inside joke he'd never shared with anyone else— "making bombs. He dug tunnels and built secret chambers all over our family home in India to hide the rebels. My aji was terrified of him being found out, because he never lied and he wouldn't have if the British had caught him. He would have hung for his crimes."

Her eyes shone. "You must be so proud!"

God, how was she so perfect?

Chapter Fourteen

India moved her twist to the other side. But she couldn't block out the way Yash was looking at her. No one else had ever looked at India like that, as though he saw everything inside her. Until this moment she hadn't realized this was what she'd been looking for in every relationship she'd been in.

Over the years she'd set up a pattern where her relationships never lasted more than six months, then a few years ago she'd given up because this full-bodied immersion in her feelings just never happened, and without it she'd felt like she was cheating herself. Her body and mind didn't function as separate entities, she'd never known how to make them.

The last man she'd been with had changed everything about himself for her. Become vegetarian, started meditating and practicing yoga. Being with him should have been filled with peace, but you couldn't have peace without truth and she'd felt like a liar. In one night, Yash had ruined her forever.

These were absolutely not things she should be thinking right now.

Yash followed her twist, his body supple for a novice and more flexible than he thought it was. He was an overachiever, and yoga was always an adjustment for the overachievers.

Something about the pride in his eyes when he'd talked about his grandfather wrapped around her heart. She imagined a man exactly like Yash. The same finely boned, slightly long face, the stubborn jaw, the most stunning eyes with a million gradations of gray radiating from jet-black pupils.

"I didn't know my grandfather either," she said, because she had to keep from focusing on the way he watched her. "Our mom didn't either. Somehow he'd made his way here from India. He worked for my great-grandparents and basically became part of their family. He was the one who brought the yogic practice into our lives. My grandma Ramona always said she was in love with him before she knew what love was. But it was illegal for them to marry, and them being together caused quite a scandal. When someone threw a burning torch into the studio, he left, to protect her and her family. He didn't know she was pregnant when he left. Mom never knew him. But in a way Grandmona—that's what we called our grandmother—made sure we all knew him."

The gray in Yash's eyes glowed with interest, with the unfiltered curiosity that made people feel completely seen when he talked to them. India reminded herself that it wasn't just her. This was how he was with everyone. A politician.

He looked around the living room as though seeing it for the first time. "That's the most fascinating history."

India followed his gaze and tried to see what he saw. Her home was such a part of her that even though so much of it was new now, to her it had made the transformation without losing itself. It looked modern, the recent update obvious, but there was so much time frozen behind it. His gaze picked it all out.

One detail at a time. He seemed to fall into its history body and soul.

The fact that saving it had cost them their ability to get Mom treatment without fear of financial ruin made India sick to her stomach.

"So this place has been in your family for four generations?" he said, with the sincerity that had made her forget herself the first time he'd spoken to her. As though the sheer amount of interest he had in her split him in half and threw him wide open in front of her. It had split her wide open too, seized her body with awareness. Now the memory warmed every sensitive inch of her. Her womb, her breasts, her skin, everything buzzed with the life force inside her.

She pulled in a breath, pulling her awareness back to this moment. "The Dashwoods came here from England in the 1930s and never moved."

"Then a young man from India came into their lives and lived here in the 1940s. Can you imagine what his life here might have been like? My mother tells stories of when she moved here forty years ago, and even that seems wildly brave to me sometimes. The fact that my parents chose to leave their home and come to a place where they were so different from everyone. I can't imagine leaving California ever." She couldn't either. "You said he left. What happened to him?"

"At first Grandmona believed he'd gone back to India. He wrote a few letters, but then the letters stopped and he never responded to her letters telling him about Tara. It turned out that the return address that she used to reply to his letters wasn't a real address."

"How did she find that out?"

"My mom went to India looking for him when she was eighteen and never found him."

For a few seconds they both just sat there, the shock of having shared something so personal hanging in the air between them. This was how it had been the first time they'd met. Breathless. Armorless. She needed to stop thinking about that night, that day. He had made his choice. His being here had to do with a bullet and the fact that someone had tried to end his life. His being here was about processing that and moving on with the life he'd chosen. Over her.

Listening to stories about her family was certainly not why he was here, but every time she thought about her grandparents' story, her foolish heart got too heavy.

He reached over and touched her hand. Then pulled away almost immediately.

"I'm sorry," he said.

The awareness of his touch stayed long after. That darned full-bodied reaction burning through her, making her mind and body yearn as one, for just another brush of his skin against hers.

She hated hearing him apologize, and she didn't know why she hated it so much.

"Let's do some pranayama," she snapped, when those were words no one should ever snap.

Without another word, he put his focus on following along as she started the practice.

For the next twenty minutes they focused on breathing patterns. One nostril at a time, anulom vilom; then hard diaphragm breaths, kapalbhati; then rolling the breath into all the various parts of the body to all the bandhas, bringing awareness to them, tightening them, opening them up. By the time they were done she felt almost entirely insulated from everything outside herself. All she could do was hope that he did too.

He looked deeply relaxed, much less wound up than he'd seemed in all the time they'd spent together this week.

For another few minutes she sat there letting him soak in what he was feeling. How he was feeling had obviously taken him completely by surprise. Then she made her way to the kitchen, ignoring the way his eyes followed her, as though in walking away she was taking whatever he was feeling with her.

He joined her, eyes studying the room again. She wondered if he would leave now. She wondered if she wanted him to.

"You've done a great job keeping the place updated. It's beautiful," he said.

"Thanks. Last year we basically gutted it and rebuilt. Without the renovation, we risked it collapsing under us. The structural integrity was damaged. It was a huge . . . well . . ." Suddenly she was weary of not being able to hold her thoughts with him. "It was a huge undertaking."

"I'll bet." He was one of those people who picked up on things far too fast. It had probably taken him seconds to calculate how much the remodel had cost and he was now trying to figure out if a yoga studio had enough business to be able to pay for it and still be financially viable.

"The alternative was to be shut down by the health department."

"Come on, India, it was never that bad." Mom came down the stairs a bit too fast, and India suppressed the urge to ask her to slow down.

"Mom! Did you need something? Why didn't you call me if you needed something?" She tried to keep her voice casual, but Yash's focus on her intensified. He seemed to register every single bit of the worry she was hiding.

Tara looked at India in that way she had of looking at her children when she was trying to figure out what was going on with them. "I'm fine," she said before turning to Yash. "I'm Tara." She folded her hands in a namaste and Yash returned it. Easily. No mocking in sight.

"Yash Raje."

"No way!" Tara smiled one of her thrilled-with-herself smiles, which, heaven help her, seemed to thrill Yash. "I know who you are. I'm so sorry about the shooting."

Instead of looking like someone had gouged out his skin the way he had every time someone mentioned the shooting, Yash nodded. "Thank you."

"India tells me there's still hope for your bodyguard."

He slid a quick look at India, and she wished there was a way to telepathically stop her mom from talking to him about that.

Impotent pain was back in his eyes. "I am very hopeful," he said, with so much conviction that India's hands itched with the urge to touch him. "The doctors were able to perform surgery in good time and he's young and healthy."

"You should take India to see him. Her Reiki is very strong."

India tried that telepathy thing again, but it washed right over Mom.

"I read that they removed the bullet from you. Good thing. You know doctors often leave bullets inside if they didn't puncture organs?" The floaty expression that said Mom was about to launch into one of her macabre stories animated her features.

"Yes, it's usually less risky than surgery," Yash said, just as India was about to stop Tara.

Tara rubbed her hands together. "Our bodies being as magical as they are, the tissue wraps up the bullet and protects the body from it. I once had a student who fainted during a session. Turns out he'd been shot ten years ago and the bullet they'd left in his elbow had mushroomed into a lead-leaking bomb." She poked a finger into Yash's elbow and made an explosion with her hand. "Boom! It was flooding lead into his blood like a pump."

Yash's eyes shone. "Wow!" The smile he threw India lit a spark inside her. "What happened?"

Tara grinned, relishing the gore as much as her captivated audience. "They dug the bullet out of him. It was five times its original size. Then they pumped him full of drugs to absorb the lead. No permanent damage. Simen ended up going to nursing school."

Yash looked like he was going to choke, but he held his laughter in and the spark inside India's chest threatened to burst into flames.

Her mother put her empty bowl in the sink and rinsed it off. "Maybe I'll have some more oats. Did you have Mr. Raje try some?"

"Call me Yash, please. And India was kind enough to offer—"

"Yash didn't find them appetizing enough to try," India said.

Tara looked horrified. Yash looked cornered.

"No one who's tried India's oats hasn't loved them," Tara said, with the kind of determination that usually went with words like, *You're getting out of this over my dead body.* She pushed the bowl India had filled toward Yash.

To his credit, he did not step back. In this moment it was clear the man had warrior ancestors.

Something ominously close to a giggle escaped India. She turned it into a cough. The look he gave her nudged awake parts of her she hadn't used in a very long time. A look hungry for her laugh. The one he had once extracted from her over and over. With far too much ease. How easy she'd been. How careless with her self. She reached for the bowl—time to stop this idiocy.

He scooped it up before she got to it. Then took a spoonful and pushed it into his mouth.

Against her better judgment, she waited, jaw thrust out, refusing to show the anticipation burning her throat. She was a terrible cook in most instances, but she loved her overnight oats, she was proud of them, and if he didn't like them, well, people had a right to their opinion.

A whole array of emotions flitted across his face. All of which boiled down to disbelief. "It's . . . umm . . . very fruity," he said, as though "fruity" were the rarest of tastes. "What's that crunch I'm tasting?"

Holding her amusement in was a losing battle. Clearing her throat, she answered, "That's chia seed."

"Ah." The future governor of California obviously had no idea what chia seeds were.

"It's surprisingly . . ." He struggled to find the exact right word.

"Delicious?" Tara was smiling too now.

"Ingestible?" India said.

"It's certainly that. But also, different from anything I've ever ingested before."

She pressed a hand to her heart. "Easy with the praise. You'll turn a girl's head."

Tara started laughing and he joined her. Something bright and shiny lit the room.

"Please tell me the future governor of California has tasted overnight oats before," Tara said. "Next you'll say you don't drink wine. California has standards, son!"

"Well, fortunately what I lack in oats I make up for with wine. And now India has fixed me for the oats-based voters. So, thank you." He took another bite, looking like the action took him completely by surprise.

India felt her cheeks warm. "Please, we're teasing you. Don't feel like you have to."

"No, you're right. This is surprisingly ingestible."

Her mother let out another laugh. "Speaking of ingestible, have you heard of Agastya Rishi? He ran a gurukul, a school that only the most brilliant scholars were admitted into."

Yash took another bite and nodded encouragingly. India gave up on trying to stop her mother.

"Once, he developed an abscess in his leg. It filled up with pus and swelled up to twice its size." She patted her calf, and India fought to hold in her groan. "It was declared that he would die unless someone sucked the pus out of his leg."

"Mom, please," India said, but Yash looked fascinated and horrified and so utterly baffled that no more words came out.

"What?" Tara said. "They didn't have medical instruments back then, so sucking on abscesses was the only way to save his life."

That couldn't possibly be true, but it was one of Mom's stories and India bit her tongue.

"Did someone?" Yash asked, throwing a wary glance at the spoon of yogurt he'd been about to put in his mouth.

"Agastya asked all his disciples if they would do it. They all refused. But there was one boy, a servant boy who had served Agastya day and night. He was devoted to the sage but was too poor to be his student. Without a moment's hesitation he offered to do it."

India groaned. Yash gasped.

"And?" they both asked together.

Tara smiled. "And he did it. But instead of pus, the sage's abscess was filled with the sweetest nectar. Not even the sweetest mango on earth had ever tasted that good. It had been a test to see which of the disciples was devoted enough to the guru to deserve to be taught his most closely held knowledge."

"Oh God," Yash said, staring at his spoon of yogurt like he was going to explode.

"True devotion is unconditional," Tara declared, "and its results are always sweet."

Yash put the spoon of yogurt in his mouth and India's shoulders started shaking with laughter. Yash and Tara joined her. Laughter filled the room. Yash spooned more into his mouth with the care and curiosity of a sommelier tasting a note of wine he'd never before encountered, and it was so ludicrous that India couldn't stop laughing.

He was watching India's face when she heard her mother's laughter change, and her own laughter dried up. A breathless coughing fit gripped Tara. India pushed her onto a barstool, trying to keep the worry that gripped her heart from her face, trying to ignore Yash's immediate alert focus on what she was trying to hide.

Grabbing a glass from a shelf, he filled it with water and brought it to Tara.

"I'm fine. Stop fussing," Tara said to no one in particular. Her pallor had turned distinctly gray, her breath more labored.

With all the gentle firmness that would set him apart in a crowd of millions, he made Tara drink, and her breathing eased.

"I'm going to get her into bed," India said, suddenly wanting him gone.

She couldn't let him get involved in her life. Already, she'd let him in more than she should have. Letting him come up here like this wasn't just reckless it was irresponsible toward her own well-being.

"Shouldn't you be taking her to a doctor instead?"

"Oh! Why didn't we think of that?" India snapped. He could take his imperiousness elsewhere, she didn't need it. "Thank you, but we got this."

"Sorry, I didn't mean to pry. Is there anything I can do?" He continued to study Tara.

India should have told him to help by leaving. Instead she said, "You can start by fixing the damn health care system, by not making compromises on the policy you've drawn up." It came out exactly as bitterly as she meant it to.

"India!" Her mother sounded horrified. "Thanks for offering to help, Yash. I just need to rest for a moment. I think I might have inhaled too much incense up there." Mom turned to her. "Walk Yash out. I'll go lie down." It was a tone that brokered no argument.

So India didn't argue, but she followed her mother and threw Yash a look. "Let me get her situated and then I'll walk you out. Is Brandy waiting downstairs?"

"I'll text her."

They were both quiet as he followed her down the long, narrow staircase. He kept his distance, but the sense that he was too close, that she could feel him with her entire body, it made her want to tell him she couldn't do this. She couldn't do this.

How could she tell him that without admitting things she had no business feeling? The man had a girlfriend. He'd probably had said girlfriend when he'd spent an entire night emptying his heart out to India. Letting her empty hers out to him.

So many times she'd almost picked up the phone and called him. *Why?* That's all she'd wanted to know. *Why did you do it?* The moment when Ashna and Trisha had returned from Sripore and told her that Yash had a girlfriend was a moment she would always remember.

Isn't it romantic that he and Naina got together at the wedding reception in Sripore?

Isn't it romantic that they've been best friends since they were little?

Why?

Why?

She could not possibly be that foolish again.

No. She wasn't being foolish. He needed her help, and she would help a stranger if a stranger needed her. Maybe if she repeated that often enough, she'd remember it.

"Is she going to be okay?" he asked as they reached the front door. His body said he wanted to hold her, comfort her.

Her body wanted that with a force that almost brought her to her knees.

She wrapped her arms around herself and gave him an I-don't-know-but-I-don't-want-to-talk-about-it shrug.

"My father is a physician. He knows some of the best doctors in the country."

Congratulations, she wanted to say, but he was trying to help, so she said, "We're taking care of it."

"At least let him or Trisha refer you to the right specialist. A second opinion is never a bad thing."

"Thank you."

"India?" he said with some impatience.

"Yash?" she snapped back.

"You're helping me. Why can't I help you?" Suddenly he was close. Too close.

"Because you came to me for help. I did not come to you."

He stepped back as though she'd shoved him, and for a moment she felt awful. It was the truth, though, and it was important for her to remember that it was the truth. And the truth was important.

"Do you ever?" he asked, his voice soft. "Do you ever ask for help?"

Only you could help yourself. When she helped people, that's what she tried to show them. She pushed the door open and waited for him to leave.

He was smart enough to know she wouldn't answer. "What you said before about the broken health care system. Does your mom not have insurance?" He always recovered too fast. Always saw too much.

He was too used to pushing until he had his way, but he couldn't have his way in this. He needed to get what he needed from her and leave. She couldn't need anything from him.

"I told you, we're okay."

"You don't look like you're okay."

That made her want to shove him, and she balled her fists, which made her even angrier at herself than at him. She was no one's charity case. "This studio is prime real estate."

Her own words shocked her as they came out and seemed to shake him more than they should have. "This is your home. You can't be serious."

Wiping every trace of softness from her voice, she looked at him with all the unyielding purpose she needed him to see. "There is nothing you can do to help except get better so we can both go back to our lives."

Something about that reached him.

What darkened his eyes this time was too much like shame.

"When is the next time you need to speak in public? Your next campaign event?" she asked, because he was still here, at her door, unable to leave.

"The debate next week."

It was clear from his face that he didn't think he could do it.

For all her bravado just now, her heart did a terrible squeeze at how unsure he looked. Before she could talk herself out of it, she reached out and took his phone and held it up to his face to unlock it. She called herself from it and then saved their numbers on both phones.

"Text me and we'll set up a time to talk." With that, she dropped the phone in his hand, fingers coming millimeters from his but not touching. Then she turned back to the stairs, wanting nothing more than to go back and let their fingers touch. Just once. "Shut the door behind you when you leave," she said as she walked away.

Chapter Fifteen

As India left him standing in the lobby of her studio, Yash felt aware of himself in a way he hadn't been for a very long time. Awareness had wrapped around his nerves as he followed her through the breathing exercises, and it lingered on. Which had made him linger as well, too afraid to leave and return to the coldness he'd been feeling.

He checked his phone to see if Brandy had responded and saw a bunch of texts from Rico, all of which said some form of "*Where the hell are you?*"

Shit. He'd completely forgotten about his meeting with Rico.

"Hey, man, sorry. I lost track of time," he said as soon as Rico answered his call.

"Where are you? We were supposed to meet an hour ago," Rico said with more relief than anger, and Yash felt a jab of guilt.

"I got caught up in something. Where are you?"

"Still at home. That's where we were supposed to meet, remember?"

Ashna's house was around the corner and Yash left the studio and started walking toward it.

"Is everything okay?" Rico asked.

"Of course everything is okay." Nothing was okay. Especially now that he was walking away from India's studio. "I'm right outside, actually. I'll be there in a minute. And, umm, hey, did you call anyone to ask where I was?" The last thing Yash needed was to set off the Raje panic dominoes.

"I'm not a fool, mate. Everyone thinks we are in our meeting. You'd actually better be right outside, because Ashna's on her way home and if she gets here before you, wherever you were that you don't want to talk about is not going to stay secret."

"It's not a secret," Yash said, but that didn't mean he was going to talk about it. "I'll see you in a moment."

Curried Dreams, Ashna's restaurant stood at the corner between the studio and Ashna's house. It used to be his uncle's, and Yash had avoided it growing up, because his uncle had always made him uncomfortable. It was closed for renovations. Ashna was finally making it her own. About damn time, if you asked him.

Construction trucks and a giant dumpster were parked outside. Yash turned around and looked at India's studio and imagined what that must have been like during the renovation. Then he rounded the corner and made his way up Ashna's driveway. His sisters had hung out at the restaurant and the house much more than he had. So much of his life had been spent in a whirlwind of fighting for one thing or another. His famous laser focus had always been aimed at something. And like a laser it had eaten through every other aspect of this life.

When he'd walked away from India all those years ago, it had been far too easy for him to make up a million excuses to let what he had felt go. Naina needed him, he had to stay focused on his goals, trusting a stranger wasn't a chance he could afford to take again. India had dug up too much of his baggage. He'd worked too hard to bury it.

Evidently he'd been right. Because his level of distraction right now was taking over everything else. The election was looming over him like a test he'd blanked out on and all he wanted was to turn around and go back through that turquoise door. He wanted to hear her voice. He wanted to feel how he felt when he was around her. Alive in a way he had been chasing all his life. In all the wrong places.

He knocked on Ashna's door. It was Rico and Ashna's now, since Rico had moved in just a month after coming back into her life. Until a couple days ago Yash had wondered if it was too soon.

"Did you walk here?" Rico asked, opening the door. "What's wrong with you? Where is Brandy? Where were you?"

"You're sounding scarily like Ashna. Could you please not?" But he'd clean forgotten that Brandy was on her way. He texted her and told her where he was and that she didn't have to come back. He still didn't think he needed security outside public events, especially not inside people's homes. Fortunately, Nisha had agreed that Brandy didn't have to wait at the yoga studio with him after getting him there safely.

"I knew working for family was going to be tricky," Rico said.

Yeah, especially their family. "Good thing you've trained for the challenge in cutthroat competitive sports."

They were now fifteen points ahead in the polls even though Yash had made no appearances since the shooting. Rico had kept the media flooded with the tragedy strategically interspersed with ads and recordings of Yash's earlier speeches.

"Listen, man, I'm sorry," Yash said. "Everything you're doing is totally saving my ass and I can't thank you enough. You want to get me up to speed?"

For the next hour they popped open a couple of Anchor Steams and settled around Rico's laptop on the kitchen island and went over every detail of all the campaigning Cruz was doing. All his press coverage, his endorsements, where his funds were coming from. Cruz had been forced to pull some of his negative ads because slinging mud at someone who had just been shot had not turned out to be good strategy. Every negative ad had bumped up the donations flowing into Yash's campaign.

Then Cruz had tried the vote-with-your-brains-not-with-your-sympathy tack and fallen even lower in the polls so fast that he'd reconsidered that too. He was going to have to face off with Yash on policy. Something he had been avoiding throughout the race. This was a huge win. Or it would be, if Yash could get himself behind a podium without passing out.

"What we're seeing right now is the unstoppable momentum of an accidental occurrence. Your assassination attempt has taken over the conscience of California, and the only thing that can stop us now is either a miracle or you dropping out of the race," Rico said, with all the satisfaction of someone who loved to win.

Yash knew Rico was right. It just felt like all this was happening to someone else. Yash had knocked on a hundred and ten doors in Orange County the day before the shooting. He'd been in TV studios a total of five hundred hours over the past year. He had been so inside his campaign that being blasted outside it now and not knowing how to get back in should've been the most terrifying thing he'd ever experienced. It wasn't.

"What would make you think I might drop out of the race?" He understood his family and his team being stuck somewhere between excitement over this unexpected *gift* and sadness over the tragedy. He just couldn't relate to the gift half.

"Your face right now, mate." Rico pointed his beer at Yash's face as though Yash didn't know where his own face was—which was fitting, because Yash didn't know where most of him was. "That is not the face of a man who wants to win. It's the face of a man who's questioning his path."

"Why would I be doing that?" That was it. That was all Yash could say. Winning was something he'd always wanted. Wasn't it?

He walked to the French doors that overlooked the backyard lined with trees. On the other side of the trees was India's yoga studio. From between the trees Yash could see the red-brick fa-cade.

"You haven't been to campaign HQ since the shooting."

He knew. He was aware of everything he wasn't doing. In great detail. "I'll go soon. I've been responding to texts and emails. They're holding up great."

Rico's face said he wanted to tell Yash that his staff were not holding up great. That they shouldn't have to hold up without him. But he said nothing and they moved to brainstorming their strategy for the upcoming debate. The two candidates had agreed to two debates, one next week and one four weeks after that. Debates were Yash's strength and Cruz had obviously wanted to get them over with a good month and a half before the election, so he could recover if he messed up, which Yash had planned on and now didn't know how to execute.

By the time they had covered all the debate topics, the front door sounded and Rico went to the door with the excitement of a boy expecting a visit from Superman or whatever superhero was cool these days. Yash's favorite superhero would always be Clark Kent, the perpetual outsider.

Instead of just Ashna's voice, a collection of voices wafted into the kitchen.

"I hope it's okay if we join you. It's like there's no privacy left at my place anymore."

"Hi, China," Yash said, joining them in the entrance foyer.

He'd never seen the uber-confident China Dashwood look embarrassed. But there it was.

"Hi, Yash," she said sheepishly, as a somewhat familiar, very beautiful woman who'd been hanging on her arm hurriedly pulled away from her.

"I'm so glad you're still here." Ashna threw her arms around him, taking care to avoid his hurt shoulder, which barely qualified as hurt any longer. Then she examined his face like a mother hen. "You're looking good. Better than the last time I saw you." She locked her arms around him and held on as though she weren't planning on letting go anytime soon.

He patted her hair. "I'm fine, Ashi." But he was glad to be held.

"You know Song?" China said, still a little embarrassed about her opening line when she didn't need to be. Yash should be the one embarrassed. He was the one who'd invaded China's home.

Song bounced on her heels in that way of those who were exceptionally excited about everything and grabbed both his hands. "We met on China's set last month." Right, she had been on a Food Network cooking show China produced that Ashna and Rico had been on.

"Of course I remember you, Song," Yash said. "Great to see you again."

She bounced on her heels some more and turned to Rico. "You look as handsome as ever. Love suits you."

"You as well. You look even more beautiful than I remember."

Song blushed and China grinned like she'd swallowed the sun. Ah.

So Rico and Ashna weren't the only ones who'd found each other on that set. Must've been something in the studio water.

China winked at him when he smiled at her and slipped her

hand back into Song's as though she couldn't help herself. Something ominously like fear flashed in Song's eyes.

"Everyone here is a friend," China said, and Song relaxed a little. "Yash is Ashna's family, and Ashna and Rico already know."

"Song is a huge television star, one of the biggest in the world," Rico whispered to Yash as Ashna rushed to assure Song that everyone here was good at keeping secrets.

Yash had always prided himself on being perceptive, but it didn't take much to see that Song was not ready to go public with her relationship with China. Whether it was a celebrity thing or a being-in-the-closet thing, Yash didn't envy her struggle. He made a zipped-lips action at Song. Putting people at ease was what he did, and she smiled.

"Everyone's staying for dinner," Ashna declared, taking her shoes off and putting them in the shoe closet. China and Song followed suit. "I made some chicken makhani. China, there's dal and vegetables for you."

"I love chicken makhani," Song said, her exuberance returning to its original turned-all-the-way-up pitch. "I can have China's share too." She made a face at China. "My poor vegetarian darling."

Just as everyone turned to head to the kitchen, the doorbell rang. Yash was closest to the door and pulled it open.

"You weren't supposed to leave the studio without me." Brandy stood on Ashna's front porch, her tone icy. Not that she had another tone.

"I'm sorry. I messed up. Won't happen again," Yash said. "But you didn't have to come all the way back here to scold me."

Brandy glared at him and held out his car keys. He'd given them to her to move his car to a longer term spot before she left.

Before he could apologize again he noticed a young girl in an oversized sweatshirt standing behind Brandy. She had a nose ring and hair tightly pulled into a curly ponytail, and that expression teens wore around their parents when they thought they were being embarrassed.

"This must be Ellie." Yash waved to the girl and she waved back excitedly.

"Ellie's been wanting to meet you," Brandy said in a tone that suggested she couldn't quite fathom Yash's popularity. "Since I had to drop the keys off, I figured you wouldn't mind."

"Absolutely. I've been wanting to meet Ellie too," Yash said just as Ashna came to stand next to him.

"Hi, Ellie," she said. "And you must be the new bodyguard." Only Ashna could say that in a tone that didn't make Brandy uncomfortable, but also didn't dismiss what had happened to Abdul. The sick sensation permanently lodged deep inside Yash rolled over.

Ashna introduced herself, then pulled the door wide open. "Come on in. I've been looking forward to meeting you."

Brandy blinked, something she tended to do when someone did something she found touching. "Thank you. But I'm not supposed to watch Yash in his family's homes."

Ashna smiled. "Good, then you can focus on the rest of us."

Brandy looked at Ellie and the child grinned, said "thank you," and came inside.

Two things happened simultaneously as soon as they walked into the living room: China and Song sprang apart, and Ellie gasped.

"Are you Song Ji Woo?" Veritable stars exploded in the teenager's eyes as she gaped at Song, who fought to suppress that terrified look again. "My mom didn't tell me you'd be here." Ellie seemed to forget all about her excitement at meeting Yash. "*Love in the Spring* is my favorite K-Drama ever!"

Song regained her composure at that. "You know that show?"

"Is there anyone who doesn't know that show? Well, maybe my mom doesn't, but she might be the only one in the world. You're my favorite actress ever, Ms. Song."

Song walked up to Ellie and took her hands in the warmest gesture. "Call me Ji Woo, and it is very good to meet you. Actually, forget that. Just call me Song. That's what everyone here calls me."

"Isn't that offensive?" Ellie asked, and Song laughed. Yash loved this generation. They gave him such hope for the world.

"It is, but only if I weren't the one asking you to. It started as a mistake, but I like the sound of Song now. But thank you for making sure."

Brandy gazed at Ellie like she might explode with pride.

China gazed at Song as though her heart might melt and trickle to her toes. "I'm China," she said. "You're Brandy's daughter?" she added with some surprise.

Ellie turned to China with something of a fierce look. "Yes, can't you see the resemblance?"

China burst out laughing. Ellie was clearly Black and Brandy was clearly not. "I love it."

Ellie groaned. "Please tell me you aren't one of those Black people who judges interracial adoption."

China looked taken aback at that.

"Ellie, I don't think Ms. Dashwood meant to be rude, and you shouldn't be either," Brandy said in the gentlest tone Yash had ever heard her use.

"No, Ellie, Ms. Dashwood most certainly did not mean to be rude," China said, grinning widely. "And I don't think you were rude at all. I was adopted from Kenya. My mother is not Kenyan."

Understanding dawned on Ellie's face. "I'm sorry I was rude."

She gave the tiniest sad smile. "My mother was Brandy's girl-friend. She died."

Awkwardness swept through the room.

"I'm so sorry to hear that." China stepped closer to the girl. "How long has it been?"

"Five years. I was nine."

Brandy threw a bunch of keys at Ellie. "All right, sport, go start the car. Time to leave."

Ellie caught them and threw a look from the keys to Song, clearly not excited about leaving her favorite star.

"Why don't you two join us for dinner?" Ashna said.

"Yes, please join us, Ashna's butter chicken is the best in the world," Rico said, making Ashna blush. Which was funny because everything he said about her sounded smitten. How was she not used to it?

Amid all the chaotic bonhomie, Yash found his eyes straying to the windows that looked out on the thicket of trees that cut off India's studio from view. A wave of restlessness swept through him.

China and Song exchanged secret glances. They were making an effort to keep their hands off each other with Ellie and Brandy here, but between them and Rico and Ashna, the pheromones in the air were thicker than Yash had the stomach for right now. He hated this strange and new bitterness all this eye-fucking was causing.

"Please stay," Yash said, because Ellie looked ready to explode with excitement at the prospect of dinner with Song.

If Brandy could resist the look Ellie threw her, Yash was going to believe she had superpowers. "Please, Mom, can we stay?"

Nope, no superpowers, the woman crumbled like so much dust. "Are you sure it's okay?" she asked Ashna.

"Come on, ninja warrior," China said to her. "The child deserves to taste Ashna's cooking. With you for a Mom she needs a break."

Ellie looked at her mother's face and burst into giggles.

Chicken makhani was Yash's favorite food and Ashna's was unarguably some of the best in the world. When everyone was done, Rico and Yash broke off pieces of roti and used them to wipe clean whatever was left in the serving dish.

After dinner, the women moved to the living room with their wine and Rico and Yash cleaned up. It gave them a chance to finish reviewing their media strategy for the upcoming weeks.

"Naina's doing the press conference with me tomorrow," Rico said loading the last of the glasses into the dishwasher.

"And you think I should be the one doing it. I mean, I'm fine. I'm here with you all, so, as someone who the public is trusting with their futures, I should be able to be with them too, right?"

Rico turned on the dishwasher. "They love Naina, they can't get enough of her. Right now it's more important for you to focus on what you need to do to get back to normal. Fast."

If he'd meant to comfort Yash, he failed.

"Do we have to involve Naina in the campaign?" Yash asked.

Rico studied him with that blank face people put on when they were trying to figure out how to handle you. It was Yash's least favorite face. "Are you trying to tell me something, mate?"

"Just that Naina was never supposed to be such a large part of the campaign. We were never supposed to get involved in each other's professional lives."

The only good saying that accomplished was to make Rico drop his kid gloves. "The public is literally obsessed with your relationship right now."

Why? How was Naina and his relationship anyone's business?

Also, why was calling it a relationship feeling like such a grotesque lie?

Because that's exactly what it is.

Rico folded his arms across his chest and pinned Yash with a look. "Please, dear God, please tell me you're not naive enough to think your relationship should be kept private during the campaign. You are fifteen points—by some polls, twenty points—ahead of that asshat. That's not an advantage we could have dreamed of when we started this. And it's because Naina's pain over your shooting was one of those *real* things that get captured by a camera once in a very rare while. Your relationship with Naina is why we have an almost sure shot at this."

Yash had no doubt of Rico's role in making sure that photograph had taken over the consciousness of the world.

"That's bullshit, Rico. Abdul taking that bullet and that fucking shooter's bigoted anger. That's why I have an almost sure shot at this. My relationship with those two, that's what you should be pushing at the public."

"Raje." Rico held his gaze. "I took this gig on because I believe in you. Because I hadn't believed in politics or politicians until I heard you speak and met you. I—every single person on your team—we all believe you should win because you are going to change the future of this state. Finally make us carbon neutral, do something to make housing fair and equitable, get every single person affordable health care. Don't treat me like I'm some sort of PR hack who's selling you cheap."

Yash dragged his hand through his hair. It was overgrown. He'd had a haircut scheduled for the day of the shooting. Now he wanted to shave it off entirely, so he wouldn't have to be bothered with not touching it the way Nisha and Ma wanted him not to.

"That's not what I meant." It's exactly what he had said, though.

"I'm sorry." He started pacing the kitchen. Laughter wafted in from the living room. He stopped at the window and willed himself not to stare across those trees again. His own reflection sat between him and where he wanted to be. White shirt buttoned all the way to the top, overgrown hair, the beginnings of a stubble—something he'd never had in his life. "I don't know what's wrong with me."

"Are you and Naina having problems?" Rico asked.

That made a laugh burst out of Yash. A cloud of breath collected on the glass and obscured his reflection. *There is no me and Naina.* But he wasn't at liberty to say those words. He shouldn't even want to say those words. "Naina and I are . . . we're fine. We're always fine. That's the whole point, right? We stay out of each other's business and all my focus stays on my work, and she does the same."

Of all things, *that* made Rico look panicked. Not like an employee, but like a family member afraid for Yash's wellbeing. If the words *Holy shit* had a facial expression equivalent, Rico's face right now was it. Not that Yash didn't feel every bit of his panic.

Instead of articulating all the reasons why he thought what Yash had just said made no sense, Rico folded his arms across his chest and fixed Yash with his coach-before-the-final-game look. "Whatever is wrong, Raje, you need to fix it. Now. The debate is next week. We're out of time."

Before Yash could respond—not that he knew how—Ashna sauntered into the room.

"Are you guys washing down my entire kitchen?" She studied their expressions and kept her reaction discreetly contained. "All well?"

"Yeah," both Yash and Rico grunted in unison. This did not at all help erase the worry on Ashna's face.

Yash was so tired of carrying the burden of everyone's worry. Tired of having everyone carry his burdens through their worry. He was fine. Or he would be soon. There was nothing to worry about.

"Is it okay if I leave? I'm . . . I'm . . ." He was exhausted, but he couldn't say the word, because he had accomplished less this past week than he usually did in half a day and there was no good reason for him to feel like he was buried under a mountain and breathing through a straw.

Ashna came to him and stroked his arm. It should have soothed him. It didn't. "Go." She threw a speaking glance at Rico when he looked like he might say something. "Get some rest."

Yash didn't move. "I don't want to go out and say bye to everyone and I don't want Brandy to ride with me."

Ashna pushed his hair off his forehead. Then she went out to the front and brought him his shoes. "Go out the back. I'll send Brandy home. But listen, just get in your car and go home. Please. If you get hurt, you know I'll never be able to live with myself."

Yash pushed his feet into his shoes and dropped a kiss on her head. "You're the best, Ashi." Then, instead of making his way around the house, he walked straight through the thicket of woods to the gate in the fence and came out in the parking lot behind the restaurant.

Shutting the gate behind himself, he leaned back on it and looked up at the studio.

A crinkly face was pressed against the upstairs window. Chutney tilted up one ear when she noticed him standing there in the light of a lamppost. He waved at her, and the pug promptly started wailing in response. Before Yash could move, as he should have, India's face appeared above Chutney's. For a moment she just stood there, that long bare neck tilted at an angle in surprise, studying him, as he studied her. Then she pulled the window open. "Yash?" she called in a loud whisper.

"India?" he loud-whispered back.

"What's wrong?"

"Why do people keep asking me that?"

She pressed a hand to her heart, then made a circling motion with it. "Do you want to come inside?"

Do you want me to? "I can't go home."

She looked like he'd punched her in the heart. Some more spinning of that hand followed, as though he didn't know that he'd have to walk around the restaurant to get to her door. It wasn't like he could fly straight up to her, no matter how badly he wanted to.

"Come on. I'm opening the door." With that, she was gone from sight and his feet moved, because he had to have her back in his sight again.

Chapter Sixteen

India's hand shook when she opened the door. Her hands never shook. She was India Dashwood. She was unshakable. Her emotions were unshakable.

"What are you doing?"

"I'm standing at your door."

She waited. Hoping her face said the *Aand . . . ?* she was thinking.

"I was craving the overnight oats. Can't stop thinking about them. Or about the sweet pus nectar." His smile was tired. So tired.

Her lips pursed, but she moved aside and let him in. He looked terrible. Haunted. Every trace of luster gone from his golden aura. Those quicksilver eyes sunken behind shadows, that usually clean-shaven jaw starting to show stubble. Okay, that part wasn't exactly unattractive. His usually meticulous hair was tousled by his own fingers, his shirtsleeves rolled up, but not in their usual let's-get-to-work way, but in an I-feel-trapped-inside-my-clothes way. Those unfair forearms on full display.

Had it been just a few hours since she'd seen him?

"Yash?" she said, her tone weary with questions.

"India?" God, his eyes. Why was he letting her see so much?

"Why did you say you can't go home?"

"I've been living at my parents' house since the shooting."

"That makes sense."

"Does it?"

"Yes." The Rajes were the most tightly knit family India knew, and no family should let someone who'd been shot out of their sight. "You shouldn't be alone." Would he be alone, though? Where was his girlfriend in all this? Why was he here right now instead of with her?

Why was India letting him in?

Because she helped people. That's why.

"I just can't go back there," he said, making her heart squeeze. She needed to get him on his feet and out of here. Fast.

Turning away, she walked to her office. He followed at a distance. Careful not to get close, but not careful enough to hide how hard it was to do.

"Sit. Are you really hungry?"

He shook his head. "Ashna just fed me to within an inch of my life. But I didn't lie. I am craving the oats."

That made her laugh, but his eyes were so tortured she sobered again. The man was a master at sticking to truth on a technicality, at Yudishtiring it. How badly he wanted to not lie, that was the part of him she couldn't look away from.

"Why don't you want to go to your parents' house?" She dropped down in the chair across from the couch.

His pause was long, his struggle to find words painful. "The last time I lived there was after my accident." His hand went to his hair, then pulled away. "Most of my sophomore and junior years in high school I was fighting to get out of a wheelchair. My senior year was spent relearning how to walk. By the time I felt like myself again, I moved to UCLA." Unlike the rest of his family, and her, he hadn't gone to Berkeley. Now she wondered if it was because he'd needed the distance. "I've only been back for overnight stays every now and again. But . . ."

"Being sick and having everyone fuss over you brings back memories."

He looked at her like she'd found an exposed nerve and plucked it. He didn't respond.

"What about your apartment?"

"I don't . . ."

"Never mind. You don't want to be alone."

Suddenly he smiled.

"What?" she asked.

"You're actually answering questions for me," he said, still smiling, and she realized that she was. She was giving him answers he should be coming up with for himself, but he'd scared her with those haunted eyes.

"What is it you need from me, Yash?" she said, somewhat harshly.

I need you, his eyes said, and if he said those words she was going to scream. "I need your help."

Springing off the chair, she went to her bonsais. One of them was out of alignment with the rest and she straightened it.

"But you don't have to help me," he said behind her, his voice falling on her skin like a caress. "I mean that. If this is a problem. Just say the words and I'll leave."

More than anything she wanted him to leave, to leave her home, to leave her thoughts. Turning around, she walked back to him. "Of course I'll help you." She sat back in the chair, because since when was she a liar? "I will always help you."

That seemed to hit him even harder, which made her angry. Why did that surprise him?

"Why? Because you help everyone who needs it?"

How dare he ask her that?

"That certainly has something to do with it." That was about as much as she was going to give him. Because obviously him needing to ask why was telling. "I saw that you canceled your public appearances."

"Only for the next week. I have to get back to it before the debate."

"And that's why you're here, because you think I can help you get back to it?"

"That certainly has something to do with it."

She wanted to tell him to stop playing games, but she knew he wasn't playing games. He didn't want to be here. He was only here because he felt like there was nowhere else he could go for help right now.

"Is the studio always this quiet?" he asked.

"It's late. We've been closed for hours."

"It was empty this evening too. Did you . . ." He studied her, in that guarded way where he was thinking about how to say what he wanted to say. "Did you cancel appointments because you thought I might need to come over?"

She wished her smile wasn't so bitter. "You have a very high opinion of yourself, don't you?"

"No, I have a very high opinion of you."

"Yash." She hated saying his name. Every time she said it, a physical ache squeezed in her chest. Craving gathered in her belly. "Please."

But suddenly he seemed in no mood to back off. "Why is it so easy for me to talk to you?"

"Is it?" Because she was in hell talking to him.

"I haven't been able to tell anyone else that I'm not sure I can do this."

"This?"

"I'm not sure I can go through with it."

She waited. If he could indeed only verbalize things to her, then he had to prove that. It was the only hope she had of helping him, which seemed like the only way to get rid of him and get back to her life.

"I'm not sure I can run anymore."

"You're not sure if you want to run for governor anymore?"

"That's what I said."

No, it wasn't, and she had to make that distinction for him. "Are you thinking about dropping out of the race?"

"That makes it sound like a conscious decision. It's more like the part of me that was running, the part that had focused on nothing but that one thing, winning, that part is dead. Not lying in a coma but dead. He's gone. And before you make me close my eyes and go back anywhere, I'll tell you that part of me was alive and well and firing on all cylinders until I woke up in that hospital."

"Was it when you woke up? Was that when you noticed that he was gone?"

He closed his eyes and leaned his head back on the couch. His Adam's apple pushed against his throat where his stubble tapered off. His shirt was always buttoned all the way to the top. The urge to unbutton him, to strip him down to the man underneath, it was hot lava inside her.

For a long time he was silent, and miles away. "The thing I haven't told you. The thing I haven't told anyone is that I can't feel anything. Not unless I'm with . . ." He closed his eyes and went silent again.

This explained so much. It explained why he kept coming back. She waited.

"Thinking back to waking up in the hospital, the only thing I remember is not feeling anything at all." His eyebrows pulled together. Pure agony tightened his face. "Did I tell you that Abdul fell on me when he was shot?"

"No, you didn't."

"After he took the bullet for me." A tear danced at the edge of his closed eyes. "I remember him pushing me out of the way and hitting his head on the podium with the force of it. When I sat up he was sprawled across my legs, blood was spurting from his neck, it was like a spring. I couldn't get it to stop."

"You tried to stop it."

"I don't know if what I did qualifies as trying. I don't know."

"What did you do?"

"I got my jacket off and pressed it against his wound. There was no way to stop it. Everything was soaked, my hands, the jacket." The tear slipped from his eye and disappeared behind his ear.

"How is he doing?"

He sat up and opened his eyes, thick spiky lashes damp at the edges. "A new doctor just saw him. But no one can figure out why he won't wake up."

"Did you find the doctor?"

"I had to do something."

"That's good. That you got to do something."

"What's that supposed to mean?" Anger sharpened his words.

"Should it mean something?"

"India, Please! Just say what you're trying to say."

"Okay. What do you think I'm trying to say?"

He grunted. "God, I hate this." She wondered if he would get up and leave again. He'd run out of here once and she'd pushed him out once. They were one-for-one.

"Are you saying that finding the doctor was for me, not for Abdul?"

"I'm saying that I hope the doctor can help Abdul."

"I know that. But you're trying to get at something. You're trying to tell me that I didn't lose that part of me when I woke up in the hospital. You're trying to say something."

A giant lump was lodged in her throat. All she wanted was to give him that answer, but she knew he had it already.

"It's when they took him away on that gurney," he whispered finally, the sound coming out raw.

She swallowed.

"That's when I lost the part of me who thought he could win. They took Abdul away on that gurney and I knew there was nothing I could do."

"Nothing you could do for Abdul?"

"No, for anyone."

Those words hung there, eating through the silence in the room, until the sounds outside the window came back into focus. The rustling of the wind. A stray whirring of a car.

"Why do you think you can control everything?" She was the one to break the silence.

"I don't."

"Okay."

"Doesn't everyone want to?"

"Yes, but not everyone believes they can."

"If you don't control your own destiny aren't you just a puppet?"

"That depends on what you mean by 'controlling your destiny.' Controlling your actions and controlling the world's reaction to your actions are two very different things."

He sat up. "You're quoting the Bhagavad Gita to me."

"I'm just answering your question."

"How can I just let him die?"

"Do you really believe that you have a say in that?"

He opened and closed his mouth, then tried again. "Will you go somewhere with me? Please. There's something I want to show you."

India stepped back. He'd said those words to her before. That night long ago she'd been willing to follow him anywhere.

"Yash, please." *There's nothing you want to show me that I want to see.* But she couldn't say those words. She wasn't a liar, but she was no longer the girl who gave everything away without any thought to self-preservation either.

"If you go with me now, I'll leave. I promise. I'll let you get back to your life. I'll get back to my own."

The fact that he meant for that to be an inducement proved he didn't understand her at all, and that's what made her nod her head.

The walk to Stanford Hospital took twenty minutes. In less than half an hour they were at the registration desk of the critical care unit. The nurse at the desk recognized Yash and asked how he was doing.

It was long past visiting hours, but she let them through with a whispered, "Just five minutes, then you have to move to the waiting area." Obviously, she and Yash had a pattern.

Yash thanked her, and led India to Abdul's room where he lay motionless and hooked up to too many machines.

For a long time they just stood there, India watching Yash as darkness wrapped tight around him, mottling his aura to a rusty brown. The need for his aura to return to its golden splendor was a prayer inside her. All she wanted was for him to have peace.

"How can I live with myself if he dies?" Someone had left a framed picture of a baby next to Abdul's bed, Yash stroked it with a finger. "He has a little girl. She's just a few weeks old. And please, please don't tell me again that I wasn't the one who pulled the trigger."

"Okay." She wanted to, though. Before she could say more, there was a sound by the door, then a familiar voice filtered in. Trisha's distinct voice speaking to someone.

Yash pushed India behind a curtain, hiding them from view just as Trisha hurried into the room.

"Hello, there, Mr. Khan. How are you this fine evening?" Trisha said, her voice so deliberately light it only made the emotion it was laced with starker.

A shudder went through Yash's body. India's own body traced it because he was pressed flush against her, sandwiching her between the cold wall and lean muscle that emitted heat like a furnace. Her face was a whisper away from his neck, just where his shirt was buttoned all the way up. One breath and her lips would kiss his exposed throat.

His smell, like his aura, was bright and warm, a perfume commercial given human form, powerful, luxuriant, more vibrant than any human had the right to be. If her knees gave way beneath her she would never forgive herself. If he felt her trembling she would never forgive herself.

"Did I say thank you?" Trisha said on the other side of the curtain, and Yash's hands tightened on India's arms. All of him tightened, sadness radiating from his body like a tangible thing.

Before she could stop herself, India's hands went around him and stroked his back, unable to keep from soothing him. He sagged into her, the weight of the world too heavy on his shoulders. Warm breath blew at her hair sending tingles skittering down her spine. If she sagged into him the way he was sagging into her, she would never forgive herself.

Her body soaked him up, shameless about how starved it was for him, aware that this was all it could get. Ever. This accidental reminder of what it had once wanted with blinding desire.

Sounds of Trisha moving got closer, the sliding of a stool, the clicking of a keyboard. A sigh. "You have to hurry up and wake up. We're running out of time," she said. "Please."

In the silence that followed, Yash's body trembled in India's arms. She held him there. Nothing else mattered but the fact that he was where she could touch him. Her hands flattened into his back, absorbing the tremors, letting all her energy flow into his pain, directing it at unraveling the knots where he'd gathered his guilt and helplessness.

Time melted around them, swelled, and stood still. A lifetime. A blink. His body melted into hers. Arousal swelled and raged through her blood, every inch where they touched throbbed. Then a stool scraped the floor again, and footsteps hurried away. There was silence again, broken only by the staccato hissing of the ventilator and monitors.

Yash didn't move, not until India dropped her arms and sagged into the wall behind her, because her legs had ignored her and forgotten how to stand. Her hands felt empty, her palms cold.

His pulling away was an abomination of the way he had held her. One had sewn her together, the other ripped apart. She was not strong enough for this. She really wasn't. What was she even doing?

Nothing.

They'd been hiding. That's all.

The moment he gave her space she slipped past him, and with one last look at Abdul and one last prayer she hurried out the door. Her hands pressed into her chest, as much a ritual as a pathetic attempt to hold something inside.

By the time Yash caught up with her she had taken the elevator down and was out of the building and hurrying down the palm-tree-lined road, half hoping he wouldn't follow her.

He fell in step next to her, only slightly out of breath. "I'm sorry."

"Don't."

If she cried now, with him watching, she'd never forgive herself.

She couldn't do this. She couldn't give him what he needed. She was wrong about her own strength.

"You were right," she said, forcing herself to keep her voice calm. "You weren't the one who pulled the trigger. But you are the one who can do something to change a world where that happens." She didn't look at him, she couldn't, she just kept walking.

"I no longer know how to do that."

When they were in preschool, China regularly pushed anyone who pissed her off to the ground. It was a terrible thing to do and she always got in trouble. Sometimes, when India was angry, she wished she was more like her sister. She wished she could shove Yash to the ground now.

"When did you start believing that you could control everything?"

He didn't answer. He just kept pace with her step for step. It was her fault, because she'd phrased the question wrong. She tried again. "Will you honestly answer something for me?"

He nodded, eager for answers.

"When was the first time you experienced feeling powerless in your life?"

It took him a moment to file through the significant events of his life. He stopped. "The accident." Two words. Spoken like he'd never said them before.

She kept walking and he followed again. "Do you remember anything about it?"

"Yes." They walked in silence for a while. Then he spoke again. "I remember being thrown. A sense of suspension, my organs feeling weightless. And . . ."

Without slowing her steps, she waited.

"And a lot of blood. A lot." His face went pale, and his aura dulled enough to match it, as though all that blood from his accident and the shooting mixed and became indistinguishable as it drained from his body. "Powerless would about describe it."

She didn't let him linger in those feelings. "And what did you do with that?"

"Nothing." He'd obviously buried the memory until this moment. "The next thing I remember is the doctor telling me that I would never walk again." His voice was stronger now. This was the part he was comfortable with.

"And what was your response?"

"To prove him wrong. Naturally. Wouldn't that be anyone's response?"

"No. You already know that's not everyone's response." She picked up the pace and he did the same. "So, you've never considered the role that forces outside your control—the universe—played in your recovery?"

They arrived at an intersection and waited for the light to turn green.

"If I had left things to *the universe*"—yes, he used air quotes—"after my accident, where would that have left me? Still in a wheelchair, that's where."

The light turned green and she started walking again. For the next few minutes they walked in silence, responses flooding her brain, but she needed to get this right.

"Consider for a moment another side of what you're saying. Don't you think there was any element of luck in the fact that your efforts paid off? Yes, you gave getting out of that wheelchair your all. The reason you were able to heal yourself was that your injuries responded to the retraining therapies you used. Yes, there was a really small chance of them working and you worked really hard to give that chance a chance. But there *was* a chance."

He followed her in silence until the studio came into view.

She stopped and turned to him. "If your injury had involved destroyed spinal nerves or something like that, then no amount of effort would have mattered. There was an element out of your control that worked in your favor. You put everything into it. But things out of your control supported that. You did your best and trusted the universe to do the rest and you didn't even know it. You just have to do the same thing again."

He was gazing down at her in that way he had as though she had all the answers, as though she were, in fact, all the answers he'd ever sought. "But how can I do something that I did without knowing I was doing it? Don't you see, I don't know how to."

"You do. You do know. You're just afraid you won't get the result you want."

A small smile touched his lips, but not his eyes. "So I'm a coward on top of being a control freak."

"Being afraid doesn't make you a coward. We're all afraid of not getting what we want. But to get what we want we *have to* combine both—doing our part *and* trusting the universe with the rest. You of all people cannot refuse to do your part because you've suddenly realized that there are parts outside your control. You don't have that luxury. Too many people trust you to have courage. Too many people have put their faith in you to fix the things they're afraid of."

"What if I'm not worthy of that faith?"

"Do you know how I know that you're worthy? Because when you told me you wanted to be a public servant and not a politician I believed you. I believed you because I saw how much you believed it yourself. You promised the people who believe in you that you'd fix things. A politician can stop running for election, but a public servant can't stop serving. Abdul did his job, you need to do yours. You might be afraid, but I know you're not a liar."

The storm in his eyes went darker. *I am a liar*, his eyes said when he couldn't say the words. There were too many things he wanted to say but couldn't. Which was exactly why she had to say the words.

"I kept my end. I went to the hospital with you. Now it's time for you to keep your end of it."

"Okay." But he didn't move.

For a while they stood there, something larger than themselves looming between them. Two bugs stuck in glue. A physical bond holding them together even as it kept them apart.

Turn around and walk away. You can do this.

The way he looked at her meant she couldn't. He had more to say. Maybe if he said it, they could both leave.

"I made a promise. I don't know how to break it." He was no longer talking about Abdul, or the election, or the promise he'd made to the people of California. He was talking about them. Him and her, and Naina, who stood between them.

Those words were what gave her the strength to step away. He did the same, then turned away from her and started down the street.

Pressing her back into the glass-paned door of her home, she tried to stop herself from calling after him. And failed. "Yash."

He spun around, face overrun with relief at getting to see her again. She knew exactly how he felt, and it made her livid.

"You're already breaking it. You being here." She moved her hands between them, tracing the thing that danced between them. "This. You're already breaking your promise. A promise isn't what you say. It's what you do. Otherwise, you're just Yudishtiring it." With that, she let herself back into the studio.

Chapter Seventeen

Why everything in a hospital cafeteria smelled deep-fried and unhealthy, Yash would never know. Why he had never before noticed this, he had no interest in digging into. Grabbing his food from the smiling cafeteria server, he took the bowl to a corner table. The lunch rush had finally passed and the cafeteria was almost empty. For the past two hours, Yash had taken selfies and shaken hands and talked to the staff about the issues that were closest to their hearts. His own heart had stayed even keeled, no racing about, no emulating a cardiac episode. India Dashwood had proven worthy of the trust his sisters had placed in her.

He hadn't met Trisha for lunch at her hospital in years. The fact that being in the hospital reminded him of having his body pressed against India's should have set off alarm bells, but everything reminded him of that. Of that moment when she'd held him and everything had felt right.

It had been a week since he'd seen her, but the smell of sandalwood-laced incense wouldn't stop tapping at his senses. For Yash physical attraction had always been accompanied by discomfort and the urge to suppress it. Now desire wouldn't stop sparking like electricity through his veins at the memories of holding her. Of her pressing into him, her arousal tangible in her breath as it kissed his throat.

You're already breaking your promise. A promise isn't what you say. It's what you do.

The sense of loss in her eyes when she'd said the words was the reason he had to stop this. He'd walked away once without thinking about what it would do to her because he'd been able to convince himself that she hadn't felt what he'd felt. Now her eyes left no doubt about how wrong he'd been.

More than anything he wanted to tell her that the promise he was breaking wasn't what she thought, what everyone thought. The only promise he'd ever made to Naina was that they would always keep their arrangement to themselves. He'd never promised her any part of him. He'd never had the urge to promise all of himself to anyone until now.

None of that changed the fact that he'd promised India that he'd leave her alone.

"Congratulations!" Trisha said, sweeping into the cafeteria and wrapping her arms around him so tightly that she freaked herself out. "I'm sorry, did that hurt? Ugh, I'm such a knob."

"Knob? Are we all talking like your boyfriend now?" Trisha's boyfriend, DJ, was as English as they came.

She punched his arm, the unhurt one, obviously.

"Okay, now, that did hurt. So, I won't argue about the 'knob' thing."

She punched him again. "So, oh my god, the debate. You usurped that stage the way the Brits usurped our ancestors."

"Trisha, beta!" he said, imitating their mother. "Does your tongue have no bone?" And he got a delighted laugh from her.

"You're so going to win."

He'd gained another five points. He now had a historically

unprecedented lead. "Uncatchable," the media kept calling it. "This election is yours to lose," everyone kept telling him.

The morning after leaving India, he'd finally gone back to his campaign office. His staff's excitement at having him back had made him feel an inch tall. Every one of them had teared up, and he'd realized how unfair he'd been in leaving them to fend for themselves while he licked his wounds.

But you're back now.

That's what India would've said. Yes, she'd taken to saying things inside his head. All. The. Time.

The past week, he'd gone back to his usual pace of work. Drowned himself in prepping for the debate, and getting caught up with his staff. Their purpose had multiplied manifold. They were raring to win this, to set things straight, to change the world. They'd all been the best in their fields when they'd given up everything to join his campaign.

Nadia had quit her job as a Kaiser surgeon. Xio had let go of her position as employee number six at a pre-IPO start-up. Xilong and Smita had given up hefty paychecks at law firms. Hari had given up partnership in his PR firm. The Fabulous Five, as they called themselves, had been working around the clock toward his victory for a year.

Every one of them had one thing in common. They had come to him and made the case to work on his campaign. They'd told him that they'd been waiting all their lives for someone like him, someone who'd made them believe again when they'd lost faith in the system.

How had he forgotten about them?

They had celebrated his debate performance—spectacular, even if he said so himself—with salted caramel ice cream from Bi-Rite and Bob's Donuts. The family had all been there too.

HRH had hugged every one of the staff and told them he loved them, which was so out of character that it had creeped the hell out of everyone and made Ma laugh until she cried.

Trisha had been in surgery and missed it.

"I'm sorry I wasn't there last night," she said.

"Don't apologize for doing your job."

Abdul did his job. Now you do yours.

Was this going to be his life now? Having India's voice run in his head all the time?

The week had felt like a year. Her words, her presence, it was all lodged inside him, but all it did was make him feel empty.

She had wrapped her arms around herself as she called him out for cheating on Naina. After the words left her, her long, perfectly sculpted arms unwrapped from around herself and fell to her sides. A letting-go.

Then she'd gone inside, leaving him staring after her, his heart hanging lopsided like a door knocker displaced after a door had been slammed too hard.

He hadn't been able to move. In the end he'd dropped down on her front step and sat there examining every word she'd said to him from every angle. Unhealed wounds had opened back up as he turned his attention to them for the first time. His own panic and numbness had slowly started to make sense to him. By the time he'd pushed himself off the cold concrete the sun had started to nudge at the sky and he'd known exactly what he had to do.

How are you? He had typed and erased those words to her innumerable times. Like a smitten teenager. Something he'd never been when he was a teenager.

It was easy to assume she was fine, to take her strength for granted. It was what he'd done from the very first time he'd met her.

"What on earth are you eating?" Trisha asked, studying the bowl in front of him.

"Lunch."

"Yash, is that . . . oatmeal?"

It tasted like throw-up, or maybe pus, and not the nectar kind either. A smile twisted his lips as he pushed it toward Trisha. "Want it?"

Trisha put a spoonful in her mouth. "It's not bad. Thanks. Should I get you something else?"

"Not really hungry." But he took a spoonful, because he had to make sure it was as bad as that first bite. *True devotion is unconditional and its results are always sweet.*

Trisha looked alarmed as she watched him swallow, but instead of commenting on it she turned to the debate. "I did DVR and watch the entire thing after my shift and you're totally back."

"I am back." He returned her jubilant smile.

There had been a moment of panic when he'd headed for the stage. But instead of what he didn't know was hiding in the crowd, he'd thought about the people he did know were there. People who supported him. People who trusted him to do this. *A public servant doesn't stop serving.*

"Do you have any idea how proud I am of you?"

"As a matter of fact I do, giraffe, and right back at ya."

She put a few quick spoonfuls into her mouth and grinned at his use of her childhood nickname.

"Anything new with Abdul?" he asked. He'd stopped by to see Abdul earlier. The trauma specialists they'd consulted had all basically repeated what the other doctors had said. That there wasn't much more they could do but wait.

"Nothing new. But there's always hope," Trisha said. When it came to medicine, she was more practical than anyone Yash knew. If she had hope, that gave him hope. Abdul had been in a coma for three weeks now. "But you know that the chances of him waking up go down the longer he stays in a coma. How is Arzu?"

"Incredibly strong. She believes he's going to wake up."

Trisha nodded. "There's something to be said about faith and belief after we've done everything we can with medicine." She put another spoonful in her mouth. "So seeing India helped, then?" she said, casually enough that he wasn't sure if it was pretend casualness or real casualness.

He *hmm*-ed in response. "A lot." *She saved me.* "You're really good friends with her, right?"

Her pause was longer than he'd have liked. Trisha wasn't spy-level intuitive like Nisha and Ashna, but she was genius-level brilliant. So maybe it was a mistake to think barking up this sister tree was the easiest option.

"I'm closer to China, but I do hang out with India when we do our Raje-Dashwood sisters hang-out once every few months. She's lovely, isn't she? There's just something weirdly *good* about her."

He almost choked on his tongue. Trisha did not want him to answer that. He *hmm*-ed again.

"That's a lot of *hmms*, Yash. What's going on?"

Yup, barking up the wrong sister tree. With his luck, they'd all be putting their heads together and swapping analysis the second he stepped out of here. "I got the feeling her mother wasn't feeling great. Do you know anything about it?"

"You know that even if I did, I couldn't talk to you about it. There are laws, counselor!"

She hadn't said no straight out. So maybe India had called her.

"All I'm saying is that, since you're friends, maybe drop by and check up on Tara?"

She beamed at him. "Sure. I'm so glad white-knight Yash is back and ready to fix all the world's problems. I'll swing by. I did want to thank her for helping you." She leaned over and pushed his hair off his forehead. "I'm so glad to have you back."

He was glad to be back too. He really was.

Trisha scraped the bottom of the bowl and pretended not to study him. "How's Naina, by the way? When does she go back to Burma?"

Unlike him, details weren't Trisha's strong suit, unless they were related to medicine. "It's Nepal. And she isn't sure about her plans."

"Are you saying she might stay here? Yash, that's amazing! You guys can finally make it official."

"What are you talking about?"

He must have snapped, because she looked all alert and wounded, like the sensitive little girl she used to be. "Well, I'm excited that your girlfriend might actually be around for a while. Especially now when you need her. Why are you upset?"

The sick panicked feeling he'd had to suppress every time he thought about Naina living in California flooded through him, but he could blame no one but himself that Trisha didn't understand.

"What makes you think I'm upset?"

She did not dignify that with an answer. Instead she fixed him with a look that would've done the sensitive little girl she'd been proud.

"Naina and I aren't looking to change anything."

"Okay."

"What?"

"Are you sure you're okay?"

"Why?" It was getting annoying that they wouldn't stop asking him that. He was back to campaigning, back to returning their calls, back to working twenty-hour days. He felt everything ten times over now. No numbness in sight. What more did they want?

"Well, you were missing all night last week."

"Missing?"

She made a funny face, as though she wasn't sure who he was anymore. "Naina is your girlfriend. You're thirty-eight. If you spent the night at her place, why would you hide it?"

"Hide what?"

Trisha straight-out laughed at that. One of those laughs annoying younger siblings laughed when they caught you in a lie.

"Please tell me there wasn't a search party out. I told Ma I was fine." He had texted his mother and told her he had work to take care of and planned on staying at his apartment. He hadn't lied, because he *had* planned to go home. It wasn't like he'd planned to spend a night dragging India to the hospital and then sitting on her front step.

Not that any of it deserved to be met with a stealth search-party mission.

"Let me get this straight. You got shot. You had panic attacks when you tried to campaign. You shut yourself off from the rest of us for two weeks. Then you disappeared for an entire night. Did you really think Ma would let it be?"

Turns out, when he hadn't answered the phone—because he was too busy having his broken brain set straight by the only person he wanted to be around right now—Ma hadn't believed that he was in his apartment. Neel had been dispatched to check Yash's apartment in San Francisco. When Yash hadn't been found where he'd said he was, they had called Naina, and she had admitted to him being with her.

"I don't understand why you're lying about it. I know you've always been private about your relationship but everyone is happy for you. Both Ashna and I live with our boyfriends. I've always been so proud of you for supporting Naina one hundred percent in what she wants to do with her life. But if she's voluntarily back, then why is that a problem?"

Instead of answering, he made an incredulous sound.

"Wait, you think she's doing it just to help your campaign. You don't want her to make a sacrifice for you. You're trying to protect her." She made one of those faces his sisters made when they thought something was romantic. As a brother of this particular cornucopia of meddlesome sisters, he knew there was no dissuading them from their fanciful imaginings after that look.

"She's not wrong," Trisha went on. "The voters love her, and having her by your side is certainly not something to push away right now. You might have to stop being a hero and let her help you this time. You've asked for nothing from her all these years."

Yash blew out a breath. "I set out to win this election by myself, without her here. I shouldn't need her here to win." It was time to end this farce. Way past time. He had to talk to Naina about it today.

Trisha looked at him like he had sprouted a horn in the middle of his forehead. Fortunately, Brandy marched up to them with her usual purpose. She'd been patrolling the cafeteria and keeping an eye out for other psychos who might want to shoot him. "It's time," she said with her usual sunny minimalism.

At least they'd all agreed that he didn't need security 24/7, but just for public appearances and media events.

Standing up, Yash gave Trisha a quick hug. "I have to get to an interview. You'll keep me posted about Abdul? And you'll check up on Tara?"

She saluted. "Yes sir. Break a leg." She threw a grateful smile at Brandy, then turned to him again. "And get over yourself. It's okay to let people take care of you."

Yash was fuming when Naina greeted him at the studio. Flying at him, she dropped a kiss on his lips as cameras went off. What the hell? This was not how they greeted each other.

"Thanks so much for being here." Anne Shobraj, the host of *Morning Mountain View*, said, an *awww* written all across her face.

Naina smiled up at him, causing the *awww* to intensify.

As soon as Anne had excused herself and hurried off to the stage, Naina turned to him, confusion written large on her face. "Will you stop looking so tortured?"

"Why did you lie to Ma?"

"Lie?"

"About me spending the night at your place."

"Yash, come on, we're almost forty, it's not like our parents think we're playing Scrabble with each other for entertainment."

He hated when she did that, bought into her own lies. "We are not a real couple, Nai. I need you to stop acting like we are."

"What are we, then? And if you say the words 'fake relationship' again I'm going to kick you in the shins. The way I did when we were kids."

He hated that he smiled at that. "We're friends who made a deal. We're partners in a lie."

"No. We're much more than that. We're friends who want to change the world. Who can be really good together."

"We can't. We weren't. We tried."

She made pouty lips. "Why can't we try again? Since when do you give up?" He rubbed his forehead and she looked around. "We can even get help for your . . . your . . . reticence."

His ears warmed. He wasn't exactly proud of the fact that he didn't enjoy sex as much as the next guy, but as a proud and vocal feminist, shouldn't she not buy into the entire oversexed machismo thing?

"I just got shot. It's not at the top of my mind. Why are you suddenly acting like we're something other than what we are?"

"Why are you suddenly acting like you're trapped in something you never wanted? You're right, we are friends who made a deal. A deal you're suddenly acting like you want out of."

Damn straight he wanted out of it. He wanted out of it more than he'd ever wanted anything, and that was saying something. "Because I do want out. Because this wasn't the deal."

"How can you say that? Now, when we almost have everything we worked for. I thought we talked about this. You agreed to this the other day." She rolled her hand between them, but there was nothing there to trace. No electricity arcing between them. No connection that felt like a lifeline.

"That's not true. You said that's what you wanted. I never agreed to it."

She pressed a fist to her waist and looked at him as though he'd lost his mind. Getting that look from everyone around him was starting to get on his last nerve. Before she could respond, a perky young man asked them to join Anne in the studio.

After the introductions, the very first thing they showed was the footage of Naina sobbing over Yash on the gurney.

"Can you walk our viewers through what that was like? Seeing Yash go down like that from the audience," Anne said.

Naina pushed a trembling hand into her chest. It took her a moment to compose herself. Seeing that teared Anne up.

"Yash and I have been friends since we were in diapers. I don't remember life without him." She met his eyes, and guilt and frustration churned up his insides. "For a moment there I thought I'd lost him forever."

"How terrifying," Anne nudged.

"*Terrifying* doesn't begin to cover it. You know those moments when you rethink your entire life and all your choices? It was one of those moments." Naina reached out and took Yash's hand and squeezed it. Was that the truth? Was that why she'd changed after the shooting?

Anne's eyes lit up. A journalistic coup flashed so bright in her eyes it sent a god-awful tremor of dread up and down Yash's spine.

Naina's tears, however, were real, and he squeezed her hand. She pulled their joined hands to her heart. "Of all the people in my life, Yash is the only one I've ever been able to be entirely myself around. He's the only one I know how to ask for what I want. And I know he'll make it happen. No matter the cost to himself. And you know what the best part is?"

Anne opened her mouth but was too overwhelmed to speak. She nodded encouragingly.

"That's Yash. It's just who he is. Not just for me, or for his family, but for anyone who needs anything." A smile wobbled on her lips. "As his fiancée, it can be annoying sometimes, but a governor like that is exactly what our state needs."

Rage swirled like nausea in Yash's stomach.

The triumph in Anne's eyes was like fireworks. She leaned forward, totally at odds with her usual laid-back style. "Did you say *fiancée*? Did we miss something?"

Naina pressed a hand to her mouth and looked at Yash with entirely too much sincerity. "That was a slip. No, you didn't miss anything. Isn't it just a label, though? You don't need a ring to prove you're committed. All I know is that I'm not spending my life with anyone but him. That's bigger than any label."

Anne turned expectant eyes on him. A million things ran through his head. The face of one person who might watch this and have her heart broken again floating to the top of everything else. He had to tell India the truth. Whatever else he did, he had to tell her the truth.

"Naina's right. I can't imagine a life without her in it. But I'm still here. I got lucky. The significantly more important thing is that every year thousands of people cry over bodies of loved ones taken by gun violence. Right now, my bodyguard, Abdullah Khan . . ." He worked hard not to let his voice crack; he would not cheapen Abdul's tragedy any more than he already had by letting it turn into a stump theme.

"Even as we sit here, Abdul lies in a coma. Every day his chance of surviving goes down. He has a family, a wife who hasn't left the hospital since it happened two days after she gave birth to their first child." The silence in the studio was deafening, but the silence inside Yash was more desolate than anything he'd ever felt. "We need to protect people better. We need to not be beholden to the gun lobby and the lies it propagates for profit. There's work to be done, Anne."

For a few seconds, no one spoke. Then Naina gave the camera a look that said, *Isn't he awesome? What did I tell you?*

A look Anne mirrored. A look that sobered the gleam in her eye. With a professional nod she switched to political questions.

At the end of the interview, Anne, now firmly in her serious journalistic stance, asked Naina about her plans. "We've talked about Yash's achievements, but you're something of a trailblazer yourself. You've dedicated the past decade of your life to bringing economic freedom to rural women across the globe." They played a clip summarizing the amazing work Naina's foundation was doing. "I believe there's some good news on that front."

"Yes, the Mehta Foundation just pledged a large endowment to us, completely changing our reach and what we can accomplish. I just accepted the position to manage research and growth here in San Francisco."

"A much easier commute to Sacramento than Nepal, right?" Anne smiled, and Yash had a sense of someone tightening a strait-jacket around him.

Naina returned Anne's smile. "It will be lovely to be closer to Yash, but really Yash and I have always put our commitment to our work above everything else. I'm sure he's happy to have me around, but California is Yash's true love."

By the time the cameras turned off, the energy in the audience had turned into a solid block of support.

Rico was waiting for them when they got off the stage, victory writ large on his face. "That might have been the most success-ful TV interview a politician has ever given." To Rico's credit, the jubilation was tempered with fierce purpose. Naina looked that way too. Her faith in him was not a lie. That much Yash did know.

The cameras had a field day as Naina took Yash's hand and they followed Rico out of the studio.

Chapter Eighteen

He's not coming back, baby." India stroked the folds on Chutney's head and she let out a whine.

India tried not to dwell on how perfectly the whine verbalized her own feelings.

Chutney had taken to sitting at the living room window on the back of the couch and staring out at the spot from where Yash had waved to her two weeks ago. Needless to say, Chutney wasn't the only one doing it.

India wrapped her arms around her dog's barrel-shaped body and rested her chin on her head. "You were a very good girl," she whispered. "You helped him get back on his feet. Remember how his eyes lit up every time he saw you, every time you let him rub your belly? That was very generous of you. To give him that." She gave her another gentle squeeze and the sweet baby squeak-purred.

"I know it hurts. I know you're not used to hurting like this. I know you always keep your emotions in perspective, yet somehow he always slips past all your defenses. But don't worry, you will figure out what to do with the hurt. You're a strong girl. The strongest."

"She might be the strongest, but can she survive you smothering her like that?" China said, coming into the room and making Chutney thump the couch with her tail.

"She needed hugs." India let go of Chutney, and she turned to lick India's face.

"She is a needy slut like that." China sank into the couch and Chutney transferred her worshipful kisses to her. "She hides it well. But maybe she's just like everyone else and does need the occasional cuddling."

India ignored China's loaded glance and pulled her knees to her chest. Her stubborn heart had taken to feeling heavy and achy, and no amount of breathing was making it go away.

"You doing okay? You've been working around the clock," China said.

India let her knees go and crossed her legs and took a long ujjayi breath. "You know I love my work, and it'll settle down soon enough." Her clients wanted to make up for the time they'd missed when she'd taken time off, and Tomas had his CPA exams and had asked for a few weeks to study for those. "Someone has to teach Mom's and Tomas's classes." India was incredibly grateful for the workload.

"Mom thinks she can get back to it soon."

They both smiled. That was Tara.

Her treatment had just started. Trisha had stopped by last week. When she'd seen Tara, and studied the liver scans, she had referred her to a hepatologist friend whom Dr. Kumar endorsed wholeheartedly.

It turned out that Dr. Ung had gone to middle school with Sid, and Dr. Ung's father had been the surgeon who'd performed the cleft lip surgeries on all three of them. Mom had taken this as a sign from the universe and instead of resisting it was now fully on board with Dr. Ung's treatment plan. They had started with a hepatitis C drug regimen. It was going to be a long road, but with Tara's heart in it, India felt like they were halfway there.

This morning Tara had declared that the bovine injury from thirty years back might have sparked the chain of events that led to her getting sick, but her lifestyle had kept it from killing her years ago, and that meant something.

India agreed that the universe had a plan for them. Until that plan showed itself, India had emptied out her accounts to make the first payment. The next one was due soon with no possible way in sight to make it.

This studio is prime real estate.

Why had she said those words to Yash? Words that had shaken him. Words she should never have spoken out loud because the studio was part of their family. How could anyone separate from something that was their identity?

"I think Mom's right. She'll be teaching again soon enough. Everything going well with the show?"

Even though China and Song were still spending all their free time holed up in China's room, this was the first time in weeks that India was bringing up China's work. Her sister was an adult and India had decided to treat her as such. She might even have avoided China, because, one, she was in pain, constantly, and she didn't want China to see it. Two, respecting Tara's wishes and not telling China and Sid about the insurance situation was becoming harder as India grew more and more desperate.

Do you ever ask for help?

Why had Yash asking her that bothered her so much?

Maybe it was time to ask China for help. But China already covered part of the mortgage.

China cleared her throat and Chutney stretched between the

sisters, offering her head to India and her belly to China for a rubdown. Both sisters complied.

"Remember how you said you were proud of me?" China said, her voice suspiciously small.

"Cee, I'm more proud of you than I am of anything else in this world."

"Even so, I guess it's a good thing that you're sitting down for this."

Okay, that was not at all what India wanted to hear.

Her sister opened her mouth, then closed it, which was so not a China move.

"You're scaring me," India said.

China reached over and took India's hand. "You know how I've always wanted to travel the world?"

Since when? China was famous for the words, "Is there a world outside Northern California?" She had refused to take a job on her favorite talk show because it was shot in Chicago. Her only explanation for refusing the job had been, "But it's not in California." She didn't even like to go to L.A.

"Okay, that was a joke. But you know how you've always said I should expand my world? How I should take some time to travel?"

"I said that because I wanted you to come with me to Costa Rica last year for the yoga retreat."

"How does it matter where I travel to? So long as I travel."

"China, to repeat myself, you are scaring me."

"I'm moving to Seoul."

"To *where*?"

"Seoul, it's the capital of South Korea."

"China!"

"Okay, fine. I'll stop being an idiot. But I'm only being like this because you're intimidating me with your disapproval."

"No one has ever intimidated you a day in your life."

China smiled such a wide happy smile that India's heart did a little skip. "Are you . . . are you and Song getting married?" Her eyes slipped to China's finger. There was nothing there.

Could a smile turn dreamy and pained in the same breath? The yearning on China's face made every one of India's big-sister instincts bristle.

"Not yet. I mean, we haven't talked about that yet. But she has this amazing role she's been offered. A dystopian time-travel fantasy love story. They're paying her twice as much as she made for the last one. I think this break really helped her."

"So Song is taking on a new project, and she wants you to go with her?"

Discomfort flitted across China's face, then excitement ran riot over it again. "How can I not go with her? The hours I spend away from her here, when we're in the same city, are hell. I know you're going to think this sounds impulsive and dramatic, but I feel like I'll die if I don't see her even for a day, let alone for weeks."

It did sound impulsive and dramatic and it was downright false. You couldn't die from missing someone. Even if the pain gripped you like a chronic burning you pushed away and pushed away and pushed away without relief.

"Has Song asked you to go with her?"

"Of course she wants me to go." China scratched her forearm. Her skin always itched when she was hiding something. It was her built-in lie detector.

"Oh, Cee."

"Don't. Fine. She hasn't asked in so many words. But I know she wants me to be there. Isn't love knowing what the other person needs without being told?"

The great white elephant in the room trumpeted for attention. There was a reason Song and China only hung out in Song's hotel room and here. Song had been very clear with China that they couldn't be seen in public romantically. China had signed a nondisclosure agreement. Song was quite firmly in the closet.

China herself had justified the nondisclosure agreement as something Song's PR team had insisted on. Since Song played heterosexual romantic leads in her shows, they believed that her audience wouldn't be open to her having a lesbian relationship.

"Her culture may not be quite as openly accepting of same-sex relationships as ours is now. Let alone interracial ones," India said.

China jumped off the couch and stomped to the kitchen. She extracted a carton of coconut water from the fridge. "Don't I know that? Do we have anything stronger than this?" It was a rhetorical question. India only drank the odd glass of wine when she went out with China and their girlfriends. They only had alcohol if China bought it.

India didn't understand how China had even considered signing that NDA, given how strong and proud she was about owning her identity. Nonetheless, India had kept her lips sealed on the matter and focused on being happy for her sister. It wasn't easy, because as far as India knew, Song had never expressed any interest in coming out, and that meant China was hurtling straight into heartbreak.

China downed the coconut water. "I know what you want to ask me, so go ahead and ask."

"If you know what I'm going to ask, why don't you go ahead and answer?"

"It's easy to judge someone from a place of privilege." China waited for India to respond to that, but she wasn't getting an argument on that from India.

China grunted, crushing the carton and tossing it in the garbage with a little too much force. "I wish you knew how I felt about Song. If you'd ever experienced feelings like this you would understand. I feel like I'm on fire from the inside out, India!" She looked at India the way one would look at a robot, with equal parts sympathy and envy. "Sometimes all your principles become meaningless in the wake of the sheer force of your feelings."

Letting China see the unrelenting icy burn tearing at her was not an option. Thinking about how seeing Yash's hand in his fiancée's on television had felt was most certainly not an option.

"Principles can never become meaningless. If they do, they aren't principles in the first place." You were the beliefs you held dear. If you gave those up, who were you?

Anger sparked in China's eyes. "How can you think it's that simple? God, I wish I could be like you. Song loves me. She has the ability to love with such intensity, such vulnerability. She gives everything. It's almost scary. It's such a huge risk for her, but she still does it. And you want me to think about principles?"

No matter how cold China thought she was, India wasn't cold enough to point out that Song was giving everything within the protection of these closed walls and a nondisclosure agreement drafted by some of the highest-paid entertainment lawyers in the world. China, on the other hand, was giving everything unconditionally and without any caution.

Nonetheless, Song did have the right to love and be loved like everyone else. "I don't doubt that Song loves you. It's obvious in the way she looks at you. Who could not love you? If bigoted social structures are keeping her from showing it publicly, then absolutely she has the right to keep herself safe, but you have to protect yourself too."

"Protect myself from what? Why, when I want to leap, do you always want to pull me back?"

How could she not, when China was leaping into an abyss of pain? Pain she knew too well.

"You might be going up against something far larger than yourself. You might even have the strength to fight it. But like you said yourself, you would be coming at this fight from a place of privilege. Everyone in your life cherishes you, always has. Your family, your friends, your colleagues, your whole world already celebrates you. That's not true of Song."

China dropped onto the floor at India's feet and looked up at her, luminous eyes glistening with tears, mass of curls spilling from her high ponytail. "She stands to lose so much by being with me and she doesn't care. How can I return that with choosing my job over her? My wanting to stay here, wanting my life to be exactly as it was before her, before *us*—how can I be that selfish?"

China had worked harder than anyone India knew to get where she was in her career. The anxiety of giving anything but one hundred percent and achieving anything less than perfection used to keep her up nights even when they were little girls. India had sat by her sister through many a night as she worked tirelessly on anything she took on.

"You've never left California."

"I'm not yet thirty. I'm growing up. Isn't that what you've always wanted for me?" She laid her head on India's lap.

India stroked her hair. "You're being very brave, and I'm very proud of you."

"Well, hold that thought until you hear the rest."

India waited.

"I quit the show."

That show was her sister's baby, and India's heart broke a little bit. She kept stroking.

"The season is about to begin. Sharon wanted me to stay until the end of this season."

"Sharon has been kind and patient these past few months." China had missed work on crucial days and her boss had done nothing more than lecture her about how important she was to the show and how much they needed her work ethic. Sharon probably suspected that China was going through some sort of personal crisis, but a boss could only make so many allowances for an employee who had suddenly decided not to show up.

"Actually, Sharon turned out to be a piece of work. She's taking this as a personal affront. She thinks I'm going to a competitor and she threatened to sue me if I did."

"What did you do?"

"I told her that I hadn't planned to, but now that she'd shown her true ungrateful colors I was tempted to. Don't look so disappointed. I've worked harder than anyone else there. My show is the first of the channel's shows that's licensed to stream in every country that has streaming services. Granted, Rico and Ashna helped with making the show a phenomenon, but I was the one who got Ashna in, which got Rico in. I was the one who made sure that we took the audience interest and mined ratings gold from it."

"You probably took her by surprise, and this is just her knee-jerk reaction to get you to stay until the end of the season."

"She threatened to end my career, India. She told me that I wouldn't work in the industry again if I quit the show now."

"Oh, sweetheart. You deserve more respect than that. How dare she?"

That made China smile for the first time today.

"But you know she has a temper, she says things when she feels threatened. You usually do such a great job managing her. Go back and tell her you'll finish up the season. Then find someone who can replace you. Do this responsibly."

"I can't. I told you I can't be separated from Song for even a day. Nothing else matters." There was fire in China's eyes. She was consumed by her feelings. "I wish you knew how I feel. This beautiful painful joy. This desperate need for someone. I'd give up my career twenty times for it. I'd give up everything. You'll never understand. It's not who you are. You have no idea how lucky you are that you don't feel things this way."

India's laugh felt bitter in her mouth. On the TV behind China, the news played on mute, showing the clip of Yash speaking to reporters, again. She was lucky indeed. So lucky that there was no respite from his smiling face and tortured eyes that sought her out relentlessly. She kept turning the TV off, then turning it back on because at least that much of him she could have.

He'd been resplendent in the debate. Brilliant with facts, decent in the face of his opponent's attacks, fiercely empathetic, fearlessly vulnerable with showing his heart and purpose.

Why had she watched? How could she not have?

China turned around and followed her eyes to the TV. "I can't believe Yash is going to be our governor. Can you believe it? Someone I've known almost all my life. He looks good, doesn't he? Not the way he looked when he was hanging around here all the time."

"It was three days."

China cocked her head at her.

"He wasn't here all the time." Just three days.

"And that's all it took for you to set him straight. You're a genius. If you weren't so laid-back, you'd be a millionaire."

India laughed again. "So I'm not just a feelingless robot, I'm also unmotivated and lazy." She got up and went to the kitchen and put the kettle on. Mom insisted on working in the incense workshop, even though the medication made her nauseated and weak. She needed to eat something. Maybe some avocado cocoa cookies with tea.

"India!" China followed her. "That's not what I said and you know it."

"You're right. I do know that's not what you said." But it's what she had meant.

China took her hands this time. "Are you really angry with me? You know I admire you more than anyone else. You're my role model. I wish I could be as solid, as dependable as you, no matter how bad the storm. That's what I meant. Please don't be angry with me. I can't have you be angry with me right now."

"I'm not angry with you. I could never be angry with you. I just want you to be careful. Please. I can't watch you get hurt." China might think India didn't feel as much as she did, but India knew that China could not survive what this felt like. Not being able to have the one person who was created for you. Knowing that with every fiber of your being and not having it.

"I won't. Song loves me. She's waiting to be able to show that to the world. She's just figuring out how to do it." She slipped her hands around India and India held her tight.

"What are you planning to do when you get there?"

"Maybe I'll find a job in Seoul. They have a huge TV industry. I shouldn't have trouble finding a job there, right?"

"Anyone would be lucky to hire you. Only a brainless person wouldn't see that as soon as they meet you."

China laughed in her arms and the world felt bearable again.

On the television screen Yash was back, his hand in his girlfriend's as she gazed at him adoringly. India squeezed her sister tighter.

"Hey, don't worry so much. I'm going to be fine." China pulled away and peered at India's face. "India? I'm going to be okay. Don't be like this."

India nodded. "I know," she said, every breath burning her lungs. "I know." She could do nothing to help herself, but China had a chance at happiness, and she'd be damned if she didn't put all her faith behind it.

Chapter Nineteen

Yash had hoped for a quiet visit with his grandmother and Esha. Even so, he should not have been surprised by the fact that his parents, Nisha, and Ashna were parked on the white couch in the living room of Aji and Esha's suite, his grandmother's tea service on a trolley between them.

Their cheerful conversation dropped into silence as Yash emerged from the wide ornate staircase. He hadn't raced up two steps at a time as he usually did, because he'd been preoccupied with contemplating another, narrower staircase suffused with the smell of incense and a warm glowing energy. Craving for it sat like a giant starved vacuum inside him.

Faces that were his life stared at him over delicate teacups suspended in midair. Unfamiliar awkwardness suffused the room.

Of all people, Esha stood and came to him and gave him a hug. He wrapped his arms around her gingerly and rested his chin on her head. She was tiny. The oldest Raje cousin was the tiniest in stature. Barely five feet and possibly ninety pounds soaking wet.

Holding her made him feel better. He tried not to think about how much she would love India and how well the two of them would get on. Something about them was the same, an ethereal quality woven together with strength.

Why couldn't he stop thinking about her?

Esha looked up at him, the curiosity in her eyes probing at him, then turning to terrible sadness. But she said nothing and let him go.

He did the rounds. Leaning over to drop kisses on his mother's and sisters' cheeks, shaking Dad's hand, and then dropping down at his grandmother's feet and leaning back into her lap as she dropped a kiss on his head.

"I'm very angry with you, Yashu," she said, not sounding angry at all.

"I'm sorry, Aji."

"It's been two weeks." She stroked his hair. "How can you do this to your grandmother?"

It had been ten days. But their grandmother always started all conversations with how long it had been since she'd seen them last. He didn't argue with her. Who in their right might would?

"I called you every day." He'd been on the road, but that didn't mean he forgot to call his grandmother.

He also understood counting the days since you'd seen someone better than he ever had. It had been four weeks since he'd seen India.

"That you did," Aji said. "That's why I'm going to forgive you. And, well, I know you've been busy," she added, with enough mischief in her voice that he knew she wasn't talking about the campaign.

The way they were all staring at him, amusement writ large on their faces, reinforced that conclusion.

He looked at Ashna and Nisha, who were both studying him with enough curiosity that if he didn't know them he'd have checked if something was stuck between his teeth.

"Tea?" His mother handed him a cup. What he needed was a damn tumbler of Philz's darkest roast, but he took the tea with a "Thanks, Ma."

Esha dropped down into the couch next to Aji. She was the only one in the room who wasn't looking like a cat with a cream mustache. "You look exhausted. You're not taking care of yourself."

"He looks like he's been working hard. It's a look of a man who's going to win an election." Dad, naturally. In all his HRH glory.

"Well, good thing he doesn't have to take care of himself by himself any longer." This from Ma, who was usually pretty rational. "Having someone living with him will help with that."

He threw Nisha a look. *What are they talking about?*

She gave him nothing, just raised a finger and pointed at Aji, who had a significant-moment-incoming look.

"It's about time. I've been holding on to my ring for far too long." She looked at Ma, and Ma made a production of walking to Aji's room and coming back with a silk pouch and handing it to Aji.

"The Kohlis want to do a little ceremony. Just a small puja and dinner for the families. They know this isn't the time for a big flashy engagement party, but we have to think—"

"Ma. What are you talking about?"

"What kind of question is that?" Ma said. "Now that Naina and you have decided to make it official, we can't fault her family for wanting to mark it with some sort of ceremony. It's taken you ten years to decide to put a ring on her finger, God knows how much longer it will take for you to make it to the altar."

His grandmother was still stroking his hair. As gently as he could, he removed her hand, squeezing it before he put it back on her lap. Then he stood, an odd ringing between his ears.

Before he could say anything, Aji extracted a small velvet box from the pouch and thrust it into his hand. "Your grandfather gave me this when we got engaged," she said, eyes going dreamy with memory. "I've been waiting to give it to you so you can finally give it to Naina."

Yash popped the box open. Nestled in aged white satin sat a deep green emerald surrounded by diamonds so brilliant he blinked.

"Thank God whatever newfangled thing you two were doing is over. What's the point of a relationship if she can't be here for you?" Dad said.

Mom clapped. "We can do a celebration at Curried Dreams when it reopens next month. It will be great publicity for Ashi too!"

Nisha said something about ordering clothes.

All Yash could manage was to open and shut his mouth a few times, but no one was paying him any attention, so taken up were they with his imaginary engagement. The ringing swallowed up their excited chatter.

"I'm in the middle of a campaign," he said finally.

No one heard him.

"I'm in the middle of a damn campaign," he shouted far too loudly, and they all went silent and gaped at him as though he were the one who'd lost his mind. Which was all sorts of backward.

"Then why did you decide to announce on network television that you were getting engaged in the middle of a campaign?" Ma said.

"I did nothing of the sort."

Nisha started punching at her phone.

"Nisha, do not pull that interview up, or help me God . . ." He shoved a hand through his hair. "I know what was said. It was twisted completely out of context. What is wrong with you?"

Nisha glared at him, but she stopped trying to pull up the blasted interview on her phone.

"I don't understand," Ma said. "Why on earth wouldn't you just get married if you love each other and if you've been together for ten years? It makes no sense."

Tell me something I don't know.

After the interview, Naina, true to form, had taken off for L.A. to meet Mehta's partners and Yash had been in the Apple Valley campaigning. Probably why the family had waited until now for this ambush.

"Someone needs to tell him," Ashna said, after being mostly quiet through this circus.

That sounded terribly ominous. "Tell me what?"

Ma glared at Ashna. Something Ma almost never did to her nieces. She saved her glarings for her biological children. Possibly the only way in which she ever discriminated among them.

"What now?" he asked.

HRH stood. "What is that supposed to mean? We're all here bending over backwards trying to honor your wishes. Instead of thanking us, you're acting like we're the ones being unreasonable. When did you turn into such an ungrateful person?"

"He's not ungrateful," Ashna, Nisha, and Esha all said.

"Thanks," he said to them. Then, "I need a minute." With that, he headed for the stairs.

"Yash, wait. Don't leave like this. At least hear us out," Nisha said.

There was nothing more he could stand to hear and he really needed a moment to clear his head, so he ran down the stairs as though he hadn't heard her.

Just as he got to the bottom, the doorbell rang and J-Auntie rushed to answer.

Nisha was right behind him. Grabbing him by the arm, she pulled him across the hall and into the den. "You need to collect yourself before you see Naina's parents." Just as she said the words, Dr. Kohli's booming voice rang through the entrance foyer. Yash squeezed his eyes shut and prayed for patience.

"What's going on, Yash?" his sister said, and pushed the door shut behind them.

"You first. What the hell is going on, Nisha? Couldn't you have warned me? You fucking work for me."

"I'm going to let that go because you look entirely too miserable. Did you and Naina have a fight?"

He turned to her. He wished he could tell her. He wished he knew what he wanted to tell her.

Who was he kidding? He wanted to tell her—tell everyone—that he did want to spend the rest of his life with someone, but it wasn't Naina.

Shit.

Shit.

Shit.

He dropped into a chair.

"Yash." Nisha squatted in front of him and took his hands.

"You are doing spectacularly well. You're working so hard. I know you're hurting about Abdul. I know you're worried about him. But you have the right to be happy. You have the right to be with someone you love, have a family."

Yash dropped his head back, his shoulders shaking with laughter, the kind of laughter that you couldn't separate from frustration, no matter how hard you tried.

"Are you crying?" Nisha sounded horrified.

Yash stood and helped her up. "You shouldn't be squatting." He pushed her into the chair and started pacing.

"Oh God," Nisha said, and Yash stopped to catch her horrified expression. "Why didn't you say something? You're having cold feet. Yash, listen, I know exactly how you're feeling."

"No, you don't."

"Haven't you noticed how similar our situations are? Neel and me, and Naina and you? Family friends, best friends since childhood." She didn't mention that Neel had dated someone else for seven years before he'd found his way back to Nisha. Or that once they'd gotten together they'd never left each other's side if they could help it. They hadn't lived continents apart for over a decade. "I know exactly what you're feeling."

"No, you don't."

"I do. It's terrifying when something is so right. I think I finally understand why you've both stayed away for so long."

"We've stayed away because we've both loved our careers too much." *And because being able to stay apart was the point of us getting together.* Because he'd needed control over his feelings, and with Naina there were none.

"That's the conscious reason. The subconscious reason is that you're too afraid that your perfect relationship is too good to be true."

Yash groaned.

"Did you know that I had serious cold feet before my wedding? I almost didn't go through with it. In fact . . . Never mind." Standing up, she faced him, the look in her eyes so filled with understanding, for a moment he thought she knew the truth about Naina and him. "You know how I know how much you love Naina?"

Well, there went that theory. "I'm sure you're going to tell me."

She grabbed his arm and looked at him the way people did when they wanted you to know that they knew a secret you thought you'd hidden well. "I saw you. I saw you when you first realized you were in love. You remember the night before my wedding?"

Yash's heart started to thud like a military parade.

"The night of my mehendi, I saw you in the gazebo with Naina."

"With Naina?"

"Yes, I remember the look on your face to this day. I'd never seen you look like that. You looked so totally smitten, like you'd been hit on the head with something, like you'd found your purpose in life. That's why when everyone else was shocked when you and Naina sprang your relationship on us, I knew you knew what you were doing. If you're scared, just remind yourself of that time, of how that felt. You'll find your way back to it. I promise. It's what I do with Neel."

Stepping away from her, he squeezed his temples. His head felt like a million little explosions were going off in it.

Nisha shook his shoulder. "What's wrong? What did I say?"

What she'd said . . . she might as well have driven a car into him. Before he could tell her that Naina wasn't who she'd seen in the gazebo with him that night, the door flew open after a cursory knock.

"Hai hai, Yash, beta, badhaiyaan badhaiyaan!" Naina's mother was an intimidatingly tall woman with a personality entirely at odds with her strapping physical appearance. She flew into the room, then stopped with her odd mix of anxiety and effusiveness.

Naina followed her in, her expression as tortured as it always was when she was in the presence of her parents. Behind her was the venerable and portly Dr. Kohli, who walked straight at Yash and grabbed him in a hug.

"Finally I am to have a son."

Naina's mother looked like she'd been kicked. She hung her head and smiled, even as her eyes teared up. This was in line with every interaction Yash had ever seen between Naina's parents.

Naina looked like she'd like to kick her father. Instead she put an arm around her mother.

Yash was sure today was the day he would explode, just blast out of his skin and splatter on the walls.

Nisha's hand stroked his back.

Behind the Kohlis marched in the Rajes, Mina leading the parade and welcoming the guests, even as she studied Yash the way she'd done when he was a boy trying to get away with something.

You're thirty-eight. You're a thirty-eight-year-old former state senator, former U.S. attorney, who's going to be the governor of California. What the hell is wrong with you?

"You okay?" Ashna came up to him. She, too, studied him like a particularly challenging chai blend she was trying to decode.

Would they stop asking him that question when they really didn't want an answer? If they kept at it, he was going to tell them the truth. How couldn't they see that there was something grotesquely wrong with him? Had he suddenly turned invisible? He was as far from okay as he could imagine being.

HRH and Dr. Kohli gave each other the kind of self-congratulatory hand pumps that made Yash contemplate several things, all of them violent. Yash was not a violent person, warrior ancestors notwithstanding.

J-Auntie brought in a silver tray filled with mithai, and Naina's mother made a squealing sound, all hurt forgotten at the sight of the sweets.

"Naina, beta, feed your *fiyancée* some mithai," she said as though Naina and Yash were a bashful young couple who'd just been set up by their families for an arranged marriage.

Naina winked at Yash and fished out the biggest ladoo from the tray. "Are you ever going to stop looking quite so tortured?" she said close to his ear as she stuffed the ladoo into his mouth.

She kept asking him that, but she hadn't once cared to ask what he was tortured about.

"We have to talk," he said. "Right now."

Her glance traveled around the room over their celebrating families. "Sure. What is it?"

"Alone."

"Okay, make it happen, then," she said, the challenge clear in her voice. "I'm right behind you."

That was it. He'd had enough of this. "Naina and I have something to discuss. Excuse us," he said, and led her toward the door.

"Really, beta? All impatient to get her all to yourself already, haan?" Naina's mother said, her eyes round with all sorts of insinuations, every one of them causing her great joy, and him nausea.

The rest of the room looked at him with a combination of alarm and curiosity.

"I think you're forgetting something," Ma said, slipping the velvet box into his hand and giving him an encouraging pat.

He didn't say anything more until they were up in his childhood room.

"Back in the old digs," Naina said, running a finger across the signed balls crowding shelves from floor to ceiling. Soccer, basketball, baseball, football, mementos from games he'd been to with his dad. "Shree Uncle really spoiled you, didn't he? Was there a game one of your teams played that he didn't take you to when you were a boy?"

She was right. HRH had spoiled him, but her attempt at reminding him how great his parents were and how much they'd done for him, that part was entirely out of line. Had she always manipulated him this way?

"Why are you being like this?" he asked, because he had to believe that his friend was in there somewhere. And because if she really had developed feelings for him, he'd have to figure out how not to hurt her.

"Are you going to say, 'This wasn't the deal,' again?"

"It wasn't. We were never supposed to take it this far. Don't you deserve to find someone you really want to spend your life with?"

She was toe to toe with him, eye to eye. "I have. You're that person."

"You don't love me, Nai."

She poked him in the chest. "There isn't anyone in the world I love as much as I love you. Not even my parents."

"Don't do that. You know that's not what I mean. You deserve to find love." The kind that hurt in the chest and made it hard to breathe. "The kind that burns in the pit of your stomach."

Bunching up his shirt in a fist, she turned suddenly horrified eyes on him. "Holy shit. That's what this is about? You're having an affair."

He removed her hand from his shirt and held it. "Come on, what's wrong with you? I wouldn't do that. Not while we're still dragging this farce out."

Pulling her hand from his, she shoved him. Hard enough that his shoulder hurt. "Farce? Are you fucking kidding me? Who is it?"

"I'm not going to tell you. Not like this. And it's not an affair." Or maybe it was. *A promise isn't what you say. It's what you do.*

She laughed. "This is unbelievable. Seriously? You fancy yourself in love? Really? Now? What is wrong with you? What are we, sixteen?"

"I was in a fucking wheelchair when I was sixteen, so I wouldn't know."

"Well, boo-hoo. You got out of the wheelchair and the only girl you ever wanted to hang out with was me. And I was always there for you."

"Because you're my damned best friend." Although she sure as hell wasn't acting like it.

"This is how you treat your friend? I've been here for you, Yash, always. I've taken care of you. Have you forgotten what happened when you trusted another woman? You ended up drugged and caught on tape fucking an underage intern. Even then I was there for you. I didn't bat an eyelid. Through all your trust issues I was there making sure you were okay, working around it, tiptoeing around all your physical issues. Making sure all your damned dreams didn't get shat on, because you have no judgment when it comes to women. Now you're telling me you've found someone else and you want me to be okay with that when we have everything to lose?"

He stumbled back. These were the words she'd said to him in Sripore at Nisha's reception. *You have no judgment when it comes to women. I'm the only woman you can trust.*

Memories of what Julia had done to him had made a god-awful churn inside him with what he'd been feeling for India, with how he'd been feeling after their kiss. It had made him feel out of control. *She* had made him feel out of control.

She had made him feel like someone he'd worked hard not to be, free and wild. The only other times he'd felt that out of control was when Julia had drugged him, when that car had tossed him in the air. It had all become mixed up inside him until it felt the same, but those things weren't the same. The loss of control he'd felt, still felt, with India was not the same.

The more you bury things, the more you have to dig to get to them.

Naina had used his need to bury things, used his trauma, to get what she wanted. All he could hope was that she had done it without knowing.

"Yash, please." Naina followed him as he moved away from her. "Don't do this. Not now, when we have everything we've ever wanted. Sleep with her if you want to, whoever she is. I won't even ask. Get her out of your system. But, please, please don't let down everyone who has their hopes pinned on you."

He'd thought she was his best friend, but she didn't know him at all. "That's who you think I am."

"Maybe you take who you think you are too seriously. Can't you get over yourself and just do what needs to be done?"

Who was she? Who was he, that he'd felt this way too? That goals justified doing whatever it took. They'd both been proud, unapologetic about their ambition and going after their dreams. But when had he lost track of what it cost him?

He studied her, unable to recognize the ruthless determination in her face. "And doing what needs to be done involves marrying me so you can get your funding as the first lady of California and win the Nobel?"

"How dare you? How dare you take away something I've worked my entire life for? That funding has nothing to do with you!" She was shaking. "I never thought I'd hear you take credit for my work."

"That's not what I was doing. But if your funding doesn't depend on us being together, then how does it matter if we end this? I don't want to lie anymore."

"How can you think it's that simple? The scandal would be too great. And . . . and . . . Mehta will withdraw the funding if there's a scandal. Any negative media attention on me or the foundation and the partnership is over. That was part of the deal."

That explained a lot. Mehta did have an ulterior motive. He'd practically told her that her relationship with Yash was a requirement for the funding. Naina just didn't want to believe it.

Before he could say that, she stepped right into his face. "Why are you making this about the funding? When it's about this woman you've met." She grabbed his jaw in both hands, holding him in place. "Does she know that you don't like to be touched? That intimacy terrifies you? Does she know that a child was able to make a fool out of you and jeopardize your entire future? Will she have the strength to bear it when Julia Wickham blows the whistle and the world explodes around you?"

Dear God, she was threatening him, and all he could do to stay standing was focus hard on who he'd thought she was.

"Look at your face. Everyone thinks you're so strong, and yet without me to pull a blanket over who you really are, what would they see?"

Pulling her hands from his face, he stepped away from her. "You can still do the work you're doing without Mehta. I can put you in touch with other philanthropists without an agenda."

There was a moment when his friend flashed in her eyes behind this stranger he didn't recognize, but it was barely a moment. Then she was angry again.

"If you dump me now, after you held my hand and pretended to love me on television, and go after another woman so close to the end of this race, the media will crucify you. You can forget about winning. You realize that, right?"

He did. That was why involving India in the mess was out of the question.

"And if I tell everyone that we lied for the past ten years about being a couple, your credibility will be entirely destroyed."

He knew that too.

"I just can't lie anymore, Nai."

She made a sound of such frustration he almost felt bad for her. "It was an arrangement, not a lie. You turned it into a lie. This is on you. But I know you, and I know you'll snap out of it when you realize what you have to lose. Now I'm going to go out there and tell our families that we need time. That you can't do this during the campaign. And when you've pulled your head out of your ass I'm going to still be here helping you, because that's what friends do."

"No," he said, because that much he knew for sure. "I'm done. We're done. I can't do it anymore."

"You can. Because if you don't set your head straight, let me remind you that Julia was sniffing around for revenge last year. Any scandal, and she'll be back. And if we're not together, don't expect me to save you again."

Chapter Twenty

India was helping China pack, while also avoiding China's questions. China's sister radar seemed to have finally kicked into gear. "Is Yash going to come back?"

India shoved a pair of sneakers into a shoe bag and pulled the cord tight. "What?"

What she was going for was distracted, but what came out was despondence, and China cocked her head.

Before India could say more, the doorbell rang, startling the sisters so much they burst into nervous giggles. Why had the doorbell suddenly become the focus of her life?

"Were you expecting someone?" India asked, absolutely refusing to let her mind consider any other possibility.

China clapped a hand to her forehead. "I totally forgot. I have a surprise for you." She hurried down the stairs to open the studio door, India hot on her heels.

The last person India expected to see was standing at her door, and India's heart soared. She clamped it down and smiled.

Brandy smiled back and threw an uncharacteristically tentative look at China. Then again, this was how she always looked at

China, as though she couldn't quite believe what was happening. "You sure about this?" Brandy asked.

India looked over Brandy's shoulder, and instead of a thick head of salt-and-pepper hair with a golden aura, and eyes she missed more than she should, she found a beautiful young girl. An explosion of curls spilled from her ponytail and she had the loveliest eyes in the darkest brown. She was standing so close to Brandy that she was obviously nervous.

"Absolutely sure. Come on in," China said, and didn't add anything rude. When had this truce happened?

"This is Ellie, Brandy's daughter," China said, and India and China moved to let the two of them in. "This is my sister, India. She runs the studio."

Ellie waved. Her smile was at once bright and shy. Her aura was a sunshiny yellow unique to the young, incipient and filled with untainted energy.

"It's lovely to meet you, Ellie."

Ellie took in the studio, her glance jumping from the giant Ganesha statue to the shoe racks, to the Buddha mural Tara was in the middle of creating, and her eyes went as round as saucers.

China explained how they had met at Ashna and Rico's and Ellie had invited China to her school for Career Day to talk about being a TV Producer. Then Brandy had taken them out for dinner as a thank-you and given China the limited edition Laurel & Hardy case she'd somehow acquired to replace the one she'd broken when they'd first met.

"Ellie's been looking for a job. She's a gymnast and has been wanting to practice yoga. We need a receptionist for weekday evenings until Tomas gets back, and you've been working yourself to the bone. I thought she might be interested." China smiled fondly at the girl, connection sparkling between them.

This was not at all like China. For one, she never took an interest in the studio. For another, recently she had been too preoccupied in her own life to take an interest in anything at all that didn't involve Song.

They could not afford to pay an intern. Brandy looked stressed enough to burst. The way India always felt when someone was about to break China's heart, or say something hurtful to Tara when she was being Tara, or when years of Sid's work was about to go down the drain because funding for one of his photography trips didn't come through.

"That would be lovely," India said. "Would you like a tour?"

Ellie nodded, but her eyes were stuck on Tara's mural.

"That's our mom's," China said, tracing a finger over the bold raised-copper swirls of the Buddha's hair.

Ellie turned worshipful eyes on China. "My mom was an artist too. All the walls of my room were covered with her murals, even the ceiling. It's scenes from my favorite book, *Where the Wild Things Are*."

"No way!" China squealed with delight. "That's my favorite book too." She'd been obsessed with the monsters India had been afraid of.

"My mom—Brandy—she had someone re-create the murals when I moved in with her. They're not the same as my mom's, but they're really good."

"I'd love to see them." China said.

"You mean that? You should come over to our house. Maybe dinner?" The look she threw her mother was so filled with excitement and pleading, India didn't know how Brandy stood it. "My mom makes the best pizza."

Emotion rolled beneath the mask that was Brandy's face. Something flared in her eyes when she looked at China, but just for an instant. Something too much like fear mixed in with . . . was that longing?

How had India never noticed this before? Or maybe she had. Longing or no longing, Brandy didn't want China to hurt her little girl, because her little girl was smitten too.

China patted Ellie's hand. "I'd love to. It sounds amazing. I never get pizza around here. My mom and siblings have no taste buds. They only eat"—she lowered her voice conspiratorially—"healthy food."

Ellie made an impressive mock-horrified face.

"Can I take a rain check, though?" China said, obviously basking in the sunshine of the child's adulation, even returning it. "I'm going to be out of the country for a bit. But when I get back, we're doing this."

Ellie looked at once excited and disappointed. "Where are you going? Is it for the show?"

"No. Not for the show." Despite China's wide smile, nervousness leaked into her voice. "I'm going to Seoul for a little while."

"You're following Song to Korea? You can't be serious!" Brandy snapped. It was more emotion than India had ever seen come out of the woman. Almost immediately she looked like she regretted it, but China had caught the heat in her voice.

"What is that supposed to mean?" China snapped back.

Brandy looked at Ellie. "Nothing. I'm sorry."

"Let me show you the rest of the studio." India took Ellie's hand and pulled her away. Or tried to, because Brandy, icy cool tone back in place, said, "It's just that . . . Never mind."

India tugged Ellie's hand again and this time she moved. As soon as they were out of sight, however, Ellie froze in place again and refused to budge.

"It's just what?" China snapped, not bothering to temper her voice now that Ellie was out of sight.

"I got the impression Ms. Song wasn't comfortable with going public," Brandy said, her voice so flat it had the opposite impact of what she intended.

China sputtered like she was going to bust a blood vessel. "Going public with what?"

Brandy cleared her throat. Silence followed, saturating the air.

India tugged Ellie into the yoga room and started explaining the types of classes they offered and asking her about gymnastics. Obviously the child, much like India, was more interested in the conversation that had started up again between her mother and China. They flew through the tour, half their attention on the indiscernible snapping outside.

By the time they came back out to the reception area, Brandy was standing by the front door, hands folded behind her military-style, and China was pretending to do work at the registration desk. The temperature in the room was tangibly colder, even though China looked like she had steam coming out of her ears.

As soon as she noticed Ellie, she softened and patted the chair next to her. "If you like, I can show you the check-in system. Most people check themselves in, but some forget their card and you have to check them in manually."

Ellie settled in next to her. "Thank you."

"I need to make a call," Brandy said. "I'll be outside." With a shuttered look at her daughter huddled with China over the keyboard, she let herself out of the front door.

India followed her out. "Ellie's a lovely girl. You should be very proud," she said.

"I am. And I'm sorry if China didn't warn you. It's okay if taking on a too-young intern doesn't work right now."

"You're right that she didn't warn me. But this studio is as much China's as it is mine, and if China thought Ellie would be a good fit here, I believe that she knows what she's talking about." China might fly by the seat of her pants, but she wasn't irresponsible.

"I'm sorry. I didn't mean any offense."

"None taken."

"I . . ." Brandy stared through the trellised glass of the door, expression so guarded it ended up giving away more than it hid. China and Ellie were absorbed in the check-in system. "I know China would never be callous with Ellie's feelings. She's been incredibly kind to Ellie and Ellie has talked of little other than China and . . ." Suddenly the mask crumpled and she looked positively stricken. "India . . ."

"What is it?"

"Aren't you concerned?"

There were so many things India was concerned about right now, which one was Brandy talking about? For a second she wondered if something was wrong with Yash and her heart did a god-awful spasm.

"China going all the way across the globe with someone who won't even acknowledge her here. Isn't that asking to have herself hurt?"

India had not expected that. "I'm not sure what you mean."

"I know it's none of my business. I know it's supposed to be some big secret, but your sister isn't great at keeping her feelings hidden. I've seen them together. Ellie and I spent an evening with them at Ashna and Rico's house. I've seen enough closeted people to know that Song is never planning to come out."

"I think you might be mistaken about the situation," India said. If Song wanted to be private about her relationship, then that was her prerogative and no one had the right to violate that.

Brandy's icy mask froze back in place. "I don't mean anyone any harm, and I'm never going to say anything to anyone else. I don't want your sister to get hurt. That's my only intention in bringing it up."

"I don't believe that is true."

Brandy stepped back and swallowed. She obviously didn't like being studied, and she certainly didn't like being seen.

"I think you might have other reasons why you think my sister is better off not going to Seoul."

"I'll admit that your sister is . . . I've never met anyone quite so . . . well, she deserves better than to have her heart broken. I also know that she doesn't return that opinion. But I promise you I'm not rooting for her to be hurt. It's just that . . ." Brandy was still staring through the glass panes of the studio door, her eyes stuck on Ellie beaming up at China. Turning away, she dropped down on the front step.

India sat down next to her.

"Ellie's mother was my best friend," Brandy said, watching the cars passing by. "Growing up, her mother was my parents' house-keeper. She and her mother lived on my parents' estate."

The only people in the world India knew who's home qualified as an estate were the Rajes. She had no idea Brandy came from that kind of wealth.

Brandy looked embarrassed, as though she wished she hadn't brought that up. "It wasn't . . . My parents weren't exactly, um, fond of who I was and I left home as soon as I could. The only good thing in my childhood was Nomi. I was always in love with her. I believe she was too, but she couldn't stop struggling with it. After we graduated high school, she got pregnant and married Ellie's father. I was heartbroken. I joined the Marines, did two tours in Afghanistan. She wrote to me. Upbeat letters, filled mostly with Ellie and what a joy she was. I never replied. I was too angry. Then the letters stopped."

There was a long silence. Long enough that India thought that was all Brandy was going to say. Then she spoke again. "After I returned from Afghanistan, Child Services found me. I had made the biggest mistake of my life by not responding to her letters, by not looking Nomi up all those years." In her eyes was so much pain that India reached out and put a hand on her back, between her shoulder blades where grief tended to collect.

Energy flowed from India's hands. Brandy shuddered but took a breath and kept going. "He shot her, then himself. Ellie was at a sleepover. They labeled it simply as a "domestic violence incident." Nomi left Ellie to my care." A silent sob escaped her. "Things in her marriage were bad enough that she made a will to make sure Ellie was taken care of. I should have been there for her. I should have tried harder to convince her that what we had was real. That we had a chance."

India focused energy into her, trying to find the dark knots of pain and directing light at them. "Ellie is lovely and you seem to be doing such a great job with her. I think Nomi knew what you had was real."

Brandy's smile was watery, and soft. It completely transformed her, shaving years off her face and stripping her of every bit of ice. "Ellie's everything to me. All I have. She's a great kid, hardworking too. I promise she'll be a big help. You don't have to pay her. Or maybe you could tell her you're paying her but I could give you the money."

India took her hands off Brandy and pressed them into her

own chest. "Of course we'll pay her. No one works here without pay. And we do need someone. Also, what you're suggesting is completely dishonest and your relationship seems based on trust. If you did pay an employer to pay her, it would break her confidence when she finds out, wouldn't it?"

Brandy looked up at the sky. India had no firsthand knowledge, but from what she'd seen China, Sid, and herself put Tara through, parenting was not an easy business. "You're right. I shouldn't have said that. I'm sorry. It's just hard to see someone you love get hurt."

"Don't I know it." India rubbed her hands together and folded them in her lap.

Brandy watched her. "That . . ." She pointed to her back over her shoulder. "That felt really good. Was that Reiki or something?"

India nodded. "It's just energy flow. I wasn't . . ."

"No, that felt great. Thank you." Then she looked terribly embarrassed, and India knew what she was going to say. "I've never shared what I just told you with anyone else. I don't know why I told you."

All India could do was smile. "Don't beat yourself up. I tend to have that effect on people. Occupational hazard."

Brandy returned her smile. "He's doing okay, by the way. In case you were wondering. Working himself to death. But he doesn't startle at sounds or hesitate before going onstage anymore."

I don't know who you're talking about, she wanted to say, but she couldn't tell a lie that stark, that significant. For all that Brandy had shared with her, *this* was what India had been waiting to hear. What kind of person did that make her?

It had been four weeks since she'd seen him. His campaign was going well, he was still far ahead in the polls. The assassination attempt was still in the news every day, but he was using it to talk about gun-sense, as he called it, and pushing affordable health care for all.

In the end, she nodded at Brandy. "Thanks. I'm glad."

The sound of laughter wafted out of the studio, and they turned to see China and Ellie cracking up about something. Brandy looked like someone had punched her in the heart.

India stood and held out her hand. "China has always known her mind, and she is stronger than you're giving her credit for." Although India had decided not to let her own worry get in the way of her sister's happiness, India hoped that China's strength would never be tested. "You're also jumping to a heck of a lot of conclusions here, all of which violate someone's right to keeping their life private."

Brandy took her hand and stood. Why had India thought of her as cold? The way she stared through the glass door at her daughter, the way she looked genuinely remorseful when her glance shifted to China, it was like looking at someone entirely different than the person India had judged her to be.

"I'm sorry. I shouldn't have interfered," Brandy said, looking like she meant it. "It's just that sometimes people who appear strongest on the outside can hurt the hardest on the inside."

Chapter Twenty-One

It had been a week since Yash had run out of the Anchorage in the middle of the attempted engagement. In an unprecedented occurrence, no one from the family had hunted him down. Possibly because they had realized how ridiculous it was to have brought this up so close to the election. But more probably because he'd been on the road again. His entire campaign strategy was a ground game. Door-to-door.

"I will explain when I'm ready. I don't have the time for it right now. Handle it," he'd texted Nisha after the first burst of texts from her.

Never before had he spoken to his sister like she was an employee. Never before had she let him get away with acting like her boss. But here they were. Obviously, she'd taken care of it.

The last debate had been yesterday in San Diego, and preparing for that while trying to counter Cruz's relentless campaign in SoCal was enough to keep everyone busy.

Naina had left for Nepal to pack up and hand over her responsibilities. He'd found out from Nisha. Naina and he hadn't communicated since she'd threatened him.

If he let himself think about that conversation, he'd never be able to stop thinking. For all these years he'd ignored what he had lost because he hadn't known what to do with his reaction to India. He'd been a coward and taken the easier way out. Now he'd dug up all he'd buried and he knew exactly what he'd lost. He knew.

The election, Abdul's treatment, managing his family's worry, those were things that needed all his focus. Those were things he couldn't risk. They were also things that he could control right now, and he needed that to keep going.

There was nothing controlled about how badly he wanted to go to India. He wanted to dive into the ocean of peace that was her presence. The deep anchor of her eyes, soothing, magical, stronger than he'd ever be. He wanted it with the kind of hunger that had no measure. Years ago it had terrified him. But he hadn't even known what fear was. Fear was knowing that living without her was living half a life.

Maybe he had healed. Or maybe the years had given him scabs that protected him. Or maybe being able to be the him he was with her again had shown him what he'd lost. He didn't know how to lose that again. He didn't know how not to. He didn't know how he could hurt her like that again, but he also knew that he already had.

Truth was that there was no way for them to be together without the risk of destroying everything. Still, his finger hovered over the number she'd tapped into his phone every moment that he allowed himself to not be entirely submerged in the campaign.

He took the hospital elevator to Abdul's floor. He was flying out to L.A. tonight to be on *Good Morning America* tomorrow morning. Constant motion was the only way for him to keep going. But he'd wanted to see Abdul before he left.

"His wife's with him right now," Myra, the on-duty nurse, said in her kind way.

"Thanks. I'll wait outside. I won't disturb her."

They had crossed the seven-week mark since the shooting. One part of Yash was terrified that it had been that long. The other part was sure that meant something.

You've done your part. Trust the universe to do the rest.

Her voice in his head was all he had of her and he embraced it.

When he passed the glass window of Abdul's room, he stopped short. Sitting next to Abdul, her hands on his chest, was India. Her eyes were closed, her face leached of color, her head bent, making her dark hair fall across her forehead. He pinched himself to make sure he wasn't dreaming her up.

On the floor next to India and Abdul, Arzu was saying prayers on a mat.

Time stilled. The constant need to spin stilled. Yash watched the scene before him, the power of what he was witnessing so strong it swallowed him whole. A weightlessness overtook his body. Every bit of helplessness that had been dragging at him stilled.

He'd been obsessively practicing the pranayama India had taught him every morning and meditating through the surya namaskar. He'd become addicted to the escape of centering his mind and body as one. That's how this felt, this letting go, this being fully immersed in something out of his control.

It felt good.

Like someone had sliced the ropes tying him up with the sharpest blade. One flick, the cut clean and quick. He was unbound.

The hypnotic hold of the moment released him when Arzu finished, folded her mat, and stood. Her prayer-heavy gaze shifted to her husband. If Abdul could see her expression, the sheer fierceness of it might wake him.

Yash was smiling when Arzu caught his eye. She smiled back,

and he made a rolling action with his hand to indicate that she should carry on, he was about to leave anyway. With a nod she sat down next to India, who opened her eyes slowly, rubbed her hands together, and took Arzu's hands in hers.

They seemed familiar with each other. When had that happened? How? Before India could catch him soaking her up with his eyes, he tried to make his escape. He almost made it too, but she caught his gaze. The feeling of peace was immediate and immersive. The hot spark that traveled through his chest brutal. For a moment he thought she'd rise and come to him. For a moment he thought he'd go to her. For a moment the world brimmed with potential, brightened with hope. Then she turned to Arzu and he left.

The off-kilter beating of his heart stayed with him when he stopped by Trisha's and Abdul's doctor's offices for an update. It didn't ease when he made his way to the lobby none the richer for any new information on Abdul, or on Tara. Trisha had gone to see her, but she wouldn't give him any details.

Minutes after he left Trisha's office his phone buzzed with a message from Nisha. *"We need to meet."*

Evidently she'd just been waiting for him to be done with the debate and to get back in town before hunting him down.

"Packed schedule today," he responded.

"You realize I know your schedule, right?" Nisha shot back. *"You have another few hours before you leave for the airport again. Your photo op at the bookstore just got canceled."*

"I told you I need space. Please."

He waited for her to tell him that he'd had a week since the engagement debacle, which was a week more than anyone else in the family would've gotten after pulling something like that.

"*I'm worried about you,*" she texted instead, using *I*, not *we*, which was telling.

"*Stop worrying. I'll call after L.A.*"

"*Fine, but I also need to talk to you about the surprise baby shower you're all planning.*"

Yash smiled. "*No idea what you're talking about,*" he typed, and then tucked his phone into his pocket.

Ashna, Trisha, and Ma were planning the shindig next month. It had been hard to find a date. They'd planned it for last month, then the shooting had happened. Ashna wanted to do it in the renovated Curried Dreams, but like all renovation projects that one had overshot its completion date. So the shower would happen at the Anchorage next month, just before Nisha finished her seventh month of pregnancy.

Trisha had just told him that Nisha had been trying to get one of them to slip up and tell her about it, because she didn't want to be caught in something dowdy just because they wanted to surprise her. Not that anyone had any idea what Nisha being dowdy would look like.

"Where to, boss?" Brandy was waiting for him in the lobby. She wasn't anywhere near as hands-off as he'd thought her to be when he'd first met her.

"The bookstore canceled so we're done for today. Rico's driving to the airport with me later." Brandy didn't travel with him. The security agency used local bodyguards for events. "Go on home. Ellie's probably waiting for dinner." They headed for the exit, stopping a few times so he could shake hands with people and take selfies, before making their way to the parking lot under a gloomy evening sky.

Brandy kept pace with him easily as they strode across the

concrete. It was an unseasonably warm day, and his sports coat felt oppressive around him. Usually, he couldn't get enough layers of clothing on his body.

"Ellie's working late today, but she'll be done soon, since India just left here. If you're sure you're headed home, I'll get Ellie from the studio before I do the same."

Being thirty-eight and having one word resonate like a gong out of a long sentence was completely and utterly juvenile.

Call him juvenile. "You saw India leave?" Just saying her name was like a pressure valve releasing.

Brandy studied him the way one studied roadkill twitching by the roadside.

"Ellie works at the studio?" he said, throwing another question at her before she'd had the time to address the first.

She nodded. "China set her up. She's a receptionist there for a few hours a day or whenever India needs her."

"That's great. She likes it?" Was he really coveting a teenager's part-time job?

"Loves it. The only downside is that having India for a boss is going to set completely unrealistic expectations of the workplace."

His face must have done something to expose how that affected him, because she cleared her throat. "I didn't mean you're not a great boss too. You are. Actually, you're both . . ." She trailed off awkwardly as they reached her car.

Part of him was relieved that she'd misread his reaction. The other part suspected that she'd done it to save him the embarrassment of being so transparent about his feelings. Especially since she, and everyone else in the world, believed him to be with Naina.

Instead of getting in her car, she lingered. "I'm glad Ellie is helping India. Especially since China's gone and she's by herself taking care of the studio and Tara." Her tone was studiedly casual.

This information shouldn't have hit Yash like a bat to the head, but it did. India was alone.

"Where's China?" he asked.

Brandy informed him, in the most clipped of monotones, that China had gone to South Korea.

She didn't add that China had gone with Song. She didn't have to. Yash had seen them together. Something about the entire business made worry for China stir inside him, which meant India had to be freaking out, and unable to show it.

Brandy cleared her throat, because Yash was frozen in place again.

"You said you saw India when she left the hospital?" Now that he'd opened those floodgates, he had to keep talking about her. "Did she say why she was here?"

"Between Tara and Abdul, she's been coming here every day," Brandy said with the friendly familiarity his sisters used while talking about India.

"Since when? And how do you know this?"

"We hang out. I see her when I drop off and pick up Ellie. I'm also taking yoga classes from her. She's very good." She rolled her shoulders. "Everything loosens right up. She's been seeing Abdul for weeks now. Arzu asked her to give him Reiki."

How had she even met Arzu? She had to have gone back to see Abdul after their foray that night. He texted with Arzu everyday. How had she not told him?

"I had no idea," he said, mostly to himself. "We haven't . . ." *Does she ask about me?* "How is she?"

Brandy looked as if she couldn't seem to decide if she wanted to shake him or feel sorry for him. "It's been tough. She's strong. But you already know that." Something about her tone made discomfort roll down his spine.

He'd been on the road almost every single day of the five weeks since he'd seen her last. He'd kept his focus on the campaign, and told himself that she was safe in her own world. Now the restlessness of knowing that she'd been alone after he'd left her again, with China gone and Tara sick, made his stomach turn.

Before he knew it, he'd opened the passenger door of Brandy's car. "Why don't I go with you? I'd love to meet Ellie again." He got in the car and waited for Brandy to get in.

If his behavior surprised her, she didn't show it. She just got in and started driving.

Yash had missed the turquoise door.

Brandy pulled it open and went inside with the ease of a frequent visitor, and Yash felt the way he often did, like an outsider looking in. It was a feeling he had always been completely comfortable with, but he hated feeling that way here in India's home, in her space. With her it had always been like being inside something that belonged to the two of them alone, their place from where they could watch the outside world together.

He followed Brandy inside. India waved to Brandy from behind the registration desk where she was working with Ellie. Her smile was like an intravenous shot of adrenaline. It woke every part of him up.

When her eyes fell on him, her smile slid right off her face. She stood, then froze as though unable to unlock her limbs.

"Hi," he said to Ellie, who threw a look from him to India and then to her mother.

Brandy waved her daughter over. "Ready to leave?"

He barely noticed as Ellie gathered her things, and they left.

India and he stood there, gazes locking and unlocking, bodies suspended in time. Complete and utter rightness braided through his being in electric bursts.

How did he keep forgetting how beautiful the sight of her was? Hair thick and shiny as spun obsidian, skin luminous, mouth lush and wide with that distinctive scar, eyes he had missed more than he'd ever missed anything in his life.

Finally she spoke. "Why are you here?" Her voice was soft the way it always was. That soft strong thing she had going on. Silk and steel, that pulled at him like a damn magnet.

"Yash?" Her eyes held his for just another second, then her gaze moved away to a point behind his head. His name on her lips, a sizzle on a hot pan.

"I don't know. I'm here to see Chutney."

"Okay, she's upstairs."

"I miss her." God, he was pathetic.

She looked like she was going to cry, or burst with frustration. She might have done a groan-sob, as though she wanted to shake him. He wanted her to. Just so she would touch him. He'd never wanted a woman to touch him. When Naina had, he'd had to brace himself, had to breathe through the coldness.

He followed India up the stairs, familiar smells engulfing him, incense and whole spices and aged wood and dog slobber. Chutney's tail went off in a spin when she saw him. With ecstatic yips she rolled over, then let out a long high-pitched whine.

"I feel exactly the same way, sweetheart," he said, rubbing her belly like a man starved for this unconditional love.

India tried to act like she didn't hear him, didn't see him.

"Brandy said China's gone to South Korea," he said, still rubbing.

"She left last week."

"Is she liking it?"

Worry tightened her mouth. "I hope so."

"Haven't you spoken to her?"

"I have."

Okay. He knew he had earned the short answers. He deserved them. He should leave. "How's Tara?"

She glared at him. "She's going to be fine."

"Were you able to figure out her health care bills?"

"Why are you here, Yash?"

Because I need to be.

"I wanted to know how you were, how Tara's doing. I've been worried about her."

"I've already told you. You don't need to worry. I've got it." But her voice wobbled and all his senses zeroed in on it.

"India, please tell me what's wrong. Please tell me you weren't serious about selling the studio."

"I told you I don't want to talk to you about it. I don't need your help."

"Why? Why won't you let someone help? Your universe is not going to save your home. You shouldn't have to lose it. This place is . . . it's you. Let me help."

"No. Help when you win the election, by changing things."

He strode to her, finally, losing the battle against this magnet. "I want to help now."

She didn't move, didn't back away. "No."

He was close enough that her smell engulfed him. Her warmth stroked his senses. "Why not?"

Her body was tight as a bow. "Because I'm not yours to help."

His hand went to his chest, because, man, that hurt. *You are.* He'd finally turned her into a liar, because that was a lie. "You're my friend. I can help a friend if I want to." His tone came out too harsh. Too filled with the things he couldn't say.

Instead of stepping back, she stuck out her jaw. "If being my friend was the only reason you wanted to help, I'd let you."

He leaned into her breath, letting his own mingle with it. Her body softened. His need to sink into her warmth came out in a sound that laid him bare.

That made her step back, put distance between them. "You have a girlfriend, Yash!" The fierceness of her tone didn't cover her sob.

No, I don't! But how could he say that without offering her more. Offering her everything. When he wasn't at liberty to risk everything. Too many people were counting on him.

"A girlfriend you chose over me," she whispered.

It was his turn to groan-sob. He was not someone who did that.

The back of her hand pressed into her mouth, like she wanted to stuff the words back inside.

"I'm sorry I said that," she said. "Can you ignore that I said that? Can you just see Chutney and leave? I have class. I can't—"

His hand cupped her cheek, and she gasped.

His thumb pressed against her lips. Her mouth was soft, softer than anything he'd ever experienced. Her lips yielded against his touch. They trembled against his skin. Trembled. The air around them trembled.

"I can't do this, Yash." But even as he pulled away she leaned into his hand, clinging as it left her, swaying into him, a wave of longing rolling from her into him.

"I'm sorry. I should not have come."

"You should not have."

"What if I said I need it? I need to come to you."

Worry broke across her face. "Are you having panic attacks again?"

Only at the thought of not seeing you. "No."

"I won't do this, Yash. I don't even know what this is."

He knew what it was. He knew. He'd always known. Even at twenty-eight when he'd first touched her, when she'd melted in his arms, when he'd tasted joy and utter and complete connection with another human being for the first and only time in his life, when sparks had exploded where he had touched her, when she'd told him her hopes and dreams and heartbreaks. He'd known.

"You do know what this is. It's . . . it's magic."

A sound of such frustration left her, he wished he hadn't said the words.

But he'd said them, and she wasn't someone who'd back away from that. "So what? So what if it is magic? It's not like this is the first time we're experiencing it. That night at Nisha's wedding"—a million memories swam in her eyes—"this magic was there then. What good did it do? You chose something else over it. You tried to control it by walking away from it." Her voice softened. "Don't you see, it doesn't matter that it's still here. You've made it impossible for the universe to give it to us."

"How do you do that? How do you see what it takes me so much longer to see?"

Her smile was the saddest thing. "It's an occupational hazard." Then she sobered again. "Trusting the universe is not code for compromise. It's the opposite of not doing your part. It's recognizing which part is yours to do."

He'd always thought he was good at doing his part. How wrong he'd been. "I never meant for it to turn out this way," he said, but she didn't look up at him, her gaze was fixed on her hands. Her chest rose and fell with her breaths. "When I asked you to wait, I never meant to—"

"There was nothing to wait for." This time she did look up, anger flashed in the dark centers of her eyes.

It wasn't like she'd called him either. "Why did you never call me? Why didn't you do your part? Why don't you ever fight for what you want?"

She shoved him. And, man, he knew she was strong, but he literally had to put all his strength into not flying across the room. "Are you seriously asking me why *I* didn't call *you*?"

"Ow. What happened to your peace and nonviolence thing?" he rubbed his chest.

She took a steadying breath and stuck one finger up in his face. "First, it's not a *thing*. It's who I am. I don't like to hurt anyone. It feels like shit. So, I'm sorry."

"India . . ."

"No. Don't. Don't, Yash. What is wrong with you? Why are you doing this? I'll answer your question. I didn't call you because you were with someone else and you never told me."

"I was not with someone else when we met. I was not with Naina when we had that night."

"Stop it. Stop with the loopholes and technicalities. Stop trying to Yudishtir this. The week after we met you were with her. How could you not have been with her when we met? You played with me, Yash. You hurt me. I didn't believe other men after that. You talk about magic? You took away my faith in magic."

"I'm sorry." He knew the words changed nothing now, but he had to say them.

She met his gaze, letting him see how little his apology meant, letting him see it all. "How can you talk to me about not fighting for what I want? Did you really want me to come to you, come after you, when you professed your love for someone else days after we met?"

"It wasn't like that. We were just . . . just spoken-for."

"What does that even mean? You announced to the whole world that you're with her."

"Not the whole world. It was meant to stay just within our families. But my sisters told you."

She looked like she wanted to shove him again. The right thing would have been to come to her and tell her himself. But he hadn't. He hadn't let himself think about it.

"Thank God your sisters told me. Because I might have just waited and waited for you if they hadn't."

"I thought you didn't wait for me."

"That's not what I said. I said there was nothing to wait for, and I was right."

"Now who's Yudishtiring it?"

"Let's not do this, Yash. There's no reason to do this."

But there was. There was every reason to do this. Why had it taken him so long to figure that out? "You were right. You were right when you said I'm already breaking my promise. I said that I didn't know how to break it. But the truth is that I don't know how to keep the promise anymore."

The look she gave him gouged out every single thing he believed about himself.

Maybe you take who you think you are too seriously.

Maybe those words Naina had said to him were true. Who he thought he was had fueled his choices. But not all of them had been right. Who he wanted to be was who he saw reflected in India's eyes.

Chutney nudged his leg and he dropped down next to her, glad for the relief. The smell of incense mixing with her Chutney smell strummed his senses. The desire to let the truth out warred against all the reasons to hold it in.

If he told her the truth, if he told her what he wanted, he had to be willing to risk the campaign.

"Yash," she said, standing over him, every bit of the kindness that set her apart filling that one word. "I'm not the person you made that promise to. I'm not the person who can help you if you don't know how to keep it. But I will not be the person to help you break it."

With that, she started moving around her kitchen, pulling things out of drawers and cabinets. "When you're done seeing Chutney, please let yourself out. I have to take this up to Mom." She walked past him across the dark wooden floors in her bare feet.

He sat there and watched her disappear up the stairs, her dog showering him with love as though she knew exactly how bad he was at it.

Chapter Twenty-Two

*I*ndia paused on the landing outside the incense workshop. The need to go back to Yash was so strong she almost put the tray down and ran back down and after him. If she went back now, she wouldn't be able to keep from wrapping her arms around him. His guilt was like a coat of thorns digging into him. All she wanted was to take it off so he could breathe.

She should hate him, she should be angry, and she was, but no one could call what was going on inside her hate. Very quietly, she let herself into the workshop.

Tara was lying on the mattress on the floor. Bamboo sticks, charcoal dust, and tree gum lay scattered across the machine tables. The heady scent of jasmine and oud filled the air from the freshly made sticks. Her grandfather had brought the composition with him. His family in India had been incense makers.

India set the tray with tea and cookies down on a table and unfolded a blanket. Knitted squares made from their old sweaters sat in a basket. Some finished, some still yarn. The past turning into a new future was always an unfinished project in the present. Through all her projects, Mom kept her focus on the present, without ever losing sight of the past or the future.

Spreading a blanket over her mother's sleeping body, India sat down next to her. The regimen of drugs was brutal. It sedated her. She insisted on working on the incense even though she was obviously struggling to get through a cycle, and India had been finishing up for her. India had found her sleeping more often than bent over her work this past week, but she was healing. The fact that there was a treatment and that she would recover, at least from the hepatitis, was all that mattered for now.

India dropped a kiss on Tara's head. Loneliness wrapped around her. She missed her mother's vibrant presence. She missed China, worried about her incessantly. She missed the man she had just left in her kitchen.

All the people she loved were in pain and she wasn't able to absorb it from them, no matter how hard she tried.

When Tara found out India was considering selling the studio to pay the bills, it was going to kill her in a whole different way, but preventing real death came first. India had checked the estimated price on Zillow and then felt queasy all day for having done it.

She hadn't been able to do anything to protect her sister either. The last time they spoke, China had just landed in Seoul and checked into a hotel, but instead of sounding excited she'd sobbed incoherently.

Song hadn't picked her up at the airport or even invited China to her home. China had been holed up in a hotel room, waiting for her. The idea of her sister by herself, hurting, made India livid.

Then there was Yash's pain, which she couldn't separate from her own. All the way down to her toes she knew there was more. He was not just a man who had tired of a relationship. She knew that was how anyone who had an affair with someone who was cheating justified it. But the way her entire self reacted to him was not a lie. She had spent her life staying in tune with her mind and body, being true to her whole self. It would never betray her that way.

Yash was not a liar.

He just couldn't give her the truth. And without the truth, they had nothing. Much as she wanted to push him to tell her so she could understand, that trust had to come from him. Everything was his to lose, that part she understood. But why they had ended up here, where she could cause him to lose everything, that part she needed to understand.

Why don't you ever fight for what you want?

She'd been sitting right here in this room, all of sixteen years old, when she'd asked Tara why Tara hadn't saved any information about her birth parents. She thought she was fighting for what she wanted.

Tara had pulled her into her lap and insisted on holding her tight when she answered.

"I spent ten years searching for my father because he put a fake address on an envelope. At least your birth parents were kind enough to leave you with no breadcrumbs to follow."

Fighting for something meant demanding a definitive answer, with no guarantee that you'd like the one you got.

"Did you choose us because we'd never be able to search for them?" India had asked.

"You chose me. Your eyes chose me," Tara had said in her Tara way. *"All I knew was that I'd never give you reason to want to search for them."*

Tucking the blanket around Tara, India made her way down the stairs, already dreading how empty her own home would feel with him gone.

When Chutney didn't immediately waddle up to her, a flash of discomfort gripped her. Just as she was about to call out to her dog, her eyes fell on Yash sitting on the floor where she had left him, Chutney cuddled up in his lap, fast asleep.

When she walked to him, he pressed a finger to his lips, as though her pug were their baby, and he'd finally gotten her to fall asleep after half a night of sleeplessness. A spasm of yearning squeezed in her heart and sent heat spreading across her body.

There was new purpose in him. He studied her reactions like someone studying sacred texts. Was the man trying to kill her?

She pointed at Chutney, and when he looked down at her, she quickly dabbed her eyes on her flowy yoga shrug. "When she's passed out on your lap like that, even screaming in her ear won't wake her up."

He smiled and scratched Chutney gently between the eyes. India sat down in front of him.

You're still here, she wanted to say, but couldn't without letting him see the tenderness flooding through her at seeing him, still here, on her living room floor.

"What if I told you it isn't what everyone thinks?" he said finally.

The determination darkening his eyes, the resolve squaring his jaw . . . it was obvious that he'd decided to give her honesty, even when he knew exactly what it would cost him.

She stroked Chutney's ear. "I know you, Yash. I know it isn't what it appears to be. If it were, if she was someone you were in love with, ever had been in love with, you wouldn't be here. If you were the kind of person who could be here after making a commitment to someone else, I wouldn't be here." He had made a commitment, but of course it wasn't what everyone believed it to be.

His jaw worked as he tried to respond but couldn't.

"But you are where you are and we can't go anywhere from here. So let's stop this."

His look said the time to stop things was long gone. "You're the only person in my life who demands nothing of me."

"I can't demand anything of you. I know that."

"Do you want to?"

"Does it matter if I want to?"

"Yes." Why did he need to hear it so badly? "I want you to want it. Because I want to give you everything."

"But you can't." At least they were talking about it, and maybe understanding why would help her let him go.

"After Nisha's wedding, when I disappeared like that I broke a promise. The first promise I broke was to you."

"You didn't actually promise to do anything more than try. I have no doubt that you did try."

"Why are you not angrier with me?"

"Angrier than you are with yourself?"

Instead of answering, he leaned over and kissed Chutney.

Her fingers itched to stroke his bent head. "I was. I was very angry for a while. But something you said to me that night kept coming back to me. You said, 'Sometimes I feel like my life isn't my own.' I knew something had happened that was outside your control."

He straightened up again. "And you accepted it."

"One part of it is what you think. That I don't question the universe. But somewhere deep inside, I didn't believe myself worthy of that magic. Maybe I wasn't ready for it. For you. For all the things you made me feel." Their knees were touching and it grounded her.

"And now?"

"And now it doesn't matter."

"Because none of that has changed? Because my life is still not my own?"

"No. Because you still *feel like* your life is not your own."

"Aren't those two the same?"

"No." This time she leaned over and kissed Chutney. For a while they both sat there, showering her dog with the love aching in their hearts.

"Sometimes I wish I could tell you that I don't care that your life isn't your own. That I'll take whatever I can get. But that's not who I am."

"I know. Because trusting the universe is not code for compromise. What you said earlier, you were right. You did make me feel out of control. My feelings scared me. I thought they would distract me from what I knew, what I had been trained to believe I wanted." He waited for her to respond. But she knew he wasn't done.

"It wasn't just the loss of control making me a coward. I was definitely a coward to walk away from you, but there is more." After that he went completely silent.

The resolve in his eyes was still strong, but it was laced with darkness. Whatever he wanted to say, digging it up wasn't going to be easy.

She stood. "Will something to eat help?"

"Overnight oats?"

She smiled. He actually sounded enthusiastic. "I thought the nectar pus story might have deterred you from them forever."

"I do think of them as devotional oats now." He smiled, then cleared his throat. "Also, I haven't felt my legs in about a half hour."

"Oh no. Chutney is heavy. I should have warned you." She picked the baby off his lap.

Chutney didn't so much as stir. India put her on the couch and turned back to Yash, who had the strangest expression on his face.

"Do you need help getting up?" She held out her hand.

"I wasn't kidding when I said I can't feel my legs," he said with such self-deprecating misery she wanted to hug him.

"I can lift you up. Standing up and straightening your legs is the only way to get the circulation back in them."

"You're going to pick me up?" he said with mock-horror. "Have you no regard for my fragile male ego?"

"Umm, maybe you can grunt and beat your chest afterward?" She walked behind him, tucked her arms under his, and lifted him to his feet.

He made a ridiculously tortured sound as blood rushed back into his legs.

"I know that tickles. Just give it a moment," she said still holding him up.

Laughter bubbled through his chest as he squeezed her hands and tried to stand and pushed back into her in involuntary jolts.

She was laughing too, because to see Yash Raje like this, felled by tickles and completely vulnerable, was something she would never forget as long as she lived.

This close, his scent, all that masculine vibrancy, made a heady mix with the gentleness with which he clutched her hands, the trust with which he leaned into her. Pain and pleasure gathered where their bodies touched.

Moving to face him, she let him go slowly, her hands taking cues from his. Finally he was standing, and she could tell that he was fine.

Her hands stayed in his.

"Better?" she asked.

His gaze dropped to their joined hands. He nodded.

"And the male ego?"

"Absolutely battered."

She found herself grinning as she left him to retrieve the oats from the fridge.

He took out two bowls from a drawer as though they'd done this a million times. "Will you have some?"

"No, thank you."

Slipping the extra bowl back, he handed her the other one. "I'm being a coward again."

She took the bowl. "Yash, not being able to talk about something that hurt you isn't cowardice, it's self-protection. You don't have to tell me. But if you want to, it will help me understand, and I do need to understand."

When she handed him the full bowl, he put it down and took her hand instead. He needed the contact. She did too.

"That night . . . *you* . . . you knocked the breath out of me. It was the first time in my life I had felt like that. You already know that I didn't exactly have a normal dating history as a young person. The accident happened when I was fifteen, and for the rest of high school I was trying to figure out how to get back on my feet and not disappoint everyone in my life and do all the things I wanted to. Through college I was trying to get rid of my limp—it made me too self-conscious to date. I . . . ." He stopped, and she knew this part was harder than the rest.

"I have scars. A . . . a lot of them. They were fresh then. And still painful." He let her hand go and touched his collar as though making sure it was there, covering him up, and she had to work hard to keep from wrapping her arms around him.

"I was also trying to get through college and law school at an accelerated pace, because I was in a hurry and because it gave me somewhere to put my energy, so I didn't have to think about the things that were broken. I let myself heal wrong, then I overcompensated for it. My first job out of law school was with the U.S. Attorney's Office. I loved that job, it was like finding myself." He stopped and took a breath, an ujjayi one, like she'd taught him.

He was fully inside himself, his face tight, his aura drained of its glow. It was the palest she'd ever seen it, almost every hint of gold gone. The desire to comfort him raged inside her, but she held still.

"I . . . I've never told this next part to anyone. Only my family and Naina know. When Trisha was at Berkeley, I spoke to a pre-law class. Afterward I took Trisha and her roommate out to dinner. Her roommate—Julia—developed something of a crush on me. She reached out for an internship and I took her on because she was bright and because she was my sister's friend." His hands shook, but he pressed them into the countertop and kept going.

"One evening she called me and said Trisha was in trouble and she wanted to meet and talk to me about it. Then she drugged me and . . . and recorded me having sex with her. I remember nothing of the actual incident except for the splitting headache and throwing up all of the next day. But I do remember the terrible sense of violation, a disconnection from myself that I didn't understand, couldn't shake off."

Rage shook inside her. Never in her life had she truly wanted to hurt someone. But what that woman had done to him made her want to hunt her down. She took his hand and he pulled their joined hands to his heart, as though he'd been waiting for her to.

"Naina and I were friends and Julia thought we were together, so she sent the video to Naina with a threat to release it to the press if Naina didn't break up with me. I was running for my first election. Naina came straight to me. She stood by me. My family took care of it. Everyone went into crisis mode. We paid Julia off, had her destroy the video, had her sign all sorts of gag orders, and basically made the threat disappear."

"But no one stopped to see how you were doing."

"That wasn't deemed a priority at the time."

"Yash . . ."

"I'm not done. Please let me finish."

She nodded.

"I never went out with anyone after that. At first if women flirted with me I felt physically ill. Naina and I were close enough that everyone assumed I didn't date because we were together. I want you to know that when I met you at Nisha's wedding, I was not with Naina. I had never even thought about her that way."

His heartbeat beneath their clasped hands was strong and steady. She pressed into it.

"You know how that night was. All the fear, all the coldness I'd felt at the thought of intimacy, I didn't feel that with you. For the first time I didn't need to control everything. I felt free and safe."

Some of the warmth returned to his gaze. "You swept me entirely off my feet. I was surrounded by people I'd known my whole life, but I couldn't keep track of conversations. Everyone kept asking me what was wrong with me. All I knew is that I didn't feel like myself. It was the headiest feeling, as though a part of me I'd never hoped to get back had returned." He squeezed her hand, a tremor going through him.

She wanted to tell him he could stop, he didn't have to relive all this. But she knew he had to say it. He'd been waiting a long time to say it.

"Then you kissed me, and it was beautiful. Too beautiful. Too much."

For ten years now, the memory of that kiss had haunted her.

His tentativeness at first, then his intensity, how it had consumed them both.

"All the darkness my mind associated with intimacy came back. Just for a flash. But the beauty of it gave me a taste of how it could be. I wanted that. After you left that night, I couldn't sleep, couldn't stop thinking about you, about our kiss. As the night wore on, my old memories kept getting tangled up with our kiss. How consumed by you I felt got tangled up with what I associated with feeling out of control. I didn't put this together until you made me think about my control issues."

How strong, how untouchable he seemed, how blessed. Yes, he was those things, but the things he'd withstood would have broken almost anyone else. "I really want you to be my governor," she said, then laughed because it was such an absurd thing to say in this situation.

It made him laugh too, and pull her hand to his lips.

When he spoke again, his gaze was locked with hers, his breath fell on her knuckles like kisses. "In the light of day, the dark feelings receded. On the flight to Sripore, you were with me. I didn't know how I was going to wait that long to see you. But after we got to Sripore everything changed again."

He told her the rest of it.

Going back to how Naina's parents had started pressuring her to get married, to "settle down," as soon as she turned twenty. Her way of dealing with it had always been to joke about it and say, "I'm only ever going to marry Yash, so you have to wait until he's ready."

Her father never thought it was a joke. He kept talking to Yash's parents about it. When Yash's parents asked him, Yash had blown them off by saying that he didn't have time for a relationship. But his father had become convinced that Naina was a match made in heaven for him. A reformer, an activist, someone who had proven her loyalty after what had happened with Julia Wickham.

"He wasn't wrong, was he?" India said.

"If anything, it was a friendship made in heaven. All the comfort we both needed, with none of the complications of feelings being involved."

Then Naina had gotten into a program that does research in Nepal. Her father refused to let her go. In his view, at twenty-eight, an unmarried daughter was already his greatest failure. He dug in his heels, she had to get married and then do whatever she wanted to do with her husband's permission, or he was cutting her off. Naina had always had a complicated relationship with her dad. Telling her parents to go to hell was just never an option for her.

"It never is," India said, and he tucked a lock of hair behind her ear.

"When we were in Sripore for the ceremony, Julia went on social media and started to like some of Naina's posts about the wedding. She sent me seemingly innocent messages about how lovely my family looked, even though it violated the gag orders she'd signed. What had happened between you and me had already dug up things that I'd repressed and Julia's messages just threw open the floodgates."

All that had been churning inside Yash when Naina and her father had fought, and she'd told her father that she and Yash were together but that Yash didn't want to get married until he won the election.

"I remember the look on Dr Kohli's face as though it were yesterday. I'd never felt such rage as I felt at everything that was behind that look. If my father had done that to my sisters, I would never have let him get away with it. For all their demanding ways, my parents have never treated their daughters' dreams and abilities as less than their sons', or any man's."

Naina's father had completely ignored what his daughter was saying and asked Yash if she was telling the truth.

"What did you say to him?" India asked, anger threaded through her voice. She was back in that moment with him, his rage her rage.

"I asked him if he'd heard his daughter, because she'd said everything he needed to hear."

"You Yudishtired it," she said, feeling pride, of all things. Pride at what he'd done for another woman, even when it had compromised their chance at happiness. The belief that she would follow him to the ends of the earth wrapped around her. She would do anything to make him happy, to keep him safe.

He saw it, and it made him drop another kiss on her fingers, sending sensation skittering across her skin.

"Our families acted like it was inevitable. Naina and I insisted we wanted to keep it private, and for a while everyone complied. Naina got to go off to Nepal and I went back to losing myself in my work. I buried that night with you, convinced myself that I had imagined it. I told myself that helping my friend was the right thing to do. But I was just choosing to run away, because it was easier than dealing with the mess in my head. I felt cornered, but I also felt relief."

A tear slid from his eye and she wiped it, when what she wanted was to kiss it away.

"I am so sorry that I didn't think about what it would do to you. I took the easier path, the path that let me keep everything I'd buried, buried. All my life I've thrived on fighting for things, but I never got to fight Julia, I never got to confront her, and the self-loathing made me lose you."

This time she pulled their joined hands close and dropped a kiss on his fingertips. Hope filled her heart so hard and fast she knew she should stop it. But, looking in his eyes, falling into the crystal gray that had not a single defense against her, against his own remorse, she knew she was lost.

"I didn't fight for you," he said. "I give you a hard time about not fighting for things, but it was me who didn't fight my own demons for you. I want to fight for us now. I don't want to do this without you."

Those words fell like a hammer between them. Reality over the magic glittering in the air.

What was she doing? If he broke up with Naina and India's role in it came out, the media and the Cruz campaign would destroy him. They'd paint him as a cheater, a liar. She tried to pull away, but he didn't let go. "Yash, please. I believe you. I know how you feel. But we can't do this. There's too much to lose."

He stepped closer, his body pulled to its full height, his shoulders square, purpose and strength radiating from him like heat. The Yash the public saw, the Yash who was strong enough to take on anything.

"I want you to trust me. I can't lose you again. I can't keep lying. I don't want to live a life in which you aren't with me. Can you?"

She shook her head, but before she could speak the alarm on his phone went off.

He reached for his phone. "Shit. I have to be at the airport in an hour. Rico and I are flying to L.A. for an appearance on *Good Morning America*. I'll be back tomorrow afternoon. It's going to be okay. I'll talk to Naina and figure out how we make the announcement. We can discuss the rest later. All of it."

Her heart was beating too fast. It was that sense again, the one she'd had when she walked around her home making sure that her family was safe, that they were still there.

"Hey," he said. "I'll cancel. I can do *GMA* later." He started to call someone, and she stilled his hand.

"No, you're not canceling. Go, knock their socks off. We'll talk when you get back." *We have time*, she wanted to say, but she couldn't.

"We have a lifetime," he said, and she went up on her toes and kissed his cheek. A quick peck, because she couldn't stop herself, because what gripped her was hot and ravenous and chased by the kind of fear she'd never known.

He wrapped his hands around her face, his touch tender, his gaze worshipful. Then, with all the conviction of someone who had made a decision and never went back once he had, he dropped a kiss on her forehead. Then her eyelids, one at a time. Then the edges of her mouth. Their breaths mingled. The breath he gave her was all hope, the breath he took from her all trust. Finally their lips met, quick and gentle. A promise for more soon. A promise that threaded through her body and awoke every cell to possibility.

"I will see you soon," he said, or she did. In that moment there was nothing that separated them. No her, no him, just them, and that promise they had uttered as one.

Chapter Twenty-Three

*I*f hope were a drug, Yash wanted everyone addicted. Because the way it beat in his heart and ran through his blood, every dream felt within reach, every moment brimmed with possibilities. He'd spent the morning on the set of *Good Morning America*, and for the first time in a very long time he didn't feel like an imposter, he didn't feel like he was taking up space from others.

He felt like he was here to fight for everyone, but for himself most of all, because *he* needed to live in a world that was more equitable. A world that took care of the sick and protected the weak while it also gave free rein to those who innovated and made the world richer, more connected, more plentiful for everyone. Those things were not separate, not mutually exclusive, and they needed to be tied back together in the consciousness of our nation, and the world, not just California. But like in everything else, California was as good a place as any to start something.

The clip of him saying all that on *GMA* had gone instantly viral. Rico had whooped so loud and been so ecstatically smug, all Yash could do was laugh.

"I know I sound like a stuck record, but only an act of God can drop your poll numbers now, mate," Rico said, leaning back in the chair across from Yash in his office. Outside, his Fabulous Five were arguing about what the best part of his appearance on *GMA* was.

An empty box of Bob's Donuts sat between them. Another, smaller box sat in his bag. He'd ordered extra to take to India after. Yes, he was going to sugar and grease her up, or die trying. Knowing her, it would be the latter.

As for the poll numbers, well, an act of love was an act of God, wasn't it? The fact that breaking up with Naina was going to take over the news cycle and tank his numbers felt oddly insignificant. He had never wanted it to be part of the campaign in the first place.

All he felt was relief. Finally he'd get to win or lose on his own, not on the basis of a lie. From everything he knew about politics, lose was the likely outcome. He didn't care. He would do this the right way or not at all.

"Anything else?" Rico asked.

They'd driven straight to the office after flying back from L.A. and had spent all afternoon working on speeches for a spate of upcoming fundraising dinners. The Cruz campaign had become frustrated with Yash's sensible gun-reform messaging and launched an attack from a not entirely unexpected quarter. The NRA was riling up the Blue Lives Matter crowd and spending a lot of dollars on targeted social media to spread disinformation about crime statistics that harmed the Black Lives Matter message. This wasn't an issue Yash was going to pussyfoot around and let them get away with. Rico and he had been trying to come up with an out-of-the-box solution that stopped Cruz and the gun lobby in their tracks.

Vansh had been on a video call with them for hours this past week, and he was getting home tomorrow to focus on it. The brat was a genius when it came to seeing things no one else did. He also understood social media outreach and had come up with some interesting ways to overlay their message on top of their opponent's.

"I think we made good progress," Yash said. "We'll pick this up tomorrow." He thought about warning Rico about the breakup, but he wanted to be fair and talk to Naina first about how to make the announcement. They'd still have time to come up with a damage control plan.

Rico stood. "Ashna was right about Vansh. He's brighter than the rest of you."

"He knows it too," Yash said with equal parts fondness and frustration. If Vansh only focused, he'd have done great things by now.

Then again, for the first time in his life Yash wasn't jealous of his brother's ability to not care about doing great things and putting himself before everyone else.

"Wait until he gets here and you see the worshipful raptures Ashna and the rest of the family go into," Yash said, smiling. "It's a full-fledged love fest."

"Even more than with you?"

"Me? Hah, you ain't seen nothin' yet, buddy."

"Oh joy!" Rico laughed. "Right. I'm off. Call if you need to talk about anything. Anything at all, okay?" He waited for a reaction from Yash, which Yash worked hard to withhold from him.

Finally, the man left.

Naina should be back from Nepal by now. She hadn't called or texted. They still hadn't spoken since the engagement debacle. Yash had moved back into his apartment. The family had backed off. There was far too much going on with the election to spend time on a drama they saw as ongoing.

Ma had sent him one message saying she was there when he was ready to talk.

Oh, Ma, you have no idea.

Then she had reverted to her usual chatty messages about how well he was doing in his appearances and interviews, along with specifics of what messaging she thought resonated. Suggestions for what to focus on, along with technique, pauses, and eye contact. It was her area of expertise, the craft of communicating through body language. *"Still too much touching of your hair. Looks fidgety and un-leader-like."*

Well, Ma, you shouldn't have touched our hair so much when we were little. Now we can't stop doing that to self-soothe. Naturally, he didn't say that to her. He just worked hard to remember not to touch his hair when he was on camera or at a podium.

On his way to the car he tried again to call Naina and didn't get an answer.

She's angry, he told himself. He knew what was coming wouldn't be easy. Naina was going to take the brunt of it, and he wished he could save her that. Needing to be with India wasn't a choice anymore, it had become him. All of him.

Just looking at her name on his phone made wild wanting twist through him. His finger hovered over the name, stroking the air between him and the sound of her voice.

The hope in her eyes when he'd left her was the most beautiful thing he'd ever seen. He wanted to see it again. He wanted to feel the way he felt only in her presence for the rest of his life.

Just as he was about to call her and tell her that he was on his way, his phone rang.

"Yash?"

"Arzu? Are you crying? What's wrong?"

Even as he asked, he knew nothing was wrong, because he had never heard Arzu cry, let alone with quite so much abandon.

The smile in her voice was as clear as her sobs. "Can you come to the hospital? Someone here wants to see you."

He was in his car and driving before he was even off the phone. Abdul had regained consciousness. Everything was going to be all right.

The first person he called was India. "Abdul woke up."

"Oh, Yash." Her smile was filled with all the relief and joy he was feeling, and he could see it, even though she wasn't near him, where she should be. "Will you call me when you get there and let me know everything?"

"Yes. We have so much to talk about." *I love you*. He didn't say it. It felt too casual to say it over the phone. His mind flew into the future, where they would have this: *I love you*'s uttered like simple words. Not words that made him feel unhinged with the weight and wonder of them.

She stayed on the phone. Happiness filling the silence as he raced down the freeway.

"You should call your family," she said finally, knowing he'd called her first. Caring that he told everyone else.

"Yes, ma'am." But she didn't hang up and for a few minutes he just listened to her breathing coming through his car speakers, and soaked up what that felt like. "India?" He loved saying her name.

"Yash?"

"I can't wait to see you again."

"I know exactly how you feel. Now go."

This time he listened. Then he called Nisha and asked her to let the family know. He'd work on the public statement himself, after talking to Arzu and seeing how she wanted it handled. Abdul was awake and Yash had never felt more happy to be alive.

Abdul was holding Arzu's hand, his baby girl tucked in next to him. His parents sat by him, rubbing his feet with their hands.

"Boss!" Abdul's smile was so vibrant that Yash almost forgot that they weren't backstage waiting to go out and campaign. He almost forgot that nearly two months of Abdul's life had been lost.

"She's gorgeous, isn't she?" the proud father said.

"Totally. Takes after her mother."

That made Abdul laugh, a deep belly laugh that made the hope already filling Yash swell to bursting.

Abdul's mother picked up a bright red box of Turkish delight and offered it to Yash. He took one. "Thank you."

The darned thing was so delicious, and he was feeling so heady, that he asked her if he could have another piece.

She handed him the box. "It's a day for celebration, have it all."

"Obviously, you don't know Yash, Ammi," Abdul said. "Because he will eat the entire box."

"Damn straight!" Yash said.

Abdul's mother patted Yash's arm. "I always trust a man who loves his sweets." Then Abdul's parents left to go home and get some rest. He'd woken up late last night, and they'd chosen to take the initial hours to themselves. Yash understood that.

For the next half hour, Arzu and Yash filled Abdul in, and played with Naaz, who was more cheery and alert than Yash had ever seen her. It was as if she knew her life had fallen back on its rails and that she was going to know her father's love. Or maybe children reflected the world around them and this was the first day that the adults around her were not weighed down with sadness.

The doctors came in and gave them an update. Abdul's scans and tests were perfectly normal. A miracle. He'd be free to go home in a matter of days. He was going to need some rehabilitative therapy to get back to normal, but he would get back to his usual healthy self soon.

"I heard your new bodyguard is a woman," Abdul said with a smile. "Arzu tells me she's totally badass." He stroked his little girl's head with a crooked finger, all the tenderness in the universe in that gesture.

"What can I say, I'm a lucky guy when it comes to my security detail."

"Naaz has a role model. She can follow in her abbu's footsteps, inshallah!"

"Hey! Naaz is going to chart her own footsteps," Arzu said.

"You're only saying that because her abbu gave you the scare of your life," Abdul said.

"Her abbu almost killed her ammi with his heroics."

"You find my heroics hot, admit it. Look at your face, you're proud of me."

Their eyes locked and it was a beautiful thing. "Mostly I was just missing your arrogance." But her lips curved and she dropped a kiss on his cheek. "Since Yash is here and I know you're dying to ask him about the campaign, I'll go grab myself some coffee. Yash, would you like some?"

"Thanks. Do you want me to get it?"

"Nah, I need to stretch my legs."

Abdul watched her leave. "My ammi said that Arzu didn't leave the hospital the entire time I was here."

"She's fierce. You're a lucky guy."

"I know. I'm also lucky to be alive. We both are."

"Abdul . . . I don't know how to say this without it sounding completely and entirely insufficient. Thank you. I owe you my life. I'm so very sorry for what I put you through, put your family through."

"You didn't put my family through that. The bastard who shot me—shot you—he did that. They hate us. They don't want us here. This is our home. You and I, we were born here. We love this country. We deserve to have it love us back. They don't care. They only care about their bullshit definition of patriotism that requires you to be white. Arzu tells me you're leading in the polls. They probably hate that."

Yeah, well, they were in luck, because his poll numbers were about to plummet.

Abdul pushed a button and his bed propped him up to sitting. It felt like a dream to watch him do it even with the white bandage on his neck. "That means you can win. You can beat them. You can make sure our families are safer, prouder, cared-for. I've been in the hospital for almost two months. My health insurance doesn't cover all that. But it covers enough that my family won't be wiped out."

"I'm taking care of your bills. Don't worry about that. Focus on getting better."

"That's not the point. Not everyone has a grateful boss who's willing to pay their way. You know what getting sick without a job is like in this country. In our state. We have to do better. You're going to do better. You cannot lose this election. Whatever happens, you cannot lose this election."

"He's not going to lose." Arzu came back and handed him his coffee, pausing in her quick, efficient movements to hold Yash's gaze. "We're counting on you, Yash. What we just went through, you cannot let that go to waste. We believe in you."

"Thanks." Suddenly Yash couldn't breathe so well.

Arzu threw a glance at the monitors Abdul was still hooked up to, making sure all was well, then she picked up the TV remote and raised the volume. "I think you guys want to see this."

Abdul's recovery was already on the news. Arzu and Abdul hadn't even had a chance to make a statement. Someone from the hospital staff had to have leaked it. There was cheering in the streets. Jubilation.

"I'm so sorry," Yash said. "I was going to make a statement after talking to you."

Abdul waved away his words. "This is all pretty touching. When does the racist shit start?"

In keeping with every single piece of coverage about Abdul's shooting, Naina crying over Yash's body splashed across the screen. The kick of sickness in the pit of Yash's stomach would not lessen, no matter how many times he watched it.

Then it started. Pictures of Abdul in his kufi surrounded by other men in kufis and thobes, which would be great if it hadn't been followed by stock images of a mosque and stock scenes of prayers. Why was that even part of this story? The anchor started talking about a nurse reporting that Abdul's wife prayed by his side five times a day. All true, but Arzu hadn't given them permission to release those private moments. The coverage was invasive, but more than that it smacked of something else Yash knew only too well.

"Wow they're othering my being alive. The exotic lens is stunning, isn't it?" Abdul said.

Arzu shook her head incredulously. "Gotta love media-wide macroaggression."

Neither of them looked surprised.

During Yash's early campaigns the media had incessantly talked about Sripore, Hinduism, and South Asian culture. Yash had always been entirely comfortable with his culture, but the constant overlay had felt deliberate in its attempt to set him apart as different, foreign. Finally, Ma and Nisha had beaten them at their own game and flooded them with tours of the estate, the cars, fashion, Yash's obsession with sports. The Assimilation Offensive they'd called it. Disingenuous as it had felt to Yash, it had worked to sidestep the *relatability* debate. And it was only as manipulative as what the media had done by focusing so singularly on his cultural roots. He was both those things, American and South Asian, and he had no interest in his identity being leveraged for either entertainment or political gain.

Now they were doing the same thing to Abdul.

On the TV, the coverage moved to how people had been leaving flowers and offerings on the soccer field where the shooting had taken place. Vigils had collected there every night. Now there was a crowd thronging the campus.

"America belongs to all of us," a young woman in a hijab said, sobbing. An Asian woman hugged her, tears running down her face. "Yash Raje is our governor. Yash Raje is us." The emotion in her voice was palpable, and the faith in her eyes lodged like a lump in Yash's throat.

"Vote!" a group of Black and White students screamed into the camera in one voice. "Integrity, respect, intelligence. That's the kind of leader we want. Someone who stands by his friends. He makes us feel seen."

"The other side is losing its shit right now, isn't it?" Abdul said.

Sure enough, the camera panned to a group with Cruz posters. "This is America, not Arabia. One nation under God." A man waved the American flag.

"What exactly is Arabia?" Arzu said.

"Isn't that the place Peter O'Toole was Lawrence of?"

They both laughed.

An altercation broke out between the two groups. The camera lapped it up.

"Idiots," Yash muttered.

Abdul picked up the remote and muted the TV. "They're not idiots. What they are is dangerous, and they will do anything to make sure you don't win. Right now I'll bet it's killing them that they have nothing on you."

"They're going to have nothing on him," Arzu said, her fierceness trained on Yash this time. "Yash is the perfect candidate."

"She's right. I can't wait to get back out there between you and bullets."

"Don't say that," Yash said. "Don't say that."

"I would, brother. Did you know that when the agency assigned me to you I begged not to be assigned to a politician? I told them to give me an actor instead, at least those guys aren't lying about lying. Politicians? I had never seen one who wasn't a liar through and through. Then I met you. At first I just rolled my eyes at you. I thought it was an act. All that sincerity. All that annoying *interest*." He stopped to smile.

"Then I got to know you. You're the real thing. I believe that with my whole heart. Everyone else is in this for personal gain. You're here because you put us, the public, before you. I never thought I'd see the day, but finally there's a public servant who's here to serve. And you're going to win." Abdul's eyes glittered with purpose, the new hollows beneath them making the impact devastating.

"And he's going to change things for those who've been waiting for change. You're the answer to so many people's prayers," Arzu said, her conviction matching Abdul's. She picked up Naaz and pressed her to her heart. "Our children will have a better world. Our pain. Everything we went through, it's all going to count for something, because you're going to win, inshallah."

YASH'S PHONE HAD been ringing off the hook. He probably had a thousand texts. They sat unopened on his phone in the passenger seat of his car, where he'd been sitting for long enough that he knew he had to move or someone was going to find him. Several of the messages were from India.

India.

To be with her he would have to admit to the world that he had lied, for his entire political career. He'd have to break up publicly with someone everyone saw as a loyal girlfriend.

How had betting it all on telling the truth felt easy just hours ago?

A man had almost died for him. Hundreds of thousands of young people, people who felt disenfranchised, othered in their own home, were counting on him. Millions of people who were afraid of falling sick, of losing their homes, of sending their children to school because they might get shot there, of having their planet die, were counting on him. He'd made them a promise. They believed him.

They believed a liar.

Pulling the car out of his spot, Yash started to drive.

Chapter Twenty-Four

India had been waiting for Yash to call, which was a little too terrifyingly déjà vu, no matter how hard she tried not to think of it that way. This was not the same as meeting a man at a wedding, getting lost in him for a day, and jumping straight to planning how many children she'd have with him. Not by a long shot.

This was knowing someone's deepest thoughts, being intimate with the fissures that cracked them open, and sharing your own cracks with them. This was about being seen all the way inside, right to where the audacious, incipient germ of hope was hidden. This was dropping armor when spears were raised.

A sense of disbelief had been nudging at her ever since Yash had told her that he wanted her in his life, that he wanted to be a part of hers. For all the skepticism mixed in with her hope, she didn't doubt that he meant it, no matter the cost. What scared her was the cost.

Abdul just woke up, she told herself. *Yash has a lot going on. He'll call as soon as he can.*

Her phone sat silent despite her hundredth demand that it give her something, anything. The front door sounded and Chutney's tail started to thud against her lap. Lifting her puppy up, she tore down the stairs and stopped short.

"China?"

Her sister stood by the door, her glittery pink suitcase standing forlornly by her side. Her always impeccable hair was a mess. Her puffy eyes were shadowed with smudged liner and mascara. She looked completely and utterly devastated.

"Oh, sweetheart." India put Chutney down and went to her, even as Chutney raced past her to get to China first.

Ignoring India completely, China dropped to her knees and let Chutney smother her with kisses. India dropped down next to them. As she let herself drown in Chutney's frantic love, not a word came out of China. India knew she would say nothing. China tended to lose her words when she was hurting.

Chutney, for her part, was out of control, her whining loud and indignant. *How dare you leave me for so long?* their puppy communicated using every skill at her disposal.

A smile stretched China's lips even as tears started streaming down her face. She fell back on the wooden floor and let Chutney have at her.

"China? Honey?" Tara came down the stairs, face lined with worry. Chutney's wailing, dialed all the way up, had to have sounded concerning upstairs.

China sprang up to sitting at their mother's voice. Tara rushed to her and they wrapped their arms around each other and China broke into sobs in earnest.

India brought her a glass of water. For a very long time, the three of them sat together in a tangle of wrapped arms, Chutney sitting atop their mess, distributing kisses as she deemed fit.

"She didn't want me there," China said finally.

Tara looked at India, eyes helpless with anger. India was going to wring Song's neck.

"Then she should have told you not to come," Tara said.

This made China cry harder. Dear Lord, Song *had* told her not to come.

"She tried to tell me. I didn't listen. I didn't understand how she could stand to be apart from me when I couldn't stand it even for a moment. I can't breathe without her, Mom, I can't."

Tara stroked her back.

India rubbed her arm.

"She introduced me to her team as a fan. As a fan!" China's pitch grew shrill. "As a fan who had chased after her all the way from America. One of them sat me down and gave me a talking-to about stalking laws. Song was right there and she said nothing." She slid her head into Tara's lap. "But the pain in her eyes . . . it was terrible. I thought I could be strong enough for both of us. But then she said . . . she said she couldn't risk everything for me. She'd worked too hard. It would disappoint too many people. Her fans . . . her fans were more important to her than me. America was just a break. *I* was just a break. When I begged, she just left me there and told her staff to take me to the airport."

"It's her loss, honey," Tara said, sounding much calmer than India felt. "Her loss."

"Then why does it feel like I've lost everything, like I'm going to die from the pain? Why does it feel like she needs me to help her, but I just don't know how?"

"It has to be her choice," Tara said. "It's not help if she doesn't want it."

Before China could respond, the doorknob jiggled and the door flew open.

Brandy's tall muscular form filled up the turquoise doorframe. She took in the scene for a stunned second, then spun around as though she'd walked in on them changing their clothes. "I'm so sorry. I didn't mean to intrude."

China got off Tara's lap and sat up, wiping her eyes on her sleeve. She tried to look stoic, which only made her look even more miserable.

India stood and pulled Tara and China to their feet. "It's okay, Brandy. China just came home, you can turn around and come on in."

Brandy turned around and threw a tortured look at China. "Are you all right? Are you ill? Can I do something?"

China scooped up Chutney and started walking to the stairs as though she hadn't even heard Brandy. Then she stopped and turned. "No. But thank you." She sniffed, unable to stop her tears. "I'm going to try and get some sleep."

"Excuse me." Tara gave Brandy's shoulder a squeeze and followed China.

Brandy stood there, her miserable gaze following China. India recognized the longing emanating from her only too well. Suddenly Brandy seemed to remember why she was here and turned to India, and India knew something was very wrong.

It was one of those moments when the air around you darkens with news you know is coming. Before India knew what she was doing, she had grabbed Brandy by the arm. "What happened? Is Yash okay?"

Brandy didn't answer immediately. She stroked India's hand, soothing her as though she were a skittish kitten.

"Brandy, please," India said, unable to keep the desperation out of her voice.

Please let him be all right. Please.

"We don't know where he is. It's been four hours since he left the hospital after seeing Abdul, and no one has heard from him. The last person he spoke to was Nisha, and now he's not answering his phone. The family is frantic. I thought maybe you'd know where he is."

India pressed a hand to her heart, needing to physically push back the sense of doom. "He hasn't called me since . . . do you know what happened when he went to see Abdul? Did Arzu say anything?"

"Just that they had a great visit. She said Yash was ecstatic to see Abdul, and Abdul was too. Yash got a little emotional before he left, when they talked about how well the campaign was going. Arzu said they told him how excited they were that he was going to win and how much they were counting on him. None of that sounds unusual. Yash has been waiting for Abdul to wake up the entire time that I've known him. He should be celebrating."

India found her hand fisting the material of her yoga top. This was what she'd been dreading. She wasn't surprised this had happened, but she was surprised by how much it hurt.

And it was never going to stop hurting. Not ever.

"I know where he is."

"Where?"

"I'll call you when I find him. Tell his family not to worry." Grabbing China's car keys, India ran out the door.

It took her no time to find the place. Because, idiot that she was, over the years she'd gotten in the habit of coming back here to think.

The sun had disappeared from the sky and the thickness of the trees along the trail made it even darker. What was Yash thinking? Why was he here alone? There were snakes here. As if on cue, something slithered in the shrubbery next to her and she sped up. India trusted almost every creature in the universe except snakes. Especially snakes she couldn't see.

There was some light from her phone flashlight, but she had it on the lowest setting because, one, she didn't want to attract snakes, and two, she didn't want to run out of charge. She would need the light to come back down the mountain. She'd need the phone if Yash was hurt. God, what if he was hurt? Surely he would have called someone if he wasn't hurt.

She broke into a run, flip-flopped feet slipping and sliding on the gravelly path. If she had stopped to think, changing into sneakers would have been the smart thing to do when she knew climbing a mountain was involved.

Yash had carried a lantern when he'd brought her here the night before Nisha's wedding. A camping lantern with the kind of white light that mirrored the moonlight and picked out the glitter in their clothes. It had turned the sequins on her ghaghra into a million stars that merged seamlessly with the silver threaded through his kurta, the endless universe of possibility inside them reflected around them.

In all the times she'd come back here by herself, India had never let herself think about the magic of that night. She'd told herself her being here had nothing to do with him. It was simply a beautiful place. The one good thing she'd gotten out of being taken for a fool.

As she emerged into the clearing at the end of the trail, India held up her phone and pointed the flashlight at the rocky cliff they had sat on. It was the end of the trail, a spot from which you got a bird's-eye view of the Raje estate, his childhood home, with all of Woodside wrapped around it like a too-expensive blanket. She had expected to see his form silhouetted against the perfectly round moon.

He wasn't there.

How could this be? "Where are you, Yash?" she whispered into the darkness. "Where are you?"

"India?" He sat up. He'd been lying on his back on the rock, legs swinging over the cliff.

A sob escaped her, relief, so much relief, and so much love for this man who was here, feeling alone in the world. Because of her. Because doing the right thing meant something to him. His eyes hitched on her and his shoulders slumped.

Going to him, she dropped down on the rock next to him and crossed her legs. Their knees touched. The light from her phone fell on his face.

Yash Raje in every one of his avatars was a thing of wonder. As a brother, a son, a friend, a public servant. Compassionate, charming, courageous, with terrible eating habits. Who with half a heart could resist any of that? But a self-aware Yash? That was someone India had not one defense against. In this Yash, who saw himself and his world with this brutal, humble clarity, in this Yash she had lost herself completely.

It was all right there, shining in his defeated face. His silver-streaked hair fell across his forehead. His eyes creased with pain. His mouth, made for putting people at ease, pursed and turned downward.

Don't be in pain, she wanted to tell him. *I understand.* But she couldn't say the words just yet. She didn't want to understand. Not just yet.

For a little bit longer she wanted to pretend that they were possible. That he didn't have to give up everything he'd ever wanted and let everyone down to be with her.

He leaned toward her and she leaned toward him. Their foreheads touched like some ancient ritual between fallen warriors.

"India!" he said suddenly, a gasp that made all the pain in his face flood his voice. "What the hell?" He reached for her feet; the light from her phone had fallen on them. They were covered in blood.

She hadn't noticed, but they'd probably been scratched up when she ran up the trail in her flip-flops. Now that she saw the blood, she felt the sting.

With trembling fingers, he stroked her feet. Her bleeding feet, of all things, broke him. His shoulders started to shake and sobs escaped him.

"Yash, it's okay, it's okay," she said, pushing his hair off his forehead. "It doesn't hurt. It's okay. They're just scratches."

He couldn't stop crying, so much shame in his sobs she couldn't bear it.

Letting her feet go, he started to unbutton his shirt, and pulled it off, leaving behind a white cotton inner shirt that glowed in the moonlight and hugged his lean athletic form. This was Yash the way she saw him, the way he always let her see him, the armor of expensive clothing never a shield.

Before she could stop him, he pressed the rich, almost silken cotton onto her scratched-up feet, so much tenderness in the act it sliced open other parts of her.

"How could you climb the trail in flip-flops?"

"You were out here by yourself in the dark," she said. She shouldn't have, because he folded over, his head pressing against the wadded-up shirt, and gave in to his sobs, body and soul.

Her own body reached for him, leaning over him and holding him. "It's okay," she kept saying. "It's okay."

"When did you turn into a liar?" He straightened up and lifted the shirt, wincing at the dots of blood. Then he reached for a bottle of water and she had to smile.

"You remembered to bring water?"

He drizzled water on her feet, washing the dirt and the streaks of blood, checking for cuts, dabbing and wiping as though the sheer strength of his focus might heal them, heal all that was ripped up.

"It really doesn't hurt." She cupped his jaw and brought his gaze up to hers. Touching him this way, as though he were hers to touch, how was she going to give this up? Sensation burst on the palm of her hand, sparks danced in her heart. "They're barely scratches. You didn't have to ruin your shirt."

"How did you even remember this place? How did you find it after all these years?"

She bit down on her lip, unable to devastate him even more.

"India," he said, voice still gruff with tears, gray eyes catching every bit of moonlight. "Please. Tell me. Don't hide things from me. I need to know. I need to know everything in your heart. I need to save it up. Please. I can't do this otherwise." *I can't let you go.*

She saw that last part in his eyes.

The need to lean over and kiss him was a storm inside her, but if she let herself do it, how would she ever let him go? "I continued to come here over the years whenever I needed to think."

His wet eyes darkened. So much regret. "I wish I had known. I wish I had known that you had sat here, breathed this air." His thumb stroked the arch of her foot. "I wish I had—"

"Yash, listen, you know how I said that you still felt like your life was not your own, that it was not the same as your life actually not being your own? I was wrong. That was my anger talking." *My need for you.* "Too many people believe in you. Too many people need you to change things for them. They need you."

"But I need you." Their foreheads were touching again, their breaths kissing. "God, I need you. I don't know how to let you go again."

"You do. That's why you're sitting here. That's why you came here and not to me. I'm not blaming you. I'm just telling you that you and I both know what you have to do."

He pulled away. "Is it really wrong to choose what I want? To choose us?"

"No. It's not wrong. But you won't. It's not who you are. You'll find a way to dull the hurt of doing what everyone else needs you to do," she said with more heat than she'd allowed herself until now. She would too. They both would, because this wasn't a movie, this was real life, and real life didn't end when you couldn't have what you wanted.

Her words shook him, but his hands stayed gentle on her feet, still dabbing and stroking. "Is that what you think of me?"

"It's what I know about you. I know you want to fight for us. I believe that. I do. You think fighting for things is what makes you *you, but* that's only half of it. You can't make decisions that center only on your wants. You care about what everyone else wants. You care. That's what sets you apart. That's what makes you a public servant and not a politician. You want to change things for everyone. A person who puts his own gains ahead of others can never do that."

This time it took him longer to answer. His thumb was still stroking her foot, and his gaze moved from her eyes to her lips, potent as worshipful kisses. He was a man weighing his life, documenting his losses.

"I do want that," he said, as though it took his life to say it. "I can't leave things that bother me alone. I can't not fix something that I know is broken. I've never been able to. I have to at least try."

She knew. But his words were still knives to her heart. "You have to change things. You will."

That meant he had to win the election, and that meant he couldn't break up with Naina. Of all the emotions in the world, India never allowed herself to feel jealousy. It ate through love. It was the opposite of trust, and love was trust.

There was no getting away from the fact that she was going to lose Yash, but the fact that someone who had used his need to help against him made her livid.

He let go of her feet for a moment and tucked her hair behind her ear. "I thought we had a shot." His fingers brushed the sensitive shell of her ear, and a shiver ran across her skin.

"We both wanted to believe that we did. But then you went to see Abdul and realized what was at stake."

If she'd run a knife through his chest he would have looked less distraught. The fact that she understood broke his heart, and seeing how badly he needed someone to understand broke hers.

All those people in his life and he didn't trust a single one of them enough to share the things that he wanted only for himself, things that weren't tied up with the wants and needs of others. How was she going to let him go when he felt so alone in his world? How was she going to process the anger it made her feel?

Chapter Twenty-Five

People around him had always understood what Yash wanted, and helped him get it. But no one had ever understood what he needed. Not like this. The fact that India understood what seeing Abdul conscious again had done to him, without him having to say a word about it, wrecked him.

God, she really was perfect. Perfect for him.

He hadn't realized quite how much he needed the way she saw through him. Now that he'd had this with her, this freedom to not have to hide, how was he going to let it go?

How do you understand?

She caught the question in his eyes and it hit her hard too.

Breaking eye contact, Yash looked down at her feet. He'd been clutching them like a lifeline. Dots of blood kept reappearing along the scratches. The sight of her bloody feet had shattered something inside him. He'd never cried in front of anyone his whole adult life. With her he'd already lost track of how many times he'd let his tears fall.

Finding a clean patch on his shirt, he dabbed at the blood as though the act were penance. It wasn't. There was no atonement for hurting her. Again. For leaving her. Again.

How badly he wanted to shield her from himself and the hurt he was causing was going to push him over the edge. How badly he wanted to stay with her forever, felt like madness.

"Tell me about your visit with Abdul," she said, so gently that he knew she was trying to tug him away from the abyss.

Everything he'd felt poured out of him, the excitement of seeing Abdul sitting up, holding his daughter, flirting with his wife. India smiled, refusing to spill the tears he saw shining in her eyes, while he couldn't stop dabbing at her wounds, spilling tears on them. All these metaphors for hurt and healing twisted and wove around them, tightening with enough force that it cut off his breath.

"I didn't come here because I didn't want to come to you," he said finally. "I came here because I didn't know how else to keep from coming to you. Because this need to come to you first, to tell you first, to not know what to do without you, I don't know what to do with it."

"Yash, please," she said. "Please." Her hand pressed against her chest again. He kept making it worse, and he couldn't stop.

"I never came back here," he said. "After I brought you here that night, I never let myself come back here."

She squeezed her eyes shut as though trying to absorb the enormity of that. "It's terrible that our time together took something so precious from you. I don't want that, Yash, I don't want you to lose things because of your guilt."

The need to pull her close had been growing inside him ever since he'd seen her standing there at the edge of the trail, searching for him with her entire body. "It wasn't guilt. It was a reminder of our connection. If I'd been reminded of it—"

"You wouldn't have been able to act like that night never happened." Instead of pulling away, she scooted closer, as though the knowledge that he was going to do it again gripped her and she wanted to hold on.

He touched her hair again, the silky thickness of her short strands soothing between his fingers. "When we sat here that night, I felt more like myself than I ever have." Until he'd seen her again.

She clutched his hand as it stroked her hair and pressed into it. Forgiveness. Which was so much more than he deserved.

Then her hands were on his chest, pressing into the very center of it. Warmth flowed from them, easing him as shame threw open wounds he should have sought help for long ago, so he could be whole for her.

"I'm sorry," she said. "When I kissed you that evening, I was only thinking of how I felt. It was like all the world had turned magical. That's how free, how bold you made me feel. I wish I had known that it would trigger something ugly for you. I should have asked. I shouldn't have assumed." She tried to pull away, but he clung on and she stayed.

"Don't say that. It was the best day of my life. That kiss was what I've needed to stay sane. It let me look in the mirror again and see someone who might be happy someday. It kept hope alive inside me when I couldn't bear my own ugliness. But I wasn't strong enough to believe it completely. Instead of dealing with the fear our time together dug up, I chose to run."

Fierce eyes locked on his, she climbed into his lap and wrapped her arms around him, not one whit of anger or judgment in her as she held him.

He tried to keep his voice from thickening with relief and regret, but failed. "I was a coward, and now I've brought us both here." Where the only future was pain.

Her lips pressed against his neck and made him tremble.

Love rose strong and hard inside him. He dropped a kiss on top of her head and caught the shiver it sent down her body.

For a moment she stayed like that, absorbing his reactions the way he absorbed hers.

At Nisha's wedding, the first time she'd smiled at him, a sense of inevitability had taken root deep inside him. He'd known he was going to kiss her. It was a thought he'd never had before that, but it had been there from that first shy, curious smile.

When he'd gone to her studio after the shooting and she'd run at Ashna with worried questions about him, that same sense of inevitability had nudged to life inside him. The inevitability that they'd have to touch, that they'd have to join. Two halves tugged together by a cohesive force that was bigger than them.

Now here they were, lips inches from each other's, and no power on earth was going to keep them from touching. No matter how much it hurt afterward.

The full impact of what they were going to have to do—untangle from each other and walk away—hit them together, slowly, muscle by muscle.

"I don't want to understand," she said, body stiffening, then softening again, emotions rolling and ebbing through her. "But I do. What have you done to me, Yash?"

He pulled away just enough to drink in the beauty of her face.

Her eyes were squeezed tightly shut, eyelashes spiking in all directions.

"Why?" he said. "How? How do you understand? What are you doing to me, India?"

She opened her eyes, and anger flashed in the molten brown depths, more anger than he'd ever seen there, anger at herself, anger at him, anger at all the world.

"These past weeks I've done everything in my power to silence my feelings for you just so I could go on. I never understood silencing your inner voice to make things bearable before, but I do now." Her gaze hitched on his lips. She blinked as it struck her that it was what she was going to have to do for the rest of her life, silence how she felt. Because of his choices.

It made that anger flare in her eyes again. "What were you planning to do about Naina once you became governor?"

"Nothing. Go on the way we'd been going on for the past ten years. It's not like you need to be married to do the job of running a state."

"So you never planned to marry?"

"I never thought about it."

Now she was angry enough to pull away. She sprung up, and he felt like something had been ripped from him. "I don't believe that for a minute."

He squatted in front of her and slipped her flip-flops onto her feet. They had stopped bleeding.

"You plan everything. How could you not have thought about whether or not you planned to marry her?" She didn't like feeling anger and he saw her struggle to shove it down.

Her rising temper was fully justified. He didn't know what to do with anger that felt this impotent either.

Standing up, he came face-to-face with her again. "We never planned for it to go this far. Neither of us ever planned to marry."

Her gaze bored into him. She knew there was more, and she wasn't letting him bypass it. Not now, not after he'd dug everything up.

"But you're right," he said finally. "There is more to it. I told you I'm a mess when it comes to intimacy. I couldn't separate intimacy from marriage, so I chose to avoid it entirely." The irony of talking about fear of intimacy seconds after she'd been sitting in his lap wasn't lost on him. Especially when he wanted nothing more than to pull her close again.

"But it wasn't a complete lie, was it? You were with her. You didn't date other women. You Yudishtired it."

"You already know that's true. But you're trying to ask me something. Just ask me."

She jutted out her jaw, determined for answers she knew would hurt her. "Did you sleep with her?"

"Yes. It was a few times, many years ago. It wasn't . . . I'm not sure how to explain it." He was too much of a coward to tell her he'd mostly blocked it out. He'd closed his eyes and waited for it to be over, even though it was Naina, someone he trusted.

Something in his voice told her more than he could say, and what she heard made her step close to him again. Their two-step routine, chasing each other's footsteps, unable to stay away.

"You don't have to say more," she said gently. "I shouldn't have pushed you. I don't know what came over me. She's a friend, you felt safe with her."

Stepping even closer, he pushed her hair behind her ear, then cupped her jaw, needing to fill his hands with her. "I thought I felt safe with her. Truth is, until I met you again, until Ashna brought me to see you, I had forgotten what feeling safe with someone felt like."

Her eyes met his, the impact of his words on her clear in them. "Yash . . ."

"India . . ." Letting her go, he tugged his inner shirt out of his pants. "I told you about my scars. They aren't just scars. It's . . . they're . . . they cover almost my entire torso." He had to stop and breathe. "No one has ever seen me without a shirt after I recovered from the accident. I could never take my shirt off around Naina, not even when we had sex. No one's seen me like this, not even in an inner shirt." He hadn't registered taking his shirt off when he saw her bleeding feet. And he didn't care.

"Even in the video with Julia I have my shirt on. I don't remember any of it, but she had to have tried and I had to have stopped her. Even in my drugged state I couldn't let it go."

He reached for the edge of his shirt, but his hands wouldn't move to take it off.

She wrapped her hands around his, strong gentle hands. The focus of his entire body shifted to her touch. "You have nothing to prove. I know how safe you feel with me. I feel it too."

He dropped his head again, their foreheads touching once more. "What if I need to show you? What if I need someone to see?"

Her hands stroked his, tracing the knuckles, the tendons, then inched to the hem of his shirt, cool fingers skimming the hot skin at his waist. "Do you?"

He shuddered, torturously hungry for her touch. "Please." Just that one word.

She slid her hands under his shirt and splayed them against his abdomen. Skin against skin. The relief was so great that bursts of light blurred his vision.

A laugh escaped her. A laugh, of all things. "Yash Raje, is that a six-pack?" She was teasing him, now, in this moment when the pressure had felt like it might split him open.

A laugh huffed out of him.

"How has no one killed you for being so perfect?" She was looking up at him, eyes bright with wonder, hands trembling on his skin.

"Someone tried," he said against her mouth, because their lips were almost touching now.

The smile slid off her lips. He felt it.

"Too soon?" he asked.

"Too dark," she answered, sliding his shirt up and off his body.

"Sorry." He watched as she took him in. Something fevered flared in her eyes at the sight of his bare ruined body.

He'd expected shock, even anger and pain for the trauma those scars made obvious, but it was her arousal that made him step into her and press his lips to hers.

She sucked in a breath at the contact, then pulled away, only the slightest bit. "Yash . . ."

"India?"

"Let's think about this for a minute." But she pressed into him.

"I feel safe with you," he said. "I feel safe with you." He pressed another barest of kisses against her mouth; nothing had ever felt so soft. "What if I don't want to think about anything but that?"

Pushing up on her toes, she returned his kiss with one of her own, as quick as his had been. Then another, this one lingering the slightest moment longer.

Then him.

Then her.

A rhythm of touches, building, nudging aside all that was in their way, setting them aflame.

The fire built as her hands traced his body. Up his torso, across his chest, caressing his body blanketed in puckered, gouged skin.

She was touching his scars.

His lips trembled against hers, the sensitivity of her fingers on him almost too much. Even the act of pulling clothes on and off still felt like something sharp dragging over raw nerves.

"Does it hurt?" she said against his convulsing breath.

He held her hand in place when she tried to remove it, pressing her smooth hand into his scarred skin. "No. It's not pain exactly. Just heightened sensation. Sensitivity."

Her kiss was harder this time, fierce. "Is this pain something that's never been treated because you've never told anyone?"

The anger in her voice, the possessiveness, he fell into it, pushing into her kiss so hard and hungry that this time she gasped.

Need exploded inside him. She opened her mouth and he was lost. His tongue dragged against hers. Lush, wet, yielding. Her hand slid over his shoulder, to his wrecked back, tracing the relentless rawness, digging up sensations he'd spent years pushing away. Her body melted into him. Heat against heat.

Everything he'd ever buried, all the pain and soreness and shame and anger at being hit by a car, at being dragged across asphalt and gravel, skin wearing off bone. He relived it in bright, brutally clear flashes. Pressing into her, pushing into her, and she opened for him, took him in, and held him as he came apart in her arms. Bit by bit, wound by wound.

When they separated, needing breath, it was like he'd never again know where he ended and she began. He was clutching her face. A drowning man. When he let go, pink streaks brightened her skin where his hands had been. He dropped kisses on them. She was still clinging to him too. Unable to let go.

"Promise me you'll see someone," she whispered. "You'll get help."

"I don't need anyone but you."

She pulled away then, panic in her eyes, her mouth swollen and wet. The delicate scar at the bow of her lip white against her flushed skin. He caressed it. Unlike his, her scar was where she couldn't hide it.

"Don't say that," she said. "Don't do this to me."

His only response was to reach for her again, fingers diving into her hair, hand shaping the back of her head, where her hair tapered into her neck. He pulled her to him. Their faces touching. Their entire bodies touching.

"How will I leave you if you do this? If you don't take care of yourself? How will I let you go?"

Just like that, he knew he had been wrong. He couldn't do it. "You won't. You can't. Not because I won't take care of myself. I will. I promise. But because I can't. I can't go back there."

The push and pull of her body, leaning into him even as she tugged away, tightened her muscles, twisted her. "You can. You have to. Back there is where all your hopes and dreams are. You may feel safe with me, but everything you hold dear isn't. I wish we hadn't met. I wish . . ."

She wanted him to agree with that. Her eyes were begging him to tell her she was right. He couldn't.

"Everything would have worked out," she pushed. "If we hadn't met again, everything would have turned out okay."

"Only if you define okay as not living. Meeting you again was the best thing that's ever happened to me. All I've ever wanted was to live honestly, to make everything I say and do matter. But I was lying to myself, I wasn't feeling anything." He grabbed her hand and pressed it against his chest, where his heart thumped under jagged skin. Already the sensations were softer, her touch soothing them the way nothing ever had. Even the pain somehow less, just for being acknowledged.

"Don't," she said, "please." As though that were the only defense she had left.

"I had pushed myself inside a box so I didn't have to deal with myself. So I could be the person everyone saw in me. You let me out. I'm not afraid of myself anymore, because someone like you can love me. Because of how you see me, inside and outside that box. How can I let that go? How can I go back inside that box?"

Her hand caressed his chest, unable to pull away. "We have no choice, Yash."

"Do you really think we can let each other go? Now?" How strong did she think they were?

As though she heard his thoughts, she pulled away, stepping back and putting several feet between them. The cuts on her feet made her wince. "How can you think we have a choice? If you lose the election, I'll never forgive myself."

He tried to get close again, but she held out her arm to stop him.

"I should be the one to decide whether or not I put my ambitions in jeopardy. That should be my choice."

"But it's my life. The last time around you made that choice without me. I was left questioning my feelings. My judgement of men and relationships." She pressed her hands into her own chest. They were trembling. "I've always been proud of being connected to my inner voice. But I learned to mute it and I didn't even know it. Now you want me to do that again."

"No, I don't. I want you to listen to it this time. I want you to be true to what we're feeling."

"You're missing the point. You want me to mute the voice that is telling me that I will destroy your dreams. How will I live with myself? If I crush your family's dreams, crush the hopes of all the people who've put their faith in you. Abdul almost died!"

Didn't she think he knew that? He'd sat here all evening reliving his conversation with Abdul and Arzu. Until he'd seen her again, seen her bleeding feet, until he'd felt her hands on his scars, until he'd kissed her, he'd thought he could walk away. But there had to be another way. "We don't know that I will lose if we're together. We'll tell the truth and let people decide."

She didn't react. Her face was set, a stubborn mask. "If you tell people that you lied about your relationship with Naina—to the world, to your family—your integrity will be destroyed. Everything you've ever said or done will be questioned as a lie."

"We don't have to tell anyone it was a lie. We'll just announce a breakup. Half the marriages in our country end in divorce. We're not even married."

"If you break up with her now, after she sobbed over your fallen body, after she took on Cruz's attacks for you, after the big deal the media has made about your unconventional love story, your credibility will still be destroyed. The media won't buy 'we grew apart,' not now so close to the election. The speculation will take the focus off your issues, it will taint you. They'll go on a witch hunt. Start digging for reasons why you broke up." New horror creased her forehead. "Once the media circus starts, Julia might come back. If she claims you forced her to sleep with you when she was your intern, no one will believe you. Not just this election but your political career will be over."

"So we'll wait until after the election. We'll leave everything as it is until then." Even as he said the words he knew he'd made a mistake.

Her eyes dimmed with sadness and she stepped away from him. "So you'll make the lie worse? You'll be with me in private and pretend to be with Naina in public? You'll start something you've been dreaming about most of your life with a deception this calculated? We'll start our relationship with a lie? That's not who I am, Yash." She stepped close to him again and reached out but couldn't touch him. "I might love you in ways that make me feel completely out of control, but I don't have the hubris to believe that our love can survive that. No love can. You know what I'm saying is true."

"India. Please. Please don't do this. Let's at least talk about this." *Don't leave me.*

"You wanted me to fight for you. This is me fighting for you. I'm the only thing standing between you and everything you've ever wanted. The only answer is for me to step out of the way." She picked her phone up from the rock and dialed.

"What are you doing?" Yash asked.

"I'm taking us back to our real lives."

Chapter Twenty-Six

If only India had known that a broken heart could hurt like this. Like a fractured bone ripping muscle and sinew from skin, but also not quite like that. Physical pain was localized; this was a full-bodied hug of pain. Her thoughts hurt, her breath hurt. Her inner self felt shattered, and acknowledging that felt like a betrayal of everything she'd ever believed.

It had been two weeks since she'd left him at the foot of the mountain. Time needed to hurry up and live up to its reputation of being a healer.

"Are you going to tell me what's wrong?" Tara asked.

India folded her mother's T-shirt with more force than was strictly necessary, when what she really wanted to do was crawl into her mother's lap and cry until she couldn't breathe.

"I spoke with Dr. Ung this morning and your viral counts are down. So it's actually really good news."

Before her mother could catch her eye, India put away Tara's folded laundry and tried to slip out of the room, because, darn it, a wave of nausea was washing through her again. Something that happened each time a Yash-related memory flashed through her—his scent, the warm pressure of his touch, the gravel in his voice.

Right now the feel of soft stretchy cotton in her hands was bringing it all back.

God, why had she kissed him? Why? Now she was stuck with reliving what that felt like. She got to feel him trembling when her fingers traced his scars. The worry that he may not get help for all the trauma he'd buried wouldn't leave her alone.

"India," her mother called after her. "Sweetheart, stay and talk to me. Just for a moment."

She turned. "Is something hurting? Do you need pain meds? Is it nausea? Try to stay in bed. Should I make you tea? Tea will help." *Stop babbling. Mom is going to see how you're feeling if you don't stop babbling.*

Fortunately her phone beeped with a text. Her heart pounded even though she knew it wouldn't be Yash. She'd taken his phone from him and deleted her number.

Her profile picture on his phone had been a bowl of overnight oats. Which was the most heartbreakingly sweet thing she'd ever seen. Also she could no longer eat oats, because, yes, it hurt too much.

"Do you really think I don't have your number memorized?" he'd asked, those stubborn eyes refusing to look away as they started down the mountain, trying not to touch on the narrow trail. Then her feet had started to bleed again and he wouldn't budge until she climbed on his back and let him carry her piggyback.

"I get to help you too. You need to accept help too. Not just give it. You tell me I need to control everything, but by never letting yourself need anyone, you're controlling everything too."

If he was right, she should never have climbed on, because

now she controlled exactly nothing. Holding him with her entire body had been the last thing she should have done. He was concerned about having memorized her number? Her body had memorized every detail of his body, her heart was already way ahead in that contest.

"When you decide to send me a text or call me, in the time that it takes you to type my number into your phone I want you to talk yourself out of it."

"I don't want to do this without you. I don't want to live a lie." Then he'd looked at her in that way he had. His Promise Eyes. *"If you trust me, if you give me a chance, I will find a way for us to be together. I swear."*

"Stop it. Stop making this harder than it is."

But when he'd leaned into her and kissed her one last time against China's car before she drove off, she'd had not one single defense.

She was human. She was giving him up. She deserved one last kiss.

You deserve all of him. You deserve to be happy.

"Who's that?" Tara asked, snapping her out of her trance.

She checked her phone. "It's China. She's been texting me silly things that are happening in the movie she's watching with Brandy." At least China was being kinder to Brandy, who'd been bringing her DVDs of Laurel & Hardy comedies that were not on any of the streaming services. They were probably the only two millennials in all the world who enjoyed black-and-white comedies.

"I think China's going to be okay."

At first China had barely left her room, and India had sat with her between her brutal schedule of classes and clients as China cried wordlessly. Because sometimes there were no words to ease the pain. Then last week China had come down to the studio and started to help Ellie with the front desk and a few days after that Brandy had started bringing movies over. Yesterday India had heard her sister laugh for the first time since she'd returned.

"I think so."

"That's one less child of mine walking around like her life is over. You two have been breaking my heart."

This was terrible. Mom needed to heal, not be sad about her children. "I'm so sorry."

Before Tara could answer, China ran into the room, Brandy hot on her heels.

"What's the matter?" Tara and India both said.

"Nothing," Brandy and China said together, and China grabbed the remote sitting next to Tara and pointed it at the muted TV and turned it off.

Unfortunately, before the TV blinked off a photograph flashed on the screen. A photograph that made India sink into the bed behind her, because her legs buckled.

Her heart was pounding so hard she could feel her entire body vibrating with it. She held out her hand to China. "Give that to me."

China blinked, slipping the remote behind her. "Give what to—"

India stood and jabbed her finger into the power button on the TV and it flashed on.

China pointed the remote at the TV, trying to turn it off again, and India yanked it out of her hand.

"India, please," China said.

The local news was talking about photographs that had been released by the *National Enquirer.* The pictures had been verified by experts as being legitimate, with no Photoshopping.

The pictures under discussion were her and Yash kissing against China's car. Like their life depended on it.

The remote dropped from India's hand.

The jaws on the three women watching her also dropped open.

Yash appeared on the screen, completely calm and composed, a picture of poise and power, his usual vibrancy tinged with just the right amount of anger for the situation. He was one hundred percent in PR mode. India felt like someone had drugged her, aware of her surroundings but too confused to know what anything was. Naina held his hand, a supportive girlfriend.

"This is all a little intrusive," Naina said to the woman doing the interview, who had an impressive air of a serious journalist. "Yash and I are private people when it comes to our relationship. We've never lied about that. This was a personal moment between us. It's completely unacceptable for the media to violate us this way and to try to profit from it."

Wait, was Naina claiming it was her in the photograph?

The journalist looked appropriately embarrassed on behalf of her profession. India could picture Rico Silva and Nisha brainstorming which journalist would have the highest damage control impact before settling on this one.

"I had just returned from a trip, Abdul Khan had just woken up from a coma, it was an emotional day," Naina went on with so much indignation that for a moment even India believed that she was the one in the pictures.

Don't pan to Yash. Don't pan to Yash.

The camera panned to Yash.

His face was set in stone. Disappointment and dignity emanated from him. In his eyes was nothing.

He slid his hand out of Naina's. "I don't believe that, when three million people in this state are without health insurance and three thousand gun deaths have happened this last year alone, this is the big news story. My opponent wants to roll back regulations and increase our carbon footprint and make our wildfires worse, he wants to cut spending on healthcare and he just got thirty million dollars from the NRA, and *this* is the big news story. I had to cut short a meeting with California Black Caucus leaders in L.A. to address *this*?"

Both the journalist and Naina smiled like proud mother hens. Then the journalist turned her gaze on him again, sympathy turning to purpose. "I want to talk about your meeting with the Black leaders and the other issues on your platform, but it would be disingenuous for me to not ask, Yash Raje, are you having an affair?"

Breathe, India told herself. *Breathe*.

Naina laughed, somehow managing to make her amusement cynical yet endearing. "I love that I'm sitting here telling you that woman is me and you need to ask a man if I'm telling the truth."

For the first time India registered that Naina had cut her long hair. It was now as short as India's, and cut exactly like hers in the picture, which showed almost none of India's face. The sick churning in her stomach rose up her throat.

"I'm immensely grateful for Naina's support," Yash said without looking at Naina. "She has supported me and my dreams since we were in grade school and I couldn't be more grateful."

Naina took his hand again and squeezed it.

His eyes rested fleetingly on their joined hands, and India thought she would cry. Then his gaze came back to the camera. "The only other thing I'll say on the matter is that there is nothing clandestine or nefarious about that picture. It was an honest and private moment, and it should not have been violated. I'm in love with the woman in that picture. And that's the truth."

India's gaze clung to his across the screen, and for a moment it was just the two of them in the world. Then they went to commercial. Never in her life had she felt so many things, but the overriding sense was one of disorientation. This could not possibly be her life.

"India?" Tara and China said together, as India stared at the brightly patterned rug on the bedroom floor. *God, please don't let them see.*

"India?" They both said again, and she heard her name in his voice. Their stupid dance: *India? Yash?*

She looked up.

"What is going on?" China asked, also sliding the question sideways to Brandy.

"You heard the woman. She and Yash were caught on camera." India picked up a throw on the bed and started folding it. "They should be a little more careful."

"India! Who is idiot enough to believe her?"

Hopefully, all of California, given that India's face was not visible in the pictures. But that was China's car they were leaning on. Those were India's clothes. The rudraksha beads on her wrist were her beads. And this was her family. They knew.

India shoved the throw at her sister. "Anyone who has an interest in Yash winning needs to believe her."

That stopped China in her tracks, and India took advantage of it. "I have a class to teach." With that, she left.

A PERIOD OF three weeks should be enough for the pain to lessen, shouldn't it? Twenty-one days was the magic number for setting a habit, wasn't it? Apparently it wasn't long enough to break a habit. Or Yash Raje was just a tough habit to break. It would happen, eventually.

After leaving him at the foot of the mountain three weeks ago, India had taught four classes a day along with seeing clients and packaging the incense Tara was churning out. If she left even a moment open, everything started to spin out of control.

Nights were especially brutal.

A lifetime of mastering how to empty her mind, how to focus her breath, how to live in harmony with the universe even when it didn't give her what she wanted, and here she was, with no clear path for how to get past this.

"You've been in here for hours." China tiptoed into the yoga room.

Before India could jump up, China sat down next to her and put a hand on her shoulder, holding her in place. "Your students have been gone for half an hour."

Had it been that long?

"Should you be teaching so many classes?" China asked, her tone gentle, careful.

"Who's going to teach the classes if I don't? Who's going to make the incense sticks? Who's going to see clients?" Not everyone could fly to the other side of the world on a whim.

Good thing she didn't say that last part, because as soon as she said what she did say, guilt gripped her.

"I'm sorry," she said.

"Don't be. You're stretched too thin. I get what you're doing."

India tried to stand, but China held her back again.

"I should have seen what was happening. I did. I saw how he looked at you. I should have asked you about it, but I was too wrapped up in myself. Can you forgive me?"

"You're misunderstanding the situation."

"India, I just spent six months with someone who made me sign an NDA to make sure no one found out about us. What

Brandy said to me the other day was true. 'NDAs just mean you can't talk about it. What's obvious is still obvious.' You and Ya—"

"China! I told you. You're misunderstanding the situation." India's heart raced and ached. The only way she knew how to bear this was to never talk about it. "The only reason I've had to work this hard is because . . . because there's something Mom and I haven't told you."

China rolled her eyes.

It was time to tell her anyway. They were behind on the payments already. The late notices would start soon. India needed help.

You need to accept help too.

"Mom canceled her health insurance."

"What? When?"

"Before the diagnosis. There's no insurance, and there's nothing to pay for her treatment with. That's why I can't cancel classes. We need every penny that comes in."

"Why didn't you tell me?"

"Mom asked me not to, and you were already dealing with too much. I'm only telling you now because . . . well, I haven't come up with a way to pay the medical bills except . . . except . . ."

China looked devastated. This wasn't how India had wanted to tell her. "Finish that thought, India."

"I've been looking for a real estate agent to come in and look at the studio."

China sprang up, almost stumbling back in her haste.

"You can't decide that! This is not your home alone." She ran out of the yoga room, and India followed her.

"Just because you run the studio doesn't mean you own it." She was yelling. "You can't sell our home."

Ellie stared at them openmouthed. Mom was sitting next to

her, helping her shut down for the day, which meant Brandy was here to get her.

Both India and China spun around and saw Brandy sitting on a bench, an open magazine in her lap.

"Who's selling our home?" Mom asked from behind them, voice eerily quiet. They spun back around to face her.

"It's just an option, Mom," India said just as quietly, because it was time to ask for help. It was past time.

She couldn't make her mother's medical bills go away.

"Except it isn't an option. Five Hundred High Street will leave the Dashwood family over my dead body."

"No, Mom. Your being alive is bigger than the studio, bigger than all the memories in this home."

Tears sprang in China's eyes. "It won't come to that."

It had already come to that. "I paid the last installment from the mortgage, which we are now behind on. There are too many bills and we have nowhere to get the money from."

"Whatever I had saved up, I spent on going to Korea. God, what an idiot I was," China said.

"You were not an idiot. You were brave enough to follow your heart," India said with too much force.

Tara and China turned matching sympathetic expressions on her.

"I can't believe I'm putting you girls through this again. After you drained everything to save the building," Tara said.

Before they could respond, Brandy cleared her throat.

They had forgotten she and Ellie were right there.

"If you don't mind me interjecting . . ."

China smiled. "We mind you using the word *interjecting*."

Brandy smiled back. "I think I might have a solution. A business proposal, if you will."

"Well, then spit it out. We kinda need a solution right now," China said.

Turned out, Brandy's parents, who had done nothing but abuse and neglect her when they were alive, had left her all their wealth after they died. She hadn't touched a penny because their only condition had been that she could not donate it to charity. Yes, that's the kind of lovely people they were.

"Let me invest in the studio. You'll have the money up-front, and I can be as silent an investor as you want me to be. I haven't touched the account since I inherited it, and if I don't soon, it's going to become an inactive account and the state will get the money. I believe the studio is a sound investment. This way I'll have a retirement fund and Ellie will have a college fund and I don't have to use the money directly. Because if I touch that money directly, I won't be able to live with myself."

For a full minute everyone was silent.

"You would do that?" China said finally. "Why?"

"That money was always a symbol of all the ugliness family was synonymous with for me. You three have taken Ellie and me in, you've become our family in such a short period of time. Using the money to help you will be perfect."

"It's like it's dirty money from the Mafia or something and you're laundering it for us with goodness!" Ellie said, and they all smiled.

China threw her hands around Ellie and hugged her, then Tara joined in. "Come on," she said to India and Brandy, pulling them into the hug. "There's plenty of time to be sad about things. This is a good moment."

India squeezed into the circle of love. Yes, this was a good moment.

"This reminds me of the time we all jumped into the sewer to help retrieve a lost medallion." Tara had her dreamy storyteller face back. "It took months to get the smell off, but things you do for love always have lingering effects."

China and Ellie started giggling so hard Brandy had to thump their backs.

"We'll think about it," India said when Brandy looked at her for an answer. "There's a lot to consider. But thank you."

Brandy nodded.

"Let's not think too hard, though," Tara said, all sorts of meaning in her eyes. "It's okay to do what feels easy and to trust that the universe won't punish you for it."

China wrapped her arms around Tara's waist. "The universe finds a way," they both said, eyes on India.

"But you can't cut it off. You have to give it options," Tara added.

They stared her down, but she wouldn't give them a reaction. She had no options to give the universe.

China squeezed her arm. "The most important thing is that we won't have to sell our home. Also, Sharon called me yesterday and I'm going to see her tomorrow about going back to work. I can probably work a good bonus into the deal."

Only China could come up with that, when she was the one who'd quit without any regard to the bridges she was burning. At least she was smiling again, and that was everything. "I will work my butt off, though. I really miss work."

"Oh," Ellie said suddenly, "Tara, are you still okay with me borrowing a sari from you for Nisha's baby shower?"

All of them slid sideways looks at India, studying her worriedly. She blanked out her face the best she could. It wasn't like she could miss Nisha's baby shower. Not only had she promised

Ashna and Trisha that she would be there, but she and China were in charge of helping Ashna with the games.

"If you don't want to be there, Brandy and Ellie can help me with the games," China said still studying her like a butterfly in a shadow box.

"Why would I not want to be there?" With that, she excused herself and went upstairs, the answer to her own question ringing in her ears.

NISHA'S BABY SHOWER was technically a dohale jevan, a traditional cravings feast for the mother-to-be. *Cravings feast* just about covered it. Between DJ and Ashna, every kind of food you could dream up was on the menu. If only India could eat with the butterflies crowding her stomach. The white tent, the garlands of lights and flowers strung across the Raje estate, it was all too much of a throwback to a night many years ago.

Ashna had called it a small celebration. So India should have expected the hundred guests. At least the estate was big enough that people were spread out and there was no dearth of places to hide. Fortunately, the man India wanted to see the most and the least was nowhere to be found.

As soon as she finished helping people pin toilet paper diapers on themselves, and guess the baby's gender from all sorts of unrelated things, she slipped past the crowd heading to the food.

She was no longer worried about running into Yash. She'd been here hours without seeing him, which meant he'd made sure she didn't have to meet him with a hundred people watching.

Thank you.

She had to stop talking to him as though he were with her.

Since those pictures had leaked, he'd been campaigning relentlessly, but only five of the ten points he'd dropped in the polls after the incident had been recovered. Possibly because the Cruz campaign kept the story in the media. Raising all sorts of doubts about whether or not Naina was even in the country when the pictures were taken. Yash refused to address it. He was protecting her. If they identified the car and then traced it back to India, life as she knew it would be over.

She looked up at the back facade of the house. All those windows. Goose bumps traveled up and down her arms. At least she got to see him on TV when she couldn't bear not seeing him.

Don't watch me, it makes it worse, she said silently to the windows that gave her nothing but reflected lights.

"It's impressive, isn't it?" A woman India had never met in person came to stand next to her. The woman had the same haircut as India. Short layers in the front and close cropped in the back. She might be an inch taller, but if her fine-boned face wasn't visible, one might mistake one of them for the other.

Naina.

The sight of her hair, of all things, made rage rise inside India. Rage. She breathed through it.

"It's really tempting to dream about inheriting all this someday," Naina said in a voice that was as polished as the rest of her.

India started walking. Engaging with her was out of the question, not with the amount of anger inside her.

Naina followed, her hot pink chiffon sari moving gracefully with her. India was wearing a white-and-silver-embroidered kurta with churidar tights, so if she wanted she could easily outrun her. Actually, she could outrun most people in any clothing. It was an immodest thought, but she needed it right now.

"I can't believe you had the guts to show up today," Naina said. Obviously she knew who India was. Yash had probably told her because of the pictures.

"Nisha and I have been friends for a long time." India kept walking, making her way into the house.

The sights and smells hit her like breaking water on a dive. The very texture of the air wrapped her in a full-bodied hug, a too-tangible reminder of the gray-eyed boy who had run through these halls as a child. He was everywhere. "And I was just leaving."

Actually, who was she kidding? He was always everywhere. He was inside her.

"Did you want me to be grateful that you're leaving?"

Among other things. At first India didn't say it. Then she did.

Naina looked taken aback. "Like what? Having another woman steal what's mine?"

India stopped and turned to her. Was she for real?

Don't engage with her.

But the look on Naina's face was too superior, too entitled. "If indeed one of us is stealing what's not theirs, it isn't me."

That shocked Naina so much she froze. India took that chance to make her escape. She had to leave before the energy of this place seeped into her lungs even more than it already had. She could smell him. She could feel him smiling against her lips.

Where was her coat? When she'd arrived she'd gone straight to the backyard and someone had taken it. Her eyes fell on a sign on a door that said COATS. She ran into the room. It was beautiful. Lined with bookshelves and with a high-frescoed ceiling. A painting covered almost all of one wall: a man in regal finery of blue and gold. He had Yash's stubborn jaw, Yash's gentle eyes.

Ram.

The man smiled down at her, the challenge in his gaze boring into her. He'd fought for what he wanted, even when he knew he could hang for it. On a brass plaque in the wide carved gold frame were the words *Victorious Through Truth*.

He never told a lie in his life.

Hair fell across his forehead and an unholy urge to push it up moved inside India.

"You know Yash and I have been engaged for ten years, right?" Naina said, letting herself into the room. Thankfully there were no other people around.

"That's a lie," India said, and turned to the coat hangers on wheels lined up along one wall. She started searching for her jacket.

"Is that what he told you? Yash made a promise to me."

India spotted her jacket. *Take it and leave.* Grabbing it, she walked past Naina without answering.

"God, you're one of those quiet pushover types, aren't you? Sometimes I just don't understand Yash."

India spun around, heart thumping.

"It's obvious you don't. If you understood Yash, this would be so much easier."

That made Naina give a condescending laugh. It was obviously how she processed things, by looking down at them. The exact opposite of how Yash processed things, by coming eye to eye with them. "Yash and I aren't exactly going for easy. We want to do hard things. World-changing things. It's not something a yoga instructor would understand. If you don't leave him alone, your selfishness is going to ruin everything."

"*My* selfishness is going to ruin everything for *you*. That's a really selfless sentiment."

That stopped Naina. Suddenly the superiority in her gaze turned to something else. Fear? For the first time she looked like she saw India as more than *just a yoga instructor.*

"You and Yash *have* done great things with your life. You will continue to. But Yash also deserves to be happy."

He deserved to be loved. He deserved not to live a lie.

"Yash loves me."

India pressed the jacket to her chest. "Yes, he does. You're family to him."

That made Naina step back. "Don't you dare patronize me. I don't need you to tell me that. Yash's happiness is in being governor of California. Then moving on to even bigger things. I'm the one who will get him there. You're the one who will get in his way."

Every time India thought she could walk away without answering, the woman said something that made it impossible. "And you don't care how you get there? You don't care that you're holding him to ransom when all he was doing was helping you? You don't care that you've turned him into a crutch?"

Naina paled at that. India had hit a nerve. But every aha moment fought you. That's what made the journey so hard.

India pointed the jacket she was clutching at Naina. "That's my hair you're wearing. That's the thing about lies, after a point you stop noticing you're telling them."

I don't want to do this without you. I don't want to live a lie.

Naina touched her hair. "You think I *wanted* to cut my hair? I was protecting him from losing everything. That was the promise we made. To help each other. He wanted me to do this."

That was a lie.

"Yash did not ask you to cut your hair." The clarity with which India knew this nudged apart the clouds that had been fogging her mind. "You did that without his knowledge." Her heart started racing. How had she missed this? "You did it because it made the lie too big to be reversible. Too public. Too premedidated." She pressed a hand to her mouth, covering the laugh that escaped her. "By claiming to be me in those pictures, you made sure any hope Yash and I had was over."

Naina paled. But she wasn't the only one who'd been forced to look in a mirror she'd been avoiding.

When those pictures first came out, India had been terrified, but there had also been a spark of hope. Hope for the truth to come out even if it was by accident. Then Naina claiming to be in the pictures had snuffed that hope out. But that hope had been there, and it meant something.

Chapter Twenty-Seven

Yash had been watching India from his childhood room. When they'd been setting up, he may or may not have manipulated the placement of the tent so he had the perfect vantage point to watch the baby shower games from his window. Ashna had let slip that India and China were helping with those.

He felt not a whit of guilt for it. Not seeing her for a month was more penance than any man deserved for any crime. Putting her in a position where they came face-to-face with an audience comprised of his entire family was something he would never do to her. Staying in his room had been easy. The family had given up on him spending any time with them and written it off as campaign stress.

Already Naina knew who she was. He'd had to tell her after those photographs. He kept reminding himself that Naina was essentially a good person and wouldn't hurt India. Her pretending to be India in those pictures had saved India from having her life turned upside down by the media. It had also saved his election. As Naina reminded him every single time they met, which was almost never when he could help it.

As the crowd made its way to the food tent, India headed for the house. She was leaving. The thought came with so much panic, he had to breathe through it. The way she had taught him.

Suddenly she looked up and studied the house. She was searching for him. In that way she had of searching for him with her entire being.

Find me, please. Fight for me.

For a few moments they were talking again, as though their gazes were locked, their bodies full of each other. Then someone came and stood next to her. It was the way India's body stiffened that made Yash look away from her to who it was.

Shit.

India stepped away from her, but Naina was in one of her belligerent moods. She followed India into the house.

Yash ran out of his room and down the corridor and down the stairs. He ran through the foyer to the entrance and out to the porte cochere. His parents were saying bye to some friends and they stopped him, bombarding him with questions about the campaign trail. Then jumping right to the one thing Indian aunties and uncles never stopped doing no matter how old you got. They reminisced about how small he'd been when they first knew him. In this case he'd already been in college, so the tearing up was a little excessive.

"You okay?" Ma said, holding his hand and studying him in that way she'd taken to studying him all the time.

"I'm looking for someone," he said without thinking about it. "Did you see Naina come out here?"

"No." Ma's examination grew even more focused.

Tugging his hand from hers and giving her what he hoped was a please-stop-worrying look, he went back into the house and pulled the door shut before he started running from room to room looking for India and Naina.

They had turned the library into the coat room. He pushed the door open and went in and was immediately struck by the full-body blow of her voice.

"That's my hair you're wearing. That's the thing about lies, after a point you stop noticing you're telling them," India said with all the calm that made her *her*. Then there was that edge under there. Also all her.

"You think I *wanted* to cut my hair? I was protecting him from losing everything. That was the promise we made. To help each other. He wanted me to do this." Naina sounded livid.

"Yash did not ask you to cut your hair. You did that without his knowledge," India said with absolute certainty. "You did it because it made the lie too big to be reversible. Too public. Too premeditated." Her hand pressed into her mouth, covering the laugh that escaped her, as though she couldn't believe that she had missed this. "By claiming to be me in those pictures, you made sure any hope Yash and I had was over."

She'd had hope?

She'd had hope.

"How were you naive enough to think you and Yash had a chance?" Naina said.

"Because truth has to . . ."

". . . count for something," Yash and India said together.

India spun toward him. And there it was, the endless peace of her gaze. Breath whooshed out of him, weight lifted off his shoulders.

"Because love has to count for something." He took a step closer, and her body sagged, mirroring all the relief he was feeling. "I breathe differently when she's around. I feel . . . I feel alive in ways I never have." Her eyes soaked him up, her gaze traveling down his body. She was checking to make sure he was okay.

"You thought we had a chance?" he said to her. "Why didn't you say something?"

"What is wrong with you, Yash?" Panic tinged Naina's always-confident demeanor. "You can't give up everything." She turned to India. "You'd let him lose everything for you?"

India froze in place at Naina's words. Only in her eyes could a million emotions flit by in the space of one breath.

"None of it means anything without you." He fell into her eyes, all those shades of brown, earth opening up for him.

"Yash, beta, what is going on here?" *Great, great, great.* The last voice he wanted to hear right now was Ma's.

India studied his expression, her own getting stronger, and he took strength from it. Her eyes moved to Ma, who had to be standing behind him.

"Mina Auntie!" Naina said. "Shree Uncle!"

Holy double shit. Yash turned around and saw his parents looking at him like they had no idea who he was. How much had they heard?

"What do you mean, none of it means anything without her?" Ma said.

India took a step closer to him, moving automatically as though she couldn't help but be his shield.

"Who is this girl?"

Oh, Dad, please, not now.

"Shree!" His mother had never snapped at his father in front of her children, let alone in front of anyone else, and HRH went utterly still. "You will let me handle this."

She went to India and took her hand. "Hi, I'm Mina Raje. Haven't we met?"

"I'm India Dashwood." India's voice was as calm as he'd ever heard it. She was breathing through this, and he followed suit.

"Ah yes, you're China's sister. Thank you so much for your help with Yash. And with Ashna for so many years. Ashna's been suggesting I come to you for my knee."

"I'd be happy to help."

Suddenly Ma realized what she might have sounded like and looked embarrassed. "I hope that didn't come across as me being rude. I was just . . ."

"You're trying to put me at ease. I appreciate it. Thank you." She turned to Yash. "I have to leave. Will you be okay?"

Yash felt something slash through him. "I'll take you home. We have to talk."

Before she could answer, HRH spoke. "Why would he not be okay? What is she talking about? What is going on?"

"Did you . . . are you hiding something from us? Did you break up with Naina and not know how to tell us?" Ma asked.

"Can we talk about this later?" Yash said. "I need to walk India out."

"No, Yash," India said, "You need to talk to your parents. You need to listen to what they have to say. Please."

"Can you stay for just a moment longer?" Ma said, then she turned on Yash. "Did we ever give you the impression that you couldn't talk to us? I thought our relationship was more open than that." It wasn't like Ma to make things about her. She didn't exactly understand boundaries, but she did understand secrets. "When did you and Naina break up? Why didn't you tell us? Naina?"

Naina's jaw was clenched. She looked devastated, but there was also something else in her eyes. Defeat? Resignation? She threw another look at Yash and India, and he had a sense that she saw something she hadn't let herself see until now.

"I think you all have a lot to figure out," Naina said. "Yash, you know where to find me if you need me." Then, in true Naina fashion, she left the scene of the mess, head held high.

"Did you cheat on her?" HRH said. "Did I teach you nothing? You're running for the bloody highest office in the state. Haven't you seen the mess an affair makes of people's careers?"

"Thanks, Dad. For telling me that cheating is wrong because it can ruin my career."

"Really, that's what you think I just said?"

"Yes, that's exactly what you said."

"Well, forgive me, what I meant to say was that I can't believe that you would be so irresponsible."

"Please stop," India said, stepping between HRH and Yash, her voice more forceful than he'd ever heard it. "Don't you know your son at all?"

Yash didn't think he'd ever seen his father's jaw drop open, or his mother look at another woman with such . . . delighted respect.

"The bigger question, young lady, is exactly how well do *you* know my son?"

"Dad!"

India met HRH's imperious glare as though he were one of her students in need of help. "I know him well enough to know that he hasn't been irresponsible a day in his life." Then she turned around and looked at Yash, everything he'd ever wanted to be reflected in her eyes. "Except when it comes to his own needs."

"What's wrong with his needs?" HRH spat out, a vein throbbing in his neck.

"I think we need to ask our son that." Ma placed a gentle hand on HRH's arm.

"I think that's a very good idea," India said to Ma, then turned to Yash again, another goodbye in her eyes. "You promised me you'd take care of yourself."

He took her hand. He didn't care that his parents were watching. Her gaze didn't flicker away from his for even a second. "You never answered my question. Did you want us to have a chance?"

"Yes," the whisper slipped out and she swallowed. "But, it's too late, Yash. There's no way to do this without admitting that you lied. And you can't do that." Then, she turned to his parents. "It was nice meeting you."

As she slipped out of the room, Yash felt her leave. With every fiber of his being.

"Into my office. Now," Mom said, leaving him and HRH to follow without turning around.

As soon as they'd shut her office door, she turned on Yash. "What is going on, beta?"

"Isn't it obvious what's going on?" HRH said. "The way he was looking at that yoga instructor—"

"Dad, for heaven's sake, her name is India." And damn if his voice didn't do a restless, worshipful thing when he said it.

"Oh, Yash." This from Ma, hand pressed to heart and everything. God save us all from Indian mothers. "Beta . . . oh, Yash." She fell into the chair behind her and placed her head in her hands.

"You're being very dramatic right now, Ma."

Although all he wanted was to go racing after India, so the moment did seem to call for drama.

"Dramatic? My whole life I've dreamt of hearing that note in your voice when you talked about Naina. And I never did. Now, when you're leading in the polls, when you're a month from winning this, and the public loves Naina . . . *now* you look like this!"

She pointed a very, very dramatic finger at his face. "And you think *I'm* being dramatic?"

"Are you encouraging him, Mina? He will mess this up over my dead body."

"Shree. It's nighttime, I'd like you not to say inauspicious things in my home."

"He's going to win this election. He just has to keep his pants on." Both Yash and Ma groaned, and HRH raised a hand. "I mean that figuratively. He's been with Naina for ten years. No son of mine betrays someone this way."

"About that . . ." Yash said. "I think you should sit down, Dad."

For once his father complied without argument, and Yash told them. At long last, he told his parents that he and Naina had lied. He told them about meeting India at Nisha and Neel's wedding. He told them how she had helped him after the shooting. He navigated the ugly parts, but they seemed to know more than he'd given them credit for.

"So if you hadn't met this yoga—fine, India—you and Naina could have turned it into a real relationship," HRH said.

Mom had been eerily quiet. She looked at Dad with an expression Yash couldn't decipher. "Sometimes you make me so angry, Shree. How can you parent as though you were never young?"

"I never lied to my parents. At least not about anything important."

Ma scoffed. It was even mean. "Really? Have we conveniently forgotten about Namrata Gadgil?"

Dad, for the first time in Yash's life, blushed.

"Well?"

"Well, I didn't bloody well have an election to lose."

Ma was standing now, hands on hips, glaring down at a man who honestly could have used a little more glaring in years past.

"We're assuming that Yash is only going to win because he was shot and because Naina was caught crying on camera. I thought you believed in our son. Those are the least of the reasons why he'd going to win."

Dad did not look happy, but those were exactly the words Yash needed to hear.

For the past ten years Yash had lied. Even as the lie became bigger, he'd let it slide. He'd put the election before the truth. He'd believed the narrative that you had to come to power first, then you could do the work you held dear. That belief had turned him into a politician. Instead of the people he wanted to work for, he'd allowed the system to become his guiding force.

"You know how our son is," Ma continued. "He becomes obsessed with what he wants and then you can't get him to back off."

"I'm standing right here, Ma."

"I know. That's why I'm saying it. So you can hear me. I'm not saying it's a bad thing. I'm saying your greatest strength is knowing what you want. Of all my children, you have the gift of clarity. It's the things you're clear about, that's what sets you apart. You only lose your way when you let what everyone else wants from you become tangled with what you want."

In all his life Yash had never felt such relief.

"Giving Julia that internship, going to see her. It was about doing what Trisha wanted you to do." Terrible sadness flashed in Ma's eyes. Yash knew her history as a child star in Bollywood was wrapped up in pain. He knew what Julia had done to him had broken Ma's heart in ways he didn't fully understand. "It took me a long time to understand this, but you can't make up for other people's evil. It's on them when they hurt you. And this farce with Naina . . . I knew something was not right. But I thought it was what you needed. I should have pushed harder for you to get therapy, but you always seemed so strong, I didn't want you to second-guess your strength. But I was being an ostrich. You gave Julia's actions even more power when you believed that it was your fault. And our actions reinforced it. I'm sorry."

He found himself squatting in front of Ma, her hand in his. "Thanks, Ma. I am going to need therapy for that. I've already set something up." India was wrong. It wasn't too late, and Yash would be damned if he didn't do all he could to be his best self for her.

"Good," she said. "Better late than never." Then she asked the million-dollar question. "What are we going to do?"

"Don't do anything reckless, son," Dad said. "The election is next month. Let's wait until it's over. Take some time to think about it."

"Don't you think he's already thought about it?" Ma said. "You just have to trust yourself, beta. Focus on what matters to you and don't let it get all mixed up with what others want."

Chapter Twenty-Eight

India hadn't heard from Yash since she'd left him at his parents' house exactly one week ago. This surprised India more than it should have. It also scared her because she knew the man, and she knew the look in his eyes when he'd said goodbye. Granted the election was three weeks away and he'd been in a different town every day campaigning, but she knew he was up to something. Her inner voice knew it too, the desolateness inside her had eased, the perpetual thoughts of him had turned hopeful instead of painful.

So when his three sisters knocked on the door of her studio, her heartbeat couldn't be blamed for doing a frenzied thing. Her last class was done, her last client had been seen. She'd been about to go upstairs and crawl into bed.

"Hey, India," the three of them said as she gaped at them and studied the empty street behind them.

"Were you expecting someone else?" Nisha asked, all innocence.

India shook her head and said nothing.

"The three of us were supposed to watch Yash's press conference at my place," Ashna said, her tone exactly as innocent as Nisha's. "But my TV blew out. Can we, you know, watch here?"

India stepped back, letting them in. "Press conference? About what?"

Their response was three synchronized shrugs.

Trisha looked at her watch. "It started about a minute ago."

India raced up the stairs without waiting for them to follow her. *What are you up to, Yash?*

China and Tara were already sitting in front of the TV, and they scooted to make space, as the Raje sisters followed India into the living room. Had China and mom been expecting them to show up? Had they planned this?

What was *this*, exactly?

The three of them squeezed onto the sectional and India dropped down on the floor.

On the screen Rico was behind a podium addressing a room full of reporters. Just behind him, Yash, flanked by Brandy and Abdul, waved and nodded to the audience as Rico urged everyone to go out and vote.

The women on her sectional, who looked entirely too comfortable, studiedly ignored her, even when she threw them an openly curious glance.

Suddenly Rico cleared his throat and everyone in the room sat up. "We wanted to announce that the California Black Caucus and BLM just endorsed Yash Raje."

The press applauded with polite enthusiasm.

The president of the California Black Caucus came to the mic and praised Yash's commitment and allyship. India's heart filled with pride.

Next Rico introduced the president of the police union. He announced that the union was endorsing Yash's plan to reorganize and retrain the California police.

How on earth had he managed that? She knew he had been

working on it, and his brother Vansh had been helping, but this was possibly the most amazing thing India had seen in politics in her lifetime.

The press went nuts. The questions were endless. Yash answered them in a way that would make even the most cynical believe again. He was in his element. Something about him was dazzling, rejuvenated. All the earnest enthusiasm of the Yash she'd met ten years ago. All the confidence and power of the Yash who'd slipped under her skin again.

With every answer he gave, her living room exploded with opinions. It was no secret that his sisters adored him. For years when she and China had met up with them, she'd had to block out their fawning. Now she soaked it up.

Why were they here?

As they chattered on, India couldn't get a word out. It didn't seem to matter, because everyone had decided to act like she wasn't here.

"There is one more thing," Rico said finally. "Yash has another announcement of a somewhat more private nature."

"Are you finally getting married, Mr. Raje?" someone shouted from the crowd.

Yash smiled. "I'm glad you asked." There was no worry in his eyes. Nothing tortured. They were clear and brilliant. He looked freer than India had ever seen him look.

What are you up to, Yash?

"Last month when I said I wanted to work with the BLM leaders and the police union to come up with a plan to restructure the department, my opponent said it was just talk. It wasn't. I've never made a promise I can't keep. Not as state senator, not as U.S. attorney. I believe that the need to tell the truth is what defines me. It's how I define myself. That and going after what I want. I want to change the trajectory of our state, and I believe that I know how to do that."

He let that sink in before he continued. "I have, however, told one lie, and I want to own up to it now, before you put your faith in me and vote for me. Even though I believe that it has nothing to do with why you should vote for me as your governor."

The audience had gone eerily silent. India squeezed her knees to her chest and reminded herself to breathe.

On the screen, his eyes bored into her. "Naina Kohli and I are not engaged. She is not my girlfriend. All we've ever been is friends." A murmur went through the audience, but Yash went on, voice strong and calm. "Our relationship has always been one of trust and loyalty. For the sake of our families we did try to have a relationship, but we've never been in love. We never intended to be life partners or anything more than friends. When the media became fascinated by our relationship I should have set the record straight, but I didn't.

"When she cried after I'd been shot, her tears were not a lie, but inadvertently that footage turned into a romantic-tragic symbol. Yes, it was tragic. But there was nothing romantic about it. Which brings me to the lie."

India gasped. *No, Yash. Don't.*

Nisha and China pressed gentle hands into her back.

Yash went on, sincere eyes locked on the camera, *locked* on her. "The pictures taken on the day when Abdullah Khan woke up from his coma . . ." He turned around and looked at Abdul, and anyone with a pulse had to feel the connection between them. "Those were not pictures of Naina and me. Naina, being a friend, wanted to prevent a scandal from ruining my campaign, and so she decided to say it was her. I should have stopped her, but I was afraid for the safety and privacy of the woman in the pictures.

She's the only woman I've ever loved. But she did not sign up to have her privacy violated with scandal. Especially when there is no scandal, because Naina and I were never together.

"As you can imagine, I was advised by my team, by my family, by my political advisers—all of whom have worked tirelessly for my campaign—to not make this announcement today, just three weeks before the election, especially considering where I stand in the polls. Everyone believed waiting until after the election would be prudent. But relationships that start with lies often lead to disaster, and I don't want my relationship with you as your governor to start with one. So there you have it. I lied. I am profoundly sorry that I did. But every promise I've made to you has been sincere. I will work every day to fulfill each one, to make California carbon neutral, to make sure every Californian has access to affordable health care, to make schools safer for our children, to address land management to control wildfires, and to make housing fairly and equitably available to all. This is my promise to you and I hope that you'll believe that I'll keep it."

India pressed her hand to her heart; she wasn't sure if it was still beating.

"That's the bravest thing I've ever seen anyone do." Tara was the first to speak. "It reminds me of that man who was stuck under a boulder and cut off his own arm."

Every one of them stared at her, completely speechless.

"What?" Tara said. "He lived. When the choice is between life and death, you have to decide what's dispensable."

India felt suspended between joy and panic. Yash had just shown her that she was the life he wanted to choose. Did that mean that he'd decided that his campaign was dispensable?

"What is her name?" A reporter from the *San Jose Mercury News* asked.

Yash smiled. "I think I owe Rico twenty bucks for calling that as the first question. I'll tell you what, let's deal with one reveal at a time. I'll ask her if she's okay with me telling you and we can set up another press conference if she's up for it."

The press wasn't happy with that answer but Yash stood strong on it and they turned back to questions about restructuring the police.

"Who do you think this mystery woman is?" Trisha asked, scratching her head, and China started to giggle.

"Oh, did I mention that they record the press conferences and play them with a half-hour lag?" Nisha said casually. "That means Yash left the studio about half an hour ago."

The doorbell rang and India jumped off the couch and flew down the stairs.

"Hello, India, I hope I'm not intruding." His mother? What on earth was going on? "May I come in?"

"Mrs. Raje!"

Mina Raje looked over her shoulder, because India had searched the street behind her and she'd noticed. "Were you expecting someone else?"

India moved aside. "I'm sorry, I didn't mean to be rude. Come in. May I help you?"

"I certainly hope so. I doubt there's anyone else who can help me right now."

India swallowed.

"Hi, Ma!" The entire lot of them were in the yoga studio lobby now.

Tara stepped forward, looking stronger than she'd looked in a while. "If it isn't the Gubernatorial Mother."

"I don't think that's a real thing, Mom," China said, and everyone laughed.

"It should be," Mina said.

They hugged, Yash's mother and hers, batik caftan and linen suit meeting in a puff of warmth and comforting scents.

The door sounded again. India wrapped her arms around herself as she walked to the door. Her face felt warm, her throat tight. The need for that to be Yash was a fever inside her.

It wasn't.

It was Brandy. Alone. "Were you expecting someone else?" she said, looking over her shoulder, blue eyes warm.

Where is he?

Chutney let out a long slow whine upstairs, then a series of yearning barks. India ran out of the door and around the building. There, leaning against his uncle's fence, waving up at her dog, was the most beautiful man she'd ever known. She flew at him.

He caught her out of the air, strong arms wrapping her up. Then she was devouring him. Or he was devouring her. Their mouths hungry for each other. Their entire starved selves ravenous.

Why did you do it? she wanted to ask, but it was the bravest thing she'd ever witnessed, and she knew the answer already. "What was that?" she asked instead.

"That was me being a public servant instead of a politician."

She was so damn proud of him. "I love you," she said simply.

"I love you." He kissed her again.

For a while there were no more words, just his lush lips, his hot taste, his sweet breath.

"Do you think they're watching us?" she asked finally, and they both looked up at the window. It was just Chutney, head tilted at an angle. So either they were all hiding behind the curtains or they were exercising amazing restraint.

"I'm sorry it took me so long to get all that worked out before the press conference. My sisters were supposed to ask China to make sure you watched, but of course they had to show up here themselves, and then Ma had to 'check up' on them because . . . because that's going to be our life now. If you choose it."

"I choose it." Her heart had already chosen it years ago. Tears started streaming down India's face. The man had finally made her cry.

He kissed her again. "You should also know that Jiggy Mehta had asked Naina out and she'd declined, but she offered to go out with him, so it looked like she did the breaking up."

"But you said no."

"That's not how I want to win. Not the election. Not you. She's not a bad person. She just doesn't see anything but her goals."

"I know someone like that." India pushed his hair off his face. "What about the election?"

"What about it? I did my part, now I just have to trust the universe to do the rest." He wiped her tears.

"What if you lose?" she asked.

He tucked her hair behind her ear. "I've already won. Because I have you."

THE WEEKS BEFORE the election were a whirlwind. As expected, Yash's poll numbers nosedived after the press conference. Cruz leveraged his advantage like the politician he was. If India had a penny for every time the Cruz campaign used the word "lies" or "liar" she might be able to pay off the debt on the studio. But the Raje campaign kept its focus on the issues and on the courage it had taken for Yash to tell the truth. In the end, Yash's lead in the polls stabilized at a little under five points.

Yash was wholly consumed by campaigning, and very little changed in terms of how much India saw him. A lot changed in terms of how much she used her phone. They had decided to take things slow until after the election. But that didn't mean they had to spend the nights he was in town apart. To no one's surprise Yash was not good at taking things slow. He was also dismally inept at holding back. Being with him was being with all of him, every bit of who he was, fully exposed, given over. His need for her, his hunger for her pleasure, it was so determined that she had not one defense against it. He unraveled her, dismantled every piece of hubris she'd ever had about knowing her body and all it was capable of feeling. Being with Yash as he discovered his desires was becoming one with her own.

As Yash had promised, he asked India if she was comfortable going public as his girlfriend. She'd said yes. All that meant was that she had to make one press conference appearance and give a couple of interviews. There were some salacious pieces about the affair that Yash and she were apparently sweeping under the carpet. Rico had assured India that most Americans didn't know the name of their governor's significant other, let alone those of their gubernatorial candidates, except in the presence of a scandal. Since the scandal had no basis in truth, their interest would pass soon enough.

On election day India spent the afternoon knocking on doors with China, who couldn't stop talking about Brandy as they urged people to get out and vote. As the polls closed, India met Yash in his office. His sleeves were rolled up, his topmost button was unbuttoned, in his eyes was the focus of an athlete in the last seconds of the closest game of his life. She'd brought in a giant bowl of mango chia overnight oats for the staff whom she'd met soon after Yash's press conference. Every one of them wore the same focus as Yash on their exhausted faces as they tracked results in what was turning out to be a nail-biter.

The entire family was there too, including Vansh, who was

the exact opposite of his brother in every way, except that both brothers were utterly calm in the storm. Something they had obviously inherited from their father. Shree Raje had completely surprised India by texting her daily updates on Yash's numbers for the past three weeks and acting like she'd been part of all this forever. As soon as India walked into the office, Shree gave her a hug and filled her in on where the returns stood, making Yash roll his eyes even as he couldn't stop smiling.

For most of the evening India sat tucked in to Yash's side and tried not to chew her nails, while he tried to put everyone at ease by teaching them how to dunk donuts into overnight oats.

At 11:00 P.M., Nisha screamed when NPR projected the winner. Yash had won with fifty-two-point-nine percentage points, one of the closest races in recent history.

But that wasn't why Nisha had screamed. At least that wasn't the only reason.

At 1:00 A.M., Ram Raje Graff came bawling into the world. Four weeks early, just like his oldest uncle, as his grandmother informed them all.

At 3:00 A.M., Yash and India stood outside Yash's condo in San Francisco. In what had to be the nth miracle that day, they were alone.

"Nisha stole our baby's name," Yash said.

"That's exactly what I was thinking," India said, and he smiled, this man who was already naming their children. Then he pressed her into his front door and kissed the breath out of her.

"Are you ever going to take me inside, or do I have to carry you over the threshold?" she said against his lips.

"I know you can."

"Of course I can."

He threw the door open, then leaned over and picked her up. "Maybe next time. This time allow me the romanticism."

She wrapped her arms around his neck, melting into his hold, melting into him. Feeling heady and winded, she picked a kiss from his lips. He pushed into it, gave everything to her, his lips hungry and pliant. All of him laid bare with just that touching of their lips.

Everything inside her was shaking when he pulled away. His eyes were intoxicated, arousal opening up the centers in dark whorls, his aura so brilliant it blinded her.

"At this point, Governor Raje, I'd allow you just about anything."

He placed her on the bed and fell to his knees in front of her, pulling off his shirt, then his inner shirt, hands sure. The beauty of his body, the confident grace, the complete and utter surrender made her belly do a flip.

God, how was he so perfect?

It was the last discernible thought India had for a very, very long time.

Acknowledgments

By all definitions 2020 was a challenging year. A year that connected people across the earth over a joint experience equally life-altering for everyone. A year when the importance of political leadership proved just as critical as personal responsibility. I was only able to get through this year with my heart and hope intact because I got to escape into Yash and India's world where both those things bore meaning. But the words did not always come easily, and I needed the help of more people than I can fit into these Acknowledgments, all of whom I am deeply grateful for.

First and foremost, my biggest thanks to Manoj, Mihir, and Annika for being the easiest people on earth to be stuck in quarantine with. To have a family you like almost as much as you love them is my greatest gift. And to my parents for being my loudest cheering squad even when all we had was the phone.

Without the help of my writing sisterhood, I'd still be rolled up in a ball believing that the anxiety of this new world was impossible to write around. Virginia Kantra, Barbara O'Neal, Jamie Beck, Falguni Kothari, Kwana Jackson, Sally Kilpatrick, Liz Talley, Priscilla Oliveras, Tracy Brogan, thank you for holding my hand every day, and Donna Kauffman whose loss is felt in every one of our conversations and always will be. Between deep-dive critiques, brainstorming, and letting me laugh and cry in your arms, I don't know how I did this before you. To my entire sisterhood of South Asian romance writers, but especially Alisha Rai, Suleikha Snyder, and Nisha Sharma, thank you for standing in this lonely space with me from the start. And to Kristan Higgins, Christina Lauren, Nalini Singh, Julia Quinn, and Beverly Jenkins thank you for your stories and your unyielding support, but even more for modeling generosity and grace, always.

To my bestie, Dr. Nishita Kothary, M.D., for letting me pick her brilliant brain for all my admittedly macabre story needs and to my Californian family for their huge—and fortuitously opinionated—love for California. Deep Sathe and Kalpana Thatte the Rajes are the Rajes because of you.

Any book is only as good as its beta readers. Uzma Jalaluddin, Suzanne Park, Swati Bakre, Nishaad Navkal, and Emily Red-ington Modak your generous hearts and eagle eyes guided me through making the story in my head come to fruition on the page exactly as I wanted it to.

As always, none of this would come to anything without the faith and excitement of my editor Tessa Woodward and my agent Alexandra Machinist, your gentle and fierce support means more than you will ever know. And the truly badass team at Harper-Collins, especially Pam Jaffee, Kaitie Leary, and Elle Keck who work tirelessly to get my books into the hands of readers.

Speaking of getting books into the hands of readers, this year more than ever, the selfless work of librarians, booksellers, re-viewers, and bloggers was what kept that connection open, and no amount of thanks feels enough. Which brings me to the very reason why I get to do this thing I love to do: *You*, Dear Readers. Thank you from the very bottom of my heart for falling with me into these stories that are pieces of my heart.

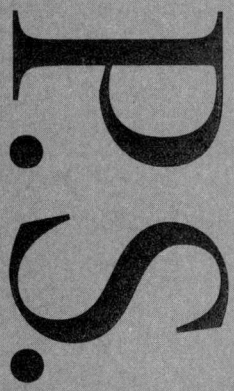

About the author

About the Book

Insights,
Interviews
& More . . .

Meet Sonali Dev

USA Today bestselling author SONALI DEV writes Bollywood-style love stories that explore universal issues. Her novels have been named Best Books of the Year by *Library Journal*, NPR, the *Washington Post*, and *Kirkus Reviews*, and she has won numerous accolades, including the American Library Association's award for best romance, the RT Reviewer Choice Award for best contemporary romance, and multiple RT Seals of Excellence. Dev has been a RITA finalist and has been listed for the Dublin Literary Award. She lives in Chicagoland with her husband, two visiting adult children, and the world's most perfect dog. ∾

Behind the Book Essay

The most basic requirement for being an author might be being a dreamer. You can't write books unless you can dream up stories. You can't survive publishing unless you take your dreams very, very seriously. Whether or not anyone else does.

Writing a series of books set under a single-story universe that paid homage to my four favorite Jane Austen novels was one of those dreams that I've carried inside me for so long that I don't even remember when the dream took birth. All I know is that it predates my choosing to follow writing as a profession. When I was a young girl growing up in India, Austen's heroines were some of the first female protagonists I read in books or watched on the screen who had a sense of self-worth despite living in a world where they had no power. Something about her stories reflected what I naturally believed about myself even when the world around me didn't reinforce those beliefs. And I credit her novels—the four that I read as a young person: *Pride and Prejudice, Persuasion, Sense and Sensibility,* and *Emma*—with teaching me how to process the world.

Like knowing for a fact that social norms and rules were often ridiculous and based on making life easier for a few. Like knowing that waiting for someone who valued you and whom you valued was always better than settling for what everyone told you was your best path simply because it was the easiest available one. Like knowing that life always gives you more chances when you mess up the ones you have. Like knowing that putting character over coolness when it comes to people you let into your life was perfectly okay.

Every one of those lessons spoke to my ability to value myself, enough to search for and prioritize what I wanted from life. They helped me put blinders on to block out the messaging around me that said otherwise. As a young mother, when I became obsessed with my own writing, my own dreams, I had a close friend tell me that she was "in awe of my ability to put my dreams before motherhood." She, on the other hand, had decided that raising her children would come before everything else.

If I had a penny for every time I've heard a mother say that, I'd be able to leave my children trust funds. Had I not mulled over subversive societal messaging and conditioning my entire life (thanks at least in part to Jane), those words would have broken me as they have been historically designed to, even though that was not my friend's intention. I heard them for what they were, the use of a tool that had given women an inducement if not an excuse to not invest in their own dreams. Not ▶

Behind the Book Essay *(continued)*

for a moment did I question my belief that motherhood and dreams were not at odds. I was fortunate enough to have learned that self-worth could exist without social reinforcement.

Being that Jane's writing had such an influence on me as a person, all my stories were always subconsciously influenced by her books in one way or another. It wasn't until the Rajes took hold of my imagination almost a decade ago that I knew exactly what I wanted to do with my dream of paying homage to her stories and tying them up in one story universe. At the time I had just signed my first contract, and my first book hadn't yet been released.

My now-adult children were middle schoolers then. My life was a twilight zone between pragmatic, suburban domesticity and the big irrepressible dreams looming on the horizon like a promise. I knew almost nothing about the business of writing, but my stories filled me up to exploding. Even though I was determined to never make a choice between motherhood and my dreams, I had made the conscious choice to always make motherhood about my children. Which didn't mean I had to hide my dreams or my stories from them. Their childhood was closely tangled with my writers' meetings, revision and rejection hell, and the highs of accolades and sales.

One evening as I drove my thirteen-year-old son to his math class, I was so filled up with my Raje story ideas that I started telling him about them. "Do you want to help me come up with titles?"

He shrugged in his bored adolescent way. "Sure."

He's always been terribly clever with words and ideas. As I explained the general plot of each book, titles popped out of him with ease. Most funny, some delightfully inappropriate.

Then we came to *Sense and Sensibility*. "She's a yoga guru . . ." I started.

Before I could even finish, he shouted out, "*Incense and Sensibility*!"

I've rarely had a more proud or smug moment in my life. "That's brilliant," I told him. And even back then I knew that when I wrote that book, that was a title I'd fight for.

I never had to. Seven years later my editor's eyes lit up when I mentioned it. So very many dreams came together at once in that moment, a simple thing like a book title popping into my child's head bringing together all the pieces that make up my life. All the pieces that have ever made up my dreams. All the validation I've ever needed for being a dreamer without compromise, a path Jane herself might have set me on. A path I can only hope reading my work might set another person on. ❧

Reading Group Guide

1. Family is incredibly important to both Yash and India. How do their perceived roles within their families impact how they see themselves and what they're willing to sacrifice? How do they hold them back?

2. Yash and Naina's relationship of convenience is a familiar trope that gets flipped on its head in this story. Discuss what you think about Naina's idea that she is a better match for Yash.

3. India's yoga practice helps keep her centered. But there are times when her self-control does not work out in her favor. How does Yash upending her hard-won equilibrium impact her character?

4. While China and India approach their love lives in completely different ways, the two sisters also have quite a bit in common. What are their similarities and differences? Do you identify more with one sister's philosophy than the other's?

5. The story of Yudishtir and his technically not-a-lie is an important theme throughout the story.

Discuss how the characters manipulate the truth. Are there situations when it is called for, or is the truth always best? What do you think each of the characters would say to that? Do you have situations in your own life when you've skirted the truth on a technicality?

6. If you have read Sonali Dev's inspiration for this novel, Jane Austen's *Sense and Sensibility*, what similarities do you see? And what differences?

7. Tara and Mina are both mothers their children take strength and support from. Discuss the way they approach motherhood and how it has impacted their children.

8. How do family legacy and history play a role in Yash's and India's identities? How does this aspect of their lives impact their choices?

9. How do you think birth order plays into each character's choices? Do you find birth order stereotypes to be accurate in your own family?

10. The book explores the role of free will versus forces out of our control (the universe). How do you think ▶

this plays into Yash's control issues and anxiety attacks?

11. Do you think you would have voted for Yash after his admission about Naina and India? Why or why not? ∾